MYCLIFF
M

We hope you enjoy this book. Please return or renew it by the due date.

You can renew it at www.norfolk.gov.uk/libraries or by using our free library app.

Otherwise you can phone 0344 800 8020 - please have your library card and PIN ready.

You can sign up for email reminders too.

D0785550

## NORFOLK COUNTY COUNCIL
## LIBRARY AND INFORMATION SERVICE

## Also by Scarlet Wilson

*Tempted by the Hot Highland Doc*
*Cinderella and the Surgeon*
*Family for the Children's Doc*

## The Good Luck Hospital miniseries

*Healing the Single Dad's Heart*
*Just Friends to Just Married?*

## Also by Fiona McArthur

*Midwife's Mistletoe Baby*
*Midwife's Marriage Miracle*

## The Midwives of Lighthouse Bay miniseries

*A Month to Marry the Midwife*
*Healed by the Midwife's Kiss*
*The Midwife's Secret Child*

Discover more at millsandboon.co.uk.

# HIS BLIND DATE BRIDE

SCARLET WILSON

# SECOND CHANCE IN BARCELONA

FIONA McARTHUR

**MILLS & BOON**

First Published in Great Britain 2020
by Mills & Boon, an imprint of HarperCollins*Publishers*
1 London Bridge Street, London, SE1 9GF

His Blind Date Bride © 2020 by Scarlet Wilson

Second Chance in Barcelona © 2020 by Fiona McArthur

ISBN: 978-0-263-28446-1

**MIX**
Paper from
responsible sources
**FSC** **FSC C007454**
www.fsc.org

Printed and bound in Spain
by CPI, Barcelona

# HIS BLIND DATE BRIDE

SCARLET WILSON

MILLS & BOON

This book is dedicated to all my fellow key personnel who've worked throughout the COVID-19 pandemic with me. Here's hoping by the time this book is out we've reached the other side.

# CHAPTER ONE

Ivy Ross CURLED up on her sofa and sighed at the messages on her phone. It was late, she was in her pyjamas, and her current foster dog, Ruff, was curled up on her lap.

He was pretending he was sleeping. She could tell, because every now and then he turned his head slightly and gave her the side-eye when she stopped rubbing his belly. He was a scruffy sort—like most of the foster dogs she looked after—and his origins were completely unknown. He looked like some kind of small terrier cross, with his short stature and sandy-coloured fur, and he was definitely a little temperamental.

But Ivy could deal with temperamental. She'd been Flight Surgeon so often, on a variety of navy vessels with mainly male personnel, that she took it all in her stride.

Ruff nuzzled into her leg as she lifted her phone again and tried to ignore the ache of loneliness that had settled in her stomach. She'd done it all. Pursued her dream career and made it in a workforce dominated by males. It had been her goal for so long. But it seemed that in her pursuit of her goal she'd lost a little of her life along the way.

Her phone buzzed again and she looked at the response on the dating app. Being away on regular deployments, often for months at a time, meant relationships were difficult.

Most guys she'd met—mainly very nice—weren't interested in a woman who often ended up working thousands of miles away, surrounded by hundreds of other men. And that suited her more than she let on to her friends. Having her heart broken once was enough. Being told she wasn't enough once was enough. Paul was now a distant memory in her past, but the scar that he'd left had made Ivy reconsider her whole outlook on dating and relationships.

Ivy had never mixed business with pleasure, and had always refused to date a work colleague. Too complicated. Too much hassle.

The dating app worked. It kept her friends happy and sometimes amused by the tales she could tell. But it also allowed her to guard her heart from any future hurt. The world could see she was dating, and potentially 'looking' for some kind of relationship, whilst secretly it saved her from a lot of awkward questions.

She had a one bed, one bath rented apartment on the bay of the island of Coronado, just opposite the city of San Diego. It was beautiful, if a little costly, and thankfully pet friendly, set in a complex with good facilities. The drive across the San Diego-Coronado bridge always gave her a rush of feelings of luck and belonging, to stay in such a beautiful city and be part of such a great organisation.

But lately coming home to a comfortable, but empty, apartment had left Ivy feeling lonely. Living in a beautiful place like this could be hard. She constantly heard life all around her. On a daily basis she caught glimpses of couples and families going about their everyday lives, all reinforcing the fact that she was on her own.

It had led her to dog fostering—taking a troublesome character from a local shelter for a few weeks at a time to try and help familiarise them with living in a home again, and hopefully making them more adoptable.

Ruff was number six. He was proving to be a bit more difficult than the rest, probably because he was older and seemed set in his bad habits, which involved chewing anything at all. His three-week furlough with her was due to end tomorrow and Ivy couldn't pretend she wasn't a little sad. But apparently the shelter had a family lined up to meet him, so it was all for the best.

Ivy shook her head as another message popped up in one of the other dating apps. Currently she was registered on three—all under pseudonyms. The last thing she wanted was to be discovered by one of the sailors she served with.

She frowned and swiped on her screen. The latest match had proved himself tasteless on the first message. Delete.

In the last month Ivy had become a bit of a master of these apps. She was looking for someone to date—not a five-minute fling or hook-up. She said so in all three of her profiles, but that didn't stop a few guys with other things on their minds sending her messages. She deleted them all quickly.

Another message buzzed onto her screen.

Hi Ali, hope you're doing well. Which city are you in currently? R x

She smiled and shifted on her sofa as Ruff gave a low growl at the disturbance. Rob. He was one of the few potential bright sparks on the horizon. They'd exchanged first general, then a few flirty texts for the last two months. Although they were both based in San Diego, both of them had careers that made it difficult to coordinate. Twice they'd planned a date, and twice they'd had to rearrange. Rob was an international banker and frequently flew across the US and to other countries for business. Ali, her alter ego on this app, was a specialist insurance agent who could be gone for weeks at a time.

Of course it wasn't true, but she was reluctant to reveal her true name or her true job until she'd got to know someone a little better. She wanted to be honest about being away a lot, so having an alternative job where she could be out of the picture for weeks at a time was handy.

She'd been texting three separate men for a few weeks now. But Rob was definitely the one who interested her most. He seemed down to earth. Fun. Cheeky and a little flirty.

Her fingers moved to answer.

Hi Rob, I'm home right now. Have been for the last three weeks. How about you? A x

She couldn't pretend that her stomach didn't give a little flip-flop.

Just landed. How about we try and finally have that date?

Ruff gave a yelp as Ivy sat upright, sending Ruff spilling from her lap. She glanced at her watch. It was late—but not too late.

Her fingers paused above the screen. If she answered straight away, would she seem too keen?

She stood up and walked through to her bedroom and pulled open the wardrobe doors. What to wear if she said yes? Ruff nuzzled into her legs, as if trying to remind her that she should be paying attention to him. 'Sorry, boy,' she said, biting her bottom lip as she scanned the contents of her wardrobe while trying to decide if she should answer or not.

She pulled out some jeans and a black strappy top with some scattered sequins across it.

Her phone gave another buzz and she smiled. He was waiting for her answer.

Well...?

Sure. Let's meet somewhere for a drink.

She definitely couldn't pretend her stomach was feeling normal. Ivy sighed as she caught sight of her appearance. Her hair was currently tied in an unruly knot on top of her head. It was clean. Just not styled in any way, shape or form. She pulled it loose and shook it out, flicking the switch at the wall for her straightening iron.

Her phone buzzed and she almost leapt on it. Rob had named a popular wine bar set right on the bay. It was about a fifteen-minute drive from where she stayed. As she was staring at the message on the app her phone started to ring.

Her friend Liz. She pressed the screen to chat as she started to get dressed.

'Hey, girl, what you doing?' asked Liz.

'I'm getting ready for a date,' replied Ivy as she tugged on her jeans.

'You're what!' squealed Liz.

Ivy grinned. She knew the response would get this kind of reaction. 'That guy I've been messaging.'

'Which one?' cut in Liz. 'I can't keep up.'

'Rob.'

'Ah...'

Ivy was changing her bra. 'What does that mean?' She turned and faced her phone as if Liz was actually in the room.

'He's the one you actually liked, isn't he?'

'He could be,' answered Ivy as she pulled the strappy top over her head.

'Didn't he cancel on you?' came the voice.

'Yeah, he did,' said Ivy, as she pulled a face at the memory. 'But I had cancelled on him first.'

'So this time it's for real?'

'Apparently.' Ivy was standing in front of the mirror, wondering if she'd made the right choice. 'Hold on,' she said, picking up her phone and snapping a selfie before sending it to Liz. 'What do you think? What does it say?'

She stared at her reflection critically, all the while wondering if she could actually pull her hair into some kind of shape before she had to leave.

Liz paused at the other end of the phone. 'It's good,' she said finally. 'It's "Look what I can throw on and look spectacular in". But please tell me you're going to do something with your hair.'

Ivy laughed as she tugged a comb through her blonde tangles, which objected to being tamed.

'What can I ever do with this hair?' she asked.

'Let your natural curls take over,' said Liz promptly. 'It only gets in that state when you've been straightening it too much.' There was a loud sniff through the phone. 'In fact, I can tell, I can smell the burning. You've switched them on already. Put them off. Spritz your hair with some water and get your diffuser out instead. Anyway, where are you meeting this guy? Somewhere central? Somewhere safe?'

Ivy smiled—knowing that if the shoe were on the other foot she'd be saying exactly the same things. Trust Liz. 'We're going to Gino's in Old Town,' she replied.

'Hmm, nice,' said Liz. 'Central enough, with some cosy booths and good wine. Does he know the place?'

'I take it he must,' said Ivy as she dotted some foundation on her face. 'He's from San Diego, but I'm not sure where he lives.'

'You haven't told him where you live, have you?' said Liz immediately, her tone wary.

'Of course not.' Ivy laughed. 'I'm feeling kind of bad. He doesn't even know my real name, or what I do yet.'

'Nothing wrong with that,' said Liz quickly. 'Make sure you're at least ten minutes late,' she added. 'That way you'll have time to scan the bar and make sure he's not actually one of your workmates.'

Ivy shuddered as she applied some eye make-up. 'Don't even say that. Not even funny. We've got a whole bunch of new marines who think they are fantastic. *Please* don't let it be one of them. That would be a disaster.'

She shook her head as she took out her mascara. 'No, I think Rob is who he says he is.'

'Have you done an internet search on him?'

Her hand froze. Of course she had. But she hadn't found him.

The silence gave way to a shriek from Liz that sent Ruff jumping in the air in fright.

'You have, haven't you? Ooh, you didn't find anything, did you? Well, that's weird, isn't it? Because if he's really an international banker he has to have an online presence somewhere, doesn't he?' There was another minuscule pause. 'Hey, want me to come along? Just in case he's not what you think?' Caution laced her words.

'Hey, boy,' said Ivy softly, as she took a few steps and bent down to pet Ruff. 'Didn't mean you to get a scare.' She rubbed both sides of his face as he scowled at her.

A tiny part of the shine about this date was starting to wear off as worry threaded its way through her head. Maybe she should be more cautious?

'Ivy? You still there?'

She gave Ruff another pat. 'Yes, I'm here,' she said as she stood up again and caught sight of her hair. Her hand went automatically to the straightening wand and she made a few half-hearted attempts to pull it through her stubborn natural curls.

She was watching her reflection in the mirror the whole time, but her eyes caught sight of the clock on the wall behind her. 'Darn it, I'll need to run. There's a trolley in a few minutes.'

'You're getting the Old Town trolley?'

Ivy nodded as she gave up on her hair. 'Why not?'

'Tourists,' said Liz with a shudder.

'I like the tourists. Plus, I always get a discount. And Elvis is usually on this shift,' she said. The green and orange Old Town trolleys covered a twenty-five-mile loop of the city.

Elvis was one of her favourite trolley drivers. A little eccentric, he dressed as Elvis every day while working, sometimes doing a little singalong while telling the tourists about the history of the city.

She grabbed her phone and her bag. 'Okay, wish me luck. I'd better go.'

'Message me,' said Liz quickly. 'And leave immediately if you think he's a creep.'

Ivy laughed. 'Liz, I'm not fifteen, and I can take care of myself.'

Liz sighed. 'I know you can, but I feel obliged to say it. Have fun!'

Ruff followed her to the door, looking hopeful. She leaned down and gave him a big hug. 'Sorry, honey.' She rubbed his coat. Truth was, she was going to miss him when she had to hand him back tomorrow, but having a dog on a permanent basis with a job like hers just wasn't on. She looked into his big brown eyes. 'Some family is just going to love you to pieces,' she said as she blinked back a stray tear and stood up again. Ruff realised at this point that she wasn't actually taking him for a walk, shot her a look of disgust and trotted off to a corner.

Ivy took a deep breath, slid her feet into a pair of gold flats, glanced at her watch and bolted out the door.

What had he done? Travis King shook his head as he strode along the street to Gino's. It was only a ten-minute walk from his apartment, and the Old Town was busy as usual. It didn't matter what night of the week it was, this part of San Diego always had a buzz in the air and jostling crowds.

He'd been flirting on and off with this particular woman for the last few weeks on the app. They'd almost met, and he still felt bad about letting her down at the last minute when he'd been called away to duty. He'd almost been tempted to tell her what his real job was, rather than the description he used online at the moment of 'international banker'. That was his brother's job, so it had been easy to pick up a few tips.

His apartment had had that odd, unused odour when he'd opened the door half an hour earlier, so he'd thrown open the glass doors to his wide balcony and left them open. He'd bought the apartment a few years back, thinking he was going to be more or less permanently based in San Diego. But he'd barely signed the deal when he'd been shipped off—first to Chicago, then Washington, then Hawaii. The life of a navy surgeon was never quiet.

His phone buzzed in his pocket. On my way. He smiled. Finally. He might actually get to meet the elusive Ali, the insurance agent who seemed to jet about almost as much as he did.

He tapped his fingers on his phone, a nervous habit, and quickly shoved it back in the pocket of his jeans. It wasn't that he was anxious about the date. Of course not. He'd been on enough dates in his life to write a dating guide—some good, some bad. In his teenage years there had been the girl who'd stayed at the end of his street and after two dates had camped out in his backyard—much to the amusement of his three sisters. Then there had been the girl who'd also been dating three of his other friends. At med school he'd met a girl at a local restaurant and gone to meet her just in time for the cops to show up and arrest her for shoplifting.

Finally, there had been all the 'friends' his three sisters had set him up with, each one nice, but just not for him. It seemed to be their mission to find him a girl. In all this, his brother was no help whatsoever. Mr International Banker had married his high school sweetheart years before and had the perfect wife and two kids.

The dating app made things easy. It was a perfect cover. Since his deployment four years ago to a war zone, followed by a catastrophic fire in a hotel he was staying in, his nights had been full of nightmares, reliving one experience or the other. Sometimes the nightmares faded and settled for a while, only to rear their heads again when he wasn't expecting them. He had no real knowledge of what triggered them. All he knew was that he hadn't had a serious girlfriend in the last four years. No relationships. No overnight stays. He didn't want to share his horror with anyone else.

His last real girlfriend had stayed in Hawaii and things had come to a natural end when he'd been stationed elsewhere. She wasn't the type to wait around when he'd been deployed to a war zone and it had turned out she'd been right not to wait for him. He'd been on his own ever since, and frequently placated his sisters by sometimes showing them who he was meeting, or chatting to on the dating apps.

On the surface, it looked as though he was putting himself out there, but if the nightmares flared up too much he could delete the apps and pull himself back, protecting himself for a while. His family had no idea about his night-time horrors, and he wasn't about to share. He was a doctor. He could deal with this himself. So he couldn't quite put his finger on why he was so edgy about this date.

Was it timing? He was hoping to be based permanently in San Diego now, and his nights had been quieter lately. Maybe things were settling down once and for all. Eventually he would like to meet someone and finally settle down to a normal life—or as much of a normal life as anyone who was in the US Navy could have.

Maybe it was his age. Most of his friends in their mid-thirties like him had met someone by now and were starting to make family plans. He'd never had those thoughts before and had no idea why they were entering his brain now.

His friends had liked the fact he seemed to go from one date to another. It seemed to brighten up their lives. But it would be nice to stop being their light relief.

He walked into Gino's, welcoming the dim lights and relaxed atmosphere. He spoke to one of the bartenders and took a seat in a booth in the middle of the bar. Jazz music filled the air, soothing but soft. By the time he finally met Ali, he wanted to actually be able to hear her talk.

She'd given him good vibes. Confident. Self-assured. Fun. Most important, she took her job seriously—just like he did. The only thing was he had no idea what she looked like. Did that even matter?

He didn't like to think of himself as a guy who would judge someone on their appearance. A few of his friends had told him the fact she didn't have a profile pic was a red flag. But he'd been quick to point out that neither did he. It was complicated. Using a pic when he wasn't using his real name could cause all sorts of issues. There were dozens of computer programs out there that could easily scan his image and search for it elsewhere. That could end up with a whole host of uncomfortable questions. Why was a navy surgeon posing online as someone else?

Plus, at some point, he felt you just had to have trust in someone. He had to hope he wasn't about to meet some-one who was thirty years older than they claimed to be, but the possibility had circulated in his head.

He sent a quick message.

I'm here. What do you want to drink?

The answer came so swiftly he couldn't help but smile.

On the Old Town trolley. Will be at least another ten min-utes. Rosé wine, please, and keep it chilled!

He raised his brows at the slightly unusual choice and scanned behind the bar to make sure they had what she wanted before he ordered. Most bars in San Diego only stocked red, white and the very occasional blush. But Gino's had a variety of rosé wines so he asked for a recommenda-tion and hoped for the best as he carried it back to the table. A woman at the next table gave him an admiring glance but he pretended not to notice. He'd dressed in a black polo shirt and jeans. Casual. And whilst admiring glances were nice, there was only one woman on his mind right now, and he was happy to wait.

'Elvis' had broken into 'Blue Suede Shoes' moments after Ivy had boarded the trolley. Within seconds most of the passengers were singing along as the trolley made its way across the Coronado bridge. Her hair was immediately ruffled in the evening breeze but Ivy didn't really care. It clearly didn't want to be tamed and it was useless to try.

She closed her eyes for a second, leaned back and smiled. She had a good feeling about tonight. That was unusual for her. Generally, she was nervous about talking on the dating app, the whole aspect of meeting someone. Probably because on a few occasions she'd felt kind of let down later. But this time felt different.

She'd chatted with Rob for a few weeks. He seemed down to earth, had a wide range of interests and a bit of cheeky flair. She liked that. There would just be those few awkward moments when, after meeting him and ensuring she felt safe, she would have to admit what her real name and job were. It paid to be cautious in this life, and she was sure she would know pretty quickly if it felt safe to be herself or not.

She grinned as a text arrived from Rob and she answered it quickly. Her timing was perfect. He was there first.

She'd just sent the text when her phone rang. It gave her such a shock she almost dropped it—even more so when she recognised the number. 'Ivy Ross,' she answered.

'Ms Ross, there's an emergency,' came the deep voice of her commander.

She sat bolt upright. 'What kind of emergency?'

'It's Flight Surgeon Davis on the USS *Calvin Coolidge*.'

Her skin chilled. The USS *Calvin Coolidge* was one of the biggest ships in the fleet. An aircraft carrier that could carry as many as five thousand personnel.

'What's wrong?'

'There's been an accident—not him. His wife and kids

have been in a serious car accident. We have to bring him home and we need a replacement.'

'What do you need me to do?'

She could almost hear her commander smile as her stomach lurched. 'We need you to be ready to deploy at zero six hundred hours.'

Her mouth went dry. It wasn't the job. She'd done it before and enjoyed it. It was the short notice. That, and the fact she'd had her fingers crossed for promotion. She was eligible, she'd been interviewed, and she'd been hoping against hope that the next call she got from her commander would be telling her she'd be Senior Medical Officer somewhere. Taking this position would likely rule her out for any immediate new role. But Ivy always did the job she was needed to do. Her stomach had a roll of regret as she said the words. 'Where is the USS *Calvin Coolidge*?'

'In the Pacific. Pack your things, Flight Surgeon Ross, you're needed.'

Her mouth was still open as the call ended. She hadn't even asked if she would be a permanent replacement or not. How long would she be deployed? Weeks or months? It wasn't that long since she'd got back from her last assignment. She loved her job, but knew rest and recuperation were essential.

Working on the aircraft carrier would mean that as Flight Surgeon she would be responsible for the welfare of thousands of colleagues, along with the senior medical officer and chief medical officer. It was a huge deal. Every minute of every day would be filled with work. She would be permanently on call—always ready to jump at the first sign of a siren. Her last assignment had been smaller, more manageable.

This one was like throwing her straight in at the deep end. She licked her dry lips. But the commander had phoned her. He'd thought of her when disaster had happened. She didn't want to believe she was the only person qualified who could fly out a moment's notice. The US Navy didn't function like that. She could almost see the list of files on his desk as he'd deliberated the job, weighing up who was most suited. He'd chosen *her*. This time her heart missed a few beats. That was good. No, that was great.

She'd spent years wanting to finally be on the radar of the commander. She admired him and wanted to impress him. He clearly thought she was up to the task. But would he consider her for a bigger task? There was so much to think about. One thing was for sure, if she said she didn't want to take this emergency job, she would automatically tumble down the ranking for any promotion.

Her stomach flipped over as she remembered Ruff. She'd need to make arrangements for a colleague to take him back to the shelter tomorrow—and it wouldn't be open before six a.m.

A photo of a glass of wine appeared on her phone. Oh, no.

Rob. She grimaced. The wine looked perfect. Chilled, with some condensation on the glass, in the midst of a dimly lit bar—the perfect place for a first meeting. How on earth could she tell him?

Her fingers started typing before she even thought.

So, so sorry, but family emergency and I need to bail. I promise, at some point, we will actually meet.

She stood up then walked to the front of the trolley, signalling to Elvis that she needed to get off. He shook his head as they were nowhere near an official stop. The trolleys weren't supposed to stop anywhere else.

'Sorry,' she pleaded. 'It's an emergency.'

After a few moments he gave a shrug and slowed down, giving her the chance to alight. 'Don't know what you're missing,' he said with a twang in his voice as he pointed towards the heart of San Diego.

She pulled up another app to grab a ride back to her apartment, and thankfully a car was only a few minutes away.

As she jumped inside, she realised that Rob hadn't replied and a wave of regret washed over. She felt terrible. She'd been looking forward to this and now, with one call, she had to walk away. But that was her job, her duty. Part of her wished she'd been a little more truthful, then she could have actually revealed why she had been called away. But it was too late now. As the car sped back across the Coronado Bridge she turned her phone over in her hands, wondering if she'd just blown it for good.

Travis had just sat down and taken his first sip of beer, letting the cool liquid slide down his throat. He was ready for this. Ready to meet this fun-sounding woman who lived in the same city as he did, and see where it went. Maybe they could have a few fun dates? His eyes kept heading to the door—even though she'd told him she was ten minutes away.

A small woman in a red coat walked in. His pulse rate quickened. But the woman let out a squeal and ran over to another table, embracing someone in a bear hug. Travis sighed and pretended he wasn't thankful. He wasn't sure she was his type. Two women around the right age wandered in, chatting and laughing conspiratorially. One brunette, one redhead, both dressed in jeans and light shirts. Maybe Ali had brought a friend. That made sense. He could understand that. But a few seconds later two men walked in behind them and joined the ladies at the bar. They were clearly two couples.

His phone buzzed. An email. He flicked it open and sighed. Peters, a friend and colleague who'd spent the last few weeks trying to convince Travis that he wanted to look to the future—encouraging him to think about leaving the navy and setting up in private practice in San Diego. Peters had a very successful practice already but one of his partners had left recently. He was anxious to fill the spot, and he'd set his sights on Travis.

In a way it was flattering, but Travis didn't even want to think about things like that. Right now, he was focused on staying in the Navy Medical Service. He liked it. No, he loved it. He slid the email away. The limited conversations he'd had with Peters had always been after a few spells of bad nightmares. Private practice would probably be in his future at some point but things were settled right now. He didn't want to make the transition before he thought he had to.

He bent his head, trying to take his eyes off the door. It hadn't been ten minutes yet. Then his phone buzzed again. He picked it up instantly, seeing the message on his screen. His first instinct was to groan and then have a quick look around. Maybe she was in the bar, watching him, and she hadn't liked what she'd seen?

He glanced down at his clothes again and at his reflection in the gantry behind the bar. His job meant that he was physically fit. Most women considered him vaguely attractive, a few had even called him outright handsome. And, no, it wasn't just his mother and sisters. Had Ali taken one look and walked away?

The thought didn't sit comfortably with him. He looked around the bar. Sure enough, as far as he could see, he was the only person right now sitting with a glass of rosé on the table.

Travis looked around again and then laughed and shook his head. Had he missed out on some kind of girl code? Was he getting too old these days to not understand the signs?

It could be something else entirely. It just seemed well… odd that as soon as he'd sent the photo of the wine glass she'd blown him off.

Maybe she was just old-fashioned nervous. There. That was a better thought. But it still left him sitting alone in a San Diego bar.

He had asked her at short notice. But she'd been quick enough to accept. Maybe Ali did have a genuine family emergency. Maybe she would message later or even tomorrow to makes excuses and rearrange. And if she did, would he agree?

He debated in his head as more people streamed into the bar. Soft jazz music was playing around him. A few couples, some groups of friends. An older, single man who sat at the bar, sipped his beer and read the paper.

The woman at the next table gave him a coy smile. 'What's wrong? Date called off? Silly girl. I can keep you company, if you like.' She flashed her teeth at him and he drew in a deep breath.

He didn't want a companion who might want to hang around overnight. He wanted something more meaningful than that. It's why he'd spent the last few weeks getting to know Ali. It's why the first thing he'd done when he'd landed had been to text her and ask her out.

He wanted the chance to finally meet face to face. Get to know if the buzz that seemed to flicker via message between them was actually there when they met in person.

He looked at the glass of wine and empty seat opposite

him, trying to think of any reason in the world why he shouldn't just look like some guy who'd been stood up. Instead, he flashed her a smile and stood up. 'Let's just say you win some, you lose some and some aren't worth waiting for.' He picked up his bottle of beer and drained it, before heading to the door and walking out into the warm evening air.

# CHAPTER TWO

BY THE TIME she reached the USS *Calvin Coolidge* Ivy was exhausted. Because the aircraft carrier was already deployed she'd had to travel via a number of different methods to get there. It was not as if she hadn't flown in a dozen naval planes before. Helicopters were more familiar. But since the *Coolidge* was in the middle of the Pacific Ocean, the distance was too far to travel in one journey.

Instead, she'd found herself going from San Diego to Hawaii and then by military jet before finally landing on the *Coolidge*. It didn't matter how many times she'd seen the fighters land on aircraft carriers before, as a passenger she still had a moment of terror when it seemed like the jet might just shoot off the end of the runway.

'Here you go, Flight Surgeon.' The cheeky pilot who'd flown her in grinned. 'Welcome to our brand-new aircraft carrier.'

'Thank you, Captain Yang.' She smiled as she waited for the steps to be put in place for her to disembark.

The sun was high in the sky above them. The Pacific Ocean unblemished and stretching for miles around them. But as soon as she stepped from the jet the wind almost knocked her from her feet. One of the crewmen grinned and grabbed hold of her elbow.

'Head down, ma'am, and move in that direction.'

The door to the carrier seemed a million miles away at the other end of the flight deck. She grabbed her bag and walked in long strides, praying she'd get out of the fierce wind soon.

It was ironic really. Most of the men and women on this aircraft carrier spent weeks below deck—there were currently eighteen decks under her feet—and would probably love to get some fresh air. But right now Ivy couldn't wait to get inside.

As soon as she got through the door she dropped her bag at her feet to give herself a few seconds to catch her breath. By the time she looked up, an older guy with grey hair was looking at her. Tony Briggs. He gave her a wide smile.

'Tony!' She leaned forward and gave him a hug. 'I had no idea you were CMO on the *Coolidge*.'

He shrugged. 'It's great to see you, Ivy. When I heard you were the replacement I couldn't have been happier.' He gave her a sideways glance. 'I thought you were moving on to bigger and better things?'

She stepped back and nodded. 'It was a bit of a surprise call but…' She looked around at the never-ending views of grey walls and said with a laugh, 'How could anyone not want to do this?' Then she sighed. 'As for the bigger and better things, I guess I'll just need to wait a bit longer.'

Tony nodded. As Chief Medical Officer on the aircraft carrier, he would be her closest colleague. It was a relief that it was someone she already knew—someone she trusted and had worked alongside in the past. He'd been one of the first doctors she'd met when she'd joined the US Navy. Steady as a rock, encouraging without overstepping the line. He'd let her learn from her mistakes on more than one occasion, but had always been ready to assist and chat. He respected her just as much as she respected him.

She gave a nervous shiver as she looked around. 'Have to be honest, didn't think I'd end up here.'

Tony gave a nod. He knew exactly what she meant without putting it into words. 'You're more than qualified. This job won't be any different than any other—just a few more people,' he added with a smile. 'Crew roll is five thousand, five hundred and thirty-two.'

She gulped and put a bright smile on her face. 'Okay.'

Tony threw back his head and laughed. 'Don't give me the "Ivy smile".'

She shook her head in confusion. 'What's the "Ivy smile"? I've never heard you say that before.'

He raised his eyebrows. 'That one where you smile at someone when it's completely clear that your brain is racing away in the background with a hundred other questions.'

She laughed and gave his upper arm a light slap. 'You know me far too well.'

He gestured his hand towards the slim corridor in front of them. 'Come on, let me show you to your quarters.'

'My closet?' she quipped back. The quarters on any navy vessel were always tiny, but she'd grown used to them.

She moved down the corridor in front of Tony, occasionally having to flatten herself against a wall to let others past, going down almost vertical stairs as they descended into the heart of the vessel.

The USS *Calvin Coolidge* was virtually new. Completed and launched the year before, it was the most modern aircraft carrier in the fleet.

Tony gave her a rundown as they moved to her quarters. 'I'll show you around the medical department and our state-of-the-art facilities once you're settled. The SMO obviously wants to meet you—you know, give you the talk about pressure and teamwork. Have you met Isaiah Bridges before?'

She shook her head. The senior medical officer would be her boss on board the carrier. He had a sterling but stern reputation. She was a tiny bit nervous about meeting him. Particularly because she wanted to be in his shoes one day.

Her phone buzzed in her pocket and she started. 'Oh, satellite's working, then?'

Tony nodded. 'Surprisingly well, unless you're in the absolute depths on the ship. You should have no problems with access.'

He pointed to a grey door to her left. 'You're in here.'

As an officer on board and with her position as Flight Surgeon, Ivy had her own quarters. To say it was compact was being kind. But since some of the crew shared with sixty other people in three rows of bunks, having a tiny bit of space to herself was a luxury.

She dumped her bag and took off her coat. The heat inside the ship was already getting to her. It only took a few seconds to retie her rumpled hair and straighten her uniform. She would change later—if she was meeting the SMO, she wanted to impress him.

Tony gave her a nod of approval and took her back down the corridor. On naval ships the med bays and theatres were always near the centre of the ship in order to ensure the most stability. On a ship the size of an aircraft carrier there were, of course, also battle dressing stations at strategic points across the vessel to be used in case of emergency. But the med bay really was in the heart of the ship.

Tony beamed with pride as he showed her around the facilities. It was clear he was proud of how modern everything was. Ivy's stomach gave a pang of pride. She believed in the service they provided for their crew. Just because they were stuck in the middle of an ocean, it didn't mean that the crew should go without care. X-rays, blood tests, even emergency surgeries could be performed on the aircraft carrier. There was an active emergency room, a physical therapy clinic, operating room, an intensive care unit, up to sixty ward beds if required, a lab, pharmacy, X-ray room, a fully equipped dental surgery and a whole range of medical, dental and nursing staff to assist.

A tiny tremor went through her at the knowledge that if some kind of mass disaster occurred, this ship could literally be turned into a floating emergency centre. Some of the crew were also trained as medical corpsmen and could assist if required.

Ivy took a steadying breath. Things were calm today. There were a few patients in the hospital ward, others in the waiting area looking for some kind of medical advice. Although surgery was her speciality, while on board she would be expected to also deliver everyday preventative medicine to the crew. She liked that. She'd discovered early in her career that she didn't want to focus too narrowly on one speciality.

General surgery was as narrow as she'd got. But as a member of navy medical personnel she'd also had the pleasure of studying aviation and aerospace medicine and been involved in some areas of research. The variety made it one of the best jobs on the planet, in her view, and she was thankful every day.

Her mind drifted. *One day, all this could be yours.* She knew it was completely and utterly fanciful, but it had always been her dream to get as far up the ranks as she could. She wanted to be the person in charge of all this.

All the medical personnel. To take responsibility for the full medical contingent on this vessel.

*I can be good enough.*

The words echoed in her head. Remnants of the mantra she'd kept repeating to herself ever since Paul had left. She'd hated him for breaking her heart. But now she was kind of glad it had happened. It had given her even more drive to be the best at everything she did. She was always striving to be the best doctor, the best surgeon, and focus on her career. Whilst she never wanted to lose her practical skills, she also wanted the respect and ability to use her organisational skills too.

Being SMO on an aircraft carrier was the ultimate job goal. She pressed her lips together for a second. She'd really hoped that would have been her next post. This one was like being put in a holding pattern, and she'd need to let her head accept that, and move on.

She watched as one of the nurses sat next to the bed of one of the patients, holding his hand and talking quietly to him. Relationships between crew members were always discouraged, but no one seemed to be paying too much attention. She could see the worry in the woman's eyes and the tremble in the hands of the male patient.

'What happened?' she said in a low voice to Tony.

He glanced up in the direction she was looking. 'Yeah. There was an accident yesterday. We're lucky our petty officer is still here. He put himself between a major piece of machinery and one of the seamen.'

Ivy drew in a deep breath. There was potential danger every single day whilst they were at sea. Accidents happened. But they were always investigated. As if he were reading Ivy's mind, Tony shot her a smile. 'Guess what your first job will be?'

She nodded. 'No problem. I'll see to it.' When a crew member was injured, a medic always took part in the investigation. Her heart gave a little pang as she continued to watch the pair. There was a real connection there. That special 'something'.

Her thoughts drifted back to two days before. She wished she'd had a chance to meet Rob. Even if it had only been for half an hour before she'd got the call. She would have liked a chance to put a face to the image she'd had in her head. To see if the easy manner translated into real life. To see if there was a little spark of attraction between them. Would a connection like the one she could currently see in front of her eyes ever be part of her life?

Would she be able to do that if—when—she was promoted next? Would there be space and time in her life for a relationship, or would the SMO role just encompass every part of her life?

Or would a spark just mean the chance of a broken heart again, and that feeling of not being good enough?

'Ivy, everything okay?'

Tony was looking at her with a frown creasing his forehead.

'Sure it is,' she said brightly. 'Let's carry on with the tour.'

An hour later she'd met a number of the crew in the hospital and med bay. Tony had gone back to seeing patients as she knocked on the door of the senior medical officer. 'Enter,' came the commanding voice.

Isaiah Bridges's dark skin gleamed a little as she entered the room. He was leaning over the desk as if he was studying something. It was only a few seconds before she realised his desk was spotlessly clean.

'Sir...' she said a little hesitantly.

He looked up and gave her a nod, pausing for a second before holding out his hand to her. 'Flight Surgeon Ross, it's a pleasure to meet you. I've heard good things.'

Relief flooded through her. 'Thank you, sir, it's an honour to be here. Thank you for requesting me. I was so sorry to hear about Flight Surgeon Davis's family.'

Her commanding officer nodded. 'I've had word. His daughter has some serious injuries and has had emergency surgery. She's in ITU now, but is stable. His wife had a spinal injury and will be required to be immobilised for a few weeks to allow healing of her vertebrae.'

'Oh, no,' breathed Ivy. The accident must have been really serious.

Isaiah Bridges nodded. 'It's going to be a long haul for him. He'll be needed at home for the next few months. We were lucky you were able to replace him so quickly. I understand his wife should make a full recovery, but his daughter might require some further surgeries in a few weeks' time. All his efforts need to be focused at home.'

'Absolutely,' said Ivy quickly. 'I'm happy to be here.'

He gave a slightly uncomfortable roll of his shoulders, as if he had a crick in his neck, then reached for a glass of water. There was silence for a few moments as she waited for him to talk again. Finally, he took a file from a drawer and handed it to her. 'There are a few checklists in here that Flight Surgeon Davis left. A few notes on crew he was concerned about, and the list of other duties still to be covered.'

'No problem,' said Ivy as she took the folder. 'I'm happy to get started.'

He paused and looked at her again. 'I also hear there could be good things ahead for you.'

The words made her skin prickle in delight, and she

couldn't help but smile. 'I hope so. You know what they say, good things came to those who wait. But for now I'm happy to be your flight surgeon.'

He gave a nod in acknowledgement.

'Dinner for my squadron is at seven. I'll see you then.'

It was a dismissal, and she was a little relieved. She walked back to her cabin and finally took a shower after all her travelling. Her body didn't know what time zone she was supposed to be in, and to be honest she could easily have curled up in her probably uncomfortable bunk. She towelled her hair semi-dry and left the rest to dry naturally. It was humid inside the aircraft carrier so any thoughts of straight hair would be a dim and distant dream.

She picked up her phone. The signal was good so she scrolled through her social media feeds. With a shake of her head she deleted two out of three dating apps. They were currently midway between Hawaii and the Galapagos Islands, two thousand miles from the nearest land. Dating would be a long way off.

Her fingers hesitated at the last app. This was the one where she'd met Rob. She hadn't even had a chance to message him again since she'd failed to show two nights ago. Ivy bit her bottom lip. If the shoe had been on the other foot she would have been furious. There was a good chance this guy wouldn't talk to her again. Her fingers hesitated above the phone. Was there even any point apologising when she might not be home again for a few months?

She could almost hear her elderly aunt's voice in her head. *Good manners cost nothing.* Of course she should apologise. It was the least she could do.

But what to say without revealing too much about herself?

She took a deep breath and started typing.

* * *

Travis was busy. Admin work was never his favourite part of the job but it still had to be done. He'd gone for a run at lunchtime, ignoring the blistering heat in San Diego, plastering himself in sunscreen, and pounded the surrounding pavements to try and work off some of his frustration at being stuck behind a desk.

He'd just stepped out of the shower when his phone buzzed. He ignored it—it was bound to be one of his sisters—as he poured himself a coffee. It was one of the few things in life he was fussy about. He should have gone to the coffee shop a few blocks from the base, but running and coffee didn't really mix. Next time he'd remember his portable cup.

His phone buzzed again and a flash of purple appeared on his screen. Travis frowned, remembering that messages that came through the dating app were purple. But he wasn't talking to anyone on the app—not after Saturday night's disaster.

He swiped the screen. Ali.

His first thought was pure exasperation and to delete it without reading. But that was the beauty of the modern phone—he could already see the first line of the message.

Hi Rob, huge apologies about Saturday night. I can't blame you if you're mad. I know I would be. But, honestly, I got called away at the last minute for an emergency that means I'm out of town for the next few months. But...

He stared in confusion at the dots. What else did she mean to say? As for the message, an apology was the least he deserved. His stomach clenched. His imagination could create a whole range of other possibilities. But maybe this was just the truth.

Recognition dawned as he saw some little dots on the screen. She was replying. Of course. She'd been checking he'd read the first message before she continued.

The truth is I was looking forward to meeting you. I'm bummed that we didn't actually get to see each other in person. You know how it is when you have a picture of someone in your head and you want to see if the imagined picture matches real life?

He set down the phone as he pulled his uniform back on and frowned. He hadn't been expecting that. Their messages had usually been fun and flirty, but this time she sounded more sincere. Almost like…she was at the same point in life that he was.

He sat back down and stared at the screen, not quite sure how to answer.

There were so many curt replies he could give. Five minutes ago that was exactly how he would have answered. But now he was curious.

And here was me thinking you caught sight of me, the only guy in the bar with a glass of rosé wine, and bailed…

She wasn't the only one who could use dots.
Her response was immediate.

What? OMG no. Absolutely no way. I would never do anything like that.

He smiled.

Really? You've never done that, ever…?

There was a slight pause.

Well, not any time lately...

So you're gone for the next few months?

The reply came quickly.

Unfortunately, yes. Duty calls. Let's just say I'm in a place where no land is in sight.

Now, that caught his interest. But before he had a chance to respond, she replied again.

How do you feel about a drink when I get back? I would like to try and meet. I was ready, and on the trolley on my way to meet you. My favourite driver, Elvis, was serenading us all with 'Blue Suede Shoes'.

There was something achingly familiar about the tale. While Travis sometimes used the regular trolleys in San Diego, he rarely used the Old Town, and knew instinctively that was the kind she was talking about. A few of his fellow crew had joked about the singing Old Town trolley driver called Elvis. The guy did actually exist.

Why don't you seal the deal by sending me a photo? Prove to me you're actually a real person and not a figment of my imagination.

He raised his eyebrows, imagining her reaction on receiving such a message. He did wonder if this was a good idea. But he was feeling bold. And it seemed Ali was too. What was wrong with asking for a photo?

The seconds seemed to stretch. Then a short reply.

Let me think about it.

No extra dots. No sentence unfinished. The phone on his desk rang and he reached over to answer it. Flirtations would have to wait.

# CHAPTER THREE

IVY'S SKIN HAD prickled with that last message—but she didn't have time to think about it much. She had a quick flick through the photos on her phone. Too many laughter lines. A dress that was a bit revealing and might send the wrong message. Her nose too big in another. Her hair all over the place in the next. She sighed, knowing that Liz would tell her every single one of these pictures was fine and she was too critical of herself.

Finally, she settled on one. Her blonde hair was sleek and shiny. She was wearing a dark top and slim cropped trousers. The picture wasn't posed. It had been taken unexpectedly and showed her sitting at an outside table at a restaurant in San Diego, wine glass in hand, and laughing. It caught all her best angles, without looking retouched. In fact, it was a relief. That was the one she would send—if she finally decided to do it.

She made her way to the mess for dinner. The officers' mess was noisy and crowded. The medical team was in the left-hand corner of the room. A few people gave her a wave as she entered. It didn't take long to see what food was on offer for the day and make her selection. She made her way over to the long table, headed by SMO Bridges. He pointed to the space next to him.

Tony was nearest her and gave a short laugh. 'Prepare

for the interrogation. And watch him, he's crafty with his questions.'

Ivy gave a good-natured smile and moved to sit next to Isaiah Bridges. She had half expected this. He wanted to make her feel welcome and part of the team. She was lucky. Not all commanders were like that.

The questions came thick and fast. Her training. Her interests. In turn she learned that Isaiah Bridges was married with a son and a daughter, and his wife worked as a producer for a TV news show. His son played basketball and his daughter planned to go to art school. He'd served for nearly thirty years and for the last fifteen he'd been SMO on an aircraft carrier. During his career he'd served on every aircraft carrier that had been in active service. How she wanted that life, and that career.

As he talked he loosened the button at his collar, giving it a little tug. The weather in the Pacific was warm, but combined with the heat of being below deck and in a crowded space she was feeling warm herself.

As it was her first night on board, she'd worn her jacket with her uniform, wondering if the officers here would be a little more informal due to the temperature around them. Everyone at her table was wearing their jackets, but she could see others from different parts of the ship in their shirtsleeves.

Isaiah's barrage of questions slowed down, and she noticed he'd only eaten a little of their delicious dinner. She passed him the jug of water on their table. 'Everything okay?'

He gave her a smile as he shook his head. 'Ah, just a little indigestion. I think I need some air. If you'll excuse me, I'm going to head along to my quarters.' He shrugged his left shoulder as if it was uncomfortable.

Ivy already knew that the corridors were likely to be

even hotter than the mess. It was easier said than done to get some air on an aircraft carrier. Most of the crew would spend their time here below decks with faint hope of feeling the brisk winds above.

She stood as he excused himself and shot Tony a look, moving swiftly from her seat as Isaiah Bridges exited the mess hall.

'Something wrong?' Tony asked her.

She gave a slow nod of her head. 'Just being cautious. Can you come with me for a minute?'

Tony nodded and grabbed the jacket that he'd put on the back of his chair. She waited until they were out in the corridor. 'I'm worried about Isaiah Bridges. I think he might be feeling unwell, but didn't want to give too much away.'

Tony's professional face fell into place straight away. 'Did he say where he's going?'

'His quarters. But I wonder if he might head to the med bay. He's not stupid.'

They started down the corridor. 'What do you suspect?' asked Tony, his steps so brisk she had to lengthen her stride to keep up.

As they turned the corner Ivy realised there was no chance to answer.

Ahead of them, Isaiah Bridges was leaning with one hand against the bulkhead in front of them, his other hand across his chest. Ivy stepped in front of him, immediately noticing the beads of sweat on his dark forehead.

'Isaiah,' said Tony, all formality lost, 'tell me how you're feeling.' He nodded to a crewman at the end of the corridor. 'Get me a chair from the med bay.'

Isaiah frowned, as if he couldn't quite process the question. 'Damn,' he muttered under his breath.

Ivy put her hand on his pulse. 'Chest pain? Indigestion? Why don't you let us take you along to the med bay and run a few tests?' She glanced around. 'Just Tony and myself. We'll look after you.'

She knew by instinct that Isaiah Bridges would hate this. She thought back frantically to this afternoon, the uncomfortable roll of the shoulders, just as he'd done at dinner this evening.

She kept talking in a reassuring manner to Isaiah as they assisted him into the hurriedly procured chair and took him along to the med bay, getting him up onto one of the trolleys.

It only took a few seconds to loosen his shirt and attach the electrodes they would need for a twelve-lead ECG. It was clear that both she and Tony were thinking the same thing. Silent MI.

Sweat continued to pour from Isaiah's forehead. They were in one of the single treatment rooms but Ivy signalled quietly to one of the senior nursing staff to assist. The nurse, Jane, gave a brief blink of recognition, then moved swiftly to take some blood.

This was what Ivy loved about her job. No matter where she was in the navy. No matter what base, what ship, the staff around her moved seamlessly, working as a team, with instructions barely needing to be given. They all knew their jobs that well. It was a privilege to be part of a team like this.

She glanced at the oxygen stats. 'Any previous asthma, or COPD?' she checked with Isaiah. When he shook his head she slipped the mask over his head and turned the oxygen flow on.

The twelve-lead printed out. 'What does it say?' said Isaiah hoarsely.

The results were clear to Ivy and she handed the printout to Tony. 'ST elevation. It looks like an inferior MI.

We won't wait for the blood work. We'll just treat you to save time.'

It was essential in the case of a myocardial infarction that it was treated as soon as possible to break up the blood clot that was blocking the blood flow and allowing part of the heart muscle to die.

Within a few seconds Jane returned with an aspirin in a medicine cup—the first-line treatment for any MI.

'Can you get me some thrombolytic?' Ivy asked, naming one of the popular clot-dissolving drugs commonly used for an MI.

Isaiah was shaking his head. 'But I haven't had any chest pain,' he said, deep furrows in his brow.

'What about that referred shoulder pain?' quipped Tony. He let out a laugh. 'Don't let it be said that you do things the traditional way.'

'I'm just glad we've caught it. We can get you treated here. Then send you to a hospital with cardiac facilities for further treatment.'

Ivy gave a slightly nervous swallow. MIs could be difficult. Lots of people required balloon angioplasty or coronary artery bypass grafting. Whilst the facilities on the ship were state of the art, they weren't as good as a specialised cardiac unit. Isaiah could well require a different kind of treatment in the next twenty-four hours. Their goal was to treat, stabilise and move him on.

'Don't worry, we'll take good care of you.'

Jane came back to the door and gave Tony a nod, handing the thrombolytic over to Ivy. It was set up in a small pump to be delivered over the space of an hour. She connected the tubing to the IV cannula that Jane had inserted while taking bloods and started the infusion.

There was a whole host of charting to be done, but Ivy pulled up a chair next to Isaiah. Right now he wasn't her boss. Right now he was a patient. And like any patient who'd just had an MI, she knew he would be anxious.

She gave him a smile. 'Okay, so let's establish that we both know our fellow doctors and nurses make the worst possible patients. What can I do to help you right now? You know we need to monitor your obs for the next hour whilst we deliver the drug.'

Isaiah rested back against the pillows and let out the biggest sigh in the world. She got it. She really did. He still really couldn't believe this had happened to him. Ivy understood that right now Tony would be reporting to the commanding officer that the aircraft carrier's SMO was undergoing treatment and would have to be airlifted from the carrier. She could only imagine how that news was going to go down.

'Would you like me to contact your wife?'

Isaiah fixed his dark eyes on her. 'Not really. You've not met my wife. She won't take this well.'

Ivy tilted her head to one side. 'Because she's predicted it for years?'

He waved one hand in the air. 'Forget it. I stand corrected. You'll get on just fine with my wife.'

Ivy gave a knowing nod. 'Okay, so we're most likely to send you back to the hospital facilities in Hawaii. Where is your wife based? Will she need transport?'

He shook his head. 'She's still on the island. Normally, we're in Maryland. But she's got some extended leave and was visiting family with the kids.'

He put his hand up to his chest. Ivy stood up quickly. 'Are you okay?' She glanced at his heart rate and BP on the nearby monitor. Both were holding steady.

He squeezed his eyes closed for a second. When he opened them again they looked a little watery. 'I'm fine. No pain. Just wondering what this will do to my career.'

Ivy was a little taken aback at the statement. But she knew instantly what it meant. She guessed Isaiah Bridges was in his mid-fifties. Many people completely recovered after an MI. But the likelihood was that he'd find himself landlocked and desk-bound for a considerable period of time after returning to work.

Ivy's action was instinctive. She reached over and squeezed his hand. 'The most important thing is that you get treated, and you get back to full health.'

He gave a hollow laugh. 'You know that I love being out here, don't you? I love the sea. It's why I joined the navy. I even did my medical training with the service. It's in my blood, you see.'

Ivy had heard this often throughout her career. Many of her colleagues came from families where naval service was a tradition—a way of life. She was different. None of her family had served. Ivy had always known she wanted to do medicine but had never tied it in with the idea of service. When a high school friend had enlisted early and had told her stories of the next few years, it had intrigued her, particularly when he'd told her what opportunities were available via the navy.

Isaiah narrowed his gaze and studied her for a second. It was unnerving. She glanced to make sure the pump was still administering the drug slowly and steadily. 'You never mentioned any family,' he said, with an edge to his voice that made it sound like a question.

She shifted in her chair. 'My family is good. My mum and dad stay in Colorado. My sister is a teacher in Columbia. My brother is currently in Australia. We're widespread.'

Isaiah shook his head and looked at her hand. 'You're not married?'

She gave a nervous kind of laugh. 'Not yet—but never say never.'

A frown creased his forehead. 'You've met someone?'

She opened her mouth to answer but wasn't quite sure what to say. She'd never been asked such invasive questions by her commander before.

As if he sensed how uncomfortable she was, Isaiah lifted one hand. 'What I'm trying to say—and sounding like an old fool—is I can take this...' He put his hand on his chest. 'I can take what's happened today, because I know at home I have my wife and kids waiting for me.' His voice trembled a little. 'If I never get back out to sea, I know I have my life back home. I've always had something to go home to.'

He paused for a second and gazed off into the corner. 'My wife and I—Adele—we literally bumped into each other in the street. I often wonder what would have happened if we'd never met that way. What I would have become without her, and my family.' He gave his head a gentle shake. 'I was ambitious. Cocky, probably a little too dangerous. She grounded me. Made me the person I am today.'

He took a deep breath. 'What I'm saying is don't leave it too long. Don't let the navy suck the best years of your life. I know it could have easily happened to me. You're a talented doctor. You must be, or you wouldn't be here. You have the potential to be a great SMO. But think about what you have at home. Don't let it just be *this*.' He held his hand up again and clicked his fingers. 'Because a moment, a second and it can be snatched away.'

She could see the emotion in his eyes. Isaiah Bridges was never this man. He was usually a commander of steel; his reputation was renowned. But there was something about a life-changing event. Something that made patients re-evaluate their lives. She'd witnessed it many times before. But this time it felt more personal. As if he was playing into the thoughts she'd had for the last few months.

She gave a conciliatory nod and glanced over her shoulder to ensure no one else was listening. 'I know what you mean.' Her mouth curved in a soft smile. 'I've been thinking about things for a while. But…' she paused '…it can be kind of hard to meet someone when you've got a job like mine. My career comes first for me. I'm hoping my next job will be the promotion I've been waiting for. That will put more pressure on me. And I can't give up on that. It's been my dream for the last few years.'

Isaiah met her smile with his own. His tone kind, he said, 'I believe there will be someone out there for you. Someone who will be just perfect. Maybe you'll turn a corner and walk into him, just like I did with Adele. Or maybe…' this time he reached for her hand and squeezed it '…there's a chance already there, and you just need to reach out and grab it. You'll get your chance for the job, Ivy. Just make sure you take your chance for life too.' He looked at the pump next to him. 'I guess I'm doing fine.'

She looked at the monitor. 'Things seem to be going smoothly. I'll stay with you until it's finished and Tony comes back, and then…' she stood up and smoothed her skirt '…I'll phone Adele. Don't worry, I'll break the news gently.'

Her phone buzzed in her pocket and she pulled it out.

Still waiting for this photo. What are you—chicken?

She bristled as she grinned. It was as if he knew her. Knew that taunting her and challenging her would bring out her competitive edge. Her fighting spirit.

Jane appeared back at the door, along with Tony. 'We'll

take over now,' she said kindly. 'You must still be tired. Go and get some rest.'

Ivy paused for a second. 'Are you sure? I'm happy to assist.' Tony walked over and put his hand on her shoulder. She knew he'd served with Isaiah Bridges for a few years. He'd just had to go and tell the commander that they would need to airlift him off the ship, and that the aircraft carrier would need a new SMO. That couldn't have been easy. He probably wanted to spend some time alone with his colleague.

She gave an understanding nod. She turned to face Isaiah. 'SMO Bridges, it's been an honour. I'll go and call your wife.'

He gave her a wave of acknowledgement. 'Flight Surgeon Ross, remember what I told you.'

She disappeared down the corridor towards her quarters. 'Well, that was some first day,' she muttered to herself. Things were starting to play around in her brain. She was here. She was ready. There was at least half a chance she'd be considered to step into Isaiah Bridges's role. It made sense. Why ship someone else to the middle of the ocean if she was already here? Part of her hated the fact that it had even occurred to her. But of course it would.

It wasn't a crime to be ambitious. She just hoped someone back at headquarters would join the dots and make the decision to give her a chance. Her steps grew more confident as she went. By the time she'd reached her quarters, her phone was in her hand.

You show me yours. I'll show you mine.

Too much? Too daring? Maybe it was time to reach out and grab something.

Didn't think we were quite at that stage. Are you that kind
of girl, because I'm thinking about being that kind of guy...

She burst out laughing at the cheeky response. It was
exactly what she needed.

You know exactly what I mean. If I send you a photo, you
need to send one back. Deal?

She had the photo ready to send if he agreed. A thought
flickered across her mind. What if he backed out? If she
sent her photo, and then he just...ghosted her? What if he
thought she wasn't good enough for him?

Panic gripped her chest for a second. That thought
was just...ugh. Then Isaiah Bridges's face flashed into
her head—his expression when he'd talked about his wife
and his kids. A warm feeling spread through her, but she
didn't have time to dwell on it as her phone buzzed again.

Deal.

One word. How could one tiny word cause her heart to
leap in her chest and her stomach do an Olympic-medal-
winning backflip?

Hesitation was for fools. She took a breath and pressed
Send.

# CHAPTER FOUR

THE CALL CUT through the dead of night and made him leap from his bed, poised for action.

Old habits died hard.

Every hair on Travis's body stood on end. It took only a few seconds to realise that it was his phone that was ringing—not a siren. He looked quickly around his apartment, which was lit only by a thin strip of light streaming through a small gap in the blinds.

It was ridiculous. He knew it was. As a doctor he'd spent half his life on call, always ready to jump at a moment's notice. But the last few years had changed things.

First he'd been on deployment with a team in a war-torn area, acting to provide healthcare and medical aid. They'd come under mortar fire. In a heartbeat he'd lost three close colleagues and had twenty injured people around him. It had been three days of being constantly under fire before another team had rescued them. And it had left scars. In the dark space at night he constantly wondered if he could have prioritised differently, maybe saved more lives, or used his scarce supplies in a different way. Every debrief told him he'd done the best job possible—but debriefs didn't give reassurance in the middle of the night.

A few months later he'd been staying in a Chicago hotel, attending a training event. The noise in the middle of the night that time had been smoke alarms as fire had ripped through the five-star building. He'd fought his way through blinding, choking smoke, assisting people, showing them the way to fire escapes and stairs, going back time and time again to retrieve others who'd been injured in the confusion.

The local fire chief had praised him, but also called him a fool. His lungs had been smoke damaged and he'd suffered minor burns. Maybe if only one event had happened, things would be different. But because the two events had happened in such a short period of time they seemed to have left an indelible mark on his brain and senses.

He ignored the way his heart clamoured in his chest—furious with himself—and picked up his phone. 'Travis King.'

He listened carefully, only asking short questions. 'When? Who? Condition?'

In his head he was already walking out the door. He finished the conversation and pulled on his uniform, lifting the bag he always had packed and near the door. He opened the side pocket and threw in some personal items. A few casual shirts, joggers, charger for his phone and a book he was midway through. As he lifted his phone to push it into his back pocket, the photo he'd been looking at before he'd gone to sleep flashed up.

Ali. Dressed in casual clothes, a black top and jeans, with a slim gold chain around her neck and long gold earrings dangling from her lobes. Her blonde hair looked as if it had been caught in the wind and she was laughing at something someone had said to her. The picture had taken him by surprise. Ali wasn't just good-looking—she was stunning, in a natural kind of way. Her lips were coral in the photo and she was holding a glass of rosé wine—it must be her signature drink—and when he'd received the photo his eyes had widened at the whole effect.

Travis wasn't quite sure what he'd expected. He wasn't the kind of guy who judged people on their looks, but he couldn't pretend that if Ali had walked into a bar next to him, he wouldn't have taken a second glance.

He pushed the phone into his pocket as he grabbed his car keys. He had a long journey ahead. He could easily drop a few messages to Ali on the way. It might even be fun, distract him a little from the task ahead.

Ivy checked the board in the hospital ward. It gave a quick view of who was working, any outstanding tasks and how many patients were currently in the unit. She had a few jobs lined up for today. A number of the crew had spent too much time in the sun. Several needed to have irregularly shaped moles and blemishes removed. A couple needed biopsies and their lab was equipped to look at those samples. Removal was a simple procedure for a surgeon like herself. Back on land, this would be done by a specialist dermatologist, but in the middle of the ocean it was her task.

Tony gave her a nudge. 'I've assigned Medical Corpsman Donnelly to the marine operation today. It will be good for him. Confidence-building.'

She nodded. The marines on board were doing an exercise at sea today. There was always a member of the medical team assigned in case of difficulties. She'd done the job on many occasions herself. But Medical Corpsman Donnelly was a good choice. He was young, enthusiastic and eager to learn. He'd be stationed at one of the battle dressing stations and could call if assistance was required. But routine exercises took place every few days at sea. A bored and unmotivated crew wasn't good for anyone. Training was crucial for all.

'What about SMO Bridges?'

Tony glanced at his watch. 'He should be landing in Hawaii any time soon. I have a colleague who'll give us a call later to let us know how things have gone. And our new SMO will be with us shortly.'

Her heart plummeted straight down into her shoes.

'Already? That was quick!'

They hadn't even considered her for the position? She couldn't pretend she wasn't devastated. All her hopes dashed in a few words.

Tony laughed. 'Anyone would think this was a military organisation.' It was clear he hadn't even thought of her to fill the position and that hurt too.

'Who is it?' asked Ivy. 'Anyone I know or have worked with?' She felt prickly. They were sending someone else to do a job that she could have taken on herself.

'I have no idea. The commander hasn't told me. Just sent me a message to say to expect a new SMO in the next hour.'

Ivy set up a trolley next to her. She put on her best Ivy smile. It was important not to let others know how put out she was. Jealousy and bitterness were hardly good team-work components. 'Well, I'm going to be busy cutting out dodgy-looking moles.'

Tony shook his head at her terminology.

It prompted her to ask, 'Do you know how many words there are for mole in dermatology?'

He shook his head.

'Seventy-two,' she said with precision. 'I did a piece of work as a medical student for a professor of dermatology. I assessed every patient his department had seen in a month. Every new referral, the outcome, diagnoses, procedures and follow-up care.'

'And that's what you learned, that there are seventy-two words for mole?'

She raised her eyebrows. 'What I actually learned was that the locum service they'd brought in to help were much more effective and efficient than the staff of eight dermatologists he had working under him. But that report?' She lifted her hand and blew into her fingers. 'Disappeared in a puff of smoke.'

'I bet it did. Well, have fun. I'm off to do some blood work on a case that's got me stumped. Talk later.'

Ivy had just finished excising her fifth mole of the day and covered the stitches with a dressing when one of the nurses stuck her head around the door. 'Have you heard?'

Ivy snapped off her gloves and started washing her hands. 'Heard what?'

'New SMO has landed. Word is he is *hot*.'

'Jenny!' said Ivy in mock disgust as she laughed. Jenny disappeared, clearly to spread the message among the rest of the staff.

*Hot.* Interesting word choice. One that she'd used herself just recently. About ten seconds after Rob had sent his picture and the absolute instant that Liz had answered her phone.

'What…?' Liz had asked dopily.

'Hot. Rob. He's just sent his photo. Wait and I'll forward it to you.'

She waited the obligatory few seconds then heard the shriek at the end of the phone. 'Girl! He's not hot—he's smokin'!'

Ivy had smiled at the photo of the broad-shouldered, tanned guy with dark hair and bright blue eyes.

'Do you think he's used a filter?' asked Liz. Ivy could imagine her tilting her phone and staring critically at the screen.

'I don't think so,' said Ivy. 'Though I did think about putting a filter on my photo.'

'You don't need a filter,' scolded Liz quickly. 'You're beautiful just as you are.' There was a pause. 'Do you think it could be an old picture? Maybe it was taken ten years ago.'

'Why do you always have to look for the worst in people?' said Ivy.

'Because there's gotta be a catch. A guy this good-looking doesn't have a girl someplace?' Liz's deep southern twang was getting more pronounced. 'Or maybe he does? Maybe he has a wife? Ten kids?'

Ivy sighed and leaned back on her bed. 'Stop it, will you? Let me have five minutes of thinking this guy might (a) actually exist, (b) be interested in me and (c) have no hidden agenda. I know it's a revelation, but I'd like to enjoy this just a few minutes more.'

'Don't say I didn't warn you,' said Liz, then she let out a deep sigh. 'But, honey, if this guy is the real deal, grab him and hide him someplace quick.'

Ivy cut the call and held the phone to her chest, closing her eyes and letting her imagination drift back to San Diego. Her dreams had been interesting that night.

The ship rocked and she was jolted back to reality as the surgical instruments she'd just used rattled on the silver tray. It wasn't often she felt the momentum of the sea. Aircraft carriers were normally so big that they were pretty stable to travel on.

She tidied away the instruments. They would be autoclaved and repackaged for use again. Curiosity was seeping through her. She desperately wanted to know who the new SMO was. It was likely someone who'd done the role for years. But would that be someone the staff would describe as *hot*?

'Whoa!' The noise came from the corridor outside.

Ivy stuck her head out as one of the nurses had both hands outstretched between the bulkheads. She smiled at Ivy. 'Just getting my sea legs. Don't know what's happening today.'

'Me either.' Ivy nodded. She glanced down the corridor but there was literally nothing to see, only grey bulkheads.

She clicked the cupboard doors and drawers closed in the treatment room. She might as well go back and check in the med bays. Make sure everything was okay there whilst they were experiencing some stormy weather. It was at times like these she sometimes wished there was a way of seeing outside.

Another swell hit and she almost slid along one wall, barely managing to stay on her feet.

As she turned the corner she pressed both her hands to either bulkhead—the corridors were slim enough to do that—just like her colleague had a few moments before.

There was noise from the bottom of the corridor and Tony appeared, laughing as he banged into the bulkhead. 'Trust you to bring the bad weather with you,' he joked to whoever was coming behind him.

There was a deep throaty laugh. Seconds later, a tall, broad man in uniform appeared at the end of the corridor, his face partially hidden by his cap.

His strides were long as he walked towards her.

She squinted, then frowned. No.

Ivy gave her herself a shake, unable to move her hands to the bulkhead because of the movement of the vessel.

She looked again.

The man's footsteps faltered as he removed his hat from his head.

He pulled back in disbelief. 'Ali?' he asked.

It couldn't be. It just couldn't be. Not on her ship. Not

in the middle of the Pacific Ocean. Her nose twitched. Maybe her blood sugar was low—it was nearly lunchtime. She probably needed to eat.

'Rob?'

Tony's head flicked back and forth between them like some kind of kids' toy, a look of both bewilderment and amusement on his face. 'What is this? Pick a new name day?'

Neither of them answered. Rob's bright blue eyes were searing into hers. His eyes…in the flesh. So much brighter than they'd been in the photo.

Tony waved his hand, realising this was probably something he didn't actually want to know about. He put one hand out towards Ivy. 'Flight Surgeon Ivy Ross, this…' he moved his other hand '…is our new senior medical officer, Travis King.' Tony cleared his throat a little. 'Try and use real names, folks, and I'll leave you to get to know each other.'

His eyebrows were raised as he walked down the corridor, beating the hastiest retreat she'd ever seen.

She couldn't stop looking at Rob. No, Travis. What kind of name was that? A warm wash of embarrassment flooded through her. He was probably looking at her and trying to weigh up if she looked more like an Ali than an Ivy.

Her tongue was stuck to the roof of her mouth and words just wouldn't form. Being lost for words was new for Ivy. She could always hold her own. But she'd never had the experience of having a man she'd exchanged flirty messages with appear in front of her as her new boss.

This was like a bad romance movie. This wasn't real life. The guy she'd been flirting with had just walked into the job she'd wanted for herself. And, no, he wasn't that old. He must have only been an SMO for a few years himself. They hadn't sent in some old sea dog with years of experience; they'd sent her a guy from a pin-up calendar with only a few more years of experience than herself. Something burned down deep inside her.

One edge of his mouth quirked upwards. They were entirely alone in the long corridor—a seldom seen event, even on a ship as large as this. 'So, how's the insurance business?' he asked.

Her tense muscles relaxed a little and her tongue unstuck itself. She pushed the brief wave of jealousy out of her head. This had to be oddest situation in the world. Was this how he wanted to play things? Thank goodness. She'd half expected him to give her a dressing-down about the online untruths. That could be military style from a boss who wanted to make his mark.

She gave him a careful look. 'There might be a spanner in the works,' she said quietly.

'Really?' He took a few steps closer. And she felt it. She actually *felt* it. A shimmer in the air between them. It was the way he was looking at her. The way his eyes connected with hers, and there was a hint of a smile on his face. A smile that lit up his whole face and made him even sexier than before. Or maybe it was his height, his presence—things that really didn't translate in a photo. The weight behind his footsteps, the bulk of muscles. Whatever it was, it was a whole lot *more* than she could ever have imagined.

'What's the spanner, then?' His voice was husky and low as he stepped closer again. 'Is it a little insurance fraud?' It was his turn to let his eyebrows rise. He was almost laughing now.

'Ouch,' she said in mock horror. 'I think there might have been some fraudulent activity in international banking, not just in insurance.'

'Touché,' he said, nodding slowly.

He was beginning to seem more like a Travis now. Rob

was maybe too traditional a name for this guy. Travis might be a whole lot more interesting than she could ever have imagined.

They both jumped as a siren sounded. She recognised it immediately. 'Emergency team, battle dressing station seven.'

Ivy let out an expletive and turned to run towards the nearby med bay and grab some supplies. For the briefest of seconds she saw a wave of something pass over Travis's eyes. It was the tiniest of moments, but it was there. It was definitely there.

As she ran down the corridor he was so close he was almost at her back. He threw his bag into a corner in the med bay and stripped off his uniform jacket, grabbing the things she thrust towards him. 'Lead the way,' he said.

Battle dressing station seven was several decks beneath them and she ran the whole way, with Travis breathing down her neck. He kept talking as they ran. 'Any ideas?'

'There was an exercise today with the marines. One of our medical corpsmen is with them. He must have sounded the alarm.'

'It must be the weather,' murmured Travis. 'My jet nearly couldn't land.'

Wow. Because she couldn't see outside, she had no idea what it looked like. But if one of their jets carrying their new SMO almost hadn't landed, the whole aircraft carrier was clearly being affected, and now, with a potential incident with one of their teams, things must be bad.

A sharp blast of strong wind hit them, along with a steep temperature drop. Tony approached, running from another direction. Their corpsman was on the deck, surrounded by dark figures. As she pushed them aside, she could see a pool of blood.

As she dropped to her knees she could barely hear a

thing through the noise of the weather outside. One of the panels in the ship was open, exposing the ship to the elements. Now she understood the noise and drop in temperature.

She immediately pressed down on the wound on the marine beneath her and shouted in Donnelly's ear, 'What happened?'

The next moment there was a bellow above her. 'Marine, is anyone still outside?'

She couldn't hear above the muffled noise, but the next minute Travis was over at the entrance along with one of the other marines and they were physically pulling someone up a line. Seconds later they pulled the man over the rim, falling back onto the floor and yelling to the other marines to seal the door.

Ivy realised there was a third guy leaning against a bulkhead with blood pouring down his forehead from an open wound.

The panel was sealed by four marines, fighting against the wind. As soon as the door was slammed, her ears popped, adjusting to the pressure change.

Travis took charge again. 'Tony,' he said, pointing to the marine with the open head wound. He himself started an immediate scan of the marine he'd just pulled back inside. 'Report, Corpsman,' he ordered Donnelly in a gruff manner.

Ivy lifted the edge of the marine's jacket, which she'd been pressing, and it only took a few milliseconds to assess the situation. 'I need a tourniquet,' she shouted, hoping someone was listening.

Donnelly started to talk next to her. 'Marine Felipe was injured during the line descent. The heavy winds threw him into the side of the ship and knocked him unconscious. Marine Ajat attempted to assist but was caught on a piece of panelling, and when they tried to pull him up, his arm was injured.'

Marine Ajat, the man currently underneath her. 'He's torn an artery,' she said, as another medical corpsman appeared and pulled a tourniquet from an emergency kit near her. She didn't need to give the woman instructions. She'd heard the conversation and immediately placed it appropriately around the upper arm to try and temporarily reduce the blood supply to allow the team to move him.

'What about you?' she asked Travis about the marine on the deck next to him.

That man was conscious but squirming under Travis's examining touch.

'Suspected fracture of the tibia,' he said. 'Can we strap this and get him up to the sick bay?' By now, their whole emergency team had arrived. All of them with equipment. When a medical emergency was sounded on the aircraft carrier the response was always immediate. No matter who was on duty or off, all responded.

'Corporal,' said Travis in a stern voice, 'I expect a full report about this.' His eyes swept to Donnelly and Ivy gave the smallest shake of her head. She could see the exchange of glances around the creased faces. She'd served with some of these men before and she could see one of the corporals was just about to challenge Travis. He was, literally, a stranger in their midst, and since he'd flung his formal uniform aside they had no idea who, or what, he was.

'This is our new SMO, Travis King,' she said as a board was slid under her marine to transport him. She kept pressing on his wound as he was lifted upwards. There was another exchange of glances. But this time there were a few nods of heads. Recognition that this was the man they wanted looking after their colleagues, and they understood the command structure.

The movement up the stairs and along the slim corridors was a little awkward. Four staff were around each patient. They reached the hospital and took each marine to a different bay. 'We're going to need to go to Theatre.' Ivy nodded to one of the nurses. 'I need to scrub,' she said, adding to another nurse, 'Dev, take over here, and, Donna, get Theatre set up.'

Everyone moved like clockwork. Ivy didn't need to spend more time examining the wound. She'd seen the spurt of blood when she'd lifted the jacket and the immediate blood loss at the scene, which was everything she needed to. Already another medical corpsman was stripping the clothes from the marine and covering him with a gown, while yet another was inserting a cannula and running through a bag of IV fluids.

On the other side of the room she could see Tony attending to the head wound and Travis reading an X-ray. Things certainly moved fast in here.

She moved through to the theatre. Her staff were already opening the packs of equipment that she'd need. The nurse anaesthetist was ready in scrubs and checking some notes. She looked up. 'Marine Ajat. I have his details. He's grouped and cross-matched. Do you need blood?'

Ivy nodded. 'Please. I can only approximate his blood loss, but at a guess around four hundred mils. He has a fluid line up. Let's start with one unit and take it from there.'

There was noise at her back as her patient was rolled into the theatre. She turned around in time to see Travis start to scrub behind her. Her mask was already tied to her face, so when she opened her mouth to speak he didn't notice. Instead, he gave her a professional nod. 'You don't mind me scrubbing in this time, do you, Flight Surgeon Ross?'

It wasn't really a question. It was a courtesy as other

people were in the room. She gave a nod of her own head.
'Of course not.'

He was the boss. How could she actually object? It
didn't really matter whether she was in a regular hospital
setting or a military organisation. If a head surgeon wanted
to scrub in, she'd be a fool to voice any kind of objection.

She needed to stay on the right side of her boss. More
than that, she wanted him to be secure in her competence
and know he could rely on her clinical judgements and
skills. He would give a report on her at the end of this.
Would he know she was in line to be an SMO like himself? She needed to make sure he could see that she was
ready. She might not like the fact that Travis had walked
into the job she wanted, but making sure she kept her nose
clean and got a good report was every bit as important.

She held out her hands for her surgical gloves and
moved over to the theatre table.

One of her nurses was poised at the marine's arm, still
pressing on the wound. Ivy swallowed. The brachial artery
was usually only injured like this from a stab or gunshot
wound. She had no idea what was happening with the outside of the aircraft carrier, but it seemed that at some point
a piece of sharp-edged panelling had lifted and this marine had suffered the misfortune of it ripping through his
arm. She could almost picture him dangling from a line
at the side of the ship, being buffeted by the strong winds
and being thrown into the sharp edge.

Ivy didn't let herself shudder. She couldn't. She was the
surgeon. She had to keep steady hands and a steady heart.

As soon as her colleague lifted the current wound pad,
it was likely that the area would flood with blood and she
would be unable to see the damage clearly. It was a tricky
procedure. Worst-case scenario was that he would pump
out blood faster than she could get it back into him…on

an aircraft carrier they didn't have a never-ending supply of blood.

'Ready with suction?' she asked the nurse next to her.

Lynn nodded. Her eyes crinkled and Ivy knew that underneath her mask Lynn was smiling. 'We've got this,
don't worry.'

The words were reassuring. Lynn had been in service
for more than twenty years. She must have sensed Ivy's
slight flurry of nerves and wanted to show support, and
Ivy appreciated that. But if Lynn had sensed her nerves,
did that mean that Travis had too?

Ivy wanted to impress her new boss. Not because of the
previous flirting. That was a whole other area she'd have
to get her head around.

But, just like with Isaiah Bridges, she wanted the SMO
to have confidence in her, and her abilities. She was good
enough. She just needed to show him that.

She didn't even look behind her to see where Travis
was, she just gave Lynn a nod. 'Let's get started.'

Travis was drawing in deep breaths. He'd been in surgery
hundreds of times, but he never forgot just how important
it was to realise the significance of having a person's life in
his hands. Most surgeons he'd met in his life had been arrogant. There was no getting away from that. He'd always
vowed never to be like that, and he liked to make sure that
the people who worked for him weren't like that either.

He watched as Ivy Ross prepared herself and conversed
with her scrub nurse. There was nothing about her actions that gave him concern, or almost nothing, right up
until that last moment when she seemed to pause before
proceeding.

Maybe she was centring herself. Focusing solely on
the task at hand. It could be that his presence was making

her nervous, but no competent surgeon should be nervous while being observed by another.

He waited, wondering if he should speak, but the moment passed and Ivy proceeded with the surgery. It was a difficult and slightly unusual task. This wasn't a surgery she would carry out every day—it would normally be carried out by a specialist vascular surgeon, but that was the thing about being a navy surgeon. Out here, she had to cover every speciality as competently as possible.

He stood silently, watching her technique. The patient was losing blood fast and tying off this artery was crucial. The number of bloodstained swabs was mounting as the scrub nurse tried to keep the blood vessel visible for Ivy to do her work.

'Got it!'

The words let him breathe a silent sigh of relief. She turned to face him, her green eyes bright. 'Well, that was a little sucker.'

He laughed—he couldn't help it—as Ivy and the scrub nurse laughed too. He stayed there, conscious of the other work he wanted to observe in the medical bay. He'd worked with Tony previously, but he'd checked the rota—he hadn't met any of the other personnel before, and he liked to know everyone on his team by name.

This was an initiation by fire, but at least he'd got to see performance of some key individuals and the teamwork in place right from the start. He'd have to look up Ivy's file later to learn a little more about his mysterious almost blind date.

He moved a little closer and watched Ivy continue with the delicate surgery. Her stitching was clear and deft, and now the crucial part of surgery was past it felt easier to move closer without making her feel uncomfortable.

The monitor gave a ping and the anaesthetist changed position. 'Blood pressure has dropped, heart rate increasing.'

Ivy lifted both hands and looked carefully into the wound. As she did, she spoke smoothly. 'Let's hang another unit of blood. I think it's a delayed response to the blood already lost. There's no evidence of another bleeder.'

Good. She wasn't panicking. She was immensely calm. She signalled behind her for a stool on wheels, which one of the staff moved closer, and she perched on it. 'I'm going to wait before I fully close. Let's make sure we can get Marine Ajat stabilised. I'd hate to have to open him twice. Everyone agree?'

She looked around the theatre, waiting until each member had nodded, before finally meeting Travis's gaze. 'What about you, SMO? Do you have an opinion?'

He looked at her curiously. It was an interesting take. Was Ivy Ross a real team player—or did she lack confidence to make a decision herself? If it was the former—that she would listen to opinions that might be different from hers—he was impressed. If it was the latter—if she needed approval from others to make a decision—then it was just the opposite and he was worried.

'You're the surgeon, it's entirely your call, Flight Surgeon Ross,' he said in a steady voice.

There was a blink of silence. 'Great,' she replied, spinning around on her stool. 'Then we wait, everyone.'

It could have been awkward. But it wasn't. Ivy chatted easily to the team around her. It only took him a few moments to remember that she'd only got here just a few days before him. Of course. She was asking the crew questions about where they lived, their families—getting to know them, the exact thing that he intended to do himself.

Apart from her eyes, the rest of her was covered. There was hardly any part of her in view, but what did seep out was her interest in her fellow crewmates, her professionalism. She asked the anaesthetist a few times for updates on Marine Ajat's condition. The extra unit of blood started to make a difference. First, his blood pressure and heart rate steadied, then eventually started to pick up. Ivy stood up. 'I'm going to close now, folks. Don't worry, I'll have you all out of here in time for dinner.'

Travis knew it was time for him to leave. He now needed to have a conversation with the commander about how an accident like this could have happened on the aircraft carrier. He glanced at the clock on the bulkhead opposite. He could take bets now that the commander had expected him to ask those questions before now. But Travis had his own way of doing things. He was going to check on all the other marines affected today and make sure he was happy with their care. Then he was going to take time to debrief Medical Corpsmen Donnelly to get a good overview of the situation, and to make sure his staff member was fine. This was his team. This was his job.

As he left the theatre he paused a moment to take a look at Ivy as she bent to close. He still wasn't sure. Was she a good team member or not?

He intended to find out.

# CHAPTER FIVE

SHE HAD THE strangest feeling that she'd done something wrong. Ivy wasn't usually unnerved at work. She was settling in well, getting to know the staff and crew and learning the different ways people worked. Because Ivy was used to moving around, she was used to quickly ascertaining the most pertinent points about her teammates.

Usually within forty-eight hours she knew who the smart-mouthed folks were, the pedantic ones, the laissez-faire types, and the two levels of confidence—super-confident and likely to overextend themselves, and can't-make-a-decision, continually second-guessing themselves.

The one person she hadn't got a handle on, at all, was Travis. Others were constantly mentioning the SMO and how he'd popped in during night shift, or done one of the general clinics, but she'd hardly set eyes on him. If she didn't know better, she might think he was actually avoiding her. But he couldn't be, could he?

She definitely hadn't imagined things. There had been a glint in his eye, a bit of teasing at the initial meeting. She'd half expected to hear from him—at least by text, if nothing else. But it seemed ridiculous that the guy who had taken up space in her head for the last few weeks, and taken the job she wanted, was now in a confined space with her, and there had been no contact at all for the past two days. She'd frantically texted Liz, asking a million hypothetical questions, and it was clear that Liz had eventually grown tired of her.

For goodness' sake, what's wrong with you, girl? Get some backbone. Go and chase that man down and ask him what the deal is!

That had exasperated Ivy beyond belief. She'd thrown herself back on her bed and sighed. Liz just didn't get it. Ivy had plenty of backbone. But this was the navy and this was her job. She could hardly chase down her commanding officer and ask him what the deal was.

Ivy sighed and sat back up on the bed. It was the middle of the night but she was still wide awake. There wasn't exactly much for her to do. There were some reports she could look at. The boring kind of stuff that she always left for last—environmental duties, or writing up the actual reports of the investigations that she'd done. The investigation part was interesting but the report? Not so much.

She pulled on a pair of scrubs she kept in her quarters—they sometimes doubled as pyjamas for her—and wandered down the corridor to the med bay.

The nurse on duty gave her a nod and a smile. 'Nothing to worry about, Ivy,' she whispered.

Ivy nodded. 'Can't sleep. I'm going to do some paperwork.'

'You must be desperate.'

Ivy rolled her eyes. 'I am.'

The nurse looked as if she might say something else but just gave a nod of her head as Ivy filled up her coffee mug and headed through to the back office.

She picked up the files and computer she needed and

bumped the office door open with her bum, balancing on top her coffee and a cookie she'd found as she backed inside.

She turned around, licking her lips at the iced cookie. She hadn't realised she was hungry, and someone had clearly bribed one of the chefs on board.

As she turned she let out a yelp. The office wasn't exactly big and there was someone sitting in her chair. As she yelped her coffee spilled and her cookie started the ominous slide to the floor. But the figure jumped up and grabbed both.

Travis. It was Travis. And he was now wearing a soft white cotton T-shirt splattered with coffee.

The only light in the room was from a small reading lamp on the table. It cast shadows around the room. 'Travis, what are you doing here?'

He gave an indignant grin. 'No, what are you doing in here?'

'I couldn't sleep.' She shrugged, looking at his T-shirt and pulling a face. 'Sorry.'

He shrugged too. 'No problem, and since you asked, I'm hiding.'

'What?' She thudded down into the other small chair next to the desk. 'Why on earth are you hiding?'

'The person in the cabin next to me is clearly having a fight on the phone with their other half. Doesn't look like it'll be stopping any time soon. Sleep was not an option.'

Ivy wrinkled her brow. 'Wait, who is in the cabin next to you?' It had to be another enlisted officer.

But Travis held up his hand. 'Don't even go there.' He pointed to her cookie. 'Do you plan on splitting that cookie?'

'Do you plan on giving me the best chair?'

He looked around the tiny office, the corner of his lip

turning upwards. 'Let me think about it while I grab a coffee and a knife,' he said.

He came back two minutes later with his coffee and she noticed that along with his white T-shirt he was wearing grey running shorts and a pair of trainers. It was a far cry from his usual uniform. Of course, he was a normal guy who wore normal clothes, but working in a place like this it became totally normal to only ever see people in a variety of their uniforms. She kind of liked it.

He held up the knife.

'Is this a murder mystery?' she asked, cupping her hands around the cookie. 'You need to know that I actually sneaked this out of a container in the ward. It's stolen property, so if we get caught, you have to take the heat with me.'

He nodded solemnly as he sat down. 'Somehow I think it might be worth it.'

His eyes connected with hers and she could swear a tiny fairy ran along the length of her spine. She couldn't help but smile. 'Okay, but I have rules about sharing.'

He laughed. 'As a guy with three sisters and a brother, I know I'm going to regret this question, but what kind of rules?'

She pointed at him. 'You cut, and I choose.'

He waved his knife in the air. 'You forget. I am a surgeon. I can cut precisely.'

She folded her arms across her chest. 'Oh, I don't doubt you can cut precisely. But can you cut *fairly*?' She emphasised the word.

Travis raised his eyebrows. 'Let's see,' he said as he leaned over the cookie. She liked this. It was totally unexpected, but from the second he'd seen her the atmosphere between them had been relaxed. Maybe she'd just been imagining that he'd been avoiding her?

'Done.' Travis sat back proudly, looking at the two halves of the cookie.

Ivy held up the plate and rotated it slowly, examining both halves before she chose. After a few seconds Travis groaned. 'Come on, my coffee is getting cold.'

Ivy kept him waiting, carefully deciding which half of the cookie she was going to select, before picking it up and taking her first bite.

She closed her eyes. 'Mmm, lovely. We're going to have to try blackmail to find out where these came from.'

Travis nodded in agreement, although his cookie lasted two bites. 'What brings you here in the middle of the night?'

She glanced at the stack of folders on the desk. 'Couldn't sleep. There's no bar about, no movies. I've already reached level one hundred and forty-four on Play-Surgeon so I decided the only thing to do is work.'

He let out a laugh. 'Level one hundred and forty-four?'

She shrugged. 'Boredom is a terrible thing. I play it while listening to an audiobook.'

'What kind of book?'

'Usually a crime thriller. Something that makes me think.'

This was the kind of chat she'd imagined they would have had back in Gino's in San Diego, and her head was struggling to marry this up with sitting in a tiny office with her new boss.

She ran her fingers down the side of her mug. 'You don't know how much I wish this was a glass of rosé.'

She looked up and his blue gaze meshed with hers. For a moment neither of them said anything, then Travis gave a sigh. 'Maybe it was for the best we didn't meet that night.'

She couldn't help the wash of disappointment that swept over her. 'Why?'

'Because if we'd already met…' he pressed his lips together and tilted his head to one side '…who knows what might have happened?'

There it was. The buzz. The one that she'd hoped and expected to be there. Electricity simmering in the air between them. The what-if question…

She gave a slow nod and crossed her legs, wishing that she was wearing something sexier than scrubs. 'That might have proved…interesting.'

He nodded. 'Would you have told me your real name?'

'Would you have told me yours?'

They were both smiling at each other again and Ivy gave a little sigh. 'I guess I might have if…' she held up a hand and raised her eyebrows '…I decided that I liked you.' She was teasing him and she could tell that he liked it.

He leaned back in his chair and put his feet up on the desk. His coffee rested in his hands. 'Oh, so it's like that, is it? What were my chances? Do you think you would have liked me?'

She leaned back and also put her feet up on the desk, clashing with his as she took a sip of coffee and looked up through lowered lids. 'Jury's still out.'

'Are you always this sassy?'

'You have three sisters and you think this is sassy?'

She could almost reach out and grab the electricity that was in the air between them. She couldn't remember the last time she'd had a conversation like this. Flirting. Fun. With lots of sexual tension. This was even better than she'd imagined.

'True.' He nodded. He took his feet back down and leaned forward. 'Truth is, I would have told you my real name, and what I did, probably within the first five minutes.'

She paused and licked her lips before mimicking his

movements. Her head rested on her hand and they were only a few inches apart.

'I think I might have done the same.'

He smiled at her. A slow, sexy kind of smile. 'Why the fake profile?'

'Probably for the same reason as you. We have serious jobs. I don't really want people to track and trace me unless I'm sure about them. One stalker was enough, thanks.'

'You had a stalker?' He pulled back and looked genuinely surprised.

She gave a brief nod. 'Bad enough that he was prosecuted. I still have a restraining order in place against him.'

'Wow. That's serious stuff.'

She nodded. 'Thankfully I live next to a whole host of marines who have my safety on their radar. They helped when needed and got me through.'

'What about your family?'

She gave a wry laugh. 'Oh, it was before he moved to Australia, so my brother did the brother thing. He came down with a baseball bat in his car. Thankfully, again, one of the marines helped him understand he couldn't help if he landed himself in prison.'

'Were you scared?'

The question took her by surprise. Not many people had the front to actually ask something like that. She paused, collecting her thoughts before she answered. 'Yes, and no,' she admitted. 'He was creepy. I worried about him sneaking his way into my house, or having some hidden camera that could watch me when I slept. But on the few occasions he approached me on the street I wasn't scared at all.' She gave a thoughtful nod of her head. 'I could take him.'

Travis looked at her with interest. 'No wonder you didn't want your real identity out there on the dating site.'

'I just wish I had thought of it earlier. It could have saved me a lot of trouble.'

Her coffee was cold now, and she hadn't done a single bit of the work she'd intended to. But her concentration was well and truly shot. The only possible thing she could think about now was the perfect specimen in front of her. He was wearing some kind of sports deodorant. It was clean and fresh with a hint of musk. She, in turn, was wearing nothing. Not a spot of make-up, or any kind of perfume or scent. Thank goodness she'd brushed her teeth before coming along to the med bay.

'I like your hair down,' Travis said quietly. 'You have waves.'

Her hand cupped her slightly straggly curls. 'In the humidity—which I'm sure we'll see—I have pure frizz. If I spend a few hours on it I have corkscrew curls, or poker-straight hair. Just depends how the mood strikes me.'

His smile was kind of lazy. 'What did you have the night you were meant to be meeting me?'

The memory flooded back to her. The nerves, the expectation, the excitement. She gave a shrug. 'Actually, I more or less had this. You didn't exactly give me much time to get ready.'

Travis held up his hands. 'Hey, I was just off a plane. I didn't want to waste any time. I thought I was about to meet some woman who'd been teasing me for the last few weeks by message. Instead, I ended up sad and lonely, sitting at a bar on my own.'

'Stop it!' The gentle slap of her hand made a connection with his warm skin, and instead of pulling away she just left it there. 'You thought you were getting some hottie, and instead you would have got me.' She gestured down at her pale blue scrubs, instantly remembering how underdressed she was. The words struck a pang somewhere in her heart.

That hidden part of her that always felt not good enough. They'd come out without much thought. Thank goodness she'd framed it as a self-deprecating joke.

Travis moved forward, back to his earlier position where his face was only inches from hers. 'I would have been delighted to get you.' His finger lifted and gently stroked the side of her face in a touch as light as a butterfly's wings.

She didn't hide her instinct. Her face leaned naturally towards his hand. 'Who says you're not a hottie?' he whispered. The words were so soft and husky they caressed her skin. Her hand came up and closed over his, holding it there against her cheek.

'There's rules against this,' she whispered.

'I know,' he replied, but he didn't move. 'But right now I'm pretending we're not aboard the *Coolidge* in the middle of the Pacific Ocean. Right now I'm pretending we're in Gino's in San Diego and you've just drunk your rosé, me my beer, and we're wondering what happens next.'

The tiny hairs on her arms prickled. She closed her eyes and let her mind carry her off to that exact place. There she was, wearing her jeans and black top, and for some strange reason a pair of black, patent, impossibly high heels. She didn't even own such a pair of shoes but, hey, it was her dream.

'What are you wearing?' she said in a low voice.

He didn't hesitate. 'Black T-shirt and a pair of jeans.'

His other hand moved, drifting over the back of hers, his fingers intertwining with hers. 'I'm liking what I see,' she whispered. His hand moved again, this time threading through her hair. Her breath caught in her throat. She knew what happened next. And she'd never wanted something so badly in her life.

'Me too.' She sensed him move closer, even though her

eyes were closed, and held her breath, waiting for his lips to come into contact with hers.

There was a noise outside. The sound of a trolley rumbling past just as the ship gave a slight roll. They both jerked apart, just in time to hear the trolley crashing off a wall.

Ivy's heart dipped in disappointment. There were voices outside. The scramble of a few of the staff catching the wayward trolley. 'Jeez, that probably woke half the patients. Get that stowed away safely. You know better than to leave equipment hanging about.'

Ivy recognised the scolding voice as belonging to Lynn, one of the nurses.

Her heart was racing in her chest, her breath pathetic gasps. She sat back in her chair—the *good* chair. 'Whoa.'

Travis looked momentarily lost. Just like he had when the alarm had gone off on his first day. And now, like then, it was so quick, so fleeting, that if she'd blinked, she would have missed it.

He gave the smallest shudder, then looked at her again. This time something had changed. No, *everything* had changed.

'Ivy,' he said in a tight voice, standing up and pulling at his T-shirt, as if he were straightening his uniform jacket. He gave a shake of his head. 'Apologies. I don't know what I was thinking. I'm your commanding officer. I'm sorry. That should never have happened. That can never, ever happen again.'

She wasn't quite sure what to say. Most of her words were stuck somewhere at the back of her throat. Her brain was working just fine. The words in there were firing back and forth. *Are you joking me? Why didn't you kiss me? What's wrong with me? How dare you? We were this close—this close!*

She stood up and swallowed, even though her mouth was bone dry.

It was as if some kind of shutter had come over his eyes. He was looking at her, without *looking* at her. Every part of her brain was telling her to be professional. Reminding her that he was her commanding officer.

Whilst there were rules in the navy, there was no coercion here. She had been a willing participant in what had just happened. But what made her stomach curl the most was the fact that if he hadn't moved she would still be in his arms.

He had changed his mind. That tiny little voice in her head spoke instantly. *You're not good enough.*

But she wouldn't listen to that voice. She wouldn't allow those feelings to flood her like they had in the past. Instead Ivy took a moment, put her hands on her hips and looked him straight in the eye. 'Don't start what you can't continue,' she said haughtily, before turning on her heel and marching out the door.

# CHAPTER SIX

Travis was truly the king of bad decisions. He shouldn't have started. And more importantly he shouldn't have stopped.

He could still sense the feel of Ivy's soft hair through his fingers and smell the fruit-scented shampoo she used in her hair.

He'd been lost. He'd been lost in the moment and lost in the person. For a few minutes they'd been in the bar they had supposed to have met in. Off this aircraft carrier, away from the rules and regulations that would frown on them getting together. Travis King had been away from trauma, away from surgery and away from the memories that stayed stuck in his head…almost.

Until that second when the loud bang had shot him back there. Back to the mortar fire and hiding while trying to tend to wounded colleagues. Travis knew exactly what was wrong with him. He knew it was PTSD from the mortar attack or the hotel fire. He suspected it was a combination of the two.

Sometimes a smell or sound made him momentarily freeze and relive one moment or another. Thing was, these events passed in a flash. Most people around him wouldn't even know that something had happened. But twice now, when he'd been with Ivy, he'd had a wave of something. And what's worse, he knew she'd noticed.

He was good at hiding things. He'd been doing it for the last four years. He didn't want to see a shrink or a counsellor. He didn't imagine that having PTSD on his medical record would allow his career to progress much further. Even though he knew that, in theory, it shouldn't, he had a more cynical view. He was a surgeon. A damn good surgeon. He was here because he deserved to be.

But…

Travis drew in a deep breath. He wasn't quite sure what had happened last night. Oh, he was exactly sure what he'd *wanted* to happen. But that noise had brought him to a clanging halt.

There was something about Ivy Ross. Her smile. Her shape. The flirting.

He'd spent a long time waiting to meet someone. She was right in front of him. But even considering being in a relationship seemed to trigger a warning in his brain. He was letting his guard down. Opening his mind to new possibilities.

And that was entirely where he was going wrong. Letting his guard down meant the chance of revealing parts of himself he didn't want to share. If things progressed with Ivy, how could he deal with his issues? The truth was that even though he used the apps, he hadn't actually thought he'd ever meet someone who would make him contemplate the future. A few dates then things were finished. That was how he'd played it for the last few years. No awkward questions. No expectations. But Ivy was peeling back parts of him that he wasn't sure he was ready to expose.

But there was more. She thankfully hadn't noticed that night, but he'd been reading her file. Ivy Ross had ambition. The navy liked her. She'd never had anything less than glowing reports and was being considered for the next SMO position that became vacant.

Tiny pieces were falling into place. She'd been on this ship, right here, when Isaiah Bridges had been taken ill. Instead of shipping him in, they could have given her the position that, from the look of her record, she'd earned. Of course, they would then have had the issue of having to find another flight surgeon for the *Coolidge*—Ivy might be good, but she couldn't do two jobs. He wasn't always sure how the top brass made their decisions. If they'd promoted Ivy, it might have been difficult for the existing team to think of her as SMO. Respect was sometimes hard to get in the navy. He could only imagine that they wanted her to take up her first SMO post right from the outset. That was how he had started his—and on a ship a little smaller than this one. They probably just wanted to let her first post be a bit easier than this one. A number of the SMOs were due to retire soon. Ivy would get her chance. But how did she feel about him stepping in here when she was, literally, waiting in the wings?

Travis groaned and leaned back in his chair. As SMO he had a cabin where he could actually reach out his arms and not touch the wall on either side of him. But it still felt claustrophobic. His phone pinged and he glanced down as his heart jumped in his chest, only to plummet instantly.

It was his family group chat. His mum and dad, brother and three sisters could talk for hours, and sometimes he preferred to sit it out and pretend there was no signal in the middle of the ocean.

He knew why he'd been so interested in his phone. He was hoping for a second that it might be Ivy. But, of course, it wouldn't be. Not after how he'd treated her last night. He shook his head. He could hear all three voices of his sisters in his head if he actually told them what had happened. They would kick his…

Every time he closed his eyes he could see the furious flash in Ivy's eyes last night. The angry tilt of her chin as she'd looked him straight in the eye and put him clearly in his place.

It had turned him on more than ever.

There was so much that could go wrong here—the first thing being that he was her commanding officer. It didn't matter that their 'maybe' relationship had started somewhere else. It didn't matter that Ivy was obviously a strong independent woman who would clearly never be influenced by him to do anything she didn't want to do. There were rules, lines that couldn't be crossed.

And he'd wanted to cross them all. Completely. Truth was, he still did.

Travis looked down at his clenched fists. It was time to hit the gym in the ship. Anywhere he could take out some of this frustration that was building in his body.


Ivy was calm. She was playing a game of imaginary dodgeball. If Travis was likely to be in a place, she made sure she was elsewhere. She had a job to do. But that didn't mean they had to overlap. She'd had to do a few minor surgical procedures on some crew members and run a few of the clinics. Healthcare and preventative medicine on the aircraft carrier was essential.

The phone was ringing as she was writing up her last set of notes. 'Flight Surgeon Ross?'

'Yes, what can I do for you?'

'This is Chief Petty Officer Cho. We've had a distress call from a boat requiring medical assistance.'

Her skin prickled. 'Any details?'

'Come topside. We'll brief you when you get here.'

She paused for a second. 'Does SMO King know about this?'

'We couldn't get a hold of him, and there's no time to wait.'

That didn't sound quite right, but Ivy didn't have time to question it. She grabbed a medical pack and shouted to one of the corpsman to accompany her. Her heart was already fluttering in her chest. Medical assistance on another vessel would likely mean her ending up at the end of a cable—not entirely her favourite place to be. But there was no time for hesitation.

Before she had a chance to think much further, she was topside, wearing her helmet and thick jacket and heading to one of the helicopters. The officer shook his head at the corpsman. 'Only room for one, and time is of the essence. Go back and try and find SMO King.'

As soon as she climbed on board, she could hear through her com. 'What do you have?'

The pilot turned. 'Call for assistance. A woman has gone into hard labour.'

He flung out his arm at the blue-and-green ocean for miles around them. 'And what a place for it.'

Ivy screwed up her face. 'Why on earth would a heavily pregnant woman be in a place with potentially no medical assistance?'

The pilot shrugged and then pulled a face. 'Who said she was heavily pregnant?'

Ivy felt her stomach clench. 'Oh, no. How pregnant is she?'

She leaned back as the helicopter took off. 'Thirty—'
She didn't catch the other figure.

The co-pilot held up his hand and signalled ten minutes.

Ivy spoke into her microphone. 'Let the carrier know we'll be bringing back a premature baby and a new mother.'

There was no way she'd be able to handle this on the vessel they were flying to. She couldn't transfer a woman in heavy labour. But she could transfer a woman who'd delivered and a baby that would likely need medical support. She swallowed heavily and leaned back even further. At least that was what she hoped she would be bringing back to the carrier. Any other possibilities just weren't allowed space in her head.

'She's gone where?'

Jane looked Travis in the eye. 'She was called to an emergency. A woman…' Jane glanced at the notes on top of the incubator she was wheeling across the room '…apparently thirty-three weeks gestation has gone into premature labour.' Jane kept walking and glanced over her shoulder at him. 'They tried to call you first but you didn't answer. Where were you?'

Her eyes looked up and down the length of his body. He was wearing a T-shirt and shorts and dripping perspiration all over the hospital floor. Travis was cursing inwardly. All the frustration he'd just taken out on a punchbag in the gym, while listening to very loud rock music through his earphones, had instantly reappeared.

'Didn't you call me over the com?'

'It wasn't me that wanted you. It was the chief petty officer.'

'Darn it.' Travis started striding up the stairs. It only took moments to reach the coms centre.

'Patch me in to my doctor. I need to know what's happening,' he said briskly.

The petty officer on duty handed him a set of headphones and gave him a signal.

'Ivy, what's going on?'

She swore at him. She actually swore at him. Someone else cut in. It took Travis a few seconds to realise who it might be. The pilot. 'Your doc is a bit busy right now. We're just putting her down.'

Travis's heart skipped a beat just as Tony joined him in the coms room. His face was red. He'd obviously heard what was happening and had sprinted here, likely from the other side of the carrier.

He put his hand over the mic. 'I missed the call. Ivy is likely about to deliver a premature baby.'

Tony rolled his eyes. 'Thank goodness it wasn't me. Been a long time since I've done a delivery.'

Travis had a sickening feeling. 'I'm not sure how long it's been since Ivy did either, or if she's *ever* done it.'

He took a deep breath and sent up a silent prayer. This could all go horribly wrong. He'd missed the call. He *did* have some experience of this, and he should have been the one on the helicopter. If he could swap places with her right now, he would do it in a heartbeat. He only hoped that Ivy would be able to deal with whatever was out there.

She could hear them as she dangled from the cable, buffeted by the Pacific winds. Talking about her as if they'd forgotten she would be listening. She was concentrating hard. But even though she was concentrating on her controlled descent, she hoped the pilot was concentrating even harder. She didn't want to end up in the blue water—no matter how calm and tranquil it looked right now.

A man was waving frantically beneath her, and he caught her feet and guided her down. There was a moment of relief as her feet hit the deck, then she unclipped and gave the helicopter a thumbs up so it could back away.

'I'm Ivy Ross. I'm a US Navy doctor. We heard your distress call. Tell me what's happening?' she asked the man quickly.

'M-my wife,' was all he stammered as he pointed at the cabin.

She didn't wait but ducked inside, unzipping the front of her flight suit. The heat was getting to her already. A woman lay on one of the side seats, panting heavily, her legs spread slightly apart.

Ivy crouched near her head. 'I'm Ivy. I'm a doctor,' she said steadily. 'Tell me your name and how many weeks you are.'

'I'm Kalia,' she breathed. 'I'm thirty-three weeks. This came out of nowhere.'

Ivy nodded, not saying all the comments that had already naturally swirled around in her head. 'How far apart are your contractions?'

Kalia gritted her teeth and grabbed for Ivy's hand.

'I need an update,' came a cool voice in her ear.

Ivy ignored it, focusing her full attention on Kalia. 'Every few minutes,' choked Kalia.

Ivy nodded. 'Okay, any history I need to know about? Problems during your pregnancy?'

Kalia shook her head.

'Is this your first pregnancy?'

Kalia nodded. 'It's too early. Will my baby be okay?'

'Update, Ivy.' She pressed her finger to her ear where her headset still was.

'Hold on.'

She turned back to Kalia. 'Your prenatal care—any problems? Did all your scans go okay?'

Kalia frowned. 'Everything has been fine. Right up

until now.' She gripped Ivy's hand as another contraction hit. Ivy could sense the panic of Kalia's husband behind her. She waved her hand at him. 'Come around here and sit with your wife. Take her hand,' she added, thinking she would need both of hers back. This delivery was probably imminent.

'Okay, Kalia. Do you mind if I examine you to make sure everything is okay?'

Kalia nodded. It only took a few minutes for Ivy to check her abdomen and determine the lie of the baby. She snapped on her gloves and did an internal examination, which showed Kalia was fully effaced and the head was already presenting.

She gave Kalia a nod and a smile. 'Everything looks good. We're going to have a baby join us soon. Do you know what you're having?'

She was talking to Kalia and her husband but she also knew that Travis could hear every word.

He started barking in her ear. 'Any issues? What do you need? How soon can you get back?'

She kept her cool and ignored him. He might be her commanding officer but this situation demanded her full attention and she was here herself. There was no backup. Everything was on her.

'Okay,' she said smoothly to Kalia. 'On your next contraction, get ready to push. We'll have this baby here soon.'

Inside she was praying there would be no immediate issues when the baby came out. She didn't have all the equipment they would normally have in a hospital, and it had been years since she'd supervised a delivery—not since back in her training days.

In her headset she heard the helicopter was back on the ship. It couldn't hang in the air above this vessel indefinitely. It would come back as soon as it was needed.

So right now, in the middle of the Pacific Ocean, it was just her, Kalia and Kalia's husband, along with an imminent arrival.

Swirls of doubt circled her like the genie coming out of a lamp. Maybe she'd got too ambitious. Maybe she would never be an SMO. Maybe she wasn't even a competent flight surgeon and was about to make a mess of all this. For the first time in forever she actually felt seasick—an unknown for her.

There was a voice in her ear. 'You can do this, Ivy.' It was as if he'd heard her thoughts and had realised that right now she was having moments of doubt.

It sent a shiver down her spine. As if he'd just read her mind—had realised she was as nervous as could be because this was all down to her.

The tone of his voice was different too from his earlier yells. Calmer, reassuring. Totally in control. Just like she was.

In the end, the arrival went smoothly. Half an hour after she started pushing, Kalia delivered a baby girl. The baby was obviously small at thirty-three weeks. Ivy guessed between three and four pounds. There were a few moments of panic in her chest as she gave the little girl a sharp rub to try and encourage her to start breathing. She had no proper suction or even an airway for a baby this size. Finally, there was a little yelp and Ivy let out the breath she'd been holding.

She spoke into her com. 'Okay, baby is here. Breathing, but might need a little extra support. Can we arrange a transfer, please?'

Now she'd checked the baby, she clamped and cut the cord and laid the baby on Kalia's chest, knowing how important skin-to-skin contact was for both mother and baby.

She could hear Travis's voice in the background, shouting instructions. The momentary encouragement was gone.

'We'll need to check your baby properly on the ship. Are you okay with that, Kalia?'

'You want to take my baby?'

Ivy shook her head. 'No, of course not. We'll take you both.' She turned to Kalia's husband. 'But we'll need to leave you here.'

'Can I come alongside?'

Ivy knew he didn't want to be parted from his wife and new daughter, but she also knew their boat couldn't be left drifting in the Pacific. 'Let me check with the captain. I'm sure he'll be able to work something out.'

She put her hand on Kalia's shoulder. 'We'll need to transfer you up to the helicopter once it comes back. Then I'll come up with the baby. It's a little tricky, but I'll help you with the harness and talk you through it.'

Ivy ignored how dry her mouth was currently feeling. There had been no time on the way here to think about how much she hated the whole process of being lowered from, then lifted back onto the helicopter. It definitely wasn't her favourite part of the job. Dangling like a spider on a gossamer strand of web, which felt as if it could snap in an instant, was the kind of thing that kept her awake at night.

A few minutes later she heard Travis's voice in her ear again and the sound of the chopper in the distance. 'We'll be above you shortly. I'm going to come down and escort our mum up, then you can come up with the baby.'

Ivy was stunned. 'You're coming?'

'Of course I'm coming. I should have been there in the first place.'

She didn't quite know what to think. Was he checking up on her? Or was he just annoyed he'd missed the call?

A few moments later there was a thud on the deck and

Travis appeared at the doorway. He had a wide grin on his face and a harness in his hand, which he placed on the floor. He extended his hand to Kalia's husband. 'Congratulations, Daddy. You have a beautiful daughter. Have you thought about a name?'

Ivy was stunned. He was acting as if it were normal to give birth in the middle of the ocean. No recriminations. No questions about how exactly they'd ended up in this position. Just immediate congratulations. It was actually kind of nice.

He turned to her. 'Have you delivered the placenta?'

She nodded. 'Completely intact.'

He stepped closer to Kalia. 'Do you mind if I get a look at your gorgeous daughter?'

Kalia shook her head and held out slightly trembling arms. 'Leila,' she said as she glanced at her husband. 'That's what we're going to call her.'

Travis unwrapped the baby from the makeshift shawl that Ivy had wrapped her in and gave her a quick check. Leila looked tiny in his large hands, but what amazed Ivy most was the way he cooed and talked to the baby. She was pretty sure he hadn't delivered a baby any time recently, but he acted as though this were an everyday occurrence. It was a whole side of him that she would never have imagined. She kind of liked it.

He handed the baby back and spent a few moments talking to the father and giving him instructions about rendezvousing with the aircraft carrier. It seemed that another larger ship would be passing the following day and could take all three passengers back to Hawaii, with their boat towed behind.

Ivy helped Kalia get herself back together, then helped her into the harness and gave her instructions for transporting up with Travis. She strapped Leila close to her chest, and waited for the harness to come back down for her.

Within a few moments she was swinging in the air, caught momentarily in a sharp gust of wind, on her way back up to the helicopter. Her heart was in her mouth, as was part of her stomach. But she lowered her head and kept talking quietly to Leila throughout the whole process, ignoring the fact she hated every second of this. The baby was bundled up in a variety of blankets that Travis had brought with him and seemed entirely unperturbed by the whole situation.

Strong arms pulled them both back into the helicopter and ten minutes later they were back on the aircraft carrier. Ivy didn't want anyone to notice that her legs were still shaking.

A whole team was waiting for them just off the flight deck. Tony gave her shoulder a squeeze. 'Okay? Do you need something?'

Travis's head turned sharply, but before he got a chance to ask the obvious question Tony spoke again. 'Ivy hates the harness. She usually ends up either wearing her lunch or with vertigo for the next few days.'

Travis's look was accusing. 'You never said anything.'

Ivy shrugged as she strode towards the door. 'I had a job to do.' Trouble was, now she was on solid ground again, it was as if all the responses she'd delayed in her body were acting at once. Thirty seconds later she was sick over the side.

As Tony and Lynn sped away with the patients, Travis put his arm around her shoulder. 'Come on, I'll give you an injection.'

She wanted to object. But she could literally feel the spinning inside her head. She already knew this was likely to trigger a migraine tonight.

She lowered her head and walked down the corridor with Travis, not talking. He sat her down in one of the treatment rooms and she stepped out of the flight suit, swaying as she did so. He caught her again and sat her back down. 'Wow, you get this bad. Why didn't you say anything?'

She kept her eyes closed. It kind of helped her head to stop spinning. 'You weren't around. I had a job to do.'

She stood up quickly and headed to the sink, putting her hands on either side of it as her stomach heaved again. He pulled back her hair, which had become disentangled from her ponytail band, and waited patiently. This was truly her at her worst. But he was still there. By her side. Later, she'd probably wonder what it all meant, but right now she just wanted to lie down. The sickness sensation passed and a glass of water was pressed into her hand.

'Let me give you something for the sickness,' he said quickly.

She opened her eyes and then shut them again. 'I'll need something for a migraine too.' Then she let out a sigh of exasperation. 'In fact, don't. I'm on duty tonight.'

'Oh, no, you're not. The only duty you might have tonight is as a patient.'

'No way,' she said as one jab, then another, nipped the skin at the top of her arms. Boy, he didn't mess around.

'If you won't stay in a hospital bed, you'll have to agree to one of us checking on you.'

Ivy sagged back down onto the hard stool. 'As long as I drink a cup of hot tea and lie down for a few hours, I'll be fine.'

Tony appeared at the door. 'She'll also need either a large slice of chocolate cake or something similar in a few hours or she gets very cranky. Believe me, I know.'

Travis looked at Tony in surprise. 'You knew about this and didn't tell me?'

Tony shrugged. 'What's to tell? It hadn't come up. Anyway, just letting you know we've had to put Leila on some supplementary oxygen. I'm sure it'll only be for a few hours but we'll keep her under observation.' As he turned to leave he glanced over his shoulder at Travis. 'I'll watch the new patients if you take care of this one. Find her some cake for later.'

Ivy grimaced. She hated being fussed over, but she was more annoyed about showing weakness in front of her new boss. A flight surgeon who hated helicopter descents was probably not on his list of prized staff skills. She expected him to say something snide, but instead he gave a big sigh. 'I'm sorry, Ivy.'

Her eyes flew open and fixed on his. 'What?'

'They put out a staff call for me, and I never heard it. I was in the gym with a set of earphones in. I missed it,' he admitted. 'It should have been me on that flight, not you.'

She gave the briefest shake of her head, knowing to keep her movements small. 'No, it shouldn't. You're SMO. This was always a task you should have delegated to one of the other doctors.'

He kept his gaze steady. 'But if I'd known about your vertigo, I would never have sent you. And when was the last time you delivered a baby?'

She swallowed, wishing she had that tea she wanted. 'About nine years ago,' she admitted.

'So, even though it wasn't your area of expertise, and it was a procedure that makes you unwell, you went anyway?'

'It's my job,' she said steadily. 'There was no time for delay.'

His gaze hadn't moved from hers. 'You didn't even try

to put out a call for me or Tony? Are you sure we haven't delivered a whole host of babies between us?'

'I know Tony hasn't. Have you?'

Travis gave a small nod. 'One or two. On my last tour of duty I think I had seven.'

'Seven!' Now she was wishing she *had* waited and tried to put another call out for either of them. Maybe then her stomach wouldn't be swishing about as badly as her head. He shook his head.

'But that was four years ago. Not recent at all.'

She closed her eyes again. The bright lights in the room were starting to nip at her eyes.

'Let me walk you back to your cabin.'

He had moved right next to her and she jumped at his soft voice. 'I should check on Leila,' she said. But even she could hear how weary her voice sounded.

His arm slipped around her shoulder. 'I'm going to walk you back to your cabin, make you tea and find you cake.'

She gave a quiet laugh and put her hand up to her head. 'Wait, did I drop into the ocean? I feel as if I'm hallucinating.'

'You didn't fall into the ocean and I don't think you're hallucinating. Or maybe you are? Need me to do a check?'

His arm felt comfortable around her shoulders, not intrusive at all. Which was odd. She'd decided she didn't like Travis any more, and he'd annoyed her. She moved her hand up to meet his, sliding her hand into his. She didn't care what it looked like, or what he might make of it. Right now, she just needed something to hold on to. 'No, don't do that. I don't need a check.' The start of the migraine was already draining her. 'I just want to get back to my cabin,' she admitted.

'Your wish is my command,' said Travis as he started guiding her down the corridor.

Ivy knew that if anyone saw them like this there would likely be talk. But she really didn't care. All she wanted to do was lie down and drink hot tea, and maybe, in a little while, eat some cake.

Before she could think much more Travis opened the door to her cabin and guided her inside. 'I'll go and get you tea. I can't give you anything else for the migraine, though.'

She nodded. 'I know. The injections are the only things that work for me. That, and sleeping for a few hours. Honestly, I'll be as right as rain in no time.'

He smiled at her expression. 'I'll also hunt you down some cake.'

She lay down on the bed once he'd left and let out a sigh. Then threw any caution to the wind and stripped off her uniform, pulling on a pair of soft pyjamas. She honestly didn't care what she looked like right now. Apart from the migraine and vertigo, she was just so grateful to relax every muscle in her body that had been tense since she'd gone out on the mission.

Within a few moments Travis came back and pressed a cup of hot tea into her hands. She sipped it gratefully. She'd been angry with him before, but he'd actually been nice to her through all of this. 'You might not be so bad after all,' she whispered as she finally drifted off to sleep.

Travis's head was all over the place. Work was fine, apart from the overwhelming guilt he'd felt that Ivy had gone on that mission instead of him. Both mother and baby were being closely monitored. Though there were a few minor hiccups, they were nothing that an extra night in the carrier's hospital couldn't solve.

He'd managed to cram all his other duties into the space of a couple of hours. He'd made a special request to the kitchen and they'd whipped up a whole cake for their hero doctor who'd gone to deliver the baby. By the time he'd collected the chocolate frosted cake and made more tea, Ivy had been sleeping for nearly three hours. He paused outside her door. Was three hours enough?

He tapped slightly at the door and pushed it open. The lights were dimmed and Ivy was still sleeping, curled on her side on top of her bed in the pair of pyjamas that hugged her body in a way he'd tried not to notice earlier. He hesitated, wondering if he should leave her, but her nose twitched and she rubbed her eyes.

She didn't change position but her green eyes blinked open and she smiled. 'Is that chocolate cake?' she asked.

He nodded.

'And tea?'

'Don't say I can't multitask.'

She smiled and pushed herself up. 'Give me a second.' She grabbed a bottle of water and her toothbrush and disappeared for a moment, looking a bit more awake when she returned. She waved her toothbrush in the air. 'Sorry, habit of a lifetime. I have to brush my teeth as soon as I wake up.'

'No problem,' he said. He'd put the cake and tea on her desk but he was sitting in her chair, so she sat on the bed opposite him.

'Okay, who did you pay to make cake for you?'

He shook his head as he lifted a large knife. 'Oh, no, I didn't need to pay anything. Ivy Ross is now a legend on board. The doctor who delivered a baby in the middle of the ocean? The whole carrier is talking about you. I just had to ask the kitchen and they were happy to oblige.'

Her blonde hair was rumpled and she had a pillow crease on her face. He tried not to think about just how cute that made her look. She stretched out her pinkie and leaned over and stuck it in the little extra frosting at the bottom of the cake. She put in her mouth. 'Mmm… delicious.'

He stared at her. 'I can't believe you just did that.'

She looked at him in mock horror. 'Of course I just did that. It marks the cake as mine. What, did you think I was going to share? I thought you said you had sisters?'

He laughed. 'Ah…the sibling move. A wise one. I might have done that myself on a few occasions.'

She nodded. 'Just be glad I didn't stick my finger right in the middle of it.' She gave a smiling shrug. 'You can have a piece from the other side.'

He cut them slices and put them on two plates, waiting until she'd settled back with her tea and the cake on her lap before sitting down again himself. She had a little more colour in her cheeks now.

After a few bites she gave him a wary smile. She was still annoyed. She couldn't pretend she hadn't been hurt by his actions, but he certainly seemed to be trying to make up for it.

A relationship on board a ship, particularly with a colleague, was probably a bad idea—a very bad idea. It was why, when other similar possibilities had raised their heads, she completely ruled them out. But this felt different because they'd been getting to know each other beforehand—before any of this, and before they'd known each other's real identities.

She took another bite of her cake. It was going down well. 'What do you think would have happened if we'd actually gone on that blind date?'

She could have kept things simple and stuck to chat about work. But she didn't want to. If she wanted to work easily with Travis, they had to deal with this.

There was no one else around so they wouldn't be disturbed. It was just her and him in her cabin. It was now or never.

Travis made a little choking noise as his cake obviously stuck at the back of his throat, and Ivy burst out laughing. 'Sorry, did I make that go down the wrong way?'

He laughed too and shook his head, leaning back in her chair. 'You just like to keep me on my toes, don't you?'

There it was. That teasing tone. The one that had completely drawn her in, whether it was spoken or in texts. The thing that had made Travis King something more than a potential blind date. Even if that had never been her intention.

She gave an easy shrug. 'Why not?' She held up her hands. 'It's not like there's much else to do around here.'

She was joking, and he'd know she was joking. But shipboard life was so different from being back at home where bars, cinemas, open air and long walks could easily fill her life.

Travis sat his tea on her desk and folded his arms. 'I think,' he started as he raised his eyebrows, 'if we'd gone on a blind date before meeting here, it would have been an absolute disaster.'

Really? What was it with this guy? Had none of his sisters taught him the art of talking to a woman? The words were like being hit with a tidal wave of icy water.

'Okay, then,' she said shortly, feeling like a fool, because in her head their blind date would never have been a disaster.

He held up one hand. 'No, wait, you didn't let me finish. Let me tell you why it would have been a disaster.'

She swung her legs off the bed. 'I don't need microscopic data on why we're a never-happened,' she said, pushing her 'not good enough' feelings away again.

He reached over and put his hand on her knee. His voice

was low and throaty. 'Our date would have been a disaster, Ivy Ross, because one meeting would have had me hooked. Who knows what might have happened? It keeps me awake enough at night just thinking about it.'

And just like that the tidal wave of icy water dashed back out the door, to be overtaken by a stampede of warm air washing over her skin.

Her gaze met his. She was sure that the noise in the room had just amplified one hundred per cent. Was that the beat of his heart she could hear?

She shuffled a little further forward. Part of her brain was screaming at her. She'd got this close before only to have the rug pulled from under her feet. She didn't want to get burned twice.

'For a guy with sisters, you certainly know how to mess with a girl's mind,' she said, tilting her head to one side.

He had the grace to look embarrassed, but it didn't stop him moving a few inches closer. 'I think if I'd already met you, and then we'd met on board, I would have had to walk back off the ship. I never actually expected to meet someone on the dating app. I was looking for some light-hearted company. Nothing serious. Just some chat. But being in close quarters with you, Ivy Ross, is an exquisite kind of torture. Particularly for a guy who is supposed to be your boss.'

Her head was swimming. His feelings about the apps were entirely the same as hers. Short-term. Not serious. No chance of a long-term relationship. And, although he hadn't said it out loud, no chance to get hurt. She licked her lips. 'What if I promise never to use that position to my advantage? You judge me on my work and my conduct.' Her eyes flickered to the door. 'Only beyond that door, of course.'

She watched him bristle at those words. He was so close

she could feel his breath on her cheek, his lips brushing against her ear as he spoke. 'This could be dangerous.'

'This could be very dangerous.' Her fingers touched the side of his face. She breathed in, inhaling his scent. Yup. She was smitten. From the smell of his aftershave to the sexual tension in the room, she would be reliving this moment for the next five years.

'Who says I kiss on the first date?' she whispered.

'I do,' he replied as his lips found hers. Warm, soft and with complete determination. His hand slid to the back of her head as their kiss deepened and her arms fastened around his neck. There was a brief movement and she found herself sitting on his lap, where she knew his intentions were far from honourable.

His hand made contact with the skin under her comfortable pyjama top and she didn't mind one bit. This could easily go much further. And the truth was, for the first time in forever, she wanted it to.

But a tiny red flag of caution waved in her mind. She couldn't pretend that her past experience hadn't made her extra-cautious. She wished she could throw that part of herself away. But it was the new her. One she had to live with. She thought she knew Travis, but did she really? And if things went downhill, she was stuck on this aircraft carrier with him as her boss for the next few months. Nowhere to run, nowhere to hide.

She pushed back gently on his shoulder.

She gave him a playful smile. 'Rob?' she said, using his fake name. 'Or Travis King, I feel as if you owe me.'

He gave her a lazy kind of smile. 'Owe you what? At this point, you can have whatever you want.'

She nodded slowly, liking those words. 'In that case, what I want is my blind date. We might need to make our own bar. But I'd like to get dressed up. I'd like you to get

dressed up too. I'd like there to be low background music.'
She pointed one finger at him. 'I'd like there to be snacks.
I'd like a chilled glass of rosé wine.' She slid her fingers
through his short hair for a moment. 'And I'd like the man
sitting opposite me to spend all his time wondering what
might come next.' She leaned forward and whispered in
his ear, 'Just like I will.'

At her last word she swung her legs off him and stood
up, giving him a few moments to collect himself.

She wondered how he would react. But Travis took it
well, readjusting his clothing as he stood up and gave her
a thoughtful nod. 'A date. *Our* blind date. I think I can do
that.' A sexy smile nudged at his lips as his nodding increased. He gave her an appreciative look. 'I kind of like
that idea.' His brow furrowed a little. 'When?'

She pulled up her phone and checked their schedules.
'Okay, Saturday night looks good.' She gave him a cheeky
wink. 'Unless, of course, I get a better offer.'

He gave a kind of half groan.

She held up her finger. 'Or, of course, if my boss sends
me out in a helicopter again on a daring sea mission.'

He rolled his eyes. 'Saturday is six days away.'

She kept smiling as she walked over to open her door,
letting her hand brush against his. 'It is, isn't it? Just think
of the anticipation.'

He didn't even try to hide his groan. 'Saturday night it
is.' He leaned close to her ear. 'Can't wait.'

His eyes drifted back across the cabin and Ivy moved
quickly. 'Oh, no. Thanks for looking after me, SMO King,
but you don't get to take the chocolate cake with you.' She
picked it up, wrapping her arms around it. 'This is definitely all mine!'

He left with a laugh and she could hear it echo as he
walked down the corridor.

Saturday night was a million miles away. But she knew this was for the best. And she was right, anticipation would make it seem even more delicious.

# CHAPTER SEVEN

HE'D BEEN PLAYED like a fiddle.

And he liked it.

It didn't matter what he told himself in his head—about how it was best if he stayed away from Ivy Ross. His body didn't listen. She was like a magnet to him. He had already been cursing himself when he'd learned she'd gone out on the mission without hesitating, but when Tony had told him that the helicopter descent and retrieval actually made her ill, he could have punched himself.

Ivy's pale, wobbly form, which she'd tried her best to hide when she'd come back, just made him admire her all the more. She hadn't even radioed in for assistance with the delivery, had just handled it calmly, while probably dreading the transfer back to the carrier the whole time. The girl had courage.

He'd checked up on Kalia and her daughter and made arrangements to get them back to Hawaii. It wasn't his job to lecture them on their journey, so he left that to the captain of the carrier. No one had mentioned him helping Ivy back to her cabin, but he had noticed a few sidelong glances.

Gossip spread fast on a ship. It was like its own little village. He could only hope that their date some days later would go unnoticed. He'd already managed to procure some rosé wine. There was a strict no-alcohol policy on aircraft carriers. But on stretches of more than forty-five days crew were allowed two drinks. By next week, that time would have arrived.

Work was busy, but he and Ivy seldom worked together. A few fights had broken out on board and he'd found himself tending to a set of broken knuckles and several broken noses and a few sailors had found themselves in the brig to cool off.

Over the last few nights Travis had suffered from terrible nightmares. A few years ago he'd had lots of broken nights but that had finally settled to only one or two a month. But now, for some reason, they seemed to have returned with a vengeance. It resulted in his feeling continually tired and occasionally snappy. He hated being like that at work. Two of his sisters had already asked him what was wrong as soon as they'd seen his face when they'd video-messaged him. He'd made a variety of excuses and brushed them off.

'Travis, can we chat?' Aileen was a qualified psychiatrist but also one of the staff counsellors on board the vessel. She had two files in her hand.

'Sure,' he said, gesturing towards his office.

She sat down in a chair and crossed her legs.

'What can I help you with?'

She handed over the first file. 'Petty Officer Brooks is demonstrating some signs of depression and anxiety. I've suggested some medications for him and wondered if you'd agree. He has a few other pre-existing medical conditions, which is why I'm checking.'

Travis glanced over the file and careful notes. 'Seems reasonable. There should be no contraindications between his meds. I'll arrange to dispense the prescription. Will you be able to review him?'

She nodded. 'For now, on a weekly basis. I'll let you know if I have any concerns.'

'Will he require a change of duties?' As SMO, Travis could ask for staff to be moved without explaining why to their commanding officers.

She shook her head. 'Not yet, but I'll let you know.' She handed him the second file. He blinked when he saw the name. It was his. The SMO's medical file was only accessible to a few people on board the ship. Aileen was one of those people.

'What's this?'

Her hands were folded in her lap. She looked him straight in the eye but her posture was relaxed. She wasn't nervous about having this conversation and weirdly that made him feel slightly nervous.

'It's been seven years since we last served together.'

He gave a nod. He remembered those days well.

'A lot has happened since then.'

'Even without this?' She pointed to the file. 'I can tell.' She let her words hang in the air between them.

'What's your point, Aileen?' He was more abrupt than he'd normally be, but all his defence mechanisms were slamming down in front of him.

One of her eyebrows rose just a fraction. 'My point is…' she took a breath '…Travis King, you might not know this, but you're human. We all are. And we are all affected, in different ways, by events we're exposed to.'

'What's that supposed to mean?' He hated how snappy he was being.

She gave a gentle shake of her head. 'It means that my door is always open, Travis, that's all.'

She stood up before he could say anything else, pausing with her hand on the door. 'Our new doctor…' she said slowly.

'Yes?'

Aileen smiled. 'I like her. I like her tenacity and her spirit. I heard her telling off one of the pilots who was trying to act like a big shot.'

'Who was it?' The words were out before he had a chance to think.

Aileen laughed. 'Oh, you don't need to know. Ivy dealt with him appropriately. All I'm saying is that she's a good fit for this crew. She's earning their respect by just being herself and gaining some admirers.'

Travis shifted uncomfortably in his chair. 'You think?'

She nodded. 'I know, people talk. Now, remember, my door is always open.'

His initial abruptness had faded. 'I know,' he said apologetically. 'Thank you.'

She gave a nod and disappeared out the door. Travis leaned back and folded his arms. He wasn't quite sure what he should worry about first. The fact that Aileen could obviously see changes in him or the fact that Ivy had more admirers than just him.

He grinned. It was a challenge. Not Ivy as such but the date. He would have to make sure he pulled out all the stops to make their new blind date as good as it could possibly be.

He could do it. And he would.

The soft navy blue dress had been found rolled in a crumpled ball at the bottom of one of her bags. She wasn't even sure why it was there. She had packed some civilian clothing, but that wasn't one of the items. It must have been there since her last trip to New York with some friends. She shook it out. The short-sleeved, knee-length dress had resembled a crumpled rag, but Ivy knew it could come out looking brand new in the laundry. At present, it was hanging in front of her. The fake wrap-around look meant the dress fell in soft folds creating a V in front, with a split near the knee to give a hint of leg.

She had a pair of small heels that would have to do. It felt strange dressing up while being on the ship. It would feel even more weird, walking between her cabin and Travis's looking like this. She might throw her uniform dress jacket over the top to try and be a little less obvious about what she was doing.

He'd insisted they meet in his cabin instead of hers—although she wasn't quite sure why. This week had been like a game of cat and mouse between them. On the very few occasions they'd been working around each other she'd tried her very best to act casual. But her body seemed to have forgotten what 'casual' was.

Every now and then their eyes would meet and one or the other of them would flash a private smile. Whenever Travis had done it, Ivy had instantly felt embarrassed, as if a siren with giant bright red arrows pointing to their heads had been wailing and flashing around them. It had sent tingles down her spine, which was entirely ridiculous.

But all this, the lead in, the anticipation, had been building on a daily basis. She'd done this. She'd wanted it to be this way. But the delicious torture had been driving her crazy.

She grabbed some long gold earrings and shook out her hair. She hadn't even attempted to straighten it. The atmosphere on the ship would mean that even though she had a gallon of product on her curls, they would edge towards frizz in a few hours. The dress hugged her curves in a way she didn't quite remember. She'd thought it was a pretty plain dress, but right now it looked anything but plain.

She glanced at the clock. The majority of the crew would be in the mess right now, drinking their two regulation beers. It was unlikely, though, that she would get down the corridors unnoticed. This was still a working naval ship, and there were always crew on duty.

Ivy finished with a slick of red lipstick and threw her jacket over the dress, stepping out into the corridor. She kept her head low as she strode along quickly. The first corridor was, luckily, empty, as was the second. The third had two men at the end of it, talking intently over something on a tablet screen.

She was beginning to think this might be easier than she'd imagined. The thought had just crossed her mind when she heard a voice behind her. 'Looking good, Doc.'

She turned and gave a nod of her head at the young petty officer second class. He had a cheeky grin on his face and she probably should have reprimanded him, but she had other things on her mind.

Her footsteps echoed down the passage, making her feel more and more self-conscious. She tugged at the dress, wondering if it was a bit too short.

Her hand paused as she lifted it to knock on Travis's door. Her stomach was doing flip-flops. Maybe she should back out? It was obvious that their feelings were intensifying in this close-knit, pressured environment. What had happened to her vow to never date a colleague?

For a few seconds she was torn. Was six days of anticipation just a smokescreen? How well did she really know Travis?

Before she had a chance to think any further the door opened and all her previous thoughts dissolved.

Travis had a welcoming smile on his face and a spark in his eye. He was dressed completely in black—black trousers and a black fitted shirt that showed off all his best assets.

Every finger, toe and hair on her body tried to cross to

prevent there being a chance of any kind of emergency on this ship for the next few hours. She wanted his undivided attention.

Travis reached out a hand and pulled her inside.

Her breath caught in the back of her throat. The whole cabin had been transformed. Not that she'd seen the inside of Travis's cabin before, but she knew it was the same as every other in this corridor.

Except this one was entirely different.

She looked around. The plain grey walls were covered in something—a printed paper with a dark wooden pattern on it. She wanted to reach out and see exactly what it was. The same paper covered his bed, which had been transformed into one side of some kind of homemade booth. A dark table was directly in front, and on the table were a covered lantern and a couple of flickering candles. There were also some plates with bar snacks, two bottles of beer and a bottle of rosé wine. All three bottles were slightly smudged with condensation, showing they'd been chilled.

As she looked around she saw there were also a couple of old-style Italian posters on the wall. Although the lighting in the room was dim, seeing the posters struck a spark in her brain.

'Gino's?' she gasped. 'You made us Gino's?'

He held out both his hands. 'You wanted us to recreate our blind date.' He gave a little bow. 'Your wish is my command.'

Of course they could never really capture the true essence of the wooden booths in Gino's and the dim atmosphere. But as she looked around in amazement Travis flicked a switch and soft Italian music drifted in the background. She was wowed. She couldn't believe he'd gone to all this trouble.

'You've done a good job,' she said appreciatively.

He handed her a wine glass. 'The good news is I'm assured this is an excellent wine, but you only get to drink two glasses.'

Ivy leaned forward and ran her finger down the condensation on the wine bottle. She couldn't help but smile. 'This is perfect,' she whispered.

Travis gestured towards the bench seat. 'So, let's imagine we're back at Gino's. I've bought us drinks and I'm sitting, waiting for you to arrive.' He gave her a sexy smile. 'And now here you are. Walking through the door and making me pinch myself with how lucky I feel right now.'

Ivy watched as he poured the wine into the glass and handed it to her. She sat down next to him, feeling the heat emanating from his body towards her.

She crossed her legs and held up her glass of wine. 'Okay, so how are we doing this? Are we doing a completely new date? Me as Ali and you as Rob? Or are we skipping to the part where we're Ivy and Travis?'

He opened one of the beer bottles and held it up, chinking it against her glass. 'How about we agree to skip to the good part?'

She leaned one elbow on the table. 'Let me think about that. It's been…' she glanced up through hooded lids '…six long, long days. We've done the introductions. We've stumbled through the getting-to-know-you part.'

He lifted his eyebrows as if he was wondering where this was going.

Her heart was racing in her chest. She knew she was about to throw caution completely to the wind. Her career could literally hang in this guy's hands if they argued at a later date. But in her head she was separating the two parts of their lives—personal and professional.

'We have the forty-five-day reprieve of having two drinks tonight. And…' she leaned over and surveyed the bar snacks '…we have chicken wings, steak fries, peanuts, chips and olives.' She leaned towards him and said in a low voice, 'Why, Travis, I think we might have struck gold.'

She'd only managed the barest sip of her wine before his lips were on hers.

'You know what?' he murmured. 'I think you might be right.'

The paper on the walls was fragile and ended up scattered over the floor. Ivy laughed when she stretched out a few hours later after falling asleep. There was no way this room would meet any kind of regulations if someone were to walk in.

She blinked as she wondered what had woken her up, thankful that something had because she really needed to get back to her own cabin. The last thing she wanted to do on an aircraft carrier was to be caught sneaking back to her cabin. Her dress was in a crumpled heap on the floor, alongside her shoes, and she swung her legs out of bed to make a grab for them.

There was a noise beside her. Then a grunt. She'd only just repositioned her underwear before she realised what was happening.

Travis was definitely a restless sleeper. But as she dropped her dress over her head and tugged it into place she realised this was something entirely different. He was murmuring, his head starting to thrash from side to side.

'No, not that way. This way. Keep your head down. Cover your mouth.'

His arms and legs started to thrash too. 'Leave it!' he yelled, and she jumped in shock.

He was having a nightmare. Travis King was having a nightmare. For the first time in her medical career Ivy wasn't quite sure what to do. She'd never dealt with anyone having nightmares before. She'd heard a few friends talk about their kids having night terrors, but she couldn't remember what she should do. Did she wake him up? Or did she let it come to a natural end?

Inwardly she groaned. If Travis made much more noise, someone would surely come by to check on him. The last thing she wanted was for them both to be reported to the captain. She might as well kiss any chance of being SMO goodbye if that were to happen. No, she needed to deal with this the best way she could. For both their sakes. She hesitated next to his bed as Travis continued to thrash his legs and arms.

'No, not that way. Here, let me help you.' He started coughing—choking almost. Whatever this dream was, it was very real for Travis.

'Travis,' she said tentatively to begin with.

Nothing. He kept murmuring and thrashing.

She tried again, raising her voice a little. 'Travis, wake up.'

Still nothing. She bent forward and gently touched his arm. 'Travis, wake up.'

It was as if she hadn't even spoken. He just kept writhing in the bed, muttering under his breath. Before she even had a chance to think or move, 'No!' he yelled at the top of his voice, his strong right arm lashing out and sending her back into the nearby bulkhead.

The noise must have disturbed him and touch must have registered with him because almost instantly he sat up, breathing fast and hard, eyes wide.

She stood frozen against the bulkhead, her arm across her chest. He hadn't hurt her in any way—she'd had worse shoves from people in the grocery store—but it was the element of surprise that took her breath away.

Travis's eyes were wide. 'Ivy?' It took him a few moments to reorientate himself. She could almost see him making sense of why she was in his cabin.

Her heart was thudding in her chest.

'Y-you…you…' she stammered, 'were having a nightmare.'

The look of horror on his face told her everything she needed to know. What she actually wanted to do was grab her shoes and jacket and get out of his cabin and back to her own, where she could make sense of it all.

But the doctor in her knew she shouldn't walk away. While she might not understand nightmares, she could understand trauma from a million miles away. Working in the armed forces meant she saw it in many forms, time and time again. She just hadn't expected it from Travis.

She took a few deep breaths, trying to let her heart rate return to normal and stop hammering away in her chest.

'Ivy, did I hurt you?' He was on his feet, stepping too close.

She flinched and she saw the pain in his eyes as he noticed and stepped back again.

She picked up the nearby chair that she must have stumbled over on her way back to the bulkhead. She pulled her dress straight and sat down, facing Travis.

'You didn't hurt me,' she said steadily. Then she took another breath. 'But you could have.'

He slumped down onto the bed. He looked as if she'd punched him in the guts.

'Travis, why don't you tell me what's going on?'

He leaned forward and put his head in his hands. She wanted to hug him. But she had to stay clear. She had to give him the space he needed to sort all this out in his head. She knew that she would need the same time later.

When he lifted his blue eyes to hers they were glistening with unshed tears. That was the moment that almost completely undid her. She tried to stay calm and rational. 'Travis, how long have you had nightmares like this?' Part of her brain shifted. This wasn't about her at all. It was about Travis. She had to treat him like a patient, not a lover. It was the only way she would be of any use to him.

His answer was throaty. 'Four years.'

'What happened four years ago?' There was no point in beating around the bush—not with a guy that a short time ago she'd been in an entirely different position with. She needed some honesty. But part of her brain stuck on the part that this had been happening to Travis for four years.

He ran his fingers through his hair. His voice shook as he spoke. 'Four years ago I was on deployment with a team that came under mortar fire. Three of my colleagues were killed instantly. Twenty were injured around me.'

She drew in a breath. She didn't need to ask where he'd been deployed. She'd spent a spell there too.

But Travis hadn't finished speaking. 'We were held down under gunfire for three days. I had limited resources and had to choose who to prioritise and who I could actually save.' He looked her in the eye. 'I relive that day every other night.'

She'd been lucky enough never to have come under direct fire, but as a surgeon in the area she'd dealt with the direct consequences of everyone else who had done. She could easily imagine the horrors of the experience.

Her skin prickled but something about what he'd said just didn't feel quite right. The words that he'd been using, the instructions he'd been shouting, had sounded more like a retreat than a lockdown.

'Is there anything else?' she probed.

He groaned, leaning back and wrapping his arms across his chest. His eyes fixed on a corner of the cabin. 'I thought I'd managed to get through things. I thought I'd got out okay. But a few months later I went to a conference at a hotel in Chicago. There was a fire in the middle of the night. The sprinkler system didn't work. Smoke was everywhere and I was on the thirtieth floor.'

These words made sense to her. The coughing and choking he'd been doing during his nightmare, the instruction he'd been shouting.

'But you got out okay?'

He gave a wry laugh as he shook his head. 'It's amazing, isn't it? The number of people who stay in a hotel and actually don't look for the fire stairs, even though they know they should? I banged on all the doors on my floor and helped everyone to the stairs. But I had to stop at every floor, yelling to others so they could actually find the escape route. On a couple of floors I found people already suffering from smoke inhalation.'

'So you stopped to help?' She knew as soon as she asked the question that he had.

He gave a horrid shiver. 'The smoke was particularly bad on some floors. I tried to check them all, but afterwards I found out that I had missed a few people already overcome.'

She could see that he blamed himself, even though there was no reason to.

He kept talking and as he lifted one arm she noticed a little puckering on the skin towards the back. Her fingers hadn't noticed that spot in her earlier exploration.

'Travis, were you physically hurt in either the mortar attack or the fire?'

She could see every muscle in his body tense. 'Barely.'

'What does that mean?'

He stood up and turned around. Under one shoulder blade was an area that had clearly been burned. The same on the top side of his left upper arm. Scattered across the base of his spine were some small areas that looked like some kind of shrapnel.

She had missed them all. She'd been to bed with a man with war wounds and burns and she'd missed them all. It seemed illogical to her but as her mind relived the previous few hours, she realised her hands had mainly been around his neck, on his face, in the middle of his back or other places.

'I'm sorry,' she said simply.

Travis was back on his feet, then kneeling before her. 'No, I'm sorry, Ivy. I never meant to hurt you. I never meant to scare you.'

She knew that. She knew all of that. But there was something more important here. 'Sit down.'

Her tone was sterner than she wanted it to be, but the best way she could help Travis right now was to keep down this path.

'Anything we talk about in this cabin doesn't leave this cabin, you understand?'

He nodded and she could see his expression change. He'd realised she'd stopped looking at him like a lover and had started looking at him as a patient.

'Travis, what just happened when we were in bed together—has this ever happened before?'

He shook his head.

She furrowed her brow. 'You're telling me that at no point in the last four years you've slept in a bed with another woman?' She gave a wry laugh. 'I don't expect you to have been a saint, Travis.'

He cringed a little and gave her an answer without looking at her. 'Of course I've slept with other women, but I've never stayed the night. I've never actually fallen asleep or spent the night with a woman in the last four years.'

'Oh.' It was the only thing she could think of to say

right now. Travis had fallen asleep with her. *Her*. The first woman in four years he'd been comfortable enough with to fall asleep with. What did that mean?

'And the reason you haven't stayed overnight with a woman for the last four years?'

He took a deep breath and she let her question hang in the air. She knew the answer to that. He didn't want to admit what the problem was. He didn't want to face up to it. Maybe he hadn't accepted he had PTSD? Maybe he just wanted to keep it secret. But right now it was the biggest problem in this cabin. Travis King was in denial. And she couldn't pretend it wasn't breaking her heart.

She took a deep breath. 'Travis. I don't need to spell this out. You need help. You must know you need help. Have you done anything about this?'

The words hung in the air between them and again he didn't answer—which was all the answer she needed.

Anger surged through her. She wanted to help him— she did. But he had to want to help himself first.

He opened his mouth to speak but no words actually came out.

Ivy stood up. 'Travis, I would like to see if this relationship has a chance. I think we could be good together. But I can't help you if you don't want to help yourself. I think the best thing I can do right now is give you some space to get some help.' She gave a sad sigh. 'And even though I'm a doctor, this isn't my area of speciality. I'm not sure that I'm the best person to help you right now, but if you need me, you know where to find me. All you have to do is ask.'

Her voice trembled as she reached out and hugged him, feeling his warm body next to hers. Part of her wanted to stay in this position. But that wouldn't help Travis—not in the long term. If he remained in denial, he would suffer like this for the rest of his life. And she truly didn't want that for him.

Tears were pooling in her eyes and she knew she had to get out of here. If he liked her as much as she liked him, she could only pray that he would reach out for help. And if he did, she would absolutely be there.

'Let me know,' she said quietly before she broke down completely. And with that Ivy picked up her shoes and jacket and walked out the door.

# CHAPTER EIGHT

HE WAS LIVING his life on autopilot and could barely look at Ivy right now.

This was all his fault. Everything she'd said to him had been fair and reasonable. She was right to walk away. All he could feel was shame and humiliation that whilst he'd been in the middle of a nightmare he might have accidentally hurt her.

But the part that had killed him most was when he'd seen the change in her eyes. When she'd started looking at him like a patient rather than the man she'd just made love with. He didn't ever want Ivy to look at him like that. He'd revealed a part of himself that he'd never shared with another, and she'd automatically gone into doctor mode.

Would he have done the same if the situation were reversed? Trouble was, he wasn't entirely sure.

Once or twice he'd thought about trying to talk to her, maybe even texting her. But how could he talk to her when he hadn't sorted himself out?

Aileen had caught him looking at Ivy a few times and raised her eyebrows in a question. He knew Aileen would be happy for him to take her up on the offer that she'd made, but as soon as he had that conversation then it was there, on his record, forever.

If he were having this conversation with any of his

friends, he would tell them not to be ridiculous. He would tell them the diagnosis wouldn't matter, that getting treatment was far more important. And he knew all that. But he also knew how the navy worked. Would he ever get another commission as an SMO with PTSD in his medical records? That was the harsh reality he was facing.

It was why he'd spent the last four years trying to pretend this wasn't actually happening to him.

Aston, one of the medical corpsman, came and tapped him on the shoulder. 'Dr King, I've got a female patient who needs to see a doctor. She's asking specifically for Dr Ross, but she's off duty. Should I go and find her?'

Travis shook his head. 'Ivy was on duty last night and had a tough case. I'll speak to the patient in the first instance. If I need to, I'll go and find Ivy.'

The medical corpsman handed over the notes. 'Room Two.'

Travis nodded and scanned them quickly. They were brief. He headed into Room Two and the young woman turned to look at him.

He gave her a smile as he sat down. 'I'm Dr King. I know you're looking for Dr Ross, but she's just gone off shift and I imagine she's sleeping right now. If it's okay with you, I can take some details and arrange for Dr Ross to see you later or some time tomorrow? I just wanted to see you to check if you need any emergency treatment.' He didn't want anything urgent for this patient to be overlooked, wanted to make sure it was safe to allow her to wait.

'Are you happy to chat with me?'

She gave a nervous nod.

'I'm Rena,' she said. 'I just wanted to see an actual doctor rather than a corpsman.'

'No problem,' said Travis. 'I'm happy to see you, but know that our medical corpsmen are fully trained.'

She didn't say anything so he continued, 'Can you tell me what brings you here today?'

She pressed her lips together. 'I just feel really tired. I can't get out of my bed in the morning, and I don't want to eat. As soon as I've finished my duties I just want to go back to bed.' She gave a laugh. 'I couldn't even drink my designated alcohol the other night. Just the smell of it…' She shuddered.

Travis gave a nod and took some notes. This could be a wide variety of conditions. He asked a few more questions. After a few minutes he started to sense where this might be going.

'Rena, how long have you been on board?'

'Since we started. It would be…twelve weeks now.'

Travis gave a nod. 'Do you mind if we run through a list of other symptoms?'

She shook her head.

'Okay, any abdominal pain?'

Her face twisted and she gave a half nod. 'Maybe a little. I just thought it was menstrual cramps. But it's a bit sharper than what it's normally like.'

Travis nodded. 'Indigestion? Nausea? Light-headedness? Headaches? Or palpitations?'

She shook her head at some and nodded at others.

'Do you mind if I ask you for a urine sample too? I'd like to rule out a urine infection.' He handed her a sample dish and Rena headed to the toilet. He wondered if he should actually go and wake up Ivy. He had a sneaky suspicion he might know what was wrong with Rena.

He stuck his head out the door and gave a shout to one of the other staff. 'Can you ask Ivy to come along? And apologise for waking her up. I want to do an abdominal scan on this young woman and think she might be happier if Ivy did that.'

Five minutes later Travis was in the treatment room, testing the urine sample.

'You called?' Ivy was rubbing her eyes. Her hair was rumpled and she was wearing scrubs that she'd clearly been sleeping in.

He gave a nod. 'I'm sorry to wake you up.'

She shook her head and stepped forward. 'No probs. Who is the patient?'

He turned the tablet around so she could read his notes. After a minute she looked up and glanced at the test strips. She gave a sigh. 'Okay, so I'm betting there's no infection, is there?'

He shook his head.

'Did you do the other test?'

He turned the pregnancy test around and she gave an even bigger sigh.

'How bad is her abdominal pain?'

'Right now it's just starting. She described as being like menstrual cramps, only sharper.'

Ivy didn't miss a beat. 'And if this pregnancy is ectopic, it's about to get a whole lot worse.' She nodded her head and paused before meeting his gaze. 'I was going to be cranky. But you were right to wake me. I'll do her ultrasound and have the conversation.'

As he nodded and turned to leave she called him back. 'Travis, you know how I hadn't delivered a baby in years?'

'Yes?'

'Well, it's been just as long since I dealt with an ectopic pregnancy. I'd feel happier if you'd scrub in too.'

A warm feeling spread across him. He knew what it was costing her to say those words out loud. No surgeon wanted to admit that something wasn't really their speciality. 'Would you like me to do the surgery?'

She shook her head. 'No, I'll do it. But I would appreciate if you stayed in case I have any questions.'

'No problem.'

She bit her lip. 'You do realise there's another issue here, don't you?'

Travis met her gaze. 'Of course. Ectopic pregnancies happen at around six weeks and we've been at sea for twelve, meaning Rena's got pregnant while she's been on board.'

Ivy's gaze dropped to the screen again. 'We all know the rules. I'm not entirely sure I feel comfortable getting a young woman into trouble for an act we both engaged in ourselves.'

Her straight talking reminded him just why he liked her so much. Ivy wasn't shy. She got right to the point. He couldn't help but smile at her. 'I guess you're right, but one of us will still need to have that conversation with her at a later date. We also need to think about contraceptive advice for her.'

Ivy leaned against the bulkhead for a minute. 'This is a tricky one. If the ultrasound confirms what we suspect, she'll need surgery. While I'm doing the ultrasound, could you ask Aileen if she might be available to counsel Rena later? I'm not sure how she'll react to the news about the pregnancy being ectopic.'

For the briefest of moments he paused as he felt a tiny moment of dread circle around him at the thought of talking to Aileen. He immediately shook it off. 'Of course I will. I'll meet you back here.'

Aileen was working in one of the other offices and gave him a wide smile as he knocked on the door. 'Travis, what can I do for you? Do you need my help?'

The look of expectation in her eyes made him want to cringe. 'Yes,' he said quickly. 'We have a young woman who probably has an ectopic pregnancy. We're not quite sure how she'll take the news and Ivy wondered if you'd be available if required.'

'Oh.' For a moment he thought she looked a bit disappointed. 'Of course, no problem at all. Eh… Travis? Anything else?'

He could say something. He could say it right now. Admit that something was wrong and that he needed help. The words were almost there, on the tip of his tongue, but…they just wouldn't go any further. He gave Aileen his best bright smile. 'No, that's great, thanks.'

As he walked back outside he thought he'd feel relief. But instead it was as if a baby whale had taken a spot on his shoulders and was pressing down. Hard.

He couldn't let this go on. Ivy had clearly been avoiding him these last few days, but just one glimpse of her, one whiff of her perfume, had made him realise how much he was allowing all this to hold him back—to steal part of the life that he really wanted.

A life with Ivy.

The impulse to lie down on the nearest bed and go back to sleep was slowly diminishing. Rena was a nice young girl who hadn't even asked Ivy any questions when she'd asked if she could do an ultrasound. The scan quickly told Ivy what she needed to know. She put the transducer back in its holder and turned to Rena. 'Okay, we need to talk about what happens next.'

'Am I pregnant?' Rena winced a little as she moved on the bed.

Ivy nodded. 'You are pregnant, but this pregnancy is unusual. The egg hasn't implanted in the lining of your womb.'

'It hasn't? What's wrong? Is that why I'm so uncomfortable?'

Ivy nodded and took the time to explain. There was a good chance that the general discomfort that Rena was feeling would rapidly increase. They had to operate as soon as possible. Ivy spoke slowly. 'Rena, is there anyone on board you would like me to get for you? A friend? A colleague? I think it's important you have someone to support you.'

She saw Rena waver before she shook her head. Maybe the pregnancy was a surprise. Somewhere on board this vessel was a man who'd shared a few intimate moments with Rena. Or it could be something else.

Ivy paused. Sexual assault wasn't unknown on military vessels. She bent forward and took Rena's hand, giving it a light squeeze. 'Rena, is there anything you need to tell me? As Flight Surgeon I'm responsible for making sure you feel safe on the *Coolidge*. I want you to know that you can tell me anything.'

A flash of recognition sparked in Rena's eyes and she shook her head. 'No, nothing like that. You don't need to worry about me.' Then her expression changed, and she laid her hand on her belly. 'So, all of this will be over once I've had the op?'

Ivy nodded. 'We'll take you in very soon. The last thing we want is for your pain to worsen and the ectopic pregnancy to rupture.'

'But you still need to take the tube away?'

'Yes, we do. There's no other way.'

'And I'll still be able to have children in the future?'

Ivy nodded. 'You should do. You have two fallopian

tubes. I'll refer you to an ob-gyn specialist that you can see once we're back on land. They'll be able to run some tests and reassure you.'

Rena gave a nod, but her eyes had a distant kind of expression.

'One of the nurses will be in to get you ready for Theatre. I'll see you in there,' said Ivy.

She walked through the door and started as she saw Travis waiting for her. 'You were good with her,' he said, giving a small nod in appreciation.

Ivy's first instinct was to brush him off. As far as she was aware, he still hadn't done what she'd asked but, then, she would never really know unless he told her.

He certainly hadn't asked her for help. But maybe he felt that wasn't appropriate. And she wasn't offended, really, more frustrated. She just wanted Travis to admit what was wrong and start the process of getting help.

She couldn't deny that, no matter what else happened, she liked Travis. He was a good guy. A good guy with a condition that needed to be treated. No matter how much she wanted to help, the first step, the denial part, Travis had to deal with himself.

She had experience of being around people who wouldn't help themselves in the first instance. One of her friends, Joss, back in university days, had Type One diabetes. Joss had continually ignored her blood-sugar results, her hypoglycaemic attacks and her secondary symptoms. Ivy had bent over backwards to help Joss, intervening on countless occasions, spending hours and hours with her friend when she had been sick, almost failing one exam in the process.

She'd finally realised that she couldn't do it for Joss. Joss had to do it for herself, and she'd slowly backed away. She'd heard later that a few years down the line Joss had self-destructed and had crashed her car while driving with low blood sugar. Luckily, Joss hadn't injured anyone else, just herself, and it had given her the wake-up call she'd needed.

Even though she was a doctor, Ivy couldn't always 'fix' someone. They had to want to 'fix' themselves. And as hard as it was to know how much Travis was hurting, he'd already been on this road for the last four years—and hadn't done anything about it. She knew how it would feel if she tried to intervene. She couldn't take sleepless nights and countless arguments—or the fear of him lashing out in his sleep again. As his blue eyes fixed on hers in the shadow of the corridor, she remembered the feel of his skin next to hers. There was so much about this guy she could actually love. There was so much potential between them. It actually felt as if she could reach out and grab it.

Deep down she knew it wasn't the way to start a relationship. But that didn't mean she couldn't be friends with him. Maybe that was what he needed most.

She gave him a smile. 'Well, I try my best.'

'I'm sorry I got you up. I heard you had a bad night.'

'I've had worse.' The words were out before she had a chance to think about them. Of course she hadn't been referring to her night with Travis. She had been thinking back to her many night shifts as an intern. But for the briefest of seconds she saw the wounded expression on his face. She couldn't leave it. She just couldn't.

Ivy reached out and put her hand on his arm. 'I didn't mean that.' She glanced over her shoulder to make sure no one could hear. 'Part of that night was very nice, as you know, and I appreciate the effort you made.'

She was trying to keep her tone light. She was just about to go into surgery with this guy and she needed them both to be on the same page.

He gave a silent nod and she tried to move on. 'Are you ready to be my wingman?'

That made his eyebrows lift in amusement. 'I'm your wingman? I don't get to be top gun?'

She shook her head. 'Oh, no, you're the wingman, absolutely. No one gets to be top gun in my theatre but me.'

'Fair enough. I'm happy to be your wingman.'

She was surprised by that. Most surgeons would never concede to another, particularly if they were senior. 'Let's go.' He nodded as the anaesthetic nurse slipped into Rena's room.

Surgery went smoothly. Whilst Ivy hoped she'd always be able to cope with any surgical emergency, it gave her confidence knowing there was someone else who could step in to help if required. They bantered easily, and she could see a number of staff exchanging glances above their masks. Ivy talked out loud, listing what she was doing and what she could see. It was what she would normally do when teaching students, but she was just outlining everything to reassure herself, and allowing Travis to add anything he felt she might have missed.

When she'd closed he stripped off his theatre garb and put his hand on her shoulder. 'Well done. Textbook case.'

And she felt it. That connection again, even though she had a theatre gown and scrubs between his skin and hers.

'Thanks for the support,' she said simply. 'It's appreciated.'

The nurse anaesthetist released the brakes on the trolley to push Rena to the post-op room. 'I can take over here and monitor our patient.' She glanced at the clock. 'Hurry on up, you two, before the mess stops serving.'

Ivy turned instantly. 'Oh, no, you go, Ellen. Grab some dinner while you can.'

Ellen shook her head. 'I have a green kale smoothie. New diet, folks. Go and live the dream for me and eat some real food.' She rolled her eyes, laughing as she pushed Rena through to the next room.

It seemed awkward to refuse to go and eat together when there wasn't much time left. Travis held the door while Ivy stripped off her theatre gown and washed her hands again. 'Shall we?'

She nodded as they walked down the corridor, ignoring the fact that she could smell his aftershave. The mess was half-empty and they grabbed what was left on offer and sat down at a table. Most of the staff from the medical department had already eaten dinner and left, so there was no one to cushion their conversation.

He waited until they'd sat down before he spoke. 'I'll sort things. I will.'

She held her breath, waiting for him to continue.

'How do you feel about waiting?'

The question blindsided her. 'W-waiting?' she stuttered.

He nodded. 'Yup, waiting. How do you feel about it?'

A whole wave of emotions swept over her. She turned her eyes to meet his. 'What exactly do you mean by waiting?' Her skin prickled at his words.

His voice was low and throaty. 'I mean, is that something you would even consider? I like you, Ivy. You know I do. Our connection feels real. It felt real even before we met, and now? Even more so.' His fork pushed his food around the plate. 'I like the thing that we've got going.' He corrected himself, 'Or *had* going. I'd like to see where it could take us. I'd like to hope that at some point we might actually have a future together.'

She felt frozen. She hadn't expected him to come out with that. They'd flirted, connected, and she'd had all the same hopes too. But was it realistic? Or were they just fooling each other this might actually have some potential.

The tick-tick of her career potential was still ticking loudly in her head. There was still so much she wanted to achieve. Would she still be able to focus her time and energy on that, as well as committing to a relationship?

Despite her words a week ago, she did still have that little piece of her heart hoping. Travis had seemed like he might actually be perfect for her. She'd spent her last few years avoiding any relationship entanglements. Could she really be contemplating one now? It was a huge leap for her. But she got the impression it might be a leap for him too.

'I haven't fallen asleep with a woman for the last four years. I haven't been relaxed enough to do so. But my nightmares and flashbacks have also never been so bad.'

'You're blaming me?' she asked with her hand on her chest.

He shook his head fiercely. 'No, of course not.' He set down his cutlery and put his hand on his own chest. 'I'm blaming me. Not you. You're the first person I've been re-laxed around. The first person I've felt a real connection with, and the first person I've opened up to.'

She couldn't breathe. They were sitting in a half-filled mess hall with chatter and laughter all around them, but all she could concentrate on was him.

He spoke again. 'You're the first person who's made me stop and question if I'm sick.'

She knew how big those words were. She knew how much they meant.

Deep down, Ivy understood that Travis had never said those words out loud before. He was finally admitting he'd been in denial.

So she went with her heart instead of her head.

She moved her hand across the table and intertwined her fingers with his. 'I'm glad you want this, Travis. But you have to be sure you want this for you, not for me. You have to want to fix yourself.'

He nodded. 'I do. I really do. And I understand you might not want to wait around for that—because I've no idea how long that might take, or if I can even do it.'

It was those words that tore at her heartstrings—that convinced her his motivations were good. The *I* word. It was the one she'd wanted to hear.

She gave him a small smile as she squeezed her fingers in his. 'I think you might be worth waiting for,' she replied in a small whisper.

# CHAPTER NINE

THE LOW-LEVEL SIREN sounded in the middle of the night and Travis sat bolt upright. For a moment he was back on the ground behind a wall as shots were being fired around him. It only took him a moment to gather himself before he was on his feet and out into the corridor.

He marched quickly to the sick bay. 'What's happening?'

One of the medical corpsman was grabbing some equipment. 'We stopped to assist a US vessel with engine trouble. But apparently some of the crew are sick.' He looked at Travis and shook his head. 'I'm sure we'll be able to cope. From what I hear, it doesn't sound too serious.'

There was a groan nearby. Travis moved into the ward area. There was an unfamiliar face curled up in one of the beds.

Jan, one of the nurses, gave him a nod. 'Abdominal pain,' she said. 'Just waiting for the ultrasound machine.'

'Any other symptoms?'

She shook her head. 'Not yet. He came in with cramps a few hours ago. We've taken some bloods.'

Travis gave a nod just as the man sat upright in bed and vomited everywhere. Both he and Jan jumped back, then exchanged glances. A few of the other staff scurried over and donned gloves and aprons.

'I know what happens next,' Travis murmured, as the man jumped from his bed.

'I need to use the bathroom,' the man said as he headed for the patient toilet.

'Lock down this area,' said Travis quickly. 'Is this one of the men from the rescued vessel—or is this one of our crew? He needs to be isolated in a single room and essentially barrier nursed right now.'

The staff moved quickly. They all knew exactly what this could mean for an aircraft carrier. Any kind of norovirus outbreak could be devastating for the working of the carrier.

'Jan, once the situation is under control we'll need an emergency meeting of the medical team. We need to control this situation.'

Tony came walking in behind him. 'There's six of them—and they are all like him.' He nodded to the guy now back on the bed. 'He was sent up for pain relief. I did say to put him in a single room.' He sighed and shook his head and looked at Travis. 'Sorry.' Then he groaned. 'But we don't have six single rooms. We'll have to put them all together and term it a red zone.'

Travis looked at Tony. They both knew that staff could already have been infected by being in contact with any of the men from the ship. If he didn't get this under control…

One hour later his whole team was in front of him—including Ivy. She looked immaculate as usual, her hair tied back and clean blue scrubs in place.

'Hi, folks, we think we could have a potential outbreak of norovirus—or something similar. All six men from the vessel that was just rescued are potentially infected. Since we didn't know that when we initially rendered assistance, we now need to track, trace and isolate any members of our crew who have been in contact with them and monitor them over the next seventy-two hours. We all know the potential here. We have to try and contain this outbreak.'

Ivy exchanged a glance with him. 'Have you briefed the captain?'

He nodded and gave her a painful smile. 'Just back from doing that.'

She winced. She knew exactly how much of a rollicking any SMO would get while telling a captain that his ship with over five thousand crew could be carrying an infectious virus. He nodded at several of his staff. 'Everyone, full protective equipment while working with affected cases. Limited personnel in that ward. Report any development of symptoms.'

He took a deep breath. 'Okay, folks, there will be an investigation into why we allowed these men onto our vessel in the first place. I want you all to know that I support you. If we'd actually known what the problem was, we could have put some precautions in place. However, five of these men are clinically dehydrated—this seems a particularly ugly strain of norovirus—and we've already had to put them on IV fluids.'

'Do you want to break us into teams?'

Tony put his arm up straight away. 'I've already had contact. I'll continue to look after the patients.'

But Travis shook his head. 'No, you're our first case of isolation. You've been exposed and will likely develop the condition yourself.' He nodded to Ivy. 'You lead the track and trace team. Find all our personnel who had contact with the men on the vessel and find a space for them to spend the next few days.'

Ivy looked at a list on her lap and pulled a face. 'I've already started. Most of the personnel were from Engineering. They went on board to try and help with the breakdown.'

Travis held in a groan. 'Perfect. Captain will love that when I tell him.' He shook his head but held up his hands. 'It is what it is. Incubation is around forty-eight hours but can be longer. If our staff have no signs or symptoms, they can be released back to their normal stations after seventy-two hours. Until then they go nowhere. First sign of any symptoms, they get shipped up here. To me.'

Ivy frowned. 'You're going to staff the ward?'

He nodded, hands on his hips. 'I was here when the first guy started vomiting. I didn't have any direct contact like Tony. But…?' He held up his hands. 'Droplets. There is a chance I've already been exposed. It makes sense for me to continue to work in here, alongside the other staff, where we'll be wearing full PPE.'

Norovirus was the kind of disease that felled cruise ship passengers and meant that ships were refused docking in ports. Having an outbreak on board the *Coolidge* would be disastrous.

Travis handed her a piece of paper. 'I've sketched out a plan of how we might have to isolate people around the ship. We have provisions to make the medical bay larger if we have to.'

She took the paper from him, her hand brushing against his.

Regret flooded through him again. 'Ivy—'

She held up her hand. 'Work, Travis. Let's prioritise work right now. We can chat later.'

He gave a nod of his head. He understood exactly why she felt this way. And he knew he needed to address the problem. He'd been allowing worries about his career to stop him taking the next steps, but as he breathed in and caught the orange-scented shampoo that Ivy used, his career was the last thing on his mind.

His job didn't define who he was, or who he could be.

He'd spent the last few years making excuses why relationships didn't really work out for him. Never allowing himself to fall asleep next to a woman was likely to be a huge factor. One that he'd been carefully ignoring. That wasn't a way to live. It wasn't a way to love.

And everything about Ivy made him feel like he was heading in that direction. The fact he'd fallen asleep next to her told him everything he needed to know. Even if his brain hadn't caught up with it yet, his body was telling him this was the woman he wanted to be around. He'd known straight away she was bringing up demons for him. But no one else could deal with those demons but him.

He'd even sent another few emails to his friend in San Diego about the private practice offer. Asking more questions, exploring the area more thoroughly, in a way he'd never really been motivated to before.

But it seemed that dealing with Ivy and his career contemplations would have to wait—for now.

'Okay, folks,' he said. 'Let's get to work.'

# CHAPTER TEN

'HE ASKED YOU to do *what*?' Liz's disbelieving voice was shrill.

'Wait,' sighed Ivy. 'He asked me to wait.'

'And you said yes?' Her tone let Ivy know exactly what she thought of that.

Ivy was beyond tired. Tracking, tracing and isolating had led to some interesting discoveries about what the personnel on the ship really got up to. As a result, she now had one hundred staff isolated in special quarters. All they seemed to do was complain. It had been forty-eight hours and all she wanted to do was sleep. But she'd been dodging Liz's messages for the last few days until finally CALL ME NOW! had appeared on her phone screen.

'I thought something was wrong,' she said, and sighed as she sagged back down on her bed.

'Something *was* wrong. My best friend was deliberately ignoring me. You only do that when you've done something you know I won't approve of.' There was a tiny pause. 'I get you're at close quarters with this guy, but do you really think you know him well enough to make that kind of decision. It sounds kind of serious to me.'

'It sounds serious to me too,' Ivy admitted. 'But...' she shifted on her bed, uncomfortable '...I can't explain it. I just feel kind of connected to him, in a way I never have before.'

'Careful,' warned Liz. 'You sound as if you're getting kind of sappy. What happened to my own Boudicca? Mistress of all around her and heading for the top job? The girl who vowed she didn't have time for a relationship.'

That prickled. 'She's definitely still here,' said Ivy defensively. 'Just because I might like a guy, it doesn't mean he'll get in the way of my career.'

'Really?' Sarcasm dripped from Liz's voice. 'Because it sounds to me like Mr Wonderful has told you he's not all that wonderful and asked you to hang around until he feels better.'

Ivy tried to butt in, but Liz just kept on talking.

'And what if he never gets better, Ivy? Are you supposed to wait forever?'

'He hasn't asked me to do that at all. He just asked me for some time to get some help, and then see how things go from there.'

'Girl, have you listened to yourself? While I get it that you're in a tiny space and feelings might be amplified because, for the first time in forever, there is a man with a hint of potential around you, what if you wait, and then finally get together, and the spark dies—like it does for a lot of romances? And you've wasted time and energy, and in the meantime your real Mr Wonderful has drifted on by?'

Ivy squeezed her eyes closed in frustration. 'But what if he's Mr Wonderful and I don't give him the chance to fulfil his role in my life?'

Liz gave the biggest sigh in the world. 'Oh, girl, you've got this *bad*.'

Ivy finally laughed. 'Let me assure you, I'm still focused on my job. I'm still chasing my dream. Travis will not get in the way of that. I wouldn't let him.' She rolled over onto her back and looked up at the grey ceiling. 'But can't a girl have a few dreams while she's waiting?'

'Sounds like you've made up your mind.'

'I have,' she admitted.

Liz was silent for a few moments and then she spoke again. 'I hope he's worth it, Ivy. I really do. Because the guy that gets you has to know just how special you are.'

Ivy knew Liz was only being protective. And she liked it. She was her best friend, and when she met Travis it was important to her that Liz and Travis liked each other.

'Thanks, honey. See you later.'

She'd barely finished the call when a text appeared on her phone.

Sleeping yet?

Travis. It was Travis. She glanced at the clock in her cabin. It was nearly 1:00 a.m. Whilst she might have been dying to snuggle up in bed, her brain had just been sparked awake again instantly.

She answered quickly.

Is there a problem on the ward?

No. Awake, but tired. Have a host of people around me, but miss you.

Her heart missed a few beats. Wow. When he wanted to be, this guy was good.

She didn't wait to reply. That was the thing about being sleepy. There wasn't time to craft answers. She didn't have the brain space for it right now.

You're still on the ward? Why aren't you in bed?

His reply took a little time to appear.

One of our staff has been infected. He's diabetic and we can't get him stabilised. Sliding scale and insulin/dextrose infusion isn't helping at all. Think I'll need to stay here all night.

She replied instantly.

You need to sleep. But maybe not in full view of everyone. I can come and take over if you like.

No way. Don't want you exposed to this.

Part of her felt warm and cosy about that response, but part of her wanted to do her job.

You can't treat me differently from anyone else and you can't be on duty twenty-four hours a day. Where's Tony?

As soon as she sent the message she could guess the response that would appear.

Man down. He had no PPE when he made first contact. He started vomiting a few hours ago. He is NOT happy being in bed in the ward, but I insisted.

Ivy didn't want to laugh but she knew Tony well. He would be a hideous patient.

Are you okay?

Her screen filled with three dots. They seemed to hover there for a while as if he'd changed his mind, deleted his response and written something else.

Truthfully? Wishing I was anywhere but here...actually, wishing I was with you.

This guy could melt her heart for real. She sucked in a breath. She would love to be wrapped in Travis's arms right now, but no matter how good her imagination was, it couldn't be a reality. How could she relax enough to fall asleep with him when he could have another nightmare? Her heart felt as though it was twisting in her chest.

She tried not to think too much. She could send all that stuff in a text, but it felt like blaming, and she didn't want to do that. She didn't want to be the person who agreed to wait, and then at the first opportunity pushed it back in his face because he hadn't worked to get better yet.

But it was as if he'd read her mind.

I'm going to speak to Aileen. She's the best place for me to start. But starting the conversation feels...huge. Bigger than me.

She wanted to wrap her arms around him in a huge hug. But before she got a chance the little dots appeared again, followed by another message.

You haven't answered, so not sure how things are in your head. Sometimes I feel like a fraud. We've both seen people affected by PTSD. Some of them we know will never be the same again because of their experiences. I'm so aware that my experiences weren't as bad as others. But the nightmares aren't going away, and I've been purposely ignoring them, pushing them away so I don't have to deal with them. But here, tonight, knowing that if I don't do something we won't be able to fall asleep in each other's arms kills me. Because it's all I can think about. I don't want to be without you.

A tear slid down her cheek. For a moment she thought about pinching herself to make sure she hadn't fallen asleep and was actually dreaming all this.

Her fingers flew across her screen, all barriers well and truly lifted. He'd told her that he didn't want to be without her. It had been a long time since someone had said those words to her. Last time she'd doubted them. But this time, no matter what else was going on, she didn't doubt them for a second.

I want to be with you too. Don't doubt that. I want you to be well. I want to be able to curl up next to you and just listen to your breathing.

Her fingers hesitated. She wasn't ready to put her heart on the line until she was sure. Sure about everything. About where she was in her life, and if she was ready to lose her heart to someone.

Not someone. Travis.

She wondered if he might be disappointed with her reply. But within a heartbeat the little dots appeared.

A man can dream. I'll get there. I promise you. Sleep well. xx

She lay back and pressed her phone against her heart. Travis King didn't want to be without her. She wanted to dance around the cabin, but her body was just too tired. So she curled up, leaving her phone exactly where it was. She might not be able to cuddle up and feel the body of the man who was, without doubt, stealing a little part of her every day, but she could fall asleep with the words and messages that he was sending her. And, for now, that would have to be good enough.

# CHAPTER ELEVEN

HE STARED AT Ivy's file again. He'd been asked for a report. One part of him wanted to opt out. He could hardly have an unbiased view of Ivy and her work. But that was unheard of. It would immediately raise red flags. Questions would be asked. Her record would be blemished by the fact her commanding officer had asked someone else to write her report.

He might as well tell the world that something was going on between them.

It wasn't as if it had never happened in the navy before. Plenty of colleagues had started and maintained relationships together. As soon as it had become known, they hadn't been allowed to serve together. It was part of the rules—and rightly so. Relationship troubles or marital debates couldn't be brought onto a ship. And military decisions could be compromised if a loved one was at stake.

That was why the navy kept things simple and said that work and love had to be separate. This was probably the first time that Travis had completely understood why.

He stared at the blank screen. He knew exactly why he was being asked for a routine report on Ivy. This time it wasn't routine. An SMO vacancy was imminent, and she was one of the candidates up for consideration.

Her record was exemplary. Anyone who knew her

would give her a report that reflected her skills and team-work abilities. The glimmers of leadership that he'd already seen would flourish in this new role. Travis felt as if his heart was currently held in a vice. If he gave Ivy a glowing report—which she deserved—and someone pointed out the fact that there were rumours of a relationship between Travis and Ivy when he'd written said report, there was a chance it could damage both of their careers.

It weighed heavily on him. He was already in the position of SMO and unlikely to be given anything more than a sharp talk and a reminder to declare any relationship between serving personnel, whereas the repercussions could be much more serious for Ivy. It could move her from the top of the list—casting doubts on her true abilities and the final report he had written on her—and let someone else take the job that should be hers.

His head sagged into his hands. Any other man might just write Ivy a glowing report and send it in. But he knew how important this would be for her. Unfortunately everyday sexism still existed in the armed forces, and any whiff of rumour about Ivy could seriously damage her career. Travis would not be responsible for that.

He leaned back in his chair as Tony knocked on the door, bringing in some reports. Tony took one look at him. 'What's up?'

It was a light-bulb moment for Travis. 'Have a seat,' he said, gesturing to the chair in front of the desk.

Tony frowned for a moment. 'Is this where I ask what I've done?'

Travis shook his head and leaned forward. 'Tony, I know you're not a fool. I've been asked to write a recommendation about Ivy.'

Tony raised his eyebrows a little. 'And, of course, you will.'

Travis nodded. 'I will, but I'd like a little input from the team.'

The frown remained on Tony's face. 'That's not entirely normal. They usually only want to know what the boss thinks—particularly if it's going to be a recommendation about a promotion.'

Travis nodded in relief. Tony knew exactly what this was about. It made it easier.

'The last thing I want is to write the glowing recommendation that Ivy deserves and for anyone to cast shade on it because my feelings towards Ivy might not be...' He looked up at the ceiling. 'How do I say it? Not entirely unbiased?'

'But if you don't do it, that will be worse.'

'I know. But what if I did a collective response? Ivy's a team player. It's one of her best attributes. Not everyone who works with her has the same bias as me.'

Tony leaned back and folded his arms, looking thoughtful. 'So you want to use this different approach to make sure everyone says how great she is, not just you?'

Travis nodded. 'I'm not sure how many people know something is going on between Ivy and me—'

Tony let out a snort. 'Try half of the ship.'

Travis kept nodding. 'In that case, over two thousand people could cast aspersions when Ivy comes up for promotion.'

'Do you think anyone would actually do that? Ivy doesn't make enemies. She's a good doctor and a good officer.'

'I know that. But do I really know the mindsets of two thousand people on this ship? The timing is awful. What I want to do is let Command know that Ivy and I are...' He paused, not quite sure what word to use.

'In a relationship,' said Tony for him.

Travis nodded and let out a long, slow breath from between his lips. Someone else saying the words out loud made it feel like a weight had been lifted from his shoulders.

'But if I do that now—just after they've asked for a recommendation—then it will instantly raise eyebrows.'

Tony leaned forward. 'And you don't want to do that. You don't want anyone to think about anything other than the fact that Ivy is worthy of promotion.'

'Exactly.'

Tony gave him a sideways look. 'It's an interesting approach.' He gave a slow nod. 'I'll ask a few key personnel if they'd like to write a contribution for Ivy's recommendation. Best not let everyone know. And I'll write one too.'

Travis gave a grateful nod. 'Thanks, Tony. I'll combine them all into one recommendation and send an email saying I thought a team approach might be a good idea for a change.' He screwed his face up. 'Maybe I'll pick some better words than that.'

Tony laughed. 'Yeah, whatever you do, don't make your recommendation look like a criticism of their process.'

Travis rolled his eyes. 'Nope. No way. I'm doing this to help her, not get in her way.'

Tony stood up, walked around and put his hand on Travis's shoulder. 'If you know her at all, you know how important this is to her. I appreciate you thinking about how to make this work best for her.' He gave another laugh. 'But you're right. Your timing does suck. Shoulda saved the loving for later!'

He was still laughing as he walked out the door.

Travis stayed in place for a few moments, his hands pressed down on the desk. He knew what he had to do next.

He'd found a kind of solution to support Ivy's promotion. As soon as that was completed he would need to talk to her to agree when they would let the powers above know that they were seeing each other. Or 'in a relationship', as the phrase went. That thought made him smile. It probably should worry him a little. But it didn't. He wanted to be able to say that. He wanted to be able to declare it to his colleagues and his friends.

It wasn't something he took lightly. An email flashed up on his screen. Peters again. His emails were becoming a weekly obsession. Travis couldn't pretend it still wasn't a little flattering. He had to admit after the string of emails he was starting to become more open to a new role. And it was nothing to do with the potential income. Peters had mentioned the possibility of them being a healthcare provider for veterans. Travis liked that idea. He knew of lots of veterans who struggled with the healthcare system once their service was finished.

Ten years ago, he wouldn't have expected to consider that kind of career until he'd completed forty years of navy service. But things had changed for him. He was questioning more. He might not have openly accepted his PTSD before. But the fact that even before he'd taken this emergency SMO post he'd already been exchanging emails with Peters told him that, subliminally, his brain had already been trying to tell him things.

Travis shook his head. He wasn't in a position to think about private practice right now. He had to do something else first. He had to start his own treatment. Take the steps he should have taken four years ago.

He ignored the fact that his hands seemed to shake a little as he pressed them harder into the desk and stood. The walk down the corridor seemed to take an age.

People were nodding and saying hello as he passed, but his mind could only focus on one thing. He didn't want to allow himself the excuse of any interruptions.

He was doing this for himself. But he was also doing

this in the hope for a new life. A life that meant he could wake up every morning next to the woman that he was starting to realise he might love.

When he reached the door he didn't hesitate, just gave a short knock and walked in.

Aileen looked up and gave him her normal warm smile. 'Hi, Travis, what can I do for you?'

He closed the door behind him and as he turned back again he noticed Aileen straighten a little in her chair. She knew. She knew what this was.

She gestured towards the chair next to her.

'Take a seat,' she said with a smile.

And he did.

# CHAPTER TWELVE

IVY WAS FEELING ANTSY. It was the only way she could describe how she was feeling right now. And she couldn't quite put her finger on *why* she was feeling this way.

Travis had started treatment with Aileen for his PTSD. Only she and Aileen knew that. Ivy wasn't foolish. She knew this could be treatment that lasted a lifetime. But at least he'd taken the first step.

They'd also started seeing each other in as discreet a way as possible. Behind the closed doors of each other's cabins Ivy had learned all Travis's habits, likes and dislikes. She'd even seen his sisters through video chat, and loved the easy, teasing relationship all the siblings had. Travis was clearly the butt of many of their jokes. They'd also taken great pleasure in regaling her with embarrassing childhood tales of their brother, all at his expense.

Most of those calls ended with Travis shaking his head and cutting the connection to his hysterical sisters. But what was clearest to Ivy was the love and affection between the siblings. It reminded her of her own relationship with her sister and brother, Neil, who had asked Travis a million questions during one of their video calls as if he were interviewing him for a job. Finally, grudgingly, Neil had conceded to Ivy that he thought Travis might be 'okay'.

It was early evening and Ivy was leaning back against

Travis as they watched a streamed talk show. It was ridiculous—one guest claimed he could see ghosts, a minor celeb was on her fifth marriage and a reality TV star was peddling her latest diet, which she claimed had helped lose her half her body weight.

Travis groaned. 'Why are we watching this mindless crap?' He was twiddling a strand of her hair in one of his fingers.

'Because I've done three minor surgeries today and seen another thirty patients, and now my brain can only compute "mindless crap", as you put it.'

Travis's warm hand slid over hers and rested on her belly. 'I can't convince you to watch a good eighties movie? *Ferris Bueller*? *The Lost Boys*? *Gremlins*?'

She laughed. 'I'm more a *Working Girl*, *Pretty in Pink* and *Mystic Pizza* kind of gal.'

He winced. 'We've missed the most obvious one, you do realise that, don't you?'

She closed her eyes and sagged back against his chest. 'If I could count on one hand the number of references people make about me to *Top Gun*, I'd be a millionaire.'

'Me too.' He laughed.

Her phone beeped and she leaned over and grabbed it, shaking her head when she read the screen.

'What is it?' he asked.

'Just a stupid online game I've been playing with friends. People send random memes with statements that you need to answer. It's all about keeping in touch.'

'So what did today's say?'

She turned the screen around to reveal a large pink cloud with words in black.

What are you doing today? What were you doing a year ago today? What do you hope to be doing this time next year?

Liz had already replied.

Eating chocolate and drinking wine. Eating chocolate and drinking wine. Eating chocolate and drinking wine. Hey? Who says I'm not progressive!

Travis shifted a little. 'So, what's your reply going to be?'

'You don't want to know that,' said Ivy carelessly.

'Actually, I do.'

She gave him a curious stare over her shoulder then settled back against his chest, knowing that he could read her reply. 'Okay, then.' She started typing on the screen.

Surgeon on the Coolidge in the Pacific. Surgeon on the George H. W. Bush in the South China Seas. Hopefully SMO on a vessel somewhere in the middle of an ocean!

'Hey,' he said gently, sliding his hand over hers again before she pressed Send. 'That's all about your job, Ivy. Not about you.'

It hadn't even occurred to her and she froze for a second. He gave her a half-playful poke in the ribs. 'Your friends want to know about your life, not the navy's.'

She twisted her head again. 'But the navy *is* my life. Just like it is yours. That's why we're both here.'

His blue eyes were twinkling. 'But it isn't. We're here because of some weird coincidence that we met online— and almost in real life. The navy didn't bring us together, we did that ourselves. This...' he held his arms wide open '...is just our playground for now. It's not the end point for us.'

Now she sat up and turned around to face him, legs curled under her, the things he was saying prickling in her brain. She looked down at her phone. 'You're right. It *is* all work related.' She hated that she hadn't noticed that herself. She hated that the thought hadn't even *occurred* to her. The response she'd given had been automatic.

She stared down at her phone again, her mouth feeling very dry. She deleted what she had written and looked up at Travis. 'If you were asked this question, what would you write?'

All of a sudden it seemed very important what his answer would be.

Travis didn't hesitate at all. 'Today I'm snuggled up with my blind-date girl.' He winked at her. 'You can bet I'll be giving that app a five-star rating. Last year...' He looked up at the corner of the cabin as if he was trying to remember the date. 'I think I was home in San Diego, probably drinking in a bar somewhere with one of my crazy sisters. And this time next year?' His blue eyes connected with hers and he lowered his voice. 'I very much hope I'll be snuggled up in bed with you.'

Ivy tried to just breathe. She wanted to cry. She wanted to book herself into therapy somewhere. When had she started to focus her whole life on her career—when had that become everything to her?

As she sat for a few moments she couldn't actually pinpoint when it had happened. Had it always actually been like this? She'd wanted to be an SMO for as long as she could remember. It had always been her long-term career goal. It had felt good to aim for a top position. For the first time she was questioning herself. Had she put her career above everything else in an attempt to feel 'good enough'?

Or was it really the first time? Had the whole road down this path—using the app, thinking about a personal life, wondering if she might like to actually meet someone—been her mind's way of telling her to think about herself?

Broaden her horizons, take some time to look at her emotional needs instead of focusing on her career goals.

Travis leaned forward and touched her arm. 'Ivy? What's wrong? I'm sorry. Did I scare you with my plans? I didn't mean to.' He stood up from her bed. 'I didn't mean to jump to any conclusions. I'm not trying to push you into anything…'

He was starting to babble and she shook her head, blinking back a few tears. 'No,' she said, shaking her head. 'It's not what you said…' She took a deep breath. 'Well, yes, it is. But I'm not scared, Travis. You're not jumping to conclusions. It's just the fact that your answers to the questions were so different from mine.' She put her hand up to her heart. 'And now you've got me thinking what kind of terrible person I am that when I get asked a casual question, my response is all about work.' Her voice was starting to shake.

Her phone pinged again as another friend responded and Ivy gave a small laugh and turned it around.

Growing a baby. Marrying the man I love. Probably having a million sleepless nights and probably relying on all my friends to assist!

Her friend was pregnant. Cassy, a mutual friend of Liz and herself, had just let them all know she was expecting. Now that definitely made a tear roll down her cheek. Cassy had a high-flying career at a bank in San Diego, but nowhere in her response had she mentioned it. Her response was all about family life.

'Hey…' Travis moved forward and pulled Ivy up towards him, wrapping his arms around her and holding her close. 'I'm sorry. Don't take this so seriously. I'm sure your friends just thought of this as a piece of fun.'

But those words just made the sob that had been stifled

in her throat erupt. Her head was buried against Travis's chest. 'But what kind of a person am I? My first reaction was all about work.' She sniffed and looked up at him with blurred vision. 'You didn't do that, Travis. Why did I?'

Travis shook his head. 'Don't do this.' His fingers went under her chin and tilted it even more towards him. 'You are a wonderful surgeon. A brilliant team player. And a fabulous human being. Ask me what I think? I'm the man that's laying my heart at your feet.'

Ivy breathed. Trying to stem the flow of panic that she felt. Her hands gripped Travis's arms. 'Give me a second,' she said, picking up her phone and tapping the screen.

On a cruise with my blind date. Living a lonely but busy life. Hopefully cuddled up with the man of my dreams. PS Congratulations Cassy—will video call you later!

She pressed Send. The words were there. But she still felt like a failure.

'Here.' She forced a smile onto her face as she turned it towards him.

Travis only gave a brief nod. She was making this worse.

Ivy sat down on the edge of her bed. 'Why don't you tell me how things are going with Aileen?'

Something flitted across his face. Annoyance? Maybe he didn't like the intrusion. Or maybe he knew she was just trying to divert attention from herself.

She saw him choose his words carefully. 'Things are going…fine. I think. I don't really know. I'm still having nightmares. But Aileen's told me not to expect any kind of instant fix. She's also told me there's a chance they might never totally go away.'

Oh, no. The expression on Travis's face told her everything she needed to know. She shouldn't have asked.

'Don't worry,' he said softly. 'I wouldn't ask you to be with me if that happens. If you can't feel safe around me, we can't be together.'

The look he gave her was the saddest she'd ever seen. He ran a soft finger down her cheek. 'Goodnight, Ivy,' he said, and before she had a chance to say anything else he slipped out of the door.

Ice poured over her heart. She'd ruined a perfect evening by being nosy, being intrusive, because Travis's selfless answers had made her take a long hard look at herself. How much was she prepared to put into this relationship?

She'd drawn a line in the sand immediately with Travis and had sealed her heart into a package, right about the same time he'd started wearing his on his sleeve.

In her head she still had him as her potential dream date. She didn't have him in her head as Travis, the real-life person and colleague with PTSD. Someone who needed a chance to heal without pressure.

And that was exactly what she hadn't done.

Reality was crushing her. She'd just acted like some weird kind of teenager. He'd inadvertently highlighted something that she felt was a shortcoming of her own, and she'd lashed out. It may not have been deliberate but it had been her natural reaction. The old *not good enough* feelings washed over her.

She hated everything she was learning about herself tonight. She had to get her act together. She had to get over herself.

Because when Travis had walked out the door, he'd taken a big chunk of her heart with him.

The report was finished. He read it over for the twentieth time. It wasn't just good, it was excellent. Better than he could ever have hoped for.

His stomach was still doing flip-flops, his finger hovering over the button to press Send. He'd seen the expression on her face last night when he'd told her Aileen had warned there was a chance the nightmares might never go away. He'd wanted to find a different kind of way to give her that news. But she'd put him on the spot and he only wanted to be honest with her.

He scanned the accompanying email and pressed Send. He did still wonder if questions might be asked, but he was confident he'd given Ivy the best recommendation he could.

His sisters had been all over him last night, instantly catching the vibe that things weren't going well. He couldn't talk to them. None of them knew about his PTSD and he could only imagine the reaction if he told them. His family were like a wrap-around blanket. He wouldn't be able to move for them, and right now what he needed was space.

Actually, not true. What he needed was Ivy. But it felt as though she was slipping away from him like grains of sands sliding through his fingers. And it was all his fault. He should have dealt with this as soon as he'd first recognised the signs. He shouldn't have let it fester and take hold for four years. And now? When he'd met a woman he actually wanted to build a future with, it might just be too late.

Aileen had talked about more than he'd revealed to Ivy. She'd asked him about his navy career—then about triggers. He hadn't thought about it before. But apparently Aileen had noticed that in certain situations she seemed to lose Travis for a second.

He'd been horrified. Because he hadn't recognised it for himself. On her advice, he'd started keeping a diary. Thinking back and recording which nights his nightmares seemed worse, along with key events in the previous days. She'd found a pattern. A pattern they'd discussed at length.

He didn't like what he was discovering. He didn't like the fact the job he'd always loved might actually be enabling his condition.

But, deep down, he knew that was what his mind had been telling him all along. It was why he'd started to respond to Peters's emails. It was as if he'd known the only way to heal was to get out.

Travis had gone into the ward that day to a full clinic of patients. Ivy was on duty but they'd both been so busy their paths hadn't crossed.

The boom came out of nowhere, reverberating through the metal carrier.

He didn't even think. His body acted instinctively, crouching on the floor as if he were hiding behind that stone wall again as the enemy let loose with a hail of bullets.

For a few seconds he relived past events. The fear, the terror, the adrenaline, the sweat, the roaring in his ears as if all other noise had disappeared.

Ivy appeared in front of him, her face close to his, her hand on his cheek. 'Travis, Travis, come back to me. You're okay.'

He could see her blonde hair and green eyes. But even though her lips were clearly moving, his brain couldn't make sense of the words. It was as if the whole world was slipping all around him.

She lifted her other hand to cup his other cheek. Her words seemed to be coming out of a fog. 'Travis. Look at me. *Look at me.* There's an accident on the flight deck. I have to go. But I need to make sure you're okay. Tell me you're okay.'

A pack was dumped right next to him, landing on the floor with a loud thump.

It brought him back to reality. Tony was already running for the door. 'Come on, Trav!' he yelled over his shoulder.

Things came back into focus. 'What…?' he asked Ivy.

She was shaking. The hands that were on his cheeks were trembling. 'Flight deck,' she said slowly. 'There's an accident. All hands.' The emergency siren was wailing.

Something clicked into place in his brain. He stood up, grabbing the pack and starting to run after Tony.

As he pounded along the grey corridors up towards the flight deck he could hear her running behind him. He couldn't believe what had just happened to him. That had *never* happened before.

He wanted to stop. He wanted to throw himself inside his cabin, slam the door behind him and try to work out why he'd had such a strong flashback. It might have only been a few seconds, but he'd been there. Back behind the wall, listening to the bullets ricocheting. Feeling the warm belly of his friend as he'd tried to stem the bleeding. His head turning from side to side as he tried to determine who he could help, and who there would be no chance for. It was probably the most sickening memory that he had. And he'd been right back there. Living it again.

Instead, he was running down the corridor, catching up with Tony as they took the stairs three at a time. A boom like that could only mean one thing. A crash on the flight deck.

Tony threw open the door and the wind that hit them was incredible. The sight was worse. The smell of burning oil. Warm orange flames licking the air. Crew on the deck. Foam and hoses already out. Twisted metal.

Travis prioritised. There were parts of the jet scattered across the flight deck. The cockpit was mainly intact and the pilot was still in his seat. Men were crowded around, trying to prise it open.

His team was by his side, Tony and Ivy racing forward with him. By the time they got there, the cockpit was covered in foam to stop it catching alight. Warm flames were flickering nearby from one of the wings, catching the high wind and coming dangerously close. Instructions were also being lost in the wind.

One of the crew lost his footing and started tumbling towards the edge of the deck. Tony dived, his whole body weight landing on his fellow crew member to stop him being blown overboard in a powerful gust of wind.

Travis felt a hand grab the belt at his waist. He looked over his shoulder. Ivy. She could barely keep upright and was using him as an anchor.

'Move!' Travis yelled to the crew member right ahead of him. The young man was trying to lever the cockpit open, but because he was slicked with foam and could barely keep his feet in the wind, he was failing miserably.

Travis put his hands on the large crowbar, gripping it tightly. It was wedged where it should be. Every muscle in his body strained as he put all his weight and strength behind it. Another man closed in between him and Ivy, pushing Ivy sideways to allow himself to press up against Travis's back and mirror his position. His hands closed over the top of Travis's and crushed down with his added weight.

This time a tiny gap appeared in the seal around the cockpit. The smell of leaking jet fuel was becoming more pronounced by the second. 'Again!' yelled Travis. He had no idea who was behind him, but the guy was the muscle that he needed. They applied leverage again, and again. Another few crew members appeared alongside him, Ivy lost in the crush. He felt her hand release at his belt. The other crew wedged their tools in next to his, and together they all repeated the motions. Finally, the cockpit cracked open, catching in the wind with such momentum that it struck a small blonde person on the other side. The crack could be heard above the wind.

It took him a millisecond to realise who the small blonde was. Travis was torn. A collar was pressed into his hands for the pilot and he started yelling, 'Ivy! Ivy! Someone check on Ivy!'

He put the collar on in less than a few seconds. The pilot was unconscious. And even though he really didn't want to be there, Travis did exactly what he should. Checked the pilot's pulse, airway, and ran his hands over the man's chest, back and limbs, checking for any obvious injuries before they moved him. It only took a few seconds before he was handed a knife to slice the harness then secured the pilot's head until they could slide him onto a stretcher. He kept his hands and the pilot's body perfectly aligned as he yelled to Tony, who he couldn't even see. 'Give me an update on her!'

It seemed to take ages to get the pilot securely onto the portable stretcher and for Tony's head to appear back in Travis's line of vision.

Travis's heart thundered in his chest. If he'd been more with it when the plane had crashed, he might have issued other orders that would have meant Ivy would have remained below decks. If he'd had time to concentrate—instead of focusing on releasing the pilot—he might have realised she'd slipped around the other side and into the path of the hood of the cockpit. If he'd delegated this task to Tony, he could be doing what he really wanted to do—checking on Ivy.

If…

Something struck him hard, like a blow to the chest.

Tony's head bobbed up. 'She's okay. Just a bad knock on the head. She'll need a few stitches.' His voice drifted away in the strong wind.

Travis knew what he had to do next. Even though it hurt his heart.

He looked up at his fellow crew members, gripping the sides of stretcher. 'Sick bay!' he yelled, and they all took off, running to the door.

# CHAPTER THIRTEEN

HER HEAD WAS pounding and she knew she was heading for another migraine. Tony had stitched her wound and sent her back to her quarters, but she was anxious to see Travis so she slipped into his office and waited.

He was still working on assessing the unconscious pilot. It was an anxious time for everyone on board. Ivy had already heard that even though the winds had been gale force, the pilot had been cleared to land. As he'd landed, his plane had caught the tail end of a squall—notorious in the Pacific—almost flipping his plane over and making one wing catch the flight deck and causing him to crash.

She could almost have heard a pin drop outside as everyone moved silently while doing their jobs, all praying the pilot would regain consciousness soon.

Ivy wished she could help but knew that right now she would probably be a hindrance. She was worried about Travis and what she'd witnessed earlier. His PTSD was worse than she'd ever imagined. She'd seen those few seconds when he'd flashed back to somewhere else. It had been real to him. She had seen the flash of fear, the way his skin had prickled, his defensive posture and the rapid pulse at the base of his throat. For the briefest of seconds she'd wondered if she could actually bring him back at all.

She'd been scared for him. Scared that he was reliving one of his worst experiences all over again.

But she couldn't pretend that part of her mind hadn't wondered if he should be doing this job. She hated herself. She really did. But if she hadn't been there to recognise what had happened and bring him back, how long would Travis have been frozen? What if another doctor hadn't been around to take the lead on the rescue? It didn't even bear thinking about.

Ivy leaned back in Travis's chair, contemplated for a few seconds then put her feet on the desk. She did feel a bit woozy and wanted to close her eyes for a few minutes. Give herself a chance not to think about all the stuff she probably needed to. Her feet accidentally knocked his laptop and the screen flickered on. It was open at his emails, and Ivy pulled her feet back down and stuck her hands out to automatically press the functions to lock the machine.

But her hands froze.

There was an email on-screen with her name on it. Her recommendation for SMO.

Her heart twisted in her chest. She knew she shouldn't look. Of course she shouldn't look. But who wouldn't when it was right in front of them?

She pressed her lips together and scanned the text. She was only past the first few sentences when every muscle in her body tensed and she stood up. Travis hadn't written her recommendation.

He hadn't written it.

Her head started to swim. She stopped reading.

It was standard procedure to ask the senior officer for a report on a candidate for promotion. It was unheard of for the senior officer to delegate that task to someone else.

If Travis hadn't written her recommendation it would raise red flags. And people could jump to conclusions about her fitness to practise, her personal conduct, her suitability for the job.

It didn't matter which one out of these was actually true. The fact he'd not written her recommendation would send a big enough message for people to ask questions. And in the navy mud and rumour had a nasty habit of sticking.

Travis King had just ruined her career.

There was only one reason for that. He didn't think she was good enough to be an SMO.

For a moment she couldn't breathe. Why would he do that to her? Why?

Didn't he want her to be promoted? Was he trying to keep her next to him or, worse than that, junior to him?

How dared he?

Her head was already thudding, waves of nausea enveloping her as tears pricked her eyes. She'd thought she loved this man. She'd contemplated a future with him. She'd even had a few wild thoughts about him proposing and them finding a place together back in San Diego. She must have been crazy.

The pain in her chest was so real. She'd had dreams, for herself and for them. And it felt as if they'd been whipped out from underneath her without a second's notice. Anger surged through her veins, along with a wave of devastation and hurt. He'd all but told her he loved her. Why would he do this?

Why wouldn't he sit her down and have an actual conversation with her, if he thought she wasn't suitable for promotion?

The hateful words swirled around in her brain again. *Not good enough. Not good enough.*

The door creaked and Ivy looked up. Travis appeared at the door, his face creased in a smile but with worry in his eyes. 'I was looking for you. I wanted to check on you. I'm so sorry. The last thing I wanted was for you to get hurt.'

He moved over swiftly next to her, lifting his hands to her brow.

She flinched and moved back. 'Don't touch me,' Ivy hissed.

He pulled his hands back and his brow wrinkled. 'Ivy? I'm sorry, it was the wind. Well, and me. I was focusing on getting our pilot out. I didn't realise you'd gone around the other side, or that the wind would catch the hood.'

'I'm not talking about this,' she said coldly, pointing to her brow. 'I'm talking about this.' She pointed her finger at the screen of his computer. She didn't care at all that his emails were private. She wasn't at all embarrassed about snooping—because she hadn't been.

'What are you talking about?' Travis looked genuinely confused.

She spun the laptop around. 'This, the recommendation you gave me—or didn't give me, as it happens. Why would you do this? You know how badly I wanted promotion. And right up until you did this I thought I was in the running.' She pressed her hand to her heart. 'And I thought you would want to support me. But no. You've deliberately thrown a spanner in the works. The man who said he cared for me, the man I loved too, has just ruined my career!'

Angry tears spilled down her cheeks. 'I'll never forgive you for this. If you didn't think I was up to the task, you should have had the decency, and balls, to sit me down and tell me.'

She bent her head and gripped the desk as a mixture of dizziness and nausea swept over her. She should be lying down. She knew that. But what she'd discovered was too important. It couldn't wait.

His hand brushed against her arm. 'Ivy, no—'

But she cut him dead. 'I helped you, I supported you when we both know that you shouldn't be functioning as an SMO right now. Not with the effects of your PTSD.' She stepped forward to him, rage enveloping her. 'I didn't tell anyone you weren't fit for duty. I made a mistake. I won't make that mistake again.'

Travis's eyes widened in horror at her harsh words.

She couldn't quite believe they'd come out of her mouth. But Ivy was no pushover.

Only a few hours ago she'd cradled his cheek in the palm of her hand, knowing he was lost to his monsters. She'd been duty-bound to report that and yet it hadn't even occurred to her. Because that was not the type of person she was.

This was the guy she loved. She wanted him to get better. She'd wanted him to get help for himself, and for them, and she'd planned to wait by his side while it happened. Her heart squeezed inside her chest. With love came trust.

Everything was gone.

Travis was stunned. He'd gone to locate Ivy but couldn't find her. His office had been the last resort and he'd been so relieved to see her at his desk.

Now her words left his head spinning. But what was worse was the look in her eyes.

He shook his head fiercely. 'No, Ivy. No. I thought long and hard about that recommendation. I even spoke to Tony about it. I want you to get that job—of course I do. You deserve it. But this?' He held up his hands. 'Us? Our timing sucked, and the last thing I wanted to do was give you a glowing recommendation that someone could cast a shadow on and say it was biased because we're in a relationship. I was stuck between a rock and a hard place because I know what it looks like when an SMO doesn't give a colleague a recommendation.

'So... I had to think of an alternative. You're a team player, Ivy. It was one of the first things I noticed about you. And I like it, it's a skill that not all surgeons have. Did you look at your recommendation? Did you read it? Mine is there, alongside a dozen others. It's the best recommendation you could ever get. Everyone thinks you should get the job. And if we are asked questions at a later date about when our relationship started, we can be honest. Things have overlapped. We can declare things. Or at least I thought we could.'

He shook his head, a confused expression on his face. 'Why would you think I think you're not good enough? That's just crazy. You're more than qualified for this job.'

The words she'd hissed at him were still being processed in his brain. She'd threatened to report him and his condition. She'd told him he wasn't fit to do the job. He was automatically and instantly offended and couldn't pretend not to be.

'You want to report me?' he asked her. 'Do it!' The response came out harsher than he intended it to. 'Report me. I froze. Yes. I froze. I admit it. But I still managed to get out there. I still managed to do my job—just like I have every day for the last four years. Should I be SMO when I have PTSD? Who knows? That's for the navy to decide. But if you don't think I'm fit for duty, say so. Don't put the safety of anyone on this ship at risk for my sake.'

He couldn't think straight. She was right in front of him, clearly not feeling well. He could see how she was holding on to the desk. She had a dressing on her head covering her stitches. Her blonde hair was dishevelled, her face flushed. Those green eyes that had flirted and teased him for the last few weeks seemed to have some kind of shield in front of them. There had been a definite flash of anger but now she looked numb. As if she couldn't believe where they'd both got to.

He couldn't either.

Last night he'd listened to his heart. He'd emailed Peters and told him he was definitely considering a change from the navy. The conversation with Aileen had struck chords exactly the way it should have. He had to accept his condition, his diagnosis, and do everything he could to heal. He would do it for himself and for the woman that he had fallen in love with.

He knew all about Ivy's career ambitions and supported them. But he was wise enough to know that both of them working for the navy would create challenges for a relationship—particularly if their spells of deployment were one after the other. His priority was to make their relationship work. He was beginning to see the light of being permanently based in San Diego. Or he'd thought he had. Now all those thoughts seemed to have vanished in a puff of smoke—or a bang on the head, as it were.

They stared at each other. Resentment simmered just under the surface. This woman, the woman he'd dreamed of spending a future with, the woman he'd risked his heart on, and who he had asked to wait for him. She was looking at him with hurt in her eyes. He'd done that to her.

He should apologise. Beg her to understand his reasoning. But as the colour drained from her face he realised he couldn't stand there and bicker back and forth with her. Ivy clearly needed to rest.

She gave a little twitch and looked at him. This time her voice was quiet. 'You're not the person I thought you were, Travis.' His gaze watched a single tear track down her face and he clenched his hands into fists to stop himself from reaching out and brushing it away.

'I'm me,' he replied instinctively. 'I've never claimed to be perfect. I can only be me. The person with baggage, and the guy who loves you. I have *never* done anything to deliberately hurt you or stand in your way.'

She remained silent, still gripping the desk with her hands before she took a deep breath and looked him in the eye.

It was like someone sticking their hand through his solar plexus and ripping his heart clean out of his chest.

'I wish I could believe that,' she said, before turning and walking out the door on shaky legs.

# CHAPTER FOURTEEN

AILEEN GAVE HER a sideways glance. 'Ivy, do you want to talk?'

Ivy was busy writing a prescription for a patient she'd just seen and hadn't even heard Aileen come up alongside her.

'No,' was her automatic response, then she breathed and looked at Aileen again. 'Why would you ask me that?'

Aileen smiled and gestured to the tablet Ivy had in her hands. 'Because you've been standing here for the last five minutes, and you've started that prescription three times, and...' she leaned over Ivy's shoulder '...you still haven't completed it.'

Ivy sighed and put the tablet down on the counter.

'I don't think we can talk,' she said, her throat feeling dry.

'Try me,' said Aileen.

Ivy had barely spoken to anyone in the last few days. She'd been ignoring calls from Liz and her family. She'd been giving monosyllabic answers and instructions to her co-workers. If Travis was in a room, she walked out. It was painful. Everything about him reminded her about the dreams she'd had.

She closed her eyes for a second and whispered, 'Is it enough if I tell you I can't wait to get off this ship?'

She didn't want to put things into words. Because then, depending on her mood, she either felt like a fool and a pushover, a heartless monster or a career-driven bitch. And every one of those thoughts amplified those not-good-enough feelings. She had judged herself to be all of those things over the last few days. She could barely eat, she couldn't sleep, and if she set foot outside her cabin, she ran the risk of running into Travis.

Her job chances were shot. But if she put in for a transfer right now, or requested to be reassigned, it would throw more red flags on her record. On top of her 'not' recommendation, that was the last thing she needed.

'You know anything you tell me is confidential,' Aileen said quietly.

Ivy turned her head quickly. 'But I'm not your patient,' she said, with an element of panic.

Aileen gave a soft laugh and held out one hand. 'Ivy, everyone on board is my patient, just like they are yours.' She gave a thoughtful pause. 'Why don't you just let me be your friend?'

Ivy felt tears brim in her eyes for the thousandth time. A friend was exactly what she needed right now. But she didn't want to involve anyone else on the ship in this. People had already noticed the atmosphere between her and Travis. She had witnessed the exchange of glances between staff and the way they were tiptoeing around her.

'I can't, Aileen,' she breathed. 'If I talk about it to you, then it's real. And I don't want it to be.'

Aileen leaned close and squeezed Ivy's hand. 'Door is always open,' she whispered, before she moved away.

It took Ivy a few moments to collect herself. She had a patient to see. She had to pull herself together and get a grip.

\* \* \*

An hour later Tony came into the treatment room as Ivy was dispensing some drugs for a patient. He folded his arms and looked at her.

'What happened?'

'What do you mean?'

'Travis is leaving.'

The tablets she was trying to count out tumbled to the floor. 'What…?'

Tony was still looking at her.

'What do you mean, he's leaving?'

The phone next to her started ringing so she picked it up. 'Ivy Ross.'

'Flight Surgeon Ross, the captain needs to see you. Report to his office immediately.'

Panic swept through her. She hadn't been ordered to speak to the captain at all on this trip. If he was calling her to his office, something was wrong.

Tony must have noticed the expression on her face. 'What's wrong?'

'I'm to report to the captain.' Her voice was trembling.

Tony gave a shrug. 'Makes sense.'

She was confused. 'Why?'

Tony glanced at his watch. 'Because Travis leaves any second now. You're about to be promoted to SMO. You were in the running for the next job. Makes sense to give it to you now.'

There was a roaring in her ears. Every cell in her body was on fire. Everything about this was so wrong. It looked as if it seemed entirely normal to Tony. But none of this seemed normal to Ivy.

'What do you mean, he's leaving now? Right now?'

Tony nodded. 'He's probably already taken off.'

She was running. She didn't even stop to explain. Her

feet were pounding down the slim corridors. 'Move!' she yelled at a few seamen to clear the way.

She climbed up ladders, heading to the flight deck as quickly as she could.

She needed to see him. She had to talk to him. Every hour of every day she felt something different about what had happened between them. It didn't make sense to her. But the one thing that hadn't changed was how she felt in her heart. She loved this guy. She loved Travis King. And she didn't want to leave things like this.

She wasn't allowed on the flight deck if take-offs or landings were taking place. But she flung open the door anyway.

As the wind whipped around her, her stomach plummeted. A helicopter was already rising high into the sky. Even from here she could recognise the familiar shape in the passenger seat. His helmet showed he was looking in another direction. She waved her hands frantically, trying to signal him.

But Travis was deep in conversation with the pilot next to him.

He didn't even see her. Didn't even know that she'd come to talk to try and catch him before he left.

Ivy was left in the middle of the empty flight deck, caught in a flurry of wind, as the man she loved disappeared out of sight.

# CHAPTER FIFTEEN

*Ten weeks later*

'TRAVIS, THERE'S A last-minute patient. She's insisting she needs to be seen today. She asked for you by name. Can you fit her in?'

Travis finished typing preoperative notes on the last patient that he'd seen. It was only 5:00 p.m., and while he knew his secretary wanted to finish for the day, he wasn't anxious to get home. 'Sure, no problem. And, Mel? You can go on home. I'll close up.'

'You sure?' He could hear the happiness in her voice through the intercom and could only imagine how much she was smiling right now.

'Of course.'

Travis finished his notes and stood up, walking over to the large window overlooking part of San Diego Bay. Peters had delivered on everything he'd promised. The partnership, the office and work that he wanted to do. He'd already seen a number of army and navy veterans with ongoing health issues.

The normal resignation process of six months had been negotiated due to his existing PTSD. He would remain in the navy reserves, but had been granted permission to take up another role while his paperwork was processed.

From here he could still see part of the fleet moored in San Diego Bay. It was like watching family and friends from afar. He loved this city. He would always stay here, and he was slowly getting used to what his new life would be.

He realised he hadn't even asked Mel anything about the new patient as he walked to the door of the waiting room.

The woman had her back to him. She'd clearly been pacing and was currently staring out at the view in the same way that he had been.

Travis's skin prickled. He didn't need to ask her name. He knew it.

Ivy.

She froze. She had clearly heard him coming into the room. She turned slowly to face him.

Her hair was sleek and smooth, and she was wearing her navy uniform.

'Hi.' Her voice was nervous and slightly croaky.

'Hi.' Ten weeks. It had been ten weeks since he'd last seen her, when she'd accused him of wrecking her job chances and not being fit for duty.

The last action he'd taken before leaving the *Coolidge* had been to recommend her for the job he was vacating.

He was sure that right now his heart was swelling in his chest as memories flooded through him. The way she'd looked at him like a patient the night she'd realised he had PTSD. She'd phoned this office as a potential patient. That was how he had to treat her. No matter what his heart dictated.

He dropped into professional mode and gestured to the office behind him. 'Come through. What can I do for you?'

He'd turned and started walking already. Trying to collect his thoughts for a moment as he held the door for her.

Ivy pressed her lips together. She strode past him in a wave of orange blossom. The scent sent a shock wave through his system. Memories of her lips, her skin pressing against his.

He did his best not to let his attention be captured by her silhouette.

He waited until she sat down and then moved around the desk to sit opposite. He was nervous. She'd sent him a few texts after he'd left, but he hadn't replied.

Travis licked his lips. 'You requested me by name. Can I assume you're here as a patient?'

Ivy took her time to reply. She shook her head. 'I landed just over an hour ago. My bags are down the hall. This is my first stop.'

He straightened in his chair. Her assignment on the *Coolidge* must have just finished. She kept going. 'I have my next deployment details.'

She pushed a letter across the table to him. He glanced down. SMO on another aircraft carrier. It would last twelve weeks.

'Congratulations.' His voice was cold. He knew that. 'You got your promotion.'

She leaned forward a little. 'I got my promotion because they told me mine was the most inclusive recommendation they'd ever seen. They are thinking of using a more three-sixty approach to recommendations in the future. They realised it's important that everyone can give feedback on a candidate, not just their superior officer.'

Travis was still. He'd heard she'd got her promotion but hadn't asked any details. He'd still been unsure if what he'd done had been the right move for Ivy or not.

He gave the briefest nod of his head but didn't speak.

'I came to say I'm sorry. I'm sorry I lost my temper with you and misjudged you. I didn't expect you to leave.

I thought… I thought that at some point on the ship we'd get a chance to talk again. Re-evaluate things.'

'But I was doing a job you didn't think I was fit to do.'

She froze, her eyes darting away from his. When she looked back she pressed her hand on her heart. 'I'm sorry, I should never have said that. You're a wonderful doctor, Travis.'

He shook his head. 'You were right. I needed to make a choice to get better. Aileen had already spoken to me about how continuing in the navy was probably triggering things for me. I hadn't taken the time to think things through. Even though, subjectively, I think I'd already figured that out. Now…' he glanced out the window again '…I have taken time to think things through properly. That's why I'm here.'

'And that's why I'm here.'

He furrowed his brow. 'What?'

'I'm here because I've had ten weeks to drive myself crazy in the middle of the Pacific Ocean. About how I can say sorry to the man I love. The man I should have told there would be no need for waiting, that I would stay by his side while he got treatment. The man I should have told that, whether his treatment worked or not, I would always be by his side.'

He stiffened and shook his head but Ivy continued.

'I want you to get better, Travis, of course I do. But I should never have walked away. I should have stayed by your side, right from the start.'

'There's a chance that I'll never be better,' he said softly. Those words were hard to say out loud. But ten weeks away from Ivy and ten weeks of counselling had made him realise it was important to be honest. 'You should feel safe to be with the person you love.'

In the blink of an eye Ivy moved around the desk to be

by his side. 'Travis, I do feel safe around you. I've had a long time to think about this. My heart keeps telling me the same thing. I have to be with the person I love. You are a good man. If you spend your nights having nightmares, we'll find a way to deal with it. I can sleep in another bed, although I'd much rather be in your arms. And if you have a nightmare, I'll be there to support you when you wake up.'

She sighed and reached out to take his hands. 'A number of years ago someone I loved told me I wasn't good enough. It doesn't matter that you never, ever made me feel like that. I had my own issues that I hadn't admitted. I always had the little voice in the back of my head, and when I thought you hadn't backed me for the job, all those feelings came flooding back. I've had weeks to think about that, and Aileen has been a great friend and support. She made me realise I had to work through those things and face up to reality.

'And the reality is, I love you, Travis King. You're a good man. The best man I've ever met and the one I want to have in my future—however that looks.'

Travis sucked in a long, slow breath. 'Ivy, I can't pretend I was happy when you told me I couldn't do my job. But you were right, and I knew I had to step away. I've been seeing a counsellor for the last ten weeks and things seem to be going well. Will my nightmares ever stop for good? I don't know. Have I thought about you every day since I left the *Coolidge*? Of course I have. But you thought I'd ruined your career, Ivy. The fact that you even considered I'd do something like that made me step back and wonder if you loved me like I love you.'

She went to speak but he shook his head. 'You see, Ivy, ever since I met you I've let my guard down. Because it seemed like the right thing to do. You were the first person I felt a real connection to. I lost my heart to you—right from the beginning—even when I knew I wasn't in a position to do that. When I thought that I'd hurt you I couldn't cope. I had to leave. I'd put off seeking treatment for my PTSD too long. I requested an emergency leave of absence and resigned from the navy. I was lucky they agreed to my request and let me leave early.'

He paused for a second. She was watching him intently, her hands still in his. 'The truth is I had wondered if I'd ever get the chance to meet someone and have something other than the navy in my life. I'd been approached a few times about going into private practice but had never even considered the possibilities. Here?' He pulled one hand from hers and held it upwards. 'I joined on the agreement that this company would offer services to veterans. I've done three surgeries every week so far. Mainly follow-ups on injuries received in service, a few surgeries on back and hip problems—long-term damage from the job.'

He looked out at the view across the bay. 'It feels good to be here. I'm getting used to sleeping in my own bed at night.' He licked his lips and looked at her again. 'But there's something missing.' His gaze locked with hers. 'A huge part of my heart.'

Ivy was glad she'd changed position. She was kneeling next to Travis's chair right now. If she'd been standing, her legs would have been shaking. From the second she'd disembarked from the *Coolidge* and started on her long journey back home, she'd had one thing on her mind. Seeing Travis King again.

She was sure he'd hate her. He hadn't answered a single one of her messages—and she didn't blame him. But she had to be here. She had to be by his side. The longer they'd been apart, the more sure she'd become. Her earlier flurry of anger had disappeared. Her rational brain had kicked in, and she'd never felt so much like a villain in her life. She loved this guy. This was the guy she'd spent the last few years dreaming of meeting. Someone with whom the spark was so vibrant it could light up the sky. Someone who had captured her mind, and her heart.

Aileen had talked her through her feelings of inadequacy, the thoughts of never being good enough, and she'd realised she had to let them go if she ever wanted to live the life she should.

She kept holding Travis's hand. Now she was here she didn't want to let go. 'Travis, I'm so sorry. All the dreams that you mention, and feeling like you're missing a piece of your heart? I feel exactly the same. Since you left, nothing has felt good. Nothing has felt right. I know what I would be asking of you. I know that this time it would be me asking you to wait—to wait while I go on assignments that will last months. We never discussed things like this. And I don't even know if that's the kind of future you imagined for us.' She blinked and swallowed the huge lump in her throat. 'But if it's not, I understand.'

He gave her an odd look. 'If you hadn't got the job, if you hadn't been given the promotion, what would you have done?'

She didn't hesitate for a second. 'This. I would still be right here.' Ivy took an enormous breath. 'I love my job— you know I do. I thought career was everything, and then I met you and realised my job didn't define me. I want a life I can live and enjoy. I want to be with the person that I love. And I have to work to make that happen. You've managed to create a new life outside the navy, and I can do that too.'

His voice was low. 'I wouldn't ask you to.'

She pressed her lips together. 'That's because you put

me first. And I need to do the same. I need to put you first. If you're willing to give me a second chance, we can work at it. I can try this first assignment. If things don't work out, I'll look at other career pathways. Ones that mean I can be by your side every single night.'

He gave a soft shake of his head. 'I'm not your patient.'

She smiled at him, noticing the tiny lines at the sides of his blue eyes. 'No, but you are my one true love. And hopefully one day you'll be the father of my children.'

His eyes crinkled in amusement. 'Are we going from blind date to children in one fell swoop?'

She shrugged. 'We've wasted enough time. A really wise woman told me that when you know, you know.'

His eyebrows rose. 'Who said that?'

'Your sister.'

His eyebrows went even higher. 'You've been talking to my sister?' Then he gave her a sideways glance, as if scared to ask the next question. 'Which one?'

'All three. They're quite a lethal combination. When you wouldn't answer my messages I contacted them all. I told them it was all my fault. And that I wanted to make things up to you.'

He gave a quiet laugh. 'Now I understand why they haven't been constantly pestering me about you.'

She gave a nod and finally let go of his hands, holding hers out. 'Think of this a recreation of our blind date. You'd just come back from deployment and the first thing you did when you arrived back in San Diego was to message me to meet. I've been waiting ten weeks to do this. It's been the longest ten weeks of my life.' She laughed and tilted her head to one side. 'Remember all the eighties and nineties movies we talked about?'

He nodded and she grinned. 'Then all I'll say is I'm

just a girl, standing in front of a guy I love, asking him to love me.'

Her heart was fluttering in her chest, wondering what Travis would say.

He stood up, gave her a smile and pulled her close. 'I think he might say, I love you right back, Ivy Ross. Best blind date *ever*!'

# EPILOGUE

THERE WAS ONLY one place they could possibly get married. The hotel on Coronado Island was famous and the gardens were currently packed with half of San Diego's resident navy personnel, alongside Travis and Ivy's families and friends.

'Ready?' asked Travis as he slid up the zip on her satin wedding dress.

They'd decided not to be traditionalists. Ivy's next deployment was in a few weeks and they wanted to spend as much time together as possible. She picked up her bouquet of orange blossoms and dark green leaves and turned to face her soon-to-be husband in his tuxedo.

She straightened his tie. 'Well, hello, handsome.' She smiled. Outside the grounds were crowded with many of their friends in uniform, but Travis didn't seem the least bit bothered that he was wearing something different.

He interlinked his fingers with hers as the sound of clinking glasses from the gardens drifted up towards them.

'Let's get out there and join in the fun.' He smiled.

'Can't wait,' she replied.

There was a huge cheer as they walked down the staircase and out into the gardens and shaded arboretum with an arch of flowers.

Travis's parents and his three sisters were at the front

of the crowd, dressed in bright colours, with Ivy's parents and brother and sister at the other side of the aisle. His brother was his best man, and Ivy's brother's kids were already off playing in a corner of the garden, smearing dirt on their yellow outfits.

Isaiah Bridges gave her a nod as they walked down the aisle, from where he was sitting along with Tony, Aileen and a whole array of personnel from the *Coolidge*.

Ivy's father stood to give her away and the gardens fell silent as they recited their vows. Love, honour and obey in sickness and health had special meaning for them. Travis was still on his journey but making good progress.

As the celebrant finished the service, Travis bent to kiss her. 'When are we talking about babies again?' he whispered.

'That ship might have sailed.' She winked as a nearby waiter appeared with a silver tray of champagne and she lifted a glass at one side. 'Secret lemonade. Let everyone else think it's champagne.'

His eyes widened. 'Really?'

She nodded and grinned. 'Really.'

Travis clasped his arms around her waist and spun her then lifted his own glass from the tray and raised it in the sky. 'Everyone, I'd like to raise a glass to Ivy King, my blind-date bride!'

\* \* \* \* \*

# SECOND CHANCE
# IN BARCELONA

FIONA McARTHUR

MILLS & BOON

Dedicated to Marion Lennox, who has written well over a hundred wonderful books and has always been one of my huge writing heroes. I feel so blessed to have you as a friend and mentor. And someone to swim with in funny bathing hats. Fi xx

# PROLOGUE

*Wednesday, eleven p.m. Private Maternity Wing, Sydney Hospital, Australia*

'SOFIA?' CLEO SPOKE quietly as she crossed to the first-time mum in the birthing unit. 'I'm Cleo Wren.'

Sofia Gonzales sat as haughty as a princess in her bed with her jet-black hair coiled in a plait on her head. Her long slender neck looked delicate against the pillows. Most telling, her elegant fingers twitched and then stiffened as she clasped them together on the coverlet with rigid tension. The girl stared unsmilingly back.

She looked fragile to Cleo. Even from that first moment she'd entered the room. So young and lost. A child, bearing a child. Alone. Cleo felt sympathy rise in her chest.

'You are the next shift?' The words were formal and surprisingly soft. The accent Spanish, her friend Jen, the previous shift's midwife, had said.

'Yes. I am. And you are Sofia?' She smiled. 'I hope we are simpatico as we will spend the next eight hours or so together until you meet your baby.'

A tiny lift of one corner of the lovely mouth. 'Jen said you are a woman of warmth, determination and strength. I need that on my side. That is simpatico enough for me.'

Despite the brisk words Cleo could see how close to

breaking this young woman was and she wanted to know why. She touched her hand and Sofia's fingers closed around hers in greeting.

Sofia nodded. 'The doctor has said he will see me to deliver this baby in the morning. He thinks I will be here in labour all night.'

'You and your baby are both well and already working together. It is quite possible we can surprise him in the morning.'

'I would like that.' Labour intruded, and with the first links of connection between the two women established, something crumpled inside Sofia and she turned her face away to hide the weakness. 'I'm scared,' the girl whispered, with her soft European cadence. Sofia grabbed tighter to Cleo's hand and began to gasp through the contraction.

Cleo placed her other hand firmly on Sofia's shoulder and concentrated on transferring calmness and strength through her fingers. Young and alone. She felt so glad she'd chosen to come in here for the extra shift now. Jen had said this woman badly needed support.

Sixty seconds later, as the contraction ended, Sofia released Cleo's hand, and Cleo mimed blowing out a deep breath to demonstrate.

'Purse your lips and blow that contraction away,' she murmured as she assessed how best to help her new initiate into the wonders of birth. 'Allow your body to sink into the bed and sigh a big sigh after each contraction.'

Sofia closed her eyes and followed Cleo's instructions obediently, and when she opened them again some of the fright had receded. She blinked and already her face appeared less tightly drawn.

'There. That one is done.'

'Many more to come, though.' Sofia tried to smile. 'I'm still scared.'

Cleo nodded. 'Doing something you've never done before asks a lot of us. But I'll stay with you. By the time you've had your baby you'll have achieved one of the most amazing things in your life. You won't be scared any more. You'll have turned into a lioness to protect your young.'

'Easy for you to say.' A little haughty impatience in the tone and Cleo held in a smile. 'I'll have been in agony and it will take hours.'

'Not agony. But hours, yes, possibly. We'll work on speeding labour up. But the journey will take as long as it needs to.'

'*Si*. The faster the better.'

Cleo glanced around the empty room. She couldn't understand the lack of support for this woman. This was a private hospital that cost bucketloads to be admitted to. Why was she alone? The previous staff had asked, and she'd just said her family were overseas. But where was the baby's dad?

'Is there anyone I can call to come to sit with you as well?'

'No.' A long pause and then quietly, 'My fiancé has left me. I am alone.'

The shock made Cleo's eyes widen. Cleo's husband had left her, too. Not as a pregnant woman in labour, thank goodness. But she understood Sofia's sadness now.

Had he left Sofia for a richer woman, more acceptable to his mother? Like hers had?

Sofia went on. 'Any family...' A pause and a definite lip curl. 'Any I would have with me are in Spain.'

So? 'I'm guessing there are family in Australia, then?'

'My cousin has destroyed my life by forcing my fiancé to leave me. He is the same as his father was. A pig.'

Well, Cleo could understand why she wouldn't want her cousin here. That was fine. She'd been thinking of female relatives or friends. 'No one else?'

'My parents are dead. Last year in a car accident.' Sofia shook her head. 'Close to me, there is just my grandmother in Spain and she is old and agreed with my cousin that he should ruin my life.' There was hurt and bewilderment as well as anger.

'You need someone here to stay with you until you give birth. May I stay until your baby has arrived?'

Sofia searched Cleo's face. 'What if my baby is not here before your shift ends?' She didn't believe her. 'Jen was here before and now she has gone.'

'Jen had already done a double shift. And she must come back tomorrow as the manager. I do these occasional shifts to stay connected to my old job when I worked here. Now I work as a retrieval nurse for patients who need a medical escort to fly home, to Australia or overseas. But I don't need to check in there again until Monday. When the new staff come on, I'll stay as a support person if your baby hasn't entered the world. I'll be here.'

'I would like that.' Sofia's eyes clung to hers. 'But why would you do this?'

Their eyes met and Cleo smiled. 'I need to be here for you at this time. Easy.' She shrugged. 'Let's check your observations and your baby's heart rate. Then, with your permission, I'll feel the position of your baby through your belly to see if it's curled itself in the best way to find a way out.'

A smile tugged on Sofia's beautiful mouth. 'Does a baby assume a position?'

Another contraction rolled over her and she moaned. Cleo held her hand through the heavy breathing and when it was done, they breathed out together.

'A position? Absolutely a baby chooses. And with the angles of your own body you can give your baby hints on slight changes that make all the difference to the length of your labour. Just by moving your centre of gravity around. We'll do that, too.'

A few minutes later the observations had been completed and found to be all within acceptable limits. 'Baby's moving down into the pelvis as expected.' They breathed through another contraction together.

Cleo sat again to chart Sofia's progress and observations on the rolling computer beside the bed. Then she saved the file and pushed the computer away.

'So now we've done that for the moment, I'll help you stand out of bed.' She pretended to frown at the bed. 'Beds are not great for healthy mums in labour because lying in bed can slow everything down.'

Sofia looked worried. 'I don't think I can move.'

'It will feel better to move, I promise. Standing adds gravity to help your baby descend even more.' She showed crossed fingers to Sofia. 'Makes labour faster!'

Sofia's eyes widened at the possibility and she rolled onto her side, suddenly eager to get up. 'Then I will stand.'

They walked around the room, pausing during the contractions, finding places of comfort before the contractions increased. The waves of labour progression were still infrequent enough for conversation.

Sofia perched gingerly on the big rubber ball when Cleo suggested it, and her eyes widened as the round softness beneath her eased her back discomfort. Together they examined the shower, and discussed the big bath in the bathroom at which Sofia looked askance.

Cleo laughed. 'You wait. If I can get you into that bath,

up to your neck in warm water, I'll have trouble getting you out again. You'll love it so much.'

She rested her hand gently on Sofia's shoulder as another contraction rolled over the woman.

Sofia gripped the bathroom doorframe and forced the breath from between her lips to stay relaxed.

'Perfect,' murmured Cleo. 'You're breathing beautifully. That was a stronger contraction.'

Sofia nodded, then sagged a little when the tightness released its grip on her. 'And closer to the last one as well.'

'Which is wonderful. Stronger and closer means nearer to meeting your baby.'

Sofia raised her brows at her. 'Easy for you to say.'

'Indeed. Though in my defence I have seen this point in labour many times and women always fill me with wonder. They keep going. Like you will. Just one contraction at a time until the most amazing thing occurs and the baby is here in your arms. Keep thinking of that.'

Sofia glanced at the bed meaningfully. Cleo shook her head. 'And try to stay off the bed. Lying down slows contractions and builds tension in your body. We talked about that. More, not less discomfort.'

'I wish I could send these pains to the father of this child.' Her eyes narrowed. 'Or my horrid cousin. Yes. I would send them to *him*. He would have dragged me back to Spain before the baby was born if he could have and then I wouldn't even have had you.'

Cleo didn't like the sound of anyone being dragged anywhere against their will. Not something she had experience of. 'Can't you say no?'

'Much good that would do me. My cousin is the head of my family now. His father was my guardian and threatened me with an arranged marriage. My parents left me financially independent enough to be able to complete university in Australia. Out of his reach. I slipped away when he was ill and then he died. I was so happy living here. Now his son has ruined my life. Bah, I hate him.'

Hate. Not what they needed in labour. Cleo touched her arm. 'Then don't think about him. Tell me the most beautiful thing about your home. I've never been to Spain. I'd like to go someday.'

With effort Sofia breathed out and almost visibly shook off the strong feelings that had upset her. 'I live in Barcelona. When I was a child my mother used to take me to the Sagrada Familia. It is a beautiful church built by Gaudi on the Carrer de Mallorca.' She smiled at the memory and the tension leaked from her shoulders. 'My mother would say, "Surely this is the most beautiful church in the world." Yet it is still unfinished more than a hundred years later.'

'It sounds amazing. I must look it up. What else?'

'I love tapas. Barcelona has wonderful food.' Her voice sounded dreamy and she smiled. 'And the dancing. I love the dancing.' She was smiling now at some distant memory. 'The men are very handsome when they dance.'

Cleo smiled, relieved Sofia had calmed down. 'They sound gorgeous. Jen's boyfriend is Catalonian and he's certainly a handsome man. They're trying to talk me into going to his nightclub where there is flamenco dancing. One day I'll go.'

'Is that this Jen? From here?'

Cleo laughed. So much for privacy. No escaping it as Jen had looked after Sofia in the previous shift. 'Yes.'

Sofia smiled. 'And one of my friends told me about this hospital and Jen. So, you and I, we were destined to meet.'

Cleo thought about Jen's cry for help for this lonely young woman. 'I'd like to think so.' And then the next powerful wave stopped all discussions.

* * *

Two hours later the contractions rolled over Sofia relentlessly but, as Cleo had promised, once she'd climbed into the birth pool, the heated bathwater lapped around and supported her. As the crashing waves of transition pushed her into second stage she breathed and moaned yet remained calm.

There was a brief pause in the labour as Sofia's body prepared for the final dance of birth. Cleo anticipated what was to come as the room rested quietly with her. Soft music underlay the steady breathing of the mother. Cleo knelt beside the bath, her gloved hands resting on the edge of the bath out of the water as she waited.

The second midwife, discreetly summoned by Cleo as birth became imminent, sat unobtrusively in the corner of the room, only rising to take and record the myriad observations as required. Cleo remained focussed on Sofia as her baby's head began to descend into the world. Her charge's previous tension seemed to have been released.

When the moment of birth arrived, it was Sofia's careful hands that reached down and lifted her own tumbled underwater baby from the depths of the pool and carried her to the surface.

In support, Cleo's hands cupped the mother's hands as she broke the surface with her new daughter to rest her tiny, blue-tinged face between Sofia's breasts. Cleo wiped the baby's eyes, nose and mouth with a soft sponge and she breathed. No cry. But blinkingly awake.

Sofia's brimming eyes met Cleo's and Cleo nodded. 'Congratulations. She's beautiful. You're amazing.'

Such incredulous wonder on the mother's face. 'She's here. I did it. Thank you.'

# CHAPTER ONE

*Thursday*

DR FELIPE ANTONIO ALCALA GONZALES, had landed in Sydney on Tuesday on his private aircraft and he'd been busy since then.

Tonight he met with Diego, another distant cousin who lived in Australia. They were heading to Diego's bar to discuss finding his cousin, Sofia, who had slipped out of sight. 'Felipe. How goes your grandmother?'

'Not well. But she is fighting her illness until I return Sofia to Spain.' Doña Luisa, the woman who had raised him when his mother had died many years ago, had asked him to retrieve his cousin, and he would do what she wished. She should not have had to ask. He would do anything for the woman who'd shown him the love he'd never received from his late father.

They'd all thought his cousin Sofia Gonzales was at university in Sydney, but instead she'd become quietly entangled with an Australian conman and was heavily pregnant by him. Diego had been watching him this last week at Felipe's request.

'Thank you, Diego. Your help has been invaluable. Though we still need to see her home to Spain before the baby is born if possible.'

'*Sí.*' Diego clenched his hand into a fist. 'And I would have liked to have thrashed the scoundrel, with his mistress watching, for their insults to Sofia. She is only nineteen!'

Felipe's eyes flared. 'As would I. But now their plans for her inheritance have been blocked by the family's bankers. They will get no more of her money.'

'Sofia is blaming you for running him off.'

Felipe nodded. 'Of course. She is young. Thought herself in love and she didn't believe the charges against the man.' And Felipe had used his own money to buy the conman off.

He understood Sofia's anger with him but the avarice he'd seen in the conman's eyes had quickly banished any reluctance to upset his cousin.

Sofia and her baby would be safer in Spain where his grandmother—for as long as she could—and he could watch over them. In time hopefully a suitable Catalan husband could be found for Sofia, if she was agreeable.

It should never have reached the stage that such a leech could attach himself to his family and enthral his cousin.

He must take some of the blame for that happening, but in his defence the last year had been absolutely crazy.

His work as medical director and oncology consultant at his hospice had been all-consuming. His father's death had left him in charge of the family. Except he had failed with Sofia.

His grandmother's terminal illness had taken most of his free thoughts. That and the sudden decline of his best friend's health, too.

Sofia had been pushed aside.

Now his cousin had gone into hiding, but he knew she deserved a moment to catch her breath after the betrayal of the man she loved. He would find her and bring her home before Monday.

But the delay was driving him insane when his grandmother was fading in health back in Spain.

On Saturday Felipe strode into the Villa Rosa flamenco club in Sydney. The one you went to for the best of Spanish dancers. The one that sold the best of Catalonian wine. The one run by Diego.

Today he had tracked down and seen Sofia and her newborn baby.

Yet, when he had finally talked to his cousin, they had achieved nothing productive.

Sofia utterly refused to accompany him in his aircraft and leave Australia. Impasse. She did not believe that their grandmother was dying or that he'd promised his grandmother to bring her home.

He could give her two more nights before he had to leave for Spain. He felt as if he would explode, having been given the disquieting news that in his absence his grandmother had become more unwell, her heart failing quickly, and he needed to return.

Damn the complications created in Australia when he wanted to be in Spain and by his little grandmother's side.

Just walking into Diego's club, though, seeing the familiar trappings, hearing the familiar music and smelling the scent of fruit-filled sangria, calmed a little of his agitation.

Monday. They would leave on Monday. He had to convince Sofia that there was little time left for their grandmother.

His eyes watched the male dancer finish the eight o'clock show and Felipe admitted the man was good. Even envied him the freedom to express himself in that manner.

Felipe could dance. Frowned on by his autocratic father, it was one thing his grandmother had been firm about when his father had scorned the idea.

Even now, at thirty-six, he could remember her whispering to him not to hold his emotions inside like his father did. 'I see you when you dance. Flamenco for you offers the release of your emotions,' she'd said.

Since then he'd incorporated many dance moves into his daily private workout routine and it soothed him. His grandmother had been amused.

Diego approached and held out his hand. 'Don Felipe.'

Felipe's anger softened momentarily at his cousin's mock deference. They had grown up together, though their lives had diverged many years ago when Diego had moved to Australia.

Diego's face saddened. 'Doña Luisa is failing, cousin?'

Felipe didn't want to talk about how much he wanted to be at home right now, but Diego knew. Had understood from the moment he'd arrived here from Spain. Instead, Felipe nodded at the Spaniard departing from the stage. 'I could stamp more than he if I let all my anger out.'

'Then why not do it?' Diego's voice was low. 'Marcos will step aside and go home early in a heartbeat to his wife. It would be good for you.' He shrugged. 'And I love to watch your passion.' A brief gesture with his hand. 'I could easily arrange for your flamenco during the last session of the evening. Perhaps enjoy the company of a beautiful woman tonight, flirt, and forget your troubles and responsibilities. I would like to see you smile before you leave.'

He didn't need the complication of a woman tonight, but to dance? Felipe's first thought of performing in the club—ridiculous. His second—he wished he could. His third—to hell with proper behaviour for his status. He'd do it. To step away from his grief, release his anger and try to go home whole on Monday.

Nobody knew him here. Perhaps his grandmother would smile when he told her.

'Do you have boots?'

At 10:00 p.m., when the time arrived for his performance, he slipped into the bar and surveyed the audience, but his gaze caught on the woman in the blue scarf and lingered. His cousin's words came back to him.

*'Enjoy the company of a beautiful woman tonight and forget your troubles and responsibilities.'*

She was tall and auburn-haired, with an aura of serenity that soothed his own jangling emotions, and he felt the pull of something quiet and real. Odd ramifications of her presence echoed all the way down to his waiting, angry, black-booted feet.

As he watched her, an inexplicable tendril of calm and peace entered his soul and rested there. Later, if she was still there, perhaps he would talk to her...

# CHAPTER TWO

CLEO SAVOURED THE odd feeling of exhilaration in her chest and the room's aroma of perfume, spicy food and fragrant wine. The wood under her finger felt warm as she traced the etched roses on the black wooden wall beside her and followed Jen deeper into the Villa Rosa flamenco club. She glanced at her watch—what the heck? Ten at night!

Like a night shift.

The small bars and restaurants of the tiny alley on their way here had seemed filled with handsome swarthy men partnering exotic women with flashing eyes and red lips. A seething nightlife unlike any she'd seen before.

It was how she imagined across-the-world Barcelona to be, rather than a neighbourhood that lay only twenty minutes from her Coogee flat. This vibrant subculture of predominantly Spanish-speaking streets felt like another dimension.

As well as another era.

Jen's Diego, her 'Spanish hunk' in Jen's words, owned and sang at the club they'd just entered. He'd been amused that Cleo, a flamenco-watching virgin, would see the last-minute guest dancer in the late show who by all accounts should not be missed.

And why not? Her painful divorce was finally through. A year in her new job had settled her. She needed a new direction now to find the fun she'd been missing out on. Jen was advocating the advantages of a Spanish boyfriend. Not on Cleo's menu but it was amusing to imagine.

The room sat expectantly in semi-darkness, the stage a golden finger of light bathing the guitarist as he strummed a lilting tune that caught at Cleo's throat and promised more.

A dark-haired waitress swung a jug of fruit-filled sangria onto their table without asking and poured their first drinks into heavy wineglasses before she sashayed away.

Cleo rested back in her chair and tried to believe this was Diego's place of employment.

This was totally exotic.

Cleo sipped the cinnamon-and-apple spiced wine, loosened the sky blue scarf she'd worn to keep the night chill off her shoulders outside and allowed her gaze to roam as the music picked up in tempo.

The guitar's song seeped into her skin and infiltrated her senses to beat in her veins.

A darkly dressed woman and a familiar man, Diego, stepped onto the stage and sat each side of the guitarist. Both began to clap rhythmically, and it was Diego's lilting voice that pierced the semi-darkness as he began to sing.

Her neck prickled.

In Spanish, the lyrics held a haunting cadence that stirred Cleo's skin to gooseflesh and she turned to see Jen staring with rapt attention at her boyfriend. Yep, she'd agree with that. He was good.

Cleo's eyes drifted back to the stage, gave up trying to decipher the meaning of the words with her only fair Spanish, and allowed the pure emotion of the music to soak into her like the sweet sangria she sipped.

Both wine and music danced in her blood and made her itch to clap her hands along with the rest of the audience.

Primitive feelings stirred against the calm and collected persona she projected. First came a young woman, dancing to the beat, her skirts swishing, hands flying, spinning and stamping.

Then came an older woman. The experience of living the dance vibrant in every gesture—another span of many minutes passed watching another world.

Wow, Cleo thought to herself. These performers were amazing.

Music beckoned to something she didn't understand as her foot began to tap. This whole night felt different. So fun. A crazy, completely wonderful thing to do for yesterday's birthday which had passed with only Jen to congratulate her.

'You look happy,' Jen said, beaming across at her.

'You're right,' Cleo said. 'This is fabulous.'

The room fell silent and the audience turned their heads as one to the bar.

A tall, dark-clothed man stood with his back toward the audience ten tables from the stage. When he spun unexpectedly to face them the guitar whispered a taunting note of promise to shift the mood.

In the dim light, Cleo couldn't distinguish the man's face, but the broad shoulders, strong chest and muscular arms under the black shirt were clearly defined. As were the long, muscular thighs clad in black jeans and strong calves in knee-high boots. He paused, poised, splendidly macho in silhouette.

Cleo's breath caught. The heels of his black boots glinted with gold and for a few beats of the mesmerising music he clicked them slowly where he stood.

Coal-black hair hung long and straight, shielding both sides of his face until his head lifted and he stared straight at the musicians on the stage. Commanding them. They clapped faster.

Now she could see his features and wondered if she would ever forget them again.

A hard face, full of angles and harsh planes, yet as primal and piercing as the howl of a wild animal on the full moon. Strong straight nose, sharp cheekbones and an unsmiling mouth. When he strode forward nobody spoke, they barely breathed, awed by his charisma—riveted by the respect he ruthlessly demanded.

She wasn't sure if it was the arrogant tilt of his head, the nonchalant looseness of his fingers as they swung at his sides or the slow haughty strides of his long legs as he passed, but her eyes locked on the coiled strength and beauty of his movement like everyone else's did. Then her gaze snagged on the taut backside unapologetically squeezed into those skin-tight trousers as he did a slow, languid climb of the two steps in front of them onto the stage.

Holy moly.

When this man moved there was no one else in the room.

He glanced neither left nor right, simply owned the space as he strode to the sphere of gold light that waited to focus on only him. His chin dropped, black hair fell forward, again obscuring his features, booted feet snapped together as he stood motionless, fingers rigidly splayed.

The guitar stopped with him.

Until music, and the dancer, began to glide slowly, precisely, rhythmically perfect, gloriously arrogant. Faster the music went. Faster he spun and stamped and whirled, a story without words. Emotion soaked the air, wrapping its ethereal hand around Cleo's heart, and she had no idea why but her mouth dried as tears gathered at the corners of her eyes.

He spun and stamped, then stopped and stared haughtily over the heads of the audience, then spun again in a wild yet fluid poetry of movement that spoke without words. Called the long history of his ancestors into the hushed room.

Cleo sat captivated by the most marvellous male she'd ever seen.

This man's carved-in-stone cheekbones and arrogant chin, the way he flung his head and flashed his eyes had an aristocratic beauty that clutched at her and refused to let go.

There was something dangerously sensual that made her feel feminine and fragile and fascinated beyond reason as she stared at him, her heart thudding in time to his gold-heeled black boots.

Her teeth grazed her lip as the rate of her breathing rose with the music.

Her breath caught when he looked her way.

Who knew even hair could be erotic? Thick strands of his black-as-night locks swung and swirled and bucked as his eyes caught and held hers.

His eyes fixed on her. Then he turned away.

She puffed out a breath she hadn't realised she'd been holding.

Struggled to remember when she'd last had shameless, erotic thoughts about a man. Had she ever?

Good grief.

She forced herself to sit back and blow out the tension. Ground herself and shift the soles of her feet back and forward to feel the wooden floor beneath her shoes.

Relationships had been scarce since the divorce. She'd dived into her overseas patient retrievals, working for an agency that mainly arranged transport and medical escorts to enable ill Australians to return home. Sometimes overseas visitors required medical supervision as well to return to their homelands. It was demanding but interesting work. Sometimes she was out of the country for a week or more at a time. Then there was the occasional labour ward shift work with Jen.

That had been enough to curtail her social life.

No time for dalliance. Let alone sex.

The only males she saw were clients or doctors—and she'd learned her lesson about doctors. She'd just divorced one after all. None were men she'd think about in that way.

This way.

At least at this moment—with this man.

Her mind imagined his sexy mouth on hers. *Oh, my*, she thought as her eyes clung like his clothes to his body. She almost laughed out loud.

A fierce cape-swirling matador who moved like liquid added heat-stoking dance gestures that reached into her soul and from across the room cupped her face with a look when he stopped.

When he snapped his heels together and focussed on her it was as if he circled her body with a wicked swirl of his large elegant hand and brushed her skin.

The last thing she'd thought she'd feel tonight was heated thighs but right now she needed to shift in her seat and squeeze her knees together.

He was looking at her.

Again.

Often.

Now almost all the time. Whenever his head came back her way his eyes were on hers.

As if speaking with his dance. Coal-black eyes bored into Cleo's through the rhythmic music and flowing movement. Her hand crept to her chest.

And always his eyes would clash and command her not to look away.

She couldn't.

The way he twirled and twisted and suddenly stopped hypnotised her like a timid creature trapped in blinding headlights.

When he finished, arms out, complete, as the music died, Cleo's pulse rate had risen to somewhere akin to a medical emergency.

The lights went on and applause and adoration rose like a tornado into the high roof. Then it finally died down as a surge of people swarmed him.

Cleo sat back and let out a long shuddering breath.

Surreptitiously she watched him speak to his adoring fans, raise his hand, bow briefly, then bend his head to speak to Diego, before striding away without looking in her direction.

Her heart thudded and her skin tingled with an after-glow of excitement, definite arousal and a strange, hollow, spreading disappointment.

Let down. Deserted. Stupid.

What had she been thinking? That he'd come see her? He'd been an entertainer and she had certainly been en-tertained. Aroused, in fact. Had she expected him to come across and chat?

And yet, out of the darkness and across the wooden floor to their table, the dancer strode her way. His heated body suddenly loomed beside her and he leaned close, the scent of steaming male and some amazing masculine cologne mixed, the sensual aroma heady. His eyes captured hers, dark and dangerous, as he held out a large elegant hand.

'I am Felipe.'

# CHAPTER THREE

FELIPE APPROACHED THE table where the woman with the blue scarf and Diego's Jen were sitting and he knew this was a bad idea. What was wrong with him?

His return to Spain on Monday had been arranged and yet the moment he'd seen this woman—felt this woman—she'd cast her net over him like that powerful woman in history. Diego had said, when he'd asked his cousin at the end of the dance, that her name was Cleo. Fitting. Cleopatra. Queen.

He wanted her. And couldn't have her. He knew that. He'd never been a believer in casual sex. But perhaps a little post-dance distraction would be acceptable. For that was all it could be—if it could even be that. He would talk to her. Find something to banish the fascination that pulled him to her.

Already he'd done something frowned upon for his station. To bare his soul in a public performance, let loose his anger and sadness, and find the hope that the dance always gave him since he'd first learned the moves. The dance allowed him to shed who he was, his responsibilities, the emotions of the last days, and yet all through that dance, every turn, he'd seen her.

Been drawn to her.

Danced for her.

Something in her eyes grabbed his chest and squeezed and he was aware that throughout the dance he'd shared that connection with her.

So here he was.

Standing beside her in the bright lights of post-performance with his hand out.

When she put her fingers into his he carried them to his lips and breathed in her scent… He closed his eyes to savour her and smiled at the small tremor he felt go through his mouth from her skin. Opened eyes again to catch her gaze and kiss her wrist.

Her hand caught warm and precious in his. Destined. Which was ridiculous.

Clear, cool sapphire-blue eyes, fine features and a determined chin… There was nothing classically beautiful but he found her face utterly arresting. Compelling. Incredibly fascinating. Her brows rose at his intimate salute.

Not so amusing was his sudden aching thirst for more than that small taste of her. To wrap himself around her and breathe her in as if she could fill his lungs with life.

'Diego says your name is Cleo. Like Cleopatra.' He lifted out the chair next to hers. 'Will you allow me to share a drink with you?' He did not give her his family name. This could go nowhere, after all.

Diego lifted his hand in acknowledgement and smiled, and then walked around the table to Jen, whose eyes were fixed on his cousin.

Felipe signalled to the waitress who had appeared with the bottle of sparkling wine he'd ordered and four empty glasses on a tray.

She put them down and opened it beside them. He indicated the bottle. 'This is Lonia Cava, from Catalonia. It tastes of white peach, melon and apple.' His eyes met Cleo's. 'I believe it is your birthday?'

He watched her eyes widen, enough to see the gold amidst the brilliant blue of her irises and then the irises expand enough for him to fall in even further. Her blue gaze seemed bottomless.

'It was. Yesterday,' she said, her voice low and pleasing. What was it about this woman that made him dream of foolishness he shouldn't even contemplate? And with a woman from the same country as Sofia's conman?

If he wasn't careful, this would end with piercing sweetness and an unfamiliar longing on his empty flight home.

# CHAPTER FOUR

CLEO STRUGGLED WITH his presence, so large and almost vibrating with heat and sex and all the images in her brain from the dance. But she tried very hard not to show it.

The music started again in the background, taped this time, and after a brief acknowledgement of the newcomer and some compliments on his dance, Diego and Jen became engrossed in their own conversation.

She was left alone with the dancer. 'Thank you for the wine.'

But under the table her hand still tingled. Just that feel of this man's lips on her wrist had made her belly kick. Which was ridiculous. She was thirty. No virgin.

She'd been married and divorced, for goodness' sake. But what she'd felt for Mark had been slow to grow and stupid in hindsight and she wouldn't do that again. On her side anyway, it had been nothing like this instant, searing awareness and aching need for him to pull her closer.

This was raw. Crazy. Pulsing with the promise of experiencing something way out of her normal world and she wondered what she'd done to draw someone like him to her. But he was here now.

There was that temptation to be mad. A magnetic pull to do something out of character for once. To consider whether she could pretend she knew the rules of the game. To feel captured and appreciated and not feel discarded afterwards.

She didn't know where it could go. Or even if it should go anywhere. 'Are you in Australia long?' It was the least she could ask.

'I leave on Monday.'

She allowed her eyelids to close as she considered that. Two days and he would be gone. Opened her eyes and nodded. 'That's too bad.' Or maybe not.

She glanced at her watch. Eleven o'clock. Not yet the witching hour but she was under some kind of spell that she didn't want to wake from. Something with no future.

She took a sip of her wine and it sparkled and fizzed on her tongue, light and delicious, and divine. Like him. 'Thank you for the wine.' She lifted her glass to him. 'And the birthday wishes. I'll just have this but then I'll have to go.'

He bent his head in her direction, apparently content with her answer, and she thought with a flicker of disappointment that he could've asked her to please stay.

His fingers waved to the door. 'It is warm. I wish to be outside. Would you like to walk from here? Along the street? Away from this room?'

And suddenly she knew she would like that. Very much. Just a walk. She wasn't planning on more, especially with a sexy Spaniard leaving on Monday, not for one night. But she did want to get out of there and spend a few moments with the man opposite and fizz and bubble like the wine and be daring.

Before she went home.

To be alone.

'I could walk with you. For a few minutes.' Whoa. And she'd actually said it. Sometimes she surprised herself.

Jen looked up, as did Diego, and they both nodded. 'I

vouch that he is a gentleman,' Diego said, and grinned that sexy, sunbeam smile that had won her friend. Then added more teasingly, 'Unless you wish otherwise.'

'A walk.' Felipe drained his glass and stood. 'A fine idea. Shall we go?'

Who said, 'A fine idea'? This sexy Spanish guy apparently. Well, then, she felt like doing something unlike Cleo Wren. Not her usual cautious behaviour.

She drank the last contents of her own glass, and the pale magic wine tingled and bubbled and made her smile as she reached for her bag.

Out on the street the alley seemed alive with laughter and the chink of glasses and the glow from streetlamps and pseudo Spanish *cantinas*. Far too alive and alert for nearly midnight in her usual world. 'Don't these people ever sleep?'

'Siesta allows the use of the night.' He took her hand. The fun came back with the rush and sizzle of a firecracker ready to explode as his fingers wrapped confidently around hers.

Her face turned up to his. 'Tell me about Spain. Where do you live?'

The dark skin around his eyes crinkled. 'Barcelona. The most beautiful city in the world.'

She tossed a smile up at him. 'How funny. I live in Sydney.' She spread her free hand in an arc in front of her. 'The most beautiful city in the world.'

He laughed and she grinned at the pleasure it gave her to see him relax. He'd seemed so self-contained and serious as he'd danced, and when he'd first come to the table as well. This outside man was easier to walk with.

Their hands swung lightly between them, entwined, warm, and she glanced down, surprised how easy she felt holding hands with a stranger. She shook her fingers. 'And why does this feel so relaxed when I don't know you at all?'

He tilted his head at her. 'You forget. We met through the dance. I saw you. It is magic when that happens.'

'Have you been dancing long?' Did he do it for a living, like Diego sang? Did he own a similar club in Barcelona? All questions she wanted to ask but she bided her time. Impatience didn't fit in with this night.

He looked away from her. Pensively. 'I have danced all my life.'

She remembered his passion and power. 'You're very good.'

He turned to look down at her and laughed at that. 'No. I am not very good. I am brilliant.'

She shook her head at his boasting but his confidence delighted her. 'Really?' She arched her brows at him. 'You're certainly not shy.'

This raised his brows. 'Do you know many Spanish men?'

She did have limited experience of the Spanish. 'I know Diego.'

'Diego is a good man. But he, also...' another amused smile '...is not shy.'

She could vouch for that. But to Jen he was kind and funny as well.

They'd walked from the alley now and onto the footpath that led to Coogee, away in the distance, past two- and three-storey houses that had glimpses of the ocean from their top balconies. Their hands still swung between them. Cars zoomed past, sweeping them with more light than that cast by the streetlamps, but the number of vehicles was slowing as the night progressed.

Each time he was illuminated she admired his presence more.

Maybe he would be back in Australia someday. 'How do you know Diego?'

'From Barcelona.'

He asked another question, instead of offering more information about himself. 'Do you live near the beach?'

'I do.' Two could play at minimal answers.

His brows went up as if aware she was retaliating in kind. 'And does anyone else live with you?'

And why would you want to know that? But she didn't say it. 'I could tell you,' she agreed, 'but then I'd have to kill you.'

He laughed. 'I like you, Cleopatra.'

Lord, she was sick of that name. 'Cleo, please. Nobody calls me Cleopatra.'

'Your mother did.' He bumped her with his shoulder. Something fun and silly and she bumped him back. As if they'd known each other for many years, not just minutes.

'True. But she was heavily into the queens of Egypt during her pregnancy. I suppose I should be glad I wasn't called Hatshepsut.'

He laughed again and she didn't know why she felt so pleased every time he did. With every chuckle a little more tension seemed to ease from his broad shoulders and his face softened. 'I like the sound of your mother,' he said.

She would have liked you as well. Or fallen for your looks at least. 'I wish I could tell her that.'

His face turned sad and she looked up at him, brows drawn, but he went on. 'I'm sorry. My mother, too, is gone. But we are adults. Is there a husband for Cleopatra?'

A roundabout way to ask. She enjoyed his odd use of English. 'There was a husband. A very conceited man. He is gone now, figuratively and legally.'

He squeezed her hand. 'My condolences. And to clarify, I am not conceited at all. Do not be concerned that I know all. I can dance. But I cannot paint or sing or write a great novel.'

'Do you have a wife?'

He laughed. 'No. Much to my grandmother's despair. There is nobody who would complain that I walk a beautiful woman home in the dark.'

It had been a long time since a handsome man had called her a beautiful woman. 'Thank you for the compliment.' She didn't believe him but it was nice to pretend. She'd needed this. 'Are you walking me home? I thought we were just walking down the hill.' Her cheeks felt hot.

He looked down at her and his eyes had warmed. 'Your husband was a fool.' Said very softly.

'Let's not discuss him.' Talk about a mood-breaker.

He snapped his fingers. 'Easily.'

She laughed. He had an unexpected humour. 'Have you been in Sydney long?'

'Four days.'

And two more until he flew out again. 'Six days seems barely enough to get over the flight.' She knew about rapid long-distance flights. 'Was there a reason for such a rushed visit?'

He looked at her and his gaze shifted away to the bottom of the hill where the sounds of the ocean were beginning to whisper to them as they drew closer. 'Yes.'

She felt the wall as a cool breeze between them. The harsh-faced man she'd first seen was back. His reasons were not for her information. She didn't know this man. What was she doing here, alone with him?

She stopped walking. Looked ahead to the lights of her unit, now in sight. Did he need to know where she lived?

'I can walk from here. Thank you.'

He closed his eyes and shook his head. Gave a crooked, apologetic smile. 'I'm sorry. I am not the open, sharing person I begin to think you are. To say what I think out loud is hard for me. Unlike you.'

'That's a sweeping statement, Felipe.' She saw something flit across his face, a bitterness, as he compressed his lips.

She decided. 'But, still, perhaps it is better if I go on alone.'

She searched his face in the gold light of the streetlamp and something in his eyes made her sad. 'It was very nice to meet you.' She reached up and very gently put her lips against his. 'Goodbye, Felipe.'

Felipe inhaled the scent of her, savoured the feather-light touch of her lips on his, and pulled her closer for a moment in time. She was right. He should let her go.

Yet he reached forward with his mouth softening, gently exploring, waiting for her to pull back.

When she remained compliant, he slid his hand around her neck and pulled her snugly against him. Gently brushed her lips with his own, back and forth, and to his satisfaction she opened to him like a flower and he explored the wonder that was Cleo.

Her taste and scent and softness warmed parts of him that had been cold for too long. Her hand, between their chests, squeezed tighter around his and he pulled her more firmly against his heart.

After many long, long moments that held the breath of time in the darkness on a footpath near the bottom of the hill, they stepped back and searched each other's faces— seeing the answer to a question that hadn't been spoken out loud.

Still her hand was held warmly and softly and they smiled at each other. 'Or I could come a little further with you?'

He slipped his hand further up her wrist to feel her pulse pounding beneath his fingers and she nodded.

A few minutes later she stopped at a door. Or at least an entry to a block of units.

In the distance he could hear the pound of crashing waves quite loudly and even taste the tang of salt, but close to her he could mostly smell the enticing scent of Cleo and feel the warmth of her skin brushing against his.

She lifted keys from her handbag and opened the bottom entry door, turning back to face him. She searched his face and something, he didn't know what it was, that she saw made her relax. 'Would you like to come in?'

'Very much,' he said softly, ignoring the voice of reason in his head that told him to move away. Step back. He could not.

He followed her straight back and charmingly rounded bottom up the stairs, admired her long, slim legs and the way her hips moved as she climbed one flight and then a second. Tension coiled inside him, his attraction to her expanding like a chemical reaction, and by the time they reached her door his heart pounded from proximity to and promise from this mesmerising woman.

She glanced back at him as she turned the key in the lock, but she didn't hesitate to push open the door.

When she moved inside, he followed. Reached back with a steady hand and removed the keys she'd left dangling, then pushed the door shut behind them with a gentle click.

To the left in the dimly lit room lay a small table and he dropped the keys on his way to reach for her.

'This is crazy,' she whispered.

'Is there something wrong with crazy between two consenting adults?'

She sighed but curled her fingers into his shirt and tugged him closer. 'No. Now is good. You'll be gone soon.'

'We have tonight. And I am prepared,' he patted his pocket, 'to keep you safe.'

He saw in her eyes that she chose to accept him and she relaxed against his chest. They kissed. His hands slid reverently over her soft breast and slid the blue scarf from her shoulders to kiss her beautiful neck.

Tomorrow he would think about Monday and going home.

# CHAPTER FIVE

CLEO FELT THE slide of silk from her neck as this tall, muscular stranger kissed her skin. Heat flooded her. She should be feeling nervous, or wary, or guilty, but the emotions most prominent were excitement and arousal, and possibly impatience.

'Beautiful,' he murmured against her skin. *'Bella.'* When she looked into his eyes they were almost black, yet warm, and totally focussed on her with a wonder she didn't expect.

When he'd kissed her before, on the street, it was as if she'd tasted the man within and trusted him without reason but with complete faith. She saw that again now. As if she recognised his moral ground as one she, too, could live with. She'd seen her own need to be someone else for the night reflected in his eyes. What was it about their connection that had brought them to this point so fast and with such a sureness that what they shared would be right? Later, perhaps, she would find the answer. If there was time. But they had all night.

'Your home is like you,' he said quietly as he stood holding her shoulders. 'Calm, welcoming and filled with a serenity that makes me want to learn how to be in your space.' His big hands ran warmly and possessively over her, stroking the skin of her arms and her shoulders as if every slide felt wonderful to him.

His hands felt just as amazing on her.

'You're in my space now,' she said softly. Reaching up and putting her hand flat on the iron of his chest above his pectorals. Pushing a little as she marvelled at the wall of muscle. Smiling at his understated strength.

'Thank you.'

'You should. I can't think of another man who has been in here since I bought the place.'

His eyes crinkled at that and he nodded in appreciation. 'I am blessed then.' He bent his head and with one hand cupping her cheek he leaned in and kissed her. His mouth gentle, then more firm as she pushed into his body to press closer. 'Do not plan on much sleep tonight.'

Her heart rate sped. Her belly kicked and the sensual woman inside her that had been hiding all these years smiled like a cat and stretched.

This man could kiss like there was no tomorrow.

She lifted curved hands to slide them around his neck to pull him into her. His tongue touched hers, dipped and teased, and she gasped at the spike of fierce, throbbing heat in her belly as his mouth seduced her.

And still they stood fully clothed! Somewhere, distantly, with the rest of her indistinct thoughts, she wondered at his patience.

Her previous experience had not included extended dalliance before the deed, and this was driving her crazy.

As if he knew, he chuckled and lifted her until her toes left the ground. She was no small woman but he was a dancer, no doubt used to twirling compliant females in his arms.

She looked down at him as he held her up and her surprise delighted him.

'This is the first time any man has twirled me,' she whispered in his ear.

'You are a woman who deserves special treatment. I wish I could teach you to dance with me. But there are other things we might do instead.' He smiled a man's smile and pulled her hips in towards him and cupped her bottom, so she wrapped her legs around him and savoured being wanton and wild.

Was this her?

He must have decided which was her bedroom, because he backed her towards it, his mouth kinked, watching her eyes, occasionally glancing ahead to keep them safe until she felt the end of her bed behind her legs.

Very, very slowly, as if to prove he had all the time in the world, he lowered her the length of his hard body until her feet touched the ground. They stood there for a moment pressed breast to chest.

Heat and need and urgency on her side, tenderness, heat and patience on his. Slowly he turned her body, slid the zipper from the top of her neck to the waist of her dress and slid one shoulder off.

She closed her eyes as his warm lips trailed along her skin. Then he pushed the other shoulder off and repeated the gesture. Her knees trembled.

He turned her back to face him and kissed her mouth as if her lips were petals he did not wish to crush and she felt the sting of emotional tears that didn't fall.

Then his fingers caught in her now rucked bodice, stroked the valley between her breasts and hooked the dress to slide it with a rustle into a colourful puddle at her feet.

'You are beautiful. Magnificent.' His voice low and reverent, and she lifted her chin. Suddenly not shy. She reached for him.

Now their movements quickened, both working the clothes from the other's body until two naked lovers lay skin to skin with strips of light through the window painting them in patches, light that shifted and rolled with them slowly into the night.

They rose and went into the shower together, soaping each other, murmuring in approval and amusement and desire.

At three they ate hot buttered raisin toast and drank tea, and he spoke of his father, a hard man who had sent him away when his mother had died. And the grandmother whom he loved, who was dying. 'My father told me to be a man and not hinder the family with emotions, and so I tried to avoid showing my feelings to others.'

'You can show me,' she said very quietly.

He smiled. 'You and my grandmother, because she would have none of it either. When I first went to her, a small boy of seven, grieving my mother silently, she demanded I not keep my thoughts to myself. She pushed me to learn the dance. From that time she has been the only person I allow to question my deeper thoughts.'

'She encouraged your dancing?'

'Despite my father.' He smiled at that. 'The dance allows me peace. She has given me so much that I cannot repay.'

She felt her heart ache with the loss she could see he was already dreading.

'Who will care for her when she is nearing the end?'

He lifted his head. Suddenly fierce. 'Me. Though there is a hospice in Barcelona, newly finished, designed for peace and tranquillity.' She could see he was thinking of it.

'A good place. Similar to the feeling I get in your home.' And she felt the warmth of his approval as a glow. But his eyes were far away. 'But enough of my sadness. Tell me of your parents.'

She told him of when they'd died in a boating accident in the harbour. Four years ago. How she'd been lost by being suddenly orphaned, and of the man who had said he loved her, had promised to honour and cherish her for ever, and yet had cheated on her and then discarded her. How she'd left her chosen profession to escape the toxic memories and start afresh.

They talked of Coogee, and Barcelona.

With his immersion in her, his concentrated attention, something shifted in her. Something had begun to heal from being torn. Mended by his wonder of her. Reminding her she was a woman this man wanted.

He fed her the last scrap of toast and carried her laughing back to bed. With renewed energy.

But not once did they talk of the morning, or the next day after that when he would be gone, and she accepted that.

At sunrise he dressed, kissed her deeply, and without further words between them he left. She was sad, disappointed, but didn't regret the night. Couldn't.

And she slept most of the day.

On Monday morning the salty breeze from Sydney Harbour pushed Cleo faster than she intended through the revolving door of the Medical Assistance Travel Escorts (MATE) offices. She liked providing safe and calm transport for those unwell and stranded. She stood breathless and disorientated after the revolution spat her out into the lobby.

Not like her usual composed self at all.

But then nothing had been the same since the early hours

of Sunday morning. In fact, her lips still felt swollen and every now and then she'd find herself smiling. Wickedly.

But today was all about work. Monday had started strange and had become increasingly odd.

Apart from the fact that today was the day Felipe was leaving. He'd told her that. And that was a good thing. She would soon stop looking to see if he was below her window again. They'd had one incredible night, which was safer, in fact, than giving your vulnerable heart away for a husband's betrayal. No wife should ever see another woman in her husband's bed.

This way there could be no betrayal, but if Felipe hadn't been leaving, then perhaps she would have asked Jen what she knew about him.

But he was leaving.

Maybe one day Felipe would be back.

Today her list of errands had taken less time than expected to complete. She always ran errands before she left on a job. This one had only just come through and she knew little about it yet. But the destination excited her beyond all reason. Barcelona. Spain must have been in her stars this month.

And today fate had smiled on her to make this morning easy. Every parking spot had appeared where she'd never seen an empty space before.

Every traffic light turned green instead of red.

And once she was parked in a prime, unmetered position, the wind had seemed to propel her here at twice the rate she would normally have walked.

All errands had been done and she was still early.

At the oak reception desk Angie Peck, pay clerk, crisis manager and unflappable international flight and transport co-ordinator, swung her brown fringe towards the new arrival and smiled.

'Look what the wind blew in. Morning, Cleo.' Angie's chocolate-brown eyes twinkled infectiously. 'Turbulent out there? What's the word for that Spanish wind?'

Cleo thought for a moment. 'No idea.' She'd been listening to her Spanish language lessons all day yesterday as she'd stared dreamily out to sea from her bedroom window. She'd wanted to learn the meaning of some of the words that her handsome dancer had whispered to her. Felipe. She didn't know his last name. But then he didn't know hers either. It had been a fleeting but fierce one-night stand and had left her feeling unsettled but glowing. Still couldn't believe that wanton woman had been her.

Angie tapped her forehead. 'I've got it, the levanter. Well, we have a small wind of change in store for you this morning, too. On your mode of transport.'

Cleo raised her brows. 'Any chance you'll tell me what it is?'

'All will be revealed inside.' Angie gave a dramatic wave at the entry to the inner sanctum. The door of the MATE inner sanctum stood shut. Odd.

The receptionist added cryptically, 'Your special calming skills will be appreciated. His nibs is already worked up.'

With a last puzzled glance at Angie, Cleo knocked firmly on the panelled fascia and waited.

She'd completed almost two dozen overseas transfers of pregnant women or new mums and their babies since she'd come to work for MATE nearly a year ago. She'd also accompanied many general patients who had been sick or injured, clients of all ages, but as the agency's star midwife she'd never been called to the office to discuss a case prior to transfer. It had always been an email or a phone call then meet the client at the hospital.

In the case of midwifery assignments, it was usual for

her to meet them at the private wing of the Sydney hospital where the rich and famous went to give birth. Like Sofia had. She wondered how the young mum was getting on. Cleo hadn't seen Jen since Saturday.

She'd thought all of the MATE clients were VIPs. It wasn't cheap to hire a midwife to travel with you, so what made this assignment so special that a face-to-face meeting was needed?

After a moment the door swung open and the tall, spare figure of Sir Reginald with his silver-grey temples and Savile Row grey suit stood back to invite her in. 'Ah, Cleo, thank you for coming.'

Sir Reginald gestured her to the seat in front of his desk, though he didn't sit down.

He paced.

That, too, was odd.

'Don Felipe Alcala Gonzales is our client.'

Amazing how many Felipes there were from Spain. The shop assistant this morning in the post office had been Felipe. And the pizza guy who'd delivered to her on Sunday night had worn a shirt with 'Felipe' on it. She'd read his name and had had to stop staring at it.

A bit like buying a red car of a certain make. You saw them everywhere after that.

Her brief liaison with her own Felipe was done. A bit of a hard act to follow despite the fact he'd kissed her goodbye and left without a word.

Best not go there. Too recent not to blush about.

Her boss went on. 'Don Felipe is the cousin of Sofia.'

'Gonzales.' Recognition flared in her brain. 'Sofia, as in the woman I looked after in labour on Wednesday night?'

'Yes. She specifically asked for you. She'd like you to escort her and her baby home to Barcelona and her cousin is the man paying the bills. He is the *cabeza de la familia—*

the head of the Gonzales family—and one of the richest families in Barcelona.'

Cleo's eyes widened. They were VIPs indeed. And still Sofia had been alone in labour?

Cleo felt glad she was escorting Sofia and not the cousin if this was what he did to the normally composed Sir Reginald. She remembered Sofia using the word 'hate'.

'Don Felipe has decided to oversee all the arrangements himself and accompany you on your flight.' Sir Reginald's words dropped into the silence between them.

Sofia would not be happy about that. She inclined her head. Hopefully she wouldn't have to see much of Sofia's ogre.

Sir Reginald fidgeted, back behind his desk now as she sat down, and if she wasn't mistaken, the usual unflappable head of the agency looked strangely nervous. 'I fear your client is very much unhappy with the Don. And now he has convinced her to go, he wishes to ensure she arrives safely in Spain. Thus, he insists on being present as well.'

'You're warning me there will be tension between them during the flight?' Why would that be a warning Sir Reginald felt he needed to give her? 'I thought my job is to ensure Sofia and her baby arrive in good health?' Cleo's comment hung in the air between them as a question. Did this Don want to micromanage Sofia? Or her?

She turned to Sir Reginald and said carefully, 'What arrangements are planned for our transfer?'

The aristocratic fingers shuffled desk papers again. 'You will be flying in Don Felipe's private aircraft.'

She didn't much like the idea of being totally under the control of anyone apart from the captain flying the plane.

Especially this Don Felipe, who agitated her boss. And her client.

She sat back and folded her hands in her lap. Sir Reginald

was always a reasonable person. 'Are you sure my presence is necessary, then?'

'Yes. It is. Sofia has only consented to return to Spain with him if she has you as her companion.'

Sofia was calling the shots, then? Their rapport had been strong in labour. And she would be delighted to accompany the young mum. Then she remembered. 'I did mention to her this is what I usually do. She must have thought about it later.'

'Sofia has decided that nobody else will do for the flight over and has requested you as her confidante for the first two weeks postnatally when you arrive, if you will agree to stay on.'

Jen would be thrilled about this. She'd wanted Cleo to fly to Barcelona with her for a year now. Ever since she'd started dating Diego.

No doubt she'd be even more adamant since Saturday night. But Cleo doubted she'd find one male dancer amongst the five point five million people who lived in Barcelona. Even she wasn't that optimistic.

Then the rest sank in. 'Two weeks?' Cleo raised questioning brows at Sir Reginald. 'It's not unusual to stay an extra day or two but two weeks seems excessive, surely?'

Sir Reginald shuffled his disarrayed papers and avoided her eyes. 'It all changed today. By the express orders of Don Felipe. And the reason Don Felipe asked me to arrange this with you. Your final say pending, of course.'

'Just how reluctant is Sofia to return to Spain?'

Her boss grimaced. 'Very.'

Reluctance was one thing, but Cleo hoped Sofia wasn't being forced in any way by her cousin. She tried another tack. 'And the baby's father? Does he have a say in this?'

'Apparently he is no longer...' a pause '...in the picture.'

Well, she'd known that already. Sofia had told her. But

she wondered if his permission had needed to be sought. She'd seen Spanish determination at first hand. Her Spanish lover had left without a forwarding address after one of the most incredible nights of her life. Still, she had no regrets.

Back to work. Not her problem. Any of the legalities could be handled by this Don.

'I hope the father of the child knows the baby is going.'

The barest hint of amusement crossed Sir Reginald's face. 'I believe so.'

Well, that was good news at least. But this was becoming clouded with what had happened to her on Saturday night and she needed to stop that. Think clearly. Probably because the ogre cousin's name was Felipe, too.

She shook her disquiet off. She needed to remain professional.

'I think I should chat to Sofia first. Just check about the two weeks. That it's really her idea and not her bossy cousin's.' Her voice remained calm and quiet, the gentle epitome of reasonableness despite her instinct screaming there was something off here.

Sir Reginald straightened and his gaze sharpened. 'You're thinking of declining the assignment?'

She looked at her boss. 'No. But there are many things to consider. The fact Sofia has agreed to go at all. The private flight, supervised by the Don. The length of time. Two weeks together with Sofia under the control of an unknown despot? Sofia and I do need to talk about this first.'

'I don't think he's a despot.' Sir Reg looked amused.

'That's not what Sofia said.' Did the young mum really want her or was everyone pushing them together? Unease grew but her sympathy for the newly single Sofia rose another notch at all these men deciding her future for her.

She glanced at her boss, who had an odd gleam in his eye. 'Are you happy to arrange that, Sir Reginald?'

'Of course. I think a meeting is an excellent idea considering the length of time and the personalities involved. I'll have Angie sort that out for this morning, as soon as possible.'

Cleo nodded.

'You can discuss the departure time after your visit,' Sir Reg said quietly, as if to himself.

Obviously, he was keen for her to go. She wondered if there was a large bonus at stake here, as well as the usual exorbitant fee charged by the agency.

The older gentleman rose.

'Thank you for the extra information.'

# CHAPTER SIX

TWO HOURS LATER Cleo pulled a hospital chair closer to the bassinet beside the bed. Studied the sleeping baby. Leaned nearer to peer in and saw the name, which was new to Cleo. Isabella.

'Congratulations again. Isabella is a lovely name. She's even more beautiful than when she was born.' The genuine warmth in Cleo's voice brought the young mother's smile back to her eyes.

Sofia's worried face softened as she looked at the sleeping baby. 'She is like a doll. Babies are so perfect when they sleep.'

Cleo's mouth tilted into a smile. 'How is she when she's awake?'

'Noisy. Petulant if I'm too slow feeding her.' A soft sigh and suddenly the young woman looked like any besotted mother. Vulnerable, protective, anxious to do the right thing by her child. 'Such big eyes watch me as she drinks and I fall more in love with her every minute.'

Cleo knew she would help Sofia despite this Don Felipe, who made even her boss nervous. 'My employer mentioned you would like me to stay for two weeks as you settle back in Spain? Is that what you want? Some assistance in the postnatal period?'

Sofia huffed out a breath. 'He says my grandmother is

very unwell. I do not really believe him, but I have decided I must return in case there is some truth in this. But I will not be bullied by Felipe. I hate his interference.'

This man certainly stirred a reaction. 'Hate's a strong sentiment to have when your baby is nearby.' As if to highlight her words the baby in the crib twisted her face and let out a mewl of distress.

Instinctively, Sofia's hand went out to smooth the covers in a gentle caress. 'Can she feel my emotions?'

'Of course. You are the most important person in the world to her. Naturally she is attuned to you.'

'I forget you are one of these new age midwives.'

Cleo laughed. 'I believe we create our own destinies if that's what you mean. And most of us can feel other people's emotions. If you want me to accompany you, then for the moment I'd like to help you create a relaxed aura when you carry your baby back to Spain. Babies respond to their mother being calm.'

She smiled again. 'And we are to travel the easy way in a private aircraft. Is it so bad to be transported in comfort, with others dealing with all the arrangements?'

'No. I have accepted that. It's Felipe I object to.'

Yet that very assurance wavered with uncertainty and Cleo's heart went out to this woman dealing with her world in turmoil. What sort of man was this older, aristocratic, interfering Felipe of Sofia's? She couldn't imagine that scenario. How did one bribe a loving fiancé away from someone? And if it happened, where did that leave Sofia? How hard would it be to be a calm mother when your world had been destroyed?

It was hard enough having a first baby when everything was smooth sailing—let alone being a single parent under someone else's authority with betrayal all around.

Sofia must be feeling she had no allies.

Well, she had *her*.

Though a voice at the back of Cleo's mind wondered if Isabella's father could be bought off so easily, then how much of a loss was he? Perhaps a man like her own not-so-dear departed ex? But that would be presuming too much.

'Well, for the next few days try to think of Don Felipe as a means to an end. Like a contraction in labour. Painful but necessary to get us safely to Spain.'

Sofia's face tightened and then she morphed into a cascade of breathy giggles that surprised them both. 'Oh…' she wiped her eyes '…I'm so glad you were there when I had my baby.'

'Me, too.' Yes, she did miss being with women at birth. It wasn't often she had time to roster in a birthing suite shift. But she loved her job now as well. Helping people find strength when they were vulnerable, support when they were desperate and safety when they felt at risk away from home. She was really enjoying the different-aged clients now, too. Especially the elderly and frail.

Those accomplishments made her work a real pleasure, and the daily change of assignments had focussed her in redirecting her thoughts very nicely from the past.

'I think the next two weeks will be easier as your bond with Isabella grows. Already I can see how wonderful you are together, and I think I can help.'

'I need someone strong on my side.' Sofia's eyes narrowed. 'Especially if I have to spend any time with *him*.' She glanced at the elegant watch on her wrist. 'He is coming to see me in two hours.'

Yes. Cleo would accompany this young woman and stand by her side for the next two weeks. And if her nemesis was coming soon they'd better get started.

Travel escorts made travelling easy for their clients. Cleo gained much of her job satisfaction in safely escorting frail or delicate clients back to their loving families, either domestic or overseas, regardless of the trickiness of the situation.

She was good at it.

Resourceful, calm, efficient and friendly with impressive medical skills. But she did not savour people with high tempers or people who created unnecessary drama out of a situation that didn't require excessive emotion.

She'd bet the next two weeks were going to be interesting. 'Would you like to tell me about how you're going with the feeding and caring for Isabella, and then we'll prepare for your flight.'

One hour later, not two, there was a knock at the door and Sofia threw up her hands. 'I don't want to see him. I'm not ready. How typical that he is early. I hate him.'

Cleo stood and then froze in horror as a tall, powerful, darkly handsome man strode in. Sofia's cousin Felipe was also *her* Felipe from Saturday night!

Cold shock widened her eyes as she tried to make sense of nonsense. The man she'd tried to forget after one night of sensual discovery and pure abandonment crossed the room to face her and she felt the blood drain from her face.

Felipe lifted his strong chin and a vein at the side of his strong jaw pulsed. There was no trace of a smile on those sensual lips. He'd known! He'd specifically arranged to hire her from the agency. Without warning her.

Mortification flooded her but the face she kept turned his way by sheer will remained expressionless. Just like his.

'Sister Cleo Wren. I am Felipe Antonio Alcala Gonzales. Sofia's cousin.'

'I see,' was all she could manage.

It really was a shame the embarrassment didn't stop

the invisible, floating warmth that settled over her like a red cape, just like a teasing taunt from the toreador, she thought bitterly. *Olé*, you goose, Cleo. Another betrayal with lies. Or enormous omissions at least. What was going on?

But that didn't stop her body thrumming with a tragic awareness of him.

Typically, his thigh-length coat fitted perfectly over immaculately tailored trousers and his long hair was tied tightly back with a plain leather thong, making his high cheekbones stand out in the bright light flooding through the window. She thought of the serious, deeply driven man of the dance and saw him in this man.

There had been no mention of great wealth or the name Gonzales when they'd met.

Nothing of the seductive lover who had charmed and then discarded her. Her legs wanted to run but Sofia would want to know why so she stayed motionless. Calm. Her face a tight mask.

He lifted one long elegant hand assertively towards her to shake hands, and she remembered that every time they'd touched she had been left with a tremor of want.

No way.

Face neutral, Cleo declined to extend her own fingers and doggedly met his dark eyes head on. His narrowed gaze bored into hers as his fingers dropped and moved to clasp together behind his straight back. A stance that suited him. Head of the family after all.

Your move, Don Felipe. I'm certainly not sure what we should do now. Her eyes narrowed at his arrogant appraisal of the situation. Yep, still a conquistador out to conquer new territory. Well, she wasn't about to be conquered. Again. Or lied to. Again.

Her usual resistance to male advances that had melted on Saturday night clanged into place like the gate of a walled city. She almost sagged with relief as she felt clean distance separating any desire she might have had to bury her head in his chest and just inhale the male scent of him. *In fact,* you *are not the man I had fantasies about.*

He'd talked of his dancing. His love for his grandmother. Nothing of his aristocratic background. Nothing of his real life. But at the time she'd accepted that for they had been strangers, and lovers for one night only.

But that was done. Finished, and here he was pretending they'd just met. And was she to do the same? Begin a lie? Like her husband had? She hated lies. Therefore she hated him. Most freeing.

Phew.

Immunity.

All that in seconds that seemed to drag on for a lifetime.

On the bed Sofia shifted and Cleo turned her head. She saw the bitter flash of defiance and the expression on her client's face made their familial resemblance more striking. And worrying.

Sofia turned a look of loathing on the man and threw up her hands. 'Pah. What are you doing here so early?' But there was a trace of tears in the loudly defiant cry. 'I change my mind and stay here.'

Looking at these two, Cleo knew she could kiss goodbye to any quiet life in the next weeks if she didn't drop this assignment. Something it would be crazy not to do now that she knew who Sofia's dastardly cousin was.

She saw the tremor in Sofia's tight fingers and felt the girl's anguish. What had he done to her? What was really going on here? Had she got her impressions of Felipe so badly wrong, everywhere? Had she made the biggest mistake ever in her assessment of the man she'd given herself to?

A tilt of Felipe's aristocratic black head. 'It is not for you to tell me to come, or go, cousin.' Said quietly and confirmed officially for Cleo that Felipe was her VIP employer.

'I don't want you here.' Sofia was crying now and edging towards hysteria and Cleo narrowed her gaze. Whatever he had done it needed to stop now.

Cleo stepped between them. 'Don Felipe.' Her voice cut across the emotion in the room with a quiet crispness. 'My client is upset. Perhaps we could speak outside in the corridor. It is not good for the baby or Sofia to be distraught like this.'

He paused. Narrowed his eyes at her and then after a long, tense pause he nodded. Gestured with his hand. 'After you.' The sardonic tone in the agreement was not lost on her.

Well, she had stepped into the line of fire. Not the first time she'd done that for a patient and it wouldn't be the last.

Unless she died of embarrassment in this hospital today.

Cleo felt his eyes on her back the whole way out the door. She didn't turn until she heard the click of the latch behind him.

Then a vivid flashback of the last time he'd come up behind her and touched her bare shoulder flashed into her brain and she spun quickly to face him.

Not happening again! 'So, you are the wicked older cousin?'

He inclined his head. 'It is my lot in life to protect my family from charlatans and that is what her fiancé was.' He ran his hands through his hair as if exasperated. 'Already the swindler had installed his mistress into Sofia's apartment.'

Good grief. Cleo raised her brows and said curtly, 'Well, I would hope that's come to an end!'

He smiled but there was no amusement in it and Cleo shivered at the implacable look in his eyes. 'Indeed.' He pulled some keys from his pocket and shook them so they rattled. 'Eviction was swift.'

Okay, but... 'Why must Sofia go to Spain now? She is still exhausted from the birth.'

His face remained inscrutable but before he could conceal the emotion, his eyes showed immense sadness. 'Because, if you remember me telling you this, our shared grandmother is dying. It is her wish that before she departs this earth she sees Sofia and has time to know her babe.'

His gaze captured hers and there was no wavering as he said very slowly and clearly, 'I will make this happen for my grandmother, the woman who cared for me like a mother.' She remembered everything he'd told her that night. For a moment she just hadn't been sure what was truth and what was lies once she'd realised who he really was. Except the devastated look in his eyes was clearly genuine.

Then he cast an impatient glance at the door before facing her again. 'Despite what is between us, Sofia trusts you. And she, too, is important, which is why I arranged for you to come. We must work with that and pretend that Saturday night never happened.'

Despite herself, she felt a stab of loss. But, yes, it would be much easier that he concurred with her own thoughts. And it was good he agreed Sofia was important. 'How ill is your grandmother?'

'The cancer has spread through her body. We are giving palliative treatment and she refuses any other care. I believe she has weeks, not months to live. If that long.'

That explained his determination to leave today. 'Thank you for your honesty.' In this instance anyway.

It looked like they were off to Spain. 'I think we can return to Sofia and help her prepare for the departure.'

He didn't answer, just stepped to the door and opened it for her.

Felipe followed her into the room. 'Your midwife will accompany you and be your advocate.' He moved to the window and crossed his arms.

Sofia's dark eyes still glinted with tears but she had composed herself and was sitting straight in the bed. '*Sí*. If I am to do this without my fiancé…' a venomous look Don Felipe's way '…I choose my own assistant. This woman is on my side!'

'Your fiancé.' A disgusted aside spoken quietly, though it carried clearly. 'He was a bad man.'

'Not until you offered him money to leave me.' Another glare from Sofia at her cousin. Then a beseeching glance at Cleo. 'See why I need you to help me leave if I decide I don't want to stay in Spain after all, Cleo?'

Cleo forced herself to keep her eyes on the young woman and not glance at Don Felipe. For she was determined that was how she would think of him now. 'Is there a reason you wouldn't be able to leave if you wished?'

'Ask him.' A jerk of Sofia's defiant head.

Now she allowed her face to turn. Met his gaze squarely. Said very quietly in question, 'Don Felipe?'

'Please. Call me Felipe.' He shrugged, though his eyes glinted with suppressed emotion.

*But which Felipe?* Cleo thought acidly. She was tempted to ask him that, but professionalism won.

'Is Sofia free to leave Spain if she wishes?'

'Sofia may come and go as she pleases. We do not kidnap people in Spain. Neither do we hold them against their will. Just as soon as she sees her grandmother, she can decide what she wants to do. Though I would prefer she stay until the end.'

The two cousins glared at each other. He continued, 'My cousin has her own resources, after all.'

Cleo suspected Felipe and Sofia's grandmother was really at the heart of their antagonism.

The question remained: Could she still get involved with this man? Again? A man who had left her without him feeling it was important enough to divulge who he really was? A man she had a weakness for? Though even now, for that affront, she could see why, if he was head of an extremely wealthy family, he'd have just been slumming it with her. A lowering thought and one that certainly took off some of the shine. And a good reason to stay at arm's length for the duration of her employment by him. Perhaps the grandmother had sent Felipe. That made sense.

Again, she assessed the young mum, the baby and the man with his arms folded across his chest.

Someone had to support Sofia.

And she knew Felipe could be ruthless in his chosen path. Obviously.

Right, then. 'Don Felipe, when were you hoping to leave?' *This time.* She wasn't calling him Felipe. He could deal with that.

'We leave today. Four p.m. If Sofia can be ready.' So reasonable. Why did she feel that reasonableness was only skin-deep?

She could be reasonable, too. 'I agree to accompany Sofia for the next two weeks. If we are to leave in a few hours perhaps you could give us a little more time alone to discuss matters pertinent to women, babies and midwives?' She glanced at her watch. 'Sofia says you are here an hour early.'

He leaned forward off the wall and raised his dark brows at her.

His face held a gentle warning and possibly, which irritated her beyond all measure, a small amount of amusement. 'I will leave and return in an hour. Or Sofia will text me when you have finished your discussion. On our way to the airport we can transport you to your lodgings to retrieve your suitcase and passport.'

Lucky she'd already packed, Cleo thought with acerbity. It wouldn't take that long to hand over her cat and empty the fridge of perishables, but she wasn't telling him that. 'That won't work. I'll need at least an hour.' His expectation that her needs were not important to him rankled. She wanted to rankle him right back.

It was as if he guessed that. 'Then we will come,' he said silkily, 'when you are able to be prepared.' There was definitely amusement at her expense in his eyes.

Oh, she was prepared—just not instantly biddable.

He crossed the room to the door in three long strides and the door closed softly behind him.

Cleo's hands tightened on the chair back for extra support where she stood.

'I hate that man,' Sofia spat.

*I think I do, too*, Cleo thought, but she wasn't quite sure.

Sofia hadn't finished. 'His father was a rich pig, powerful and arrogant. Hard. I ran away from him. I had not thought Felipe was just the same, but I can see now he is.'

'Is Felipe really so powerful?'

'Very. The family has a massive fortune and Felipe manages most of it now my grandmother is old. She wants him to marry and has been parading aristocratic Catalonian women in front of him for years.'

Cleo refused to think about that for the moment.

'And she is dying, your cousin said.'

Sofia's beautiful eyes clouded. '*Sí*. But I don't want to believe him.'

Cleo had seen his face when he'd told her. She believed him.

# CHAPTER SEVEN

FELIPE WALKED AWAY from his cousin's room and stabbed the elevator button with controlled force.

Cleo Wren.

The woman he had seduced, and been seduced by. He had risen from her bed before dawn yesterday. He had stood outside her flat and looked up at her window like a lovelorn fool. He, who never looked back at his rare, brief liaisons. He was still shocked at himself, picking up an unknown woman and sleeping with her. Or rather not sleeping. It had been as if he could not get enough of her. What was it about Cleo that had made her so irresistible to him? Now was not the time to find out.

His mind had drifted, too, during his busy day on Sunday, and he had looked back at the night before with sweetness and yearned, in the few brief moments he'd had to himself, to see her again. But no time had landed in his lap.

He had known he could not stay in Australia and he did her no favours by extending their connection. Responsibilities had slapped him from the time he'd left her door.

To his disgust, being near her again still nipped at his skin like static electricity and drew his eye with instant recognition of the beat between them.

Memories pounded him again of that night. Those brilliant blue eyes, and the flash of matching colour below her chin. He remembered slowly pulling the blue scarf from that sweet throat.

It felt like only an hour ago and he could still feel the softness of her skin beneath his fingers. The shock of actually seeing her again had been almost as great as that on her own face when she had seen him.

And he'd had prior knowledge that she would be there. Had sanctioned it with the agency.

There could surely be only one midwife called Cleo in the area. He had immediately recognised the name when Sofia had mentioned her, had put the pieces together, and at least had had a few hours' incredulous warning.

She'd refused to shake his hand.

He knew why. He had known they would meet again and not warned her. The unexpected trust he'd been gifted on Saturday night had been shattered and he felt its loss keenly.

Further entanglement would only hurt them both. And be professionally unsound.

For now, sadly, he feared the affront to Cleo had been greater than he'd intended from an albeit incredible and mutually sharing one-night encounter. Now they both would have to put such thoughts and actions behind them.

Forget.

He almost laughed out loud at that.

Her sweetness could never be forgotten. He'd thought distance would help there but even that was not to be now.

If there was to be any time to explore further what lay between them, it would be after his cousin's safe arrival in Spain, and definitely after Cleo's fortnight in his employ was complete.

It would be best if the time didn't come at all, for he feared to create an imbalanced disaster between two people who lived on opposite sides of the world and came from completely different cultures. Her life was one of freedom of choice, while his was filled with duties and responsibilities. Yet for one night she had allowed him to be the dancer, the lover, the man, and not the doctor of terminally ill patients, the evil cousin, the director of many companies or the head of his ancient family.

With Cleo he could be just Felipe.

His driver, a small, dark, impassive-faced man, opened the door of the car as he strode towards it. 'Take me to the hotel, Carlos. I will remain there until they call. Then proceed to Sofia's flat.' He tossed the keys to his man. 'You will acquire my cousin's luggage, which should be packed by now, and stow it in the boot and then return for me.'

'*Sí*, Don Felipe.'

Felipe climbed into the rear of the vehicle and closed his eyes as he rested his head back against the seat.

Yet it wasn't the enormous list of tasks he needed to complete before they left today that occupied his mind. It was the almost overpowering urge to sweep the midwife up in his arms and hold her against his chest. To thank God he'd found her again.

Fifteen minutes ago everything in his power had been used to stop that action.

She had seemed immune to him, yet he'd sensed she was angry and hurt behind her so-professional face. The watchful eyes and smooth lines of Cleo's cool face had remained outwardly calm and he'd been unable to read anything. But she'd refused to touch his hand.

Yes, she was an independent woman who stood for everything Diego loved about the liberated Australian society. A society's laxness his grandmother was so sure had ruined his cousin Sofia for ever.

When all this was over, and Cleo had returned back

to her own country, he doubted he would ever forget the place he had met this woman.

For now, he must not allow himself to think of Cleo, because his loyalties lay elsewhere with his work, his family and his responsibilities. He had to continue to callously walk away.

No wonder she wouldn't allow his touch.

Yes, it was his family he should be thinking of. Sofia's sudden engagement should have overridden his daily life and his hospice work. It was his responsibility to watch over the decisions of his family and his grandmother's large estate, and he had failed his cousin.

So he had come to make matters right.

And had found Cleo.

Fate was definitely laughing at him. He hoped not at her, too. Because she didn't deserve it.

He grimaced at his grandmother's insistence that he had to be the one to come for Sofia. She knew how much he'd disliked leaving her now the cancer was back. Though there was truth in the fact his cousin would have refused to go with Diego, which was the solution Felipe had initially suggested.

They'd be back in Spain in twenty-four hours and they would be bringing with them an adorable newborn great-granddaughter and a smile to his grandmother's face.

They would also be bringing Cleo Wren and what the ramifications of that would be only time would tell.

# CHAPTER EIGHT

REFUSING TO BE distracted by thoughts of a certain man, and with the discussion of the needs of babies and the cares of women who had just given birth, Cleo and Sofia regained their warm understanding of each other. And Cleo practised her Spanish. Though apparently Spanish was different to Catalan.

Baby Isabella had taken to breastfeeding with gusto but the baby's idea of settling after her feed still needed some work.

When Cleo glanced at her watch she saw that their allocated sixty minutes had already passed.

Dark strands of Sofia's hair had fallen across her forehead and she brushed them back petulantly as Cleo reminded her of the time.

'Should you ring him?'

'If I must. But I prefer to text.'

'The sooner we leave here, the sooner you and Isabella can find some routine again in your new home. That's important.'

The young woman nodded and pulled out her phone.

When she'd finished stabbing at the screen she threw the object onto the side table as if it annoyed her.

Cleo studied her thoughtfully. 'Why don't you relax in

the shower while we wait for your cousin to arrive? I can watch Isabella and you will feel fresh for the flight.'

Sofia's grimace lightened. 'Yes. I would like that. And to dress in my travel clothes, not pyjamas.'

'Indeed. You are a powerful lioness, after all.' They smiled at each other.

'When you are ready, I will go as I need to close up my flat before he tells me I am not prepared and scoops me up from the footpath,' Cleo said.

Sofia looked up from assembling her bathroom bag. She smiled over her shoulder. 'You think he will scoop you up?'

'Like a big black falcon coming in to land.' Cleo laughed.

Sofia said, 'I like you.'

'And I like you. We will have a very pleasant time settling you back in Spain.'

Sofia raised her hand to her throat and closed her eyes briefly. 'As long as they do not try to marry me off to someone suitable when we get there. Like his father tried to do. I may not wish to stay then.'

'Then you will go elsewhere.' Cleo saw the worry on her face and felt for her. 'I will help you with whatever you need.'

'Yes.' Sofia nodded thoughtfully. 'I am surprisingly reassured by that.' And turned away to enter the bathroom.

Cleo watched her go. 'I'm glad.' She just hoped she could hold up her end of the bargain. When all was said and done she would be under the authority of an influential and prominent family, in a foreign country with a man who had known her intimately.

She just hoped nobody else knew about that.

And she'd be alone to deal with it all.

No. She wasn't really alone. There was phone access to Sir Reginald and Angie if she needed it.

* * *

When Sofia reappeared from the bathroom with impeccable make-up, in a comfortable dress of divine cut with front buttons for easy breastfeeding, it coincided with the tall form of Don Felipe framed imposingly in the doorway.

Cleo decided he did it on purpose and chose to show she wasn't impressed. 'Ah. My lift has arrived.'

The 'lift' blinked at her dismissive tone and she smiled sweetly. It seemed the disadvantage at which she found herself whenever she was with him brought out the worst in her.

He tilted his head, an amused glint in his eye. 'My driver will transport you.'

'Have I offended you?' Damn it. She would not be overawed that he was her employer. And that that was all he could be.

'Me? Offended? Why would you think that?' Then he smiled sardonically. 'I've told him where you live.' His mocking drawl made her eyes narrow and she turned back to her client, hoping she hadn't heard the exchange.

But in all honesty she shouldn't have baited him first.

Thankfully, Sofia was busy with Isabella, who had woken and was gazing wide-eyed up at her mother. Sofia could not hear or see anything except her daughter at that moment. Thank goodness.

'I'll see you at the airport, Sofia. Do we need to stop at the shops on my way home? I know we have baby supplies for the flight but is there anything else you wish for?'

Sofia looked thoughtful. 'This is Australia. Vegemite and Tim Tam biscuits?'

'I'll get some at the airport. I saw a huge stand there last week.'

Don Felipe lifted his head. 'We will not go through that part of the airport.'

'Oh.' More sweet smiling. 'Well, then, I'll ask your driver to stop on the way to my flat.'

Sofia shot her cousin a smug look. '*Gràcies*, Cleo.'

'*De nada*, Sofia.' The equivalent of *You're welcome* in Spanish fitted so perfectly there.

They smiled at each other. Felipe looked on impassively at the rapport between the two women and she hoped he felt outgunned.

Cleo waved. 'I'd better go.' She glanced at the man at the door. 'I have a few things to finalise.'

'*Sí*. One hour's worth,' he said dryly.

She nodded coolly as she walked past him.

'While we wait for you, I will ensure Sofia has been discharged by the doctors.'

Cleo had already checked but she said nothing. It would stop him following her.

Exactly an hour after she'd been dropped off at her flat a black car pulled up beside her on the footpath. The large male in the rear seat alighted to tower over her. Her one small cabin bag made Felipe's eyebrows rise.

'You travel lightly.'

'Yes.' She stepped back as if checking to see if the door looked shut behind her but really to increase the space between them. 'A useful skill in my profession.'

The driver had scurried to the rear door and was holding it open. Felipe returned to the other side of the car.

There were four large seats in the back, Sofia and Isabella in her safety bassinet in the two rear-facing seats.

That left her to sit next to Felipe facing forward. She wondered if she could ask to sit in the front with the driver. She called herself a coward under her breath and slid in.

Once seated and settled she concentrated on Sofia. 'Did you have any issues strapping Isabella into the safety harness?'

The young woman rolled her eyes. 'My cousin took control of that.'

'I have done this before,' Felipe stated impassively as his driver shut Cleo's door.

'Ah. You have children, Don Felipe?'

A narrow gaze. 'No.'

He'd already told her he was unmarried but he had kept plenty of other things from her. Perhaps he had a brood of children by other women he wasn't married to? Probably not. She smiled at her own silliness. Cleo checked the baby. 'She looks nicely settled.'

Not how the mother looked, Cleo thought. Mutinous described that better. Obviously there'd been some dispute between the cousins.

Barely any words passed between the occupants during the trip to the airport but the closeness of Felipe's hip to hers brought a warmth to her belly that she tried unsuccessfully to banish. Sitting next to a stranger she'd had passionate sex with pinged right outside her comfort zone. She didn't know where to look.

His strong, muscular thigh next to hers reminded her how easily he'd carried her to her bedroom.

Those long, elegant fingers reminded her he'd stroked every inch of her.

While bulging biceps that almost touched her own reminded her how he had leaned over her with the weight of his hard, muscular body on those very arms.

Good grief, this was crazy thinking! What on earth was she doing, working for this man?

By the time they arrived at the airport Cleo hoped the

flight would be less fraught with tension or they would all
have dull pains in the middle of their foreheads when they
landed in Barcelona.

They passed swiftly through customs and returned to
the car to drive across the tarmac to their aircraft. This
was Cleo's first private flight, though she had escorted
patients in smaller commercial aircraft.

Once on board, the cabin crew met Felipe and Sofia
with warmth and respect, and kindness towards Cleo,
who thought again how little they needed her with all this
back-up available. But then she thought of Sofia's vulner-
ability and was glad she'd come.

Felipe had disappeared almost immediately after they
came on board and stated he would see them later.

She wasn't sure if he was working or resting but he
proved true to his word as they prepared for take-off.

Which made everything much more relaxed at the rear
of the aircraft.

As they flew into the night the baby travelled well,
soothed by the slight rocking of the aircraft near the tail,
and they'd managed perfect privacy for Sofia to feed Isabella and then get some sleep, which helped everyone.

Cleo had even managed four straight hours of sleep
herself, in the reclining seat adjacent to her charge. The
delightful cabin stewardess had promised to wake Cleo
if Isabella stirred, and had proved wonderfully reliable
in her promise.

After the next feed Cleo tucked mother and baby in
to sleep once more but found herself awake and restless.

Peppermint tea. Her tongue felt glued to the top of her
mouth. She'd kill for peppermint tea.

The stewardess had disappeared and Cleo wasn't a
bell-pusher so she walked quietly towards the curtains
ahead. When she pulled aside the curtain, instead of a

galley for meal preparations, as she expected, she found a small circular lounge room and Felipe.

He looked up. Black eyes and black lashes, a flash of remembered heat in his harsh gaze and then it was gone, though his mouth had softened. Apparently whatever business he'd been concentrating on hadn't been fun.

She touched her hair. Smoothed the bump over the band that held it free of her face. Okay, she thought when the strands had been tidied, she looked as professional as possible.

The look he gave her was anything but professional. Though, to be fair, he hadn't expected her.

And she'd just waltzed in. Heat rushed to her cheeks but before she could pull back, he stood.

'Come in. I owe you an apology.'

She wanted to turn her back on him. Hide her hot face at least. Of course, as an employee, she didn't do any of those things. She lifted her chin instead. Smiled slightly, although it felt like it needed to crack through layers of cement before it broke through. 'I'm just looking for peppermint tea. Not an apology.'

'How like the Cleo I met. So straight to the point,' he mused.

That irked her but her voice stayed level. 'How would you know what I'm like? We barely spoke.'

The heat returned to his eyes and his slow smile, though not disrespectful, brought heat flooding back like a blowtorch against her skin.

'Let's not talk again, then.' There, there was that softer, more playful Felipe she remembered.

Unwanted memories flooded her and her fingers clenched by her sides. 'No, we can't do that. Your cousin is my client. She has appraised me of your many influential connections, and I am just the nurse.'

Peripherally she saw those beautiful shoulders rise and fall in a careless shrug but she couldn't take her eyes off his face. He waggled his brows. 'My family is old and distinguished, yes, but you will never be just a nurse.'

He was making fun of her. Being silly. The spell broke. 'I'm going home to Australia in two weeks. The less indepth we "not talk" the better.' She glanced around. 'I'll just find some tea and go.'

He studied her for a long moment, then reached over and pressed a bell. The stewardess appeared instantly. 'Peppermint tea for Sister Wren, please, Mari.'

She nodded at him and smiled at Cleo. 'At once, Don Felipe.' The woman disappeared.

'Please, take a seat. At least have your tea here.'

Cleo didn't want to drink tea with him watching her. She wanted to take her tea and hide. Blow this.

Her chin lifted. 'I believe I don't deserve to feel at a disadvantage. I'm doing a job and, if I'm allowed the space, I will do it well.'

His face turned serious as he leaned forward. 'My apologies if you feel at a disadvantage. There is no disadvantage to you that I am not feeling as well. Please, stay for a few moments.' He waited for her to consider that.

Reluctantly, she sat, straight backed, on one of the lounges. It wasn't comfortable in that position but at least there was a shelf to put her tea on when it came. And it wasn't within reaching distance of him.

'How are Sofia and the baby?' His voice was quiet. Conversational. As if considerate of her equilibrium. Well, thank goodness for that. Maybe they had got off on the wrong foot today with all the underlying emotions.

She didn't want to be the creator of the unneeded drama she disliked so much. They were both in this together, after all.

She collected her thoughts. Concentrated on providing a sensible answer. 'Settled. They have slept well between feeds.'

'And you?'

She looked up. 'A couple of hours as well. Thank you. Your aircraft is comfortable and your staff very helpful. Do you sleep on flights?'

'I don't sleep much at all.' Another raised brow. Again, her cheeks heated. She could attest to that.

Darn it, she just knew that when she lifted her eyes from her lap he would be watching her with a wicked smile on his face. One that she badly wanted to wipe off. She looked up. Yep.

Instead, to the surprise of both of them, she laughed. 'Boy, this is awkward.'

The tension in his shoulders seemed to fall away. A slow smile, his austere face softening into that of another man. That other man. 'Thank you for your honesty. You are good for me, Cleo. I try not to be so serious with you.'

'Can I ask a question?'

He shrugged, the smile still playing around his lips. 'I do not have to answer you but yes.'

'Why didn't you tell me who you really were and why you were in Australia?'

He was silent and she thought he wasn't going to answer. She hadn't really expected him to. 'Because that was not who I was when I was with you. And it felt good.'

She remembered the look in his eyes when she'd changed her mind about shutting him out to inviting him into her home. The connection of two damaged people that had shimmered between them. And that's enough of that, she told herself, or she'd be feeling sorry for him and she wasn't ready for that.

She changed the subject quickly. 'One more.'

He nodded.

'Was it the right thing to remove Sofia from her fiancé at this crucial time?'

'Yes.' No hesitation. Implacable. He leaned closer. 'The man…' his lip curled over the word 'man', his voice pitched very low so as not to carry '…apart from the mistress I already mentioned, had already begun to siphon money from her bank account. Large amounts Sofia had not agreed to. His removal was just in time.'

Cleo blew out a long breath. What a sleaze. Poor Sofia. No. Lucky Sofia. She had a family who supported her, even if autocratically. When Cleo's ex-husband had left her broke and broken-hearted for another woman, she'd had no family to save her. But she'd had her friends. Jen, for one.

'Let us talk about ourselves instead of Sofia.' Felipe's voice cut into her thoughts. She stilled at the velvet tone of his words.

Brought her head up. 'I don't think so.'

He leaned forward. 'Do not be embarrassed.'

With a swish of the curtains the stewardess arrived with a loaded tray and Felipe sat back. Even from a few paces away Cleo could smell the peppermint. A selection of tiny sandwiches sat on a plate to the left and round sugar biscuits to the right.

Cleo forced a smile. 'Thank you.'

The stewardess nodded. *'De nada.'* Then turned and disappeared again. Could Cleo pick up the tray and walk away? She could.

But she didn't. 'I'm not embarrassed.' Much. 'As you said at the time, what happened was between consenting adults.' She waved her free hand. 'Now that night is over, and there is no more consent.'

But she didn't quite meet his eyes.

'But it is hard to pretend that I did not taste your sweetness or spend a night in your bed.'

Now she stood. To heck with the tea. 'I'm sure you are perfectly capable of subterfuge, Don Felipe.' She raised her own brows pointedly. 'What's the alternative?' That she be at his sexual beck and call while in Barcelona? Not happening.

'Of course. You're right.' He made a low noise in his throat. 'But I wonder now if this can be hidden? When I watch you move I can think only of what lies beneath your clothes.' She gasped and his hand immediately wiped that comment away. 'I should not have said that. My apologies again.'

She couldn't rid herself of it so easily. 'I regret that you are in this position,' she said stiffly. But it wasn't like she hadn't thought about it herself. Repeatedly.

'And yet I do not regret anything.' He stood. 'Except not being more honest with you. I will leave you to have your tea in peace.'

The steam from the ornate spout of the teapot rose between them like a wall. 'Thank you.' Cleo looked away from him to the waiting cup, then back.

Felipe turned as quietly as she knew he could. And the way he walked carried her straight back to a steamy flamenco dance floor and a serious case of the wants.

Had she done the right thing in shutting him down?

Shutting down any discussion about something that could only bring discomfort to both of them. She didn't think so. There had been a spark, well, a roaring flame, actually, between them, which left an ache somewhere in her chest, but he was of the aristocracy and lived in Spain.

She had her own life, seventeen thousand kilometres away from him. And to cap it all off, she was temporarily working for the man.

But most of all, she suspected, with how quickly she had fallen under his spell, she could be hurt far worse than her ex-husband had hurt her if she let herself get in any deeper.

# CHAPTER NINE

FELIPE WALKED AWAY from Cleo because if he didn't, he could quite conceivably reach out and pull her into his arms and forget all restraint. Apart from being morally despicable, it would be the absolute worst thing he could do in view of the coming two weeks of forced proximity.

Yet a part of him said this was his aircraft, his staff, and as long as she agreed to him kissing her then most of those with them were asleep and would not know.

He could have pressed the button for privacy so nobody would have entered the lounge, and once he had her in his arms she would have been his.

Which was exactly the sort of thing his father would have done. He had used women and discarded them, including those who'd worked for him. Both for pleasure and for political gain. This lack of principles was not Felipe's way and had strengthened the rift between father and son when Felipe had made his disgust known. It was not how he wanted to live his life.

But morality was a good enough reason not to take Cleo into his arms again.

He paused at one of the exit doors and leaned his hand against the bulkhead. Stared blindly out through the oval window into the blackness beyond and searched for answers.

Even now, he could feel the soft weight of her in his

arms, the warmth beneath his fingers as he traced the line of her shoulder, the curve of her cheek, the feel of a pulse beating in secret places and the absolute silk of her thighs.

He shook himself. This was not normal. He'd never felt such honesty between himself and a woman as he had on Saturday night—and now that was shattered because she felt he had tricked her by withholding his real identity.

Certainly, Cleo had not been chasing the Gonzales name or fortune, unlike many others in his past. And even now, when she knew who he was, he could tell that wealth was the least of his attraction to her. But there was still that sizzling chemistry between them, that moment when she'd looked at him and spoken with absolute truth, 'Boy, this is awkward.' He smiled at the memory. His Cleo. She remembered his body as well.

Something of this woman had attached itself to him and created a bond that he'd walked away from, and now fate had sprung him back to her side like an elastic band. Snapping them together in the closeness of Sofia's orbit.

The question was, did he fight to stay or fight to get away?

Carlos appeared beside him. 'Don Felipe? May I do anything for you?'

'No. Rest, Carlos. I will go to my suite.' For a cold shower, though he didn't say it. 'Thank you.'

# CHAPTER TEN

BARCELONA GREETED THE travellers with blue skies, a gentle tepid breeze and a blaze of colour as they stepped onto the tarmac from the aircraft.

Travelling via private jet had been a whole new experience for Cleo and certainly less bothersome than following a wheelchair through customs.

Except for the fact that the man she'd slept with owned the plane and twenty-four hours flight time was a long time in Felipe's aircraft.

She still wasn't sure how she was going to stay sane for the next two weeks.

She appreciated the fact that Felipe had left her to drink her tea in peace.

Unfortunately, peace had been hard to come by and she'd spent many hours nervous she would run into him again.

You couldn't just forget about a man you'd recently shared the most intimate moments with.

The most improbable thing about this whole situation was that she'd actually had her first one-night stand, for goodness' sake. She'd have to blame it on the flamenco. The wicked dance was probably designed for just that reason. Blatant sensual arousal.

Now, watching the muscled back and strong shoulders

of the man in front as he carried the baby's bassinet, there were tantalising glimpses of that stalking arrogant walk that had so mesmerised her that night.

But she was here for two weeks to help Sofia. She needed to stay concentrated on that goal. She could do that. She was a professional. Her gaze shifted to Sofia, who followed her baby's bassinet mutinously. Cleo dropped back to allow the warring parties to go ahead.

Sofia had shared her disquiet already, at returning to Spain, and Cleo had felt like saying, *Why don't the two of us just go home to Australia, then?* Man, she'd been so tempted.

But that wasn't her job.

Her job was to ignore any awkward past between the boss and herself and get Sofia settled so she could see her grandmother. Then her client could decide what she wanted to do.

Five minutes later they were gliding through heavy traffic as they were swept from the airport to the city in another of Felipe's cars. Same driver.

Unlike Felipe's black limousines, everywhere else in Barcelona lay with a palette of colour. Flower beds, apartments, avant-garde artworks standing in parks or at street corners, bright hues shone and lifted the ordinary to the extraordinary. Even advertising billboards seemed bigger and more vibrant.

Cleo had seen photos of the city online, but in the frolicsome flesh Barcelona pulsed with sunshine and fun. She wished she'd come with Jen and not with Felipe and Sofia.

Before she'd realised who paid her wages, she'd hoped to explore Gaudi's gardens and architecture towards the end of her stay. She did wonder if keeping her head above the emotional water of avoiding Felipe would impact on any light-hearted sightseeing. She'd just have to push through that because she could see now there was so much more of this amazing city to soak in.

Across from her, Sofia fidgeted with a slim diamond ring on her finger and Cleo's heart went out to her. Sofia had told her she didn't believe everything Felipe had said about her ex-fiancé or that he'd taken her money. So he'd arranged for her to see her bankers soon after their arrival here. Despite everything that had happened between herself and Felipe, Cleo did believe him.

Sofia would undoubtedly feel the eyes of the gossips on her. For Sofia, a member of an elite family in the city, she'd be known to many. It would not be comfortable to return home after being heartbroken and made a fool.

Cleo silently agreed it wasn't at all comfortable from the midwife's point of view either.

Though she was far from heartbroken. And she didn't believe Felipe was a bad man. There were no hearts involved in their situation. No, siree. Just a night between two consenting adults. She couldn't even blame alcohol as one glass hadn't caused her to fall into Felipe's arms.

But no one knew, she reassured herself.

As long as Sofia had no idea how hard Cleo worked not to feel embarrassed by Felipe's hip next to hers every time they drove somewhere, then all would be well. She had to believe that.

The tingle of Felipe's gaze infiltrated her awareness, but she refused to turn her head away from the window to acknowledge him. It was hard enough shutting him out. So she stared at the city and gave Sofia privacy with her thoughts as well.

Thankfully, the scenery flew past in myriad colours and surprises and Isabella lay asleep in her bassinet to allow everyone their own thoughts.

Felipe touched her arm. It seemed he would not be ignored.

She turned her head. He sat forward and indicated the streetscape with his long, elegant fingers. 'The most beautiful city in the world.' His smile and his words carried her back to their first walk together.

Ah. A warm memory. She was sorry now that she'd ignored him. It wasn't like her to be petty. 'Just like Sydney.' Their gazes locked. Both smiled and she looked away. That way lay dragons.

Sofia, who'd leaned towards her own window, also wore a slight smile on her parted lips. Perhaps not all her memories of Barcelona were uncomfortable.

The further they drove into the city the brighter Sofia became. Cleo could see Felipe noted his cousin's unconscious uplift of mood but thankfully didn't mention it.

*Small mercies*, Cleo thought. If these two could forget their differences, life would be easier for all of them.

'We will come back this way later when Sofia has rested. My grandmother lives in the city. My place of residence is a little farther up the mountain at Sarrià-Sant Gervasi.'

'And where am I to be staying?' Sofia asked with a tinge of bitterness that flattened Cleo's hopes of peace.

'You will stay with me in your own apartments for now, until your plans are decided, as will your nurse.'

'Midwife,' Cleo corrected mildly. 'Sofia doesn't need a nurse.' Then before he could answer she said, 'Do we pass your grandmother's home on the way?'

She wondered if Sofia had a Spanish home of her own or other relatives as well as Felipe, even distant ones. Others who could agree with him and help Sofia see she'd needed to come back at least to see her grandmother. She knew

Sofia's parents had passed away, but why had Felipe been chosen to go and get her?

'No. Doña Luisa has an apartment in the Eixample Dreta. We do not pass it. Tonight, possibly, we will visit my grandmother once I have ascertained that she is well enough for guests.'

Sofia scowled and turned her head away but didn't say anything. Isabella gave a mewl of distress and Sofia and Cleo both looked across at the bassinet.

The young woman gave an audible exhalation and relaxed her shoulders. 'Like a contraction,' she murmured.

*Good girl*, Cleo thought, but the comment left her struggling not to laugh out loud.

Felipe's brows furrowed at the joke he was clearly not included in but nobody enlightened him.

'You said you have visited Spain before?' Felipe's voice broke into her thoughts.

'Yes, but not this part of Spain. I've escorted patients from Madrid and Valencia but both were rapid extractions of ill clients and all my concentration was on them.'

'Perhaps after Sofia has found her feet you will have an opportunity to explore.'

'Perhaps. It's up to Sofia.' And how badly I'll need to get back home and away from you for my own peace of mind. Maybe she wouldn't see much of him even if they lived in his house. 'Do you have a place of work?'

'*Sí*. The hospice. Perhaps I will show you.'

She waited but nothing else came. 'Do you have a normal day-to-day job there? What do you do?'

'Ah, I should have said earlier in the aircraft. I am a doctor. Do you have much knowledge of oncology?'

What? The dancer in her mind moved even further away. The unexpected offering of information made her blink. 'A little.'

She thought about two more recent clients she'd met and become friends with. 'Occasionally terminal clients require support to return home after a more rapid decline in health than expected. I believe nothing is more important than to make their comfort and fulfilment of their wishes a priority at the end of life.'

'Yes. Thank you.' Then, almost to himself, 'I should not be surprised you say that.'

'You are an oncologist? And…a hospice director?'

'*Sí*. Both.'

Not a dance artist in your spare time? Oh, she wished she could say that out loud. But Sofia would hear and ask questions. But he saw the mischief in her eyes and raised his brows in silent query. She shook her head. An oncologist? She wouldn't have guessed it. Yet another contradiction.

'Oncologists and oncology nurses are special people,' she murmured. Well, she'd already guessed he was special.

'*Sí*. As are those who deal with the beginning of life.' Was that a compliment to midwives? Or was that to atone for the 'nurse' comment he'd made earlier?

'We have just completed building a new hospice. Named after my grandmother.'

It all came back to her then from their night together. He'd mentioned the hospice but not that he ran it and had been involved in its creation. She looked at him, seeing his commitment to his job, and another tiny piece of the wall that she'd erected between them fell away.

He didn't notice her change. 'It has taken up a large portion of the last few years. Then when my father died there were even fewer hours in the day as family business intruded.'

Any softening that had lightened the harshness that seemed to be his default expression was gone, though for her peace of mind it was better when he wore an expression of aristocratic hauteur.

It had been recent, his father's death? His role as family head was new, too, then. 'I'm sorry to hear your father also has passed away.' She remembered he had said his mother was gone. So they were both technically orphans, though he was clearly suffering no monetary hardship. Sofia had said he was rich. And he owned his own international aircraft. So why did he make her feel that he needed her?

His face shifted and she felt a wave of sadness emanate from him. 'My grandmother is not a feeble woman and has hung on as long as she could, hence the necessity to speed up Sofia's return.'

'So you said. I'm sorry she is so unwell.'

He inclined his head but didn't look at her. She would have liked to see his face but he'd turned to stare out the window. 'She does not leave her bed much now. I think she will enjoy meeting you. Her contentment at this stage is very important to me.'

'I look forward to meeting her.'

Now he turned his head and studied her. 'Good!'

Was that a warning to not upset his grandmother?

'To your right is the ocean.' And there it was. The end of that subject and the distraction of viewing the port of Barcelona.

Talk about having topic changes on speed dial.

Dutifully she studied the famous Barcelona seafront. But she accepted it as a good enough place to find some mental space from the man beside her.

Tall white cruise ships and the port. Mountains in the distance, front and back. A blue diamond sea.

They drove through the city, past more brightly painted artworks on street corners, a multifaceted face, an outstretched and oversized hand, and away in the distance on the mountain in front of them she could see a white church high up overlooking the city.

They wound their way through close streets and began to climb in a sweeping motion through avenues to the summit of the mountain. The higher they climbed, the more ornate the iron and stone entries to semi-hidden houses grew.

When they reached one of the most imposing gateways the tall wrought-iron gates swung ponderously open to fold back against the overarching greenery of tree branches.

A short tree-lined gravel road swept them into a circular driveway and the stone villa soared above them in curves, balustrades and high windows that seemed to reach to the sky.

The base of the mansion sat amidst roses, hundreds of flowering roses. It took her breath away.

The house itself ascended three storeys yet seemed higher and spread out backwards. The sparkling bow windows each side of the front door were open and fluttering curtains seemed to wave and flicker a welcome home to its master.

The dozen or so steps that began wide at the driveway where they'd stopped and narrowed as they rose to the huge double door at the top created a grand ascending entrance.

A problem if you were injured or ill, Cleo thought, but noted another, smaller ornate door away to the right at ground level. Maybe that led to a less strenuous entry or perhaps even a lift.

Balconies along each floor above them promised wonderful places to sit with a view over the city below.

She turned to Felipe beside her on the rear seat. 'You have a beautiful house.'

'*Sí*. My grandfather built this for his wife.' His face softened as he looked past her to his home. 'But my grandmother prefers living in the city now that he has gone.' His face stilled as the car halted. 'She lived here until I was old enough to establish my own household then moved to the city.'

Cleo thought it would be lonely living here by yourself. 'Great view,' she murmured as the driver alighted and opened her door.

Some space from Felipe's big body was welcome. She eased out so Sofia could also climb out and by the time the women were standing beside the car Felipe had removed the infant carry part of the bassinet and had lifted Isabella from the car.

A small dark-haired woman glided down the steps, her thin face serious. Another larger blonde woman, who certainly didn't glide but had ramrod-stiff shoulders and the apparent strength to carry them all up the stairs if she wanted to, followed. They were shadowed by two burly younger men in matching waistcoats whom Cleo presumed would bring the luggage.

'*Hola*, Rosa,' their host greeted the thin dark-haired woman.

She dipped a curtsey. '*Buenos días*, Don Felipe.'

'Sister Wren, this is my housekeeper,' he said to Cleo. 'Leave your bags. Rosa will arrange everything.'

Cleo followed Sofia up the steps, Felipe carrying the bassinet, but she was uncomfortably aware that she'd never stayed in such a palatial home before. She was learning so much about the man she'd shared her bed with. Too many more reasons why he had planned to leave her behind.

Once through the large doors he stopped and placed the bassinet gently on a carved wooden chair against one of the walls.

Cleo barely took in the stretch of Italian marble floor and the soaring painted ceiling as she followed Sofia to her daughter.

Sofia began to undo the straps and Cleo slid the young woman's handbag from her shoulder and held it. The infant grizzled and whimpered until she was lifted into her mother's arms and settled.

Finally, Cleo could observe the tension drain from Sofia's shoulders as she held her baby.

She turned her head sideways to note if Felipe had observed the same. Their eyes met.

It seemed he had. But all he said was, 'Rosa will take you to your rooms and Maria will attend to any laundry needs or other requirements. I have not engaged *mainadera*.' He paused and glanced at Cleo, explaining, 'A nanny...' then back to Sofia '...as you have your own midwife.'

Yes, she'd understood the word for nanny. She had some Spanish, even less Catalan. And French, Italian and German because she needed it in her job. And languages were easy for her to learn.

Sofia drew herself up and faced her cousin. 'You are correct. My child does not need a nanny, she has a mother, but Cleo is my guest.' The words were directed at Felipe.

Cleo smiled at the young mum. 'I can be both. And here's Rosa to show us to your apartment.' Thank goodness.

Felipe ignored Sofia and directed a dark glance at Cleo. 'I will send a message later this afternoon in regard to this evening and my grandmother's ability to receive visitors.'

'Of course,' Cleo agreed, with a careful glance at Sofia and the baby. She'd be glad to get out from between the two warring parties.

# CHAPTER ELEVEN

FELIPE WATCHED THEM GO. In fact, he couldn't help watching Cleo's shapely legs and straight back as she easily climbed the stairs. Again. He'd watched her do that before, at her home. He suppressed the sigh he wanted to expel at the stubbornness of his cousin and the stupidity of his libido.

It was his awareness of the midwife that caused him the most distraction. Which was not part of the plan.

Once he was busy with his life, the board meetings, patient consultations, the family businesses, everything that had been interrupted by his grandmother's request to find and bring Sofia home, it would settle down once more, and he needed to resume all that now.

Perhaps he should have arranged for Sofia's parents' house to be prepared and staff installed there rather than bring her here. He told himself that in her present frame of mind whomever he engaged she would have suspected they could not be trusted. Hopefully her rancour towards him would lessen soon, as he was growing weary of it. He was still not sure she'd stay, even if he had made her house available to her, though she'd at least have had her independence, and her midwife to settle her in.

Which meant he wouldn't have had the distraction of Cleo staying in his own house. She still tempted him every time their glances met. Each time he noted the tiniest shift of her body beside him in the car.

A phone buzzed in his pocket and he slid his hand down and lifted it to his ear.

His mouth softened. '*Sí*, Àvia.' He listened as his grandmother launched into excited questions and leaned back against the wall with a slight smile on his face. It had been the right thing to bestir himself and fly to Australia. He hadn't heard her this animated for many weeks. When she finally ran down he gently suggested their plans for the evening if she was up to it. Again, he heard the excitement in her voice and even a proposed menu was shared.

He smiled. 'Shall I bring the Australian midwife, too? Sofia would prefer it if I did, I think.'

He listened as his grandmother agreed. 'As long as you are well enough for her as well, then. Good, and we will see you with your new great-granddaughter at seven for tapas.'

# CHAPTER TWELVE

CLEO FOLLOWED SOFIA up the stairs.

Below them she could hear Felipe answer his phone.

With her hand on the ornate wooden rail Cleo had a chance to look around the enormous space that comprised the front door, the entry, with places to sit and wait before you were invited into the inner sanctum of the house, and the soaring dome of the ceiling.

The magnificent angels painted above her head on the ceiling she couldn't study on the move but would take some time later to appreciate the works of art.

When they reached the landing, Rosa turned left and down a hallway, and at the end of the corridor she pushed open a green panelled door.

The room inside opened to a lounge area with a bow window looking over Barcelona away in the distance below. On the opposite side of the room windows showed trees and gardens and blue sky.

The room, in mint green and white, provided a restful air and obviously feminine overtones and spread larger than Cleo had expected for guest apartments.

'There are three bedrooms here,' Rosa said, in accented English. She nodded at Cleo. 'Yours is to the left, the child next and Doña Sofia has the front room.'

There was a knock at the door and a footman entered at

Rosa's call. 'Would you like me to send Maria to unpack for you?' she asked Sofia.

Sofia shook her head, though she drooped as she stood there. 'No. Thank you, Rosa, we will be fine.'

'Then I will order light refreshments to be brought up.' She turned to Cleo. 'And you. Do you require anything?'

'No. I'm fine, thank you, Rosa,' she said. 'Thank you for your assistance. Your English is wonderful.'

'Don Felipe's mother spoke English.' She left abruptly and the door closed behind her.

Sofia sank down into a chair, clutching her baby, and one lone tear slid down her cheek. 'I don't want to be here. I'm in his house. With his servants. And the father of my child is across the other side of the world.' She looked at Cleo. 'I fell in love with him. He spoiled me, encouraged me to do what I wished, unlike anyone in my family had, and I liked having my own apartment and being able to go where I wished when I wished. Now I am back in Spain. A prisoner in Felipe's house.'

'You are not a prisoner. You are here to see your grandmother.' Cleo crossed to her and perched on the edge of the nearest chair to lean towards her. 'Which is why you insisted I come. To support you. You're tired. It's been a huge twenty-four hours.'

'No kidding,' Sofia grumbled.

'You've kept Isabella happy during a very long flight. Perhaps top up her feed, which will help you feel more relaxed, and then both of you could rest. Build up your strength for tonight.'

Sofia nodded. Sat down with her baby and undid her shirt.

Cleo turned to the luggage. 'I'll unpack the bags while

you feed. Then maybe I could settle Isabella to sleep while you lie down and rest.'

Sofia nodded. 'I may feel better if all goes as you say.'

By evening Sofia seemed quite settled in the apartment and her smile had returned. Isabella played model baby with her mother's full attention.

Cleo had discovered Sofia had a house just outside Barcelona, inherited from her parents, but that it was currently closed and without staff.

So perhaps Don Felipe had done the correct thing to bring her here. A house out of town, without friends or family, might have proved daunting for a new mum with only her baby as company, she thought, but hoped it wouldn't be in her remit to arrange any moves.

Cleo showered and donned her simple cream shift, the one that washed like a dream and never looked as if it had come out of a suitcase. The high-necked style could be a formal floating knee-length frock or almost a uniform if she gathered it in with a belt.

She wore her favourite blue lapis bead necklace and she pulled it out to sit at the neck of the dress to give herself extra confidence. She shouldn't feel she needed it, but who knew how grand Felipe's grandmother was. Especially now she knew how grand Felipe was. This was his world and she wanted to keep her head held high.

'Your necklace is pretty,' Sofia commented as she walked past to take a cup of fresh tea that had arrived.

'It was my mother's. Blue at my neck always helps my thoughts turn into words that flow more easily. I wear it most days.'

'Perhaps I should get myself one so I can tell my cousin what I think of him.'

Cleo laughed. 'I think you do very well without any help. Tell me about your grandmother. How old is she?'

'Doña Luisa is in her early eighties. Though you wouldn't think it to look at her. She has a beautiful home in the centre of the city. It will be good to show her Isabella. As long as she doesn't harp at me about finding a Catalan husband. And if she is unwell, perhaps I could stay and help her until she is well again.'

She wasn't going to get well again. For some reason Sofia was refusing to believe that. Cleo wasn't going there. Tonight they would see. And as for a husband for Sofia, she had no idea how upper echelon Spanish families arranged marriages and didn't particularly want to know.

'If she is very ill, mortality can make people adjust their needs. Don Felipe mentioned your grandmother is failing fast now. Perhaps the idea of the next generation with a full life ahead of them is a comfort for her at this time.'

Sofia looked suddenly frightened and very young. 'We will see.'

# CHAPTER THIRTEEN

A MESSAGE CONVEYED by Rosa arrived after their rest. Felipe had left the house to attend the hospice, but requested everyone to be prepared to leave at seven to visit Doña Luisa.

At five to seven Isabella, in the way of breastfed babies, created last-minute irreparable damage to the delightful frock she'd been dressed in. Sofia looked as though she would cry. 'She looked so beautiful. We'll be late now.'

Cleo wrapped a bunny rug around the disaster until they could start on the repair. 'She'll need a bath. These things happen. I can help.'

'No. You go down. I will bath her and choose another dress. But you tell my cousin he will have to wait.'

Cleo wondered who'd got the worst job. 'Of course he will wait.'

All afternoon it had sunk in that she was in the principal residence of a Spanish aristocrat she'd slept with. And still fancied. With the suspicion he still fancied her as well. How had she got herself into this?

Cleo blocked the nervous flutter at being the one descending to find the master of the house and checked her handbag. She had everything. More than everything, really. She was a bit of a girl scout and always prepared.

Of course, a minute later when she did pause at the top

of the stairs, before searching to find him, Felipe was waiting at the bottom to watch her descend.

Her skin heated enough to know he observed her with
extreme concentration. She didn't plan to give him the excitement of tripping and making a fool of herself so she
went carefully. No, sedately.

When her shoes touched the marble floor at the bottom
of the stairs she lifted her head and, as expected, his gaze
sat firmly on her face.

'*Bona nit*, Cleo.'

'Good evening, Don Felipe. Isabella has made her
mother late. I've been sent to offer apologies while Sofia
changes Isabella's clothes.'

Instead of the impatience she'd half expected, though
maybe she was channelling Sofia there and not her own
experience, a smile softened his firm features.

'Babies run to their own timetables.'

She tilted her head. 'And how do you know that?'

He shrugged his shoulders and looked at her quizzi-
cally. 'I have friends with children.'

'You are the doting uncle type?' It was a question that
came out as a statement of disbelief bordering on amusement.

'You don't believe me?'

A shrug. 'Not my place as your employee.' Primly.

'And here I was thinking you were Sofia's guest.'

Now, that was funny. She laughed. His face softened
and he smiled back at her.

'Would you like a drink while we wait?' he asked.

Of all the people who needed to stay sober and keep
their wits about them it was probably her. 'I don't think
so. Thank you.'

'This is Spain. Wine is an institution.'

'Not at this time for me.' Or she'd end up in an institution.

He studied her for a moment longer and then withdrew his phone from his pocket. 'I will let Doña Luisa know we will be a few minutes late.'

He stepped back and Cleo took the opportunity to re-assemble her battered shield under the guise of examining the entry. She knew Felipe could be charming when he wished but she had to guard against that. It made him nearly irresistible.

She concentrated on the blue swirls in the marble floor that had been picked up in the columns that ringed the circular room. Towering columns every six feet, floor to ceiling, and she assumed they carried the weight of the dome above. That was some weight.

She moved to one of the spindly-legged velvet three-seaters and sat on one end so she could lean her head against the wall and admire the ceiling. Calm settled over her as she drank in the scene. Truly amazing artwork. This was good. A quiet minute to collect herself and some time to breathe.

In the distance she could hear Felipe murmuring in Catalan but most of her attention stayed on the ceiling above. Rich, vibrant colours depicted gliding angels with red capes. Glorious pale-skinned cherubs with golden curls reached out to a triumphant warrior on his horse holding up a shield and sword. She wondered how he didn't fall off the horse while holding both.

Felipe came and sat down beside her to lean his head back against the wall beside hers, his eyes on the ceiling, too. She felt he was smiling but no way was she going to turn her head to find out. He was too close.

The masculine scent she now associated with him drifted over her, bringing back far too many memories. Still resting her head back against the wall, she asked, 'One of your ancestors?'

'Yes. We're a bloodthirsty lot, my countrymen.' She turned her face to him and noted the glint in his eye when he said, 'And we like to win the wars we engage in.'

'Take the spoils and run?' Their eyes met. Her cheeks warmed. She wouldn't mind taking those words back.

His eyes widened but he resisted teasing her, a small mercy, and she changed the subject. 'Did your grandmother understand why we will be late?'

'Of course. *A baby is a baby.*' He smiled. 'Her words.'

'You are all very patient. Why is Sofia so angry with you? Why doesn't she believe anything you say?'

'Smoother tongues than mine have filled her head with lies. She will eventually learn the truth.' He closed his eyes briefly as if weary. 'I am not patient with that subject. Enough about my silly cousin.' He turned his head and their eyes caught and held. 'There is another subject I am not tired of.'

He smiled and she felt her own lips curve despite the warning bells that began to ring, at first quietly and then more stridently, in her head. A pulse beat in his strong jaw and she had the ridiculous impulse to lift her hand and feel its beat. He was so beautiful a man.

His irresistible mouth came closer.

At that moment they heard a door open upstairs and then footsteps along the corridor above. Sofia, with Isabella in her arms, appeared at the top of the stairs.

Felipe stood abruptly and Cleo sagged back in what she told herself was relief. She needed to snap out of it.

'Take care, there's plenty of time.' Felipe's voice carried easily up the stairs and ironically Cleo wondered if he was talking to Sofia or to them. She saw the young mum pause as if collecting herself.

Yes, the last thing they needed was Sofia to rush down

the steps and fall. Or for Cleo to accept a kiss in Felipe's house while working for the man.

By the time they were all in the car Isabella had gone to sleep and Sofia had her own head resting on the cushions with her eyes shut.

Cleo had her own thoughts to occupy her and was glad Sofia didn't need her input on anything. It was important that her client feel relaxed when they arrived.

Even Felipe seemed to have appreciated that fact.

Twenty minutes later the car stopped in a typical Barcelona street with motorbikes parked in the centre of the road and more mopeds under the trees along the edges of the footpath.

The occasional delivery van zoomed past the tall cream buildings, all seeming to be six to eight storeys high with ornate balconies and roof scrolling. This was obviously one of the quieter and more exclusive inner-city streets. Though on the corner a gorgeous café with tables on the sidewalk had people spilling out onto the street—a family with young children were eating gelato and the parents were laughing as they wiped dribbles of coloured ice from their youngest's face.

For a second Cleo felt the catch in her heart at all the things she'd lost thanks to her own shattered marriage, but she pushed it away. Not here. Not now.

The entrance to Doña Luisa's house lay behind a tall spiked gate that swung inwards when Felipe pushed it.

Beyond lay white marble steps with a red carpet disappearing into the distance. At the sides, speckled grey marble columns matched the grey of the marble walls but frames of cream plasterwork covered the higher reaches and kept everything light as another steeper set of stairs twirled away in a circular climb.

To the right sat an ornate elevator, round roofed, all gleaming wood and brass and glass like something out of an ancient hotel. The doors clanked as Felipe closed the three adults and one baby snugly inside.

With a jolt they shifted upwards, and their cage creaked as it rode to the third floor. The faint aroma of furniture polish and age wasn't unpleasant.

When Felipe opened the ancient elevator doors, they stepped out into an entry hung with red velvet curtains and intricate grey wallpaper, lit by lamps in sconces. A double door opened to the entrance of a large salon.

A massive fireplace, cold and filled with precious brass art objects rather than wood, held a mantel hung with a huge gilt mirror. On the wall priceless paintings broke up the wallpaper and everywhere spindly chairs were empty as if expecting hordes of visitors.

Instead a maid waited. She curtsied to Felipe and Sofia. 'Your grandmother is in the salon.'

Felipe gestured with his hand for them to follow him. 'We'll find our own way, Alba.' The woman inclined her head again and disappeared through a door.

Cleo followed the two cousins and couldn't help the widening of her eyes as her silenced feet trod the glorious Aubusson carpet runner over the paved marble and past glowing ornate furniture. Shimmering oil paintings were lit softly by windows to the outside. It was like a private museum.

The corridor ended in a wood-panelled room with a white sectioned ceiling that curved and drew her eye to the magnificent chandelier in the centre of the roof.

At first she saw the gilded screens, the marble-topped tables and velvet-upholstered chairs sitting on polished parquetry intricately inlaid with different shades of gold and red-brown timber and reflecting the light.

Don Felipe crossed to the chair in front of another unlit fire and leaned down to kiss the wrinkled cheek of the woman who now turned their way.

That was when Cleo saw the small white-haired woman sitting with a dark shawl around her shoulders. She seemed ethereal in her frailty.

'Àvia, Grandmother, I have brought Sofia and Isabella.'

'*Sí.* And you would have been in trouble if you hadn't.' There was a hint of amusement in the dry voice. The woman's gaze went to the dark-haired baby in Sofia's arms. 'She has her mother's hair.'

'And her father's eyes,' Sofia muttered.

Doña Luisa's gaze moved from the child to the mother. 'I hope not. For his were full of avarice.'

'Àvia,' Felipe murmured placatingly, 'Sofia is upset.'

'And I am old and have no patience. Or time.' The white head swivelled. 'And who is this pretty other lady?'

Cleo felt her face flush. Nobody had called her pretty in years.

'The midwife I mentioned,' Felipe said. 'Cleo Wren.' And, yes, there was amusement under his introduction as if he found her blush a reason to smile.

'Miss Wren.'

'It's a pleasure to meet you, Doña Luisa.' Now that she was closer Cleo could see the underlying yellowish tint to the skin. The sunken eyes. Yes, this woman was terminally unwell.

'My grandson tells me you have much experience in caring for the ill and stranded...?' The question hung at the end.

'Indeed. I find it satisfying to help people return home safely when they are vulnerable. At those times people need their family.'

'And you have brought Sofia back home. I am grateful.'

'Your grandson has done all the arranging.'

'Yes. I can see.' Her eyes twinkled as she glanced between Cleo and Felipe. 'I heard this.'

Felipe's head snapped up at that. But Doña Luisa just smiled blandly at him and cast one last look at Cleo. 'You are a sensible woman.'

She turned to Sofia. 'But you, my grandchild...' Her voice trailed off and Cleo had the impression that Doña Luisa did not think Sofia was a sensible woman. 'Forgive me, child. You have suffered a betrayal. I have forgotten what it was to feel strong emotions for a man.'

She looked across and raised her brows at Felipe. 'Except for you, dear grandson. Though sometimes my emotion is frustration. You spend too much time giving to others when I would like to see you care more for your own happiness.'

Her thin arm stretched towards the waiting chairs. 'Sit, Sofia, here next to me, and tell me of your little daughter. She is truly beautiful.'

And Cleo could finally release the tension she'd held over this meeting.

This was why they'd come all this way. For this ill and elderly woman to meet Isabella. As Sofia sat down with the baby in her arms Cleo stepped back.

Felipe had moved behind her to pour a glass of wine and she almost bumped into him. She edged sideways and increased the distance between them.

'Are you sure you wouldn't like to taste my grandmother's Cava?' he murmured.

'Cava?' Words from the past played in her head. *Like Lonia Cava from Catalonia. Wine that tastes of white peach, melon and apple...* His first words to her. After he'd pretended to be a dancer. Didn't he remember?

'Someone offered me that once before.' She pretended she, too, didn't remember it was him.

He frowned at her, as if he sensed her disappointment in him. 'Cava is one of the Catalonian Designation of Origin products. Nowhere else in the world can produce it and call it Cava. My grandmother buys from a local restaurant who make their own.'

She needed something to do with her hands. 'A small one, then. Thank you.' She could at least pretend to unwind.

He reached for another glass and poured an inch of the wine into the glass. At least he was listening.

'Come, we will sit near the window and watch the world go by while they talk.'

He gestured to two large winged chairs with an ornate side table between them.

The red velvet curtains shed a pink glow into her lap as she sat and looked out onto the street above the leafy tops of trees.

The view filled the room with soft light. Peaceful.

The man opposite was not.

'Have you settled into my home?' That sounded very determined.

Cleo looked at him in pretended surprise. 'Yes, thank you.' Why wouldn't she feel settled in the house of a man she'd slept with when she'd thought he was a dancer and who had actually turned out to be a Spanish nobleman pursued by hordes of panting women? 'I'm fine.' She lifted the glass to her lips. 'You?'

His mouth kicked up. She really wished he wouldn't do that.

'I am home.'

'Your grandmother dotes on you.'

An elegant shrug, dismissing any emotion she might have glimpsed. 'My *àvia* and I have spent a lot of time together.'

His raised brows suggested he'd given her something, so now she could also share. 'And you? Was your childhood happy?'

They'd discussed some things that night in Australia, but hadn't gone into detail. They had been barely acquainted, after all. Why did he want to stretch those boundaries now? She had to say something. 'My parents were happy most of the time, though finding enough funds to live on was always an issue for them.'

She shrugged. 'When I entered the workforce I studied hard and ensured my savings were adequate. My ex-husband was a doctor, although not a thrifty one, and it's taken me several months to climb out of the debt he left me with, but I finally managed it. I am a woman determined to find myself secure.'

'A sensible person?' He tilted his head at her. 'I don't think I know any thrifty women.'

'Poor you.' Dryly. She tilted her own head. 'I am prudent.' She thought about what she'd done with him and added, 'Mostly.' She'd told him too much. Though Jen had always said her relationship with her ex had been one-sided. She'd saved, he'd spent. She'd cared for him more than he'd cared for her. She wouldn't be doing that again, ever. 'Enough about me, tell me more about your grandmother.'

'Taste the wine.'

She inhaled the fruity aroma of the wine and then took a sip. 'Very nice. About your grandmother?'

He sat back and gave her one of those half amused, half warning glances. 'When my grandfather died many years ago, my grandmother took over the family empire until she could hand it on to her three sons. She has had much grief in her life and far too many deaths. Now there is only me, Sofia and Isabella left. And lots of distant cousins like Diego.'

Ah, so Diego was a distant cousin of his. She wondered if Jen knew that. Cleo could quite believe it was an empire judging by the wealth that surrounded Felipe and Luisa.

Felipe went on. 'Before he died, my father managed his and Sofia's part of the business and I managed my grandmother's and my own. She was an astute businesswoman and very used to making decisions for the family. It was her contacts who first discovered Sofia was in trouble. Her fingers are in many pies.'

He glanced with affection and obvious respect towards Doña Luisa. 'For the last ten years I have been telling her it is time for her to sit back and savour the time she has left.'

'I'm sorry. I can see she is unwell. You said you would care for her.' That night. 'Will she move back in with you when she needs more care?'

'She has refused. Though, as I said before, we have thankfully completed the new oncology hospice that she has consented to consider when she requires twenty-four-hour care.'

'We have completed', as in just his family, or 'we' as in Barcelona has completed? she wondered. She strongly suspected the former.

He shrugged. 'Though I would prefer she stayed in her own apartments with full assistance but that is up to her.'

She remembered their discussion about oncologists. 'And this is the building, the new centre you spoke about before? Where you work?'

'Sí.'

Felipe's phone buzzed quietly in his pocket and he excused himself to walk to a window. A rapid one-sided conversation and then he moved across to his grandmother.

'Àvia, there is something I must attend to at the hospice. I will be no more than an hour. Can you stay from your bed that long?'

'I am not dead yet, Felipe. Go. Take your midwife. She would be more interested in your building there than sitting in a corner, watching us talk. Show her your pride and joy.'

The frown he sent his grandmother made Cleo cringe with embarrassment. He didn't want to take her.

But he said, 'Would you like to see the new hospice, Cleo?'

And she could say nothing except, 'If you are sure that will be acceptable.'

His astonished look said it all. 'Who would complain?'

She laughed at his arrogance. She probably shouldn't. She was in his sandpit now. But she couldn't help herself. She had nothing but her courage to shield her. 'I'm sure no one would dare,' she said, her voice dry.

He raised his brows but his eyes smiled. He shook his head but didn't comment. They rode down in the elevator, and when they emerged she had to skip a little to keep up, but he didn't seem to notice. He was on a mission. Typical.

His usual driver waited with the car, and she wondered if he'd had warning or just…always waited around until he was needed.

The driver opened the rear door for her and she wondered again whether to slide across or just sit and make Felipe go to the other side of the car, but he was always there before she could make a decision.

Then she thought of all the aristocratic women she'd ever watched on TV and none of them had ever slid across a back seat. So she assumed Felipe expected her to stay put.

Good to get that sorted in her head.

Too many unknown areas with the weight of such a long, distinguished family history and the ridiculous wealth that surrounded these people. She looked forward to being home in her own humble yet comfortable environment.

'Where is the hospice?' she asked as the car pulled away from the kerb.

'Ten minutes from here. One of my patients is asking for me. He is a very dear friend of mine and I would never ignore any request he made.'

As a lead oncologist he must have many other demands on his time. 'It must have been difficult for you to get away for the week to go to Australia.'

'Yes. Though nobody is irreplaceable. My departure created yet more work for those who had no need to expand their duties. Sometimes Doña Luisa forgets how busy I am, but in this case she was right to send me instead of anyone else.'

So, he hadn't chosen to retrieve Sofia. She could see how much he cared for his grandmother and she wasn't surprised he had gone. She'd already decided he wasn't the ogre Sofia proclaimed so loudly.

'I am constantly looking for the right staff for the hospice.' He turned in his seat to give her his full attention. 'Why are you wasting time shuttling people in aircraft between countries? Your kindness would fit well in my field.'

His comment warmed her. And confused her. How had he come to that conclusion in their short acquaintance? Yes, she wanted to hear more about his work; she wanted to hear anything except that there was no future for them. She needed to banish those ridiculous thoughts.

'As you said, there is a similarity between the care of those at the beginning and the end of life. It is interesting you say that because I had thought about doing oncology nursing when I first moved from midwifery.'

'*Sí.* I could imagine you there.' He tilted his head to

study her. 'I could see you as one who stands at the gate and comforts those going and those who must bid them goodbye.'

'I've had no experience with that.'

'I'm not sure if you understand my hospice. It is not only for the old and infirm. It is for all ages, all terminal souls, from infant to child to adult to elder as they leave their families. It's about simple beauty and peaceful surroundings to pass from this world into the next.'

She frowned. Did he mean euthanasia? Her face must have registered the question.

'Not like a certain clinic in Switzerland but a place of quiet, comfort and solace for nature to take its course. With excellent support. But I do need someone who could impart the secrets of the midwife to those who think efficiency is the same thing.'

There was a thread of frustration in his voice. 'Someone who can fulfil the needs of others and work to make that happen without cold competence and too little understanding. Most of my staff are wonderful but some need more guidance in compassion.'

The car pulled up in front of a large white building with tall standard roses in ceramic pots that stood like soldiers on both sides of the path to make a floral corridor. Marble steps, as well as a ramp to the side, led to the oval doorway and the automatic doors. A discreet sign read 'Hospicio Luisa'. Named after his grandmother, he'd said. Of course.

Inside the doors, warm brown mosaics on the floor and artistic silver branches adorned the eggshell-blue walls like a tree growing from the doorway and curving away on the left towards some elevators.

A glowing parquetry desk with soft pale blue leather chairs sat in front in welcome and to the right a fountain tinkled beside two stunning life-size statues of angels.

Flowers scented the air and created a foyer less like a medical facility and more like an elegant apartment block lobby for the rich and famous.

The woman at the desk smiled and inclined her head respectfully at Felipe. She looked curiously at Cleo.

'Good morning, Elisheba,' he said. 'Please ask the nursing supervisor on duty to meet me in Raymond's apartment.'

The woman nodded. '*Sí*, Don Felipe.' Her respect was coloured by her warmth towards him and Cleo could see her delight in seeing him. Curiouser and curiouser. A different side again to this multifaceted man, and he intrigued her even more. She had seen the Spanish lover, the autocratic head of the family, the caring grandson and now the respected professional doctor.

Felipe directed her to a pair of white elevators and they rose to the third floor.

When they came out again there was more warm brown flooring, pale green walls of early summer, and flowers.

Every time they passed staff the response was the same delight as the woman from downstairs had shown. Felipe knew all their first names and enquired occasionally about family members. From the warmth of those who hailed him, he was a much-admired and looked-up-to doctor.

Unlike the rich and famous Felipe, this person she could relate to. She thought of the conversation in the car on the way here. There was definitely something they had in common. A passion for their work in helping others.

She stood beside him as they passed many rooms, all different pastel colours with plush chairs and large windows, and he paused frequently to share a particular vantage point, or luxury fitting, or pleasing colour scheme with her, and she saw and couldn't help but appreciate his fierce dedication and passion for his hospice.

At the end of the long corridor he knocked on a partially closed door.

A name on the door read, 'Don Raymond Ruiz'. The faint voice of a man bade them enter.

Two sides of the room held large windows that overlooked the cityscape and on the third wall hung a glorious print of a rainforest beside a door that she assumed led to the bathroom. In the corner was a small kitchenette and a bar fridge was tucked away.

The man in the bed looked gaunt and very pale, but of an age with Felipe, terminally ill well before his time. Yet despite his obvious frailty, his eyes danced with amusement and interest at seeing Felipe with Cleo.

'Who is this you have brought to meet me, my friend?' The educated accent was similar to Felipe's and his English as impeccable as her escort's.

Felipe crossed the room and took the man's skeletal hand in his. 'Raymond. You summoned me.' He smiled warmly at him. 'This is Cleo Wren. A midwife and nurse from Australia, and companion to my cousin Sofia who has just returned from Sydney with her new babe.'

'A pleasure to meet you, Cleo.' He looked from one to the other and his eyes shone with mischief. Cleo liked him immediately. He certainly wasn't awed by Felipe.

'A pleasure to meet you, too, Don Raymond.'

'Raymond.'

There was a knock at the door and a tall calm-faced woman around Cleo's age came in. She nodded at Mr Ruiz. 'Don Raymond. Don Felipe?'

'Thank you for your call, Maya. This is Sister Cleo Wren from Australia. I would appreciate if you offer her a tour of our facility while I speak to Raymond.'

The woman smiled at Cleo. 'With pleasure. We are

very proud of the hospice.' She turned to Felipe. 'How long would you like us to be?'

Felipe glanced at his friend, who flashed ten fingers at him. 'A quarter of an hour would be sufficient for a brief showing.'

He looked at Cleo. 'I would like your opinions on the facility, please, Cleo.'

She nodded and went with her minder out the door, secretly delighted to have the chance to explore Felipe's world and not intrude on what was obviously a private and important conversation.

By the time Cleo returned with Maya fifteen minutes later, she'd learned several things.

First, that Felipe was held in awe by the staff. When she'd questioned Maya on the reason it had come across as his determination to overcome all obstacles and his single-minded dedication to create this peaceful world for those at the end of their lives.

She'd also discovered that a lot of the capital expenditure had been donated by Felipe, but more importantly Felipe made himself available day and night for the patients and the staff. The relatives, he saw through the day.

As they traversed two more floors, the hospice itself continued to amaze and delight Cleo with the calm colours, soft furnishings and attention to tiny details, like curtains, bed lights and nurse call, which could be managed by voice technology or buttons by the bed.

Each room held a tiny kitchenette and the actual kitchen downstairs was available for the staff, visitors and, of course, the patients, and served delicious and nutritious snacks and meals twenty-four hours a day. All could be summoned by a push of the bell.

Towards the end of the tour Cleo couldn't help asking a more direct question. 'Is it very expensive for the patients?'

Maya laughed. 'It depends. To spend your last days here would cost the same as the public hospital for those who cannot afford to pay, and is very, very expensive for those who can,' Maya said with mischief. 'The idea is to have both kinds of clientele in residence.'

'And do you have enough staff?'

'*Sí*. Almost. It is an excellent place to work but the interviews are thorough for those who wish to work here. We are looking for a certain type of person.'

Cleo guessed that was the royal 'we' and it was Felipe who was looking for a certain type of nurse and doctor. He'd said as much in the car on the way here.

Maya went on. 'We have only a short time to care for these souls, but it is one of the most important times of their lives.' Her sincerity was obvious, and Cleo nodded her head. It was how she felt about midwifery.

'I totally agree. Thank you so much for showing me around.'

'It is rare that I have the chance.' The curiosity in the other woman's eyes made Cleo smile but what could she say? His grandmother made me come? She didn't think so.

When they arrived back at the room Felipe held Raymond's shoulder with a firm grip as their gazes held. Felipe dropped his hand. 'Goodbye, my friend.'

'And you, Felipe,' Raymond said. 'Find happiness.'

Cleo hung back at the charged atmosphere and Maya looked sad for a moment as she observed the two men. She waited quietly until she had Felipe's attention. 'Is there anything else you wish me to do?'

'Keep me updated.' Felipe's eyes were shadowed and

Cleo wanted to take his arm and offer support. His friend was clearly dying, though apparently with a calmness and serenity Cleo had rarely seen.

'Cleo?' Raymond's tired voice held amusement. She turned and smiled at him. He beckoned so she went across to the bed and leaned down. 'Make my friend smile,' he whispered.

Cleo nodded. Kissed the pale, dry cheek gently. Said very softly, so nobody else could hear, 'Someone needs to not take him so seriously.' But she had learned that others deeply appreciated Felipe Gonzales and now more than ever she wanted to know more about the man she could see. But then he would be so much harder to resist.

Raymond relaxed back in the bed and closed his eyes. But his lips curved in a smile. Cleo stepped away from the bed and found Felipe beside her. He took her arm. 'We need to get back.'

Maya had gone, and when they left, the sleeping man was alone in the room. She wasn't sure if it was a trick of light but there seemed to be sunshine playing on the path through the rainforest picture and the room held a golden glow.

When the car drew away from the hospice Felipe turned his face to the window. She touched his arm, the expression in his eyes showing for a moment his distress, but it shuttered as he looked her way.

'What did you think of my clinic?' He gestured back the way they'd come.

'I thought it was beautiful. Perfect for the care of those who need comfort and tranquillity.'

'Yes. It is satisfying to see the dream become a reality.'

'Your staff are rightly very proud of the service offered. And of you.'

He waved his hand as if discounting that. His mouth
tightened.

'Don't wave it away.' She remembered his grandmother's words. How she wanted him to take time for his
own happiness. 'They love you. You obviously deserve
their respect and appreciation.' When he didn't answer she
said, 'I'm sorry that your friend Raymond is so unwell.' She
wanted to add, *He's far too young to die, but when was age
a barrier to loss of life?* 'He told me to make you smile.'

He looked up. Shook his head. And his expression softened as he smiled. For a moment he wasn't the far more
reserved man she was seeing so much of in Spain.

'Ah, there he is,' she teased softly, suddenly desperate
to do as Raymond had asked her. Felipe, the less austere
Felipe, reacted to her tone, relaxing a fraction more, the
smile still playing around his wicked mouth. She wondered which facet of this fascinating man was more real.
The dancer, the doctor or the Don?

'There is who, Cleo?' His voice was low and sexy.

His eyes were dark, and dangerous, and he leaned her
way. She was mad but she said it anyway. For the smile
she'd promised, she told herself. 'The flamenco dancer.'

His smile widened and he reached long fingers across
and captured her hand in his. He already held her gaze.
Drew her wrist slowly to his mouth until his lips bowed
and he kissed her sensitive skin, making her shiver with
the long, leisurely promise. 'I could certainly show you
that man.'

The car stopped. They'd arrived. *Oh, my goodness,* she
thought, and with difficulty dragged her eyes away from
his to look at the escape hatch.

\* \* \*

When they arrived back at Doña Luisa's house Cleo had to fight to clear the fog that particular version of Felipe had created in her mind. They had arrived just in time for the meal.

'Come,' Doña Luisa called out. 'We go through for tapas.'

Tapas was a good thing. An excellent diversion from the swirl of emotion she'd been left with from the hospice. And most definitely from the volcanic reaction she'd unleashed in Felipe in the car.

That Felipe, Sofia's cousin, wanted comfort, safety and peace for others, which was clear at the hospice named after his grandmother, Cleo had no doubt now that he wanted the best for his cousin, too.

She needed time to think, some distance between herself and Felipe, for her fluctuating emotions to settle down. She needed to concentrate on the job and not think so much about the powerful, seductive man beside her.

While they had been away rapport had been renewed between Sofia and Doña Luisa because the younger woman was smiling as she helped her grandmother to her feet. A pram, possibly one almost as old as their hostess, had appeared, and Isabella reposed quietly amidst its ancient splendour.

# CHAPTER FOURTEEN

FELIPE LIFTED HIS hand towards the small of her back to usher her through to the dining room but she skipped ahead like a frightened doe. He allowed his hand to fall again and smiled. He'd liked that glimpse of a different Cleo. The one he'd met in the flamenco club and who had been markedly absent ever since they'd met again in Sofia's hospital room.

She walked swiftly to increase the distance between them and though they entered the dining room together they moved apart like ripples on a pond. He turned to assist his grandmother into her chair.

Cleo went to stand beside Sofia.

His grandmother touched his hand and inclined her head. 'You watch her. Always. I see your eyes.' Said very quietly as she shot him a wicked grin. 'I thought you didn't like Australians?'

He frowned at her and lifted his head to see if Cleo had heard the word *Australians*. She was talking to Sofia and they were both admiring the pram.

'Enough, Àvia, you tease me. She is help for Sofia.'

'Is she? No attraction there?' A quirk of white eyebrows. 'There is nothing between you at all?' She made a derisive sound. 'I have eyes.'

He turned his shocked gaze to her, sincerely hoping she

was talking about her own eyes and not others who might have been watching him in Australia. 'You are mistaken.'

'Me?' She laughed and then coughed and turned pale enough to worry him. But slowly the colour crept back into her cheeks.

'You are changed since you came back.' Said a little breathlessly. 'I will find out why.' Short sentences. 'Then.' A breath. 'We will discuss it.' His grandmother composed herself into her chair and called to Sofia. Patted the seat beside her.

There was nothing to discuss. But his grandmother's seating arrangements left him to sit next to Cleo. What was his *àvia* playing at?

Thankfully the food arrived, so he could pretend to divert his attention to the array of small dishes that circled the middle of the table.

But his grandmother's words swirled in his head. She could see his intense attraction to Cleo. Why would he be so surprised? His grandmother's passion had always been watching others. Of course she'd seen. Next she'd be investigating Cleo from her deathbed.

This wasn't good. He had no doubt Cleo would be unimpressed as well.

He looked across at his cousin. Another accurate observation by his grandmother. In this instance he was thankful she'd uncovered it and still felt guilty as hell that he'd allowed Sofia to slip unnoticed into a disaster. He should have checked on her himself as soon as his father had died.

And in an indirect way his grandmother's meddling in her grandchildren's lives had also brought him to having the woman he could not ignore beside him. A woman who had infiltrated his senses like the subtle scent she wore. Aware of every move of her arm. Every turn of her head. The way Raymond, and even Maya, had tacitly given a nod of approval for the woman he had brought with him to the hospice.

He saw all the good in Cleo, but he had to keep her at arm's length for now because he had enough on his plate without starting a torrid affair with someone who was going to fly back to Australia in two weeks. And it *would* be torrid if their one night together was any indication.

There were several minutes of silence as delicacies were eaten, though throughout his meal his awareness increased that neither his grandmother nor Cleo was eating very much.

He turned to study Cleo's plate and asked quietly, 'Is the food not to your liking?'

'It's wonderful.' A crease lay between her brows. 'Though I'm afraid I don't know what half of the things are.'

He pointed with his finger. 'Green peppers.'

'Not chillies, then. I'm so pleased. They smell amazing but I was afraid to be mistaken.' She smiled and took one with the fork provided.

'*Sí*. Tiny green peppers, not chilli peppers. They are roasted soft, flavoursome, and that touch of coconut is very tasty.'

He watched her face as she tried the different dishes, eating slowly. Savouring. Concentrating. Serious. As if learning the tastes. Cataloguing. She made him smile. There was nothing wrong with just enjoying her company while she was here.

He would really like to see her laugh again, like they had that one night in Australia.

'Where does the word *tapas* come from?' Cleo asked.

It was as if she needed to understand everything with her curiosity. She made him curious as to why she was like that. '*Tapas* is the word for a lid.' He gestured with his hand so she understood. 'A small empty plate that the barman would put on top of the beer glass to stop flies from landing on the rim of the glass.'

He leaned towards her. 'They say that one day, a barman put a piece of meat on top of the empty plate, to eat with the beer, which the patrons enjoyed.'

He shrugged. 'The story goes that then different things were placed on the plate on top of the glass and so a sophisticated tapas culture grew in Spain.' He spread his hands. 'The best is in Barcelona.'

She laughed and he congratulated himself just a little smugly on drawing her out.

'You think Barcelona has the best of everything.'

'Of course.'

She shook her head. 'So, what are those?' she asked, pointing at a dish.

'That is my favourite. Cured duck breast with fresh figs, rosemary and honey.'

She looked intrigued. He pointed.

'That is Iberian pork fillet with pears.' A wave of his hand towards the shellfish. 'You must recognise the oysters.'

She nodded. 'The Iberian coast surrounds you, so seafood should play a strong part in your tapas menus.'

A sudden loud squealing of tyres followed by a crash from the street below made Felipe hurriedly rise from his chair, muttering, 'Excuse me.' He crossed to the window to pull back the curtains. His grandmother's usually peaceful street lay in chaos. Tables and chairs from the footpath outside the café on the corner had been flung around and a car was buried nose first in the doorway of the café.

Alba appeared beside him. He turned to her. 'Call the police and the ambulance. I will go down to see if I can help.'

Cleo appeared at his shoulder. 'I'll come with you.'

His first instinct was to decline, to protect her from the chaos below, but of course she was a trained nurse with valuable medical skills. He would need help until the emergency services arrived and together they had the skills to benefit any accident victim.

And she was calm. It seemed to him that she was always calm. 'Thank you.'

When they reached the lift it had returned to the ground floor and he cursed. It was not a fast lift. 'Let us take the stairs.'

She nodded with instant agreement and he glanced at her shoes, which were low-heeled and sensible. *Sensible like her*, he thought, and after the pampered women he'd been exposed to for so many years he knew why that drew him so much.

On the ground floor, they crossed the street and saw a small crowd had gathered and voices were being raised.

Felipe pushed through them with Cleo behind him. 'I am a doctor,' he said. 'Was anyone on the chairs?' Perhaps under the car? 'Has anyone been hurt apart from the people in the car?'

'No, a woman and man. In the car,' someone offered.

Thank God the chairs had been empty, Felipe thought. He crossed himself because earlier there had been children there. Steam rose from the fractured radiator of the car but despite the loudness of the impact it didn't look too bad.

A man stumbled from the driver's side of the car and almost made it to the passenger side before he crumpled to the ground groaning and holding his head. Blood trickled down his face beneath his fingers.

Felipe moved towards him and turned to Cleo. 'There is a woman in the car. I think perhaps she is in need of a midwife.'

'No, no, no.' The woman's cries could be heard more clearly now. 'The baby is coming.' No doubt about the cry this time.

He opened the passenger door and spoke gently to the labouring woman. 'Are you hurt? Apart from being in labour?'

The woman settled briefly as her contraction eased. 'No. I am not hurt.'

'I am a doctor and I will be with you shortly. This woman she is *llevadora*—a midwife. I must help your husband.'

The woman struggled to get out of the car to see to her husband then leaned back in her seat, sobbing. '*Idiota!* He drove too fast when I said the baby was coming.'

Felipe turned. Where was Cleo?

'*Soy enfermera,*' he heard her say quietly. I am a nurse. The onlookers parted.

The younger woman's frantic gaze latched onto Cleo and something she saw in Cleo's calm gaze seemed to allow her some relief.

# CHAPTER FIFTEEN

CLEO ARRIVED BESIDE the car at the same time as the next contraction caught the woman. She moaned and pushed at the same time.

Cleo had no doubt birth was imminent, which she considered a good thing after an accident like this.

Trauma to the uterus and/or rapid deceleration could be silently dangerous for pregnancy. The placenta could shear from the wall of the uterus and cut off the blood supply to the baby. Or the mother could bleed badly and yet feel no pain. No, she wasn't going there. They would have a healthy baby born.

'Are you hurt?'

The woman held her stomach, glanced down at it, but shook her head. She glared in the direction of her husband. *'Idiota!'* she said again, and then sighed. 'I hope he is not badly hurt.'

'Perhaps just a little bit hurt,' Cleo said, and suppressed a smile.

The woman shook her head but she smiled. Until the next contraction and the woman bore down again. She heard the small grunt and Cleo looked for a place to ease the birth.

She met the woman's eyes and gestured to the road.

'Can you move out of the car?' she asked, thinking giving birth might be awkward in the car.

The woman shook her head. Cleo didn't want to move her either, really, in case something else was hurt. It was unlikely, but the impact hadn't been near the fuel tank and she had no doubt if they needed to exit the area swiftly Felipe would tell them so in no uncertain terms.

The woman grunted again.

Cleo pulled the husband's jacket from beside her feet onto the road and knelt on it. 'I'll try to push the seat back, but can you help me do that?' She gestured to help explain what she meant.

Cleo leaned down to push the small bar under the seat and the woman gave a small jerk with her body backwards and thankfully the seat slid easily and created some room in front of the woman, except for a large, soft overnight case jammed next to her feet.

It would have to be enough. Felipe was busy with the bleeding man, who appeared to have a shoulder injury as well. The woman leaned forward with her hands on her knees and breathed.

Cleo had nothing to wash her hands with, no gloves, no towels. But they had a conscious and alert mother. It could have been worse. The woman could slide forward to the edge of the seat. That would work. She was more worried the baby would be compromised than she was about the awkwardness of the actual birth, but she had Felipe there, too. Hopefully, soon emergency medical help would arrive. 'I am Cleo. What is your name?'

'Elena.' A downward grunt of late labour. 'Not how I was supposed to have my baby.'

'No.' Cleo smiled warmly. 'Is this your first?'

'No. Third.' An experienced mother, then. A bonus. They could do this together. 'Elena,' she said slowly, 'some babies are impatient. Yours is one such. May I put your bag behind you to lean against so you can sit forward at the edge of the seat? To make room for the birth?'

Elena grunted again and Cleo squeezed the bag out of the small space while Elena shuffled forward on the seat.

Felipe edged in quietly beside her. 'I'll push it in while you help her stay forward.' With relief she nodded, and he spoke quietly to Elena while they both helped her move forward and he pushed the bulky bag down with the other hand until the woman sat perched at the edge of the seat with the bag supporting her back.

'Like a birthing stool,' Cleo said with a slight smile.

Elena grimaced. 'Though it is better.'

Cleo touched Elena's arm gently. 'If you have your baby here now, I believe all will be well. Then the ambulance will come and take you all to the hospital.'

Elena said something too fast to understand but Cleo didn't need all the words. She understood the word 'idiot' again and had the feeling Elena's husband was in serious trouble with his wife! But first the baby.

'It will be soon.' She spoke calmly. 'Can you lift up so I can remove your underwear? Pantaloons?' She hoped that was the right word. The contraction had eased but Elena was panting, her eyes glued to Cleo's. She nodded quickly and reached up to the small handgrip above her head and lifted her bottom.

With a discreet shuffle under the voluminous skirt Cleo managed to hook the pair of knickers and slide them down Elena's legs. She left one side on at the ankle.

Felipe said beside her, 'I have phoned Alba to send down some washcloths and towels.'

'And my handbag.' She did have handwash in there, but it would be too late to use it before the birth. And one pack of gloves. But there was a twin pack of small plastic disposable cord clamps because she never knew which country she'd end up in or when a baby would decide to come. Not that she had scissors to cut the cord with. 'And scissors.' Though perhaps she'd wrap the placenta for the hospital to separate it from the baby later.

She asked Elena for the scarf she had around her neck. 'For the baby.' Elena stared and then nodded and tore the colourful cashmere scarf off her throat.

Felipe spoke rapidly into his phone and the two women settled themselves more comfortably. The scarf was handed to Cleo. She heard Felipe behind her instructing the crowd to turn their backs and form a circle to give privacy to the two women.

Elena's face contorted and as her breaths were expelled she said loudly, 'The baby is coming.'

Cleo discreetly lifted her skirts. She couldn't help the smile that grew at the sight of the dark bulge of the baby's head. The mother was always right.

She nodded calmly. '*Sí.* Your baby is coming. All is good.'

Felipe murmured beside her and Elena nodded sharply and gripped the edge of the seat. The sound of a mother bearing down became unmistakable in the silence of the small space.

A gush.

A splash as more waters escaped. Poor car.

The birth of the head and then a tumble of damp limbs. It was over very quickly.

The rush of a tiny body into Cleo's waiting hands, which were suddenly heavy, though the baby lay still in a frozen moment after birth.

But there was tone in the small limbs. Rapid birth would cause a baby some shock. And was to be expected under the circumstances.

'He is stunned. Give him a moment.' Calmly Cleo leaned forward with the scarf and brushed it over the baby, wiping it firmly in long strokes. She crooned to it. 'Nice big breath, baby. You can do it.'

The limbs tensed, pale eyelids quivered and blinked, and his neck stiffened.

The newborn coughed and first a weak cry broke the silence and then a louder one. His eyes opened in round surprise.

Cleo heard the sudden expulsion of breath behind her as Felipe exhaled in relief. She heard the mother's gasp as she reached for her baby, and the murmurings from the small crowd that had gathered, though after one quick glare from Felipe they didn't turn around to look.

In the distance she heard the wail of an ambulance. But the sound of the escalating baby's cries was the best of all sounds.

'You are very clever, Elena,' Cleo said to the mother as she lifted the other woman's blouse to expose the skin of her soft abdomen and laid the still-connected baby across her warm belly.

The umbilical cord was short and unless she cut it, Cleo couldn't lift the baby higher onto his mother's chest.

Felipe murmured in Spanish and the amusement in his voice was tinged with relief.

The father had crawled to where they were, inside the circle of turned backs, and leaned his head against the door of the car.

Alba pushed through the onlookers with towels and Cleo's handbag.

*'Mare de Déus!'* she exclaimed at the scene. And dropped the towels beside Cleo and waved the handbag uncertainly.

Cleo turned to Felipe. 'My hands are no use like this.'

They were wet and bloody, though she'd wiped them on the scarf when she'd dried the baby.

Now she reached for a clean towel and wiped the part of the baby she could get to. She laid another fresh towel across the infant and mother to keep them warm.

She turned her face Felipe's way. 'There's a small black purse in the zipped compartment at the back of the bag. Can you open it and remove the cord clamps, please?'

He shook his head in disbelief. Said something to the new mother. Cleo didn't bother translating, and Elena and her husband laughed weakly through their tears. The husband stared in awe at the baby then with immense gratitude at Cleo.

'What did you say?' Cleo asked Felipe.

'I said how many people do we know who carry such things as these in their handbags?' He held up the see-through sterile packet of two blue plastic cord clamps.

'And they're even the right colour,' Cleo said matter-of-factly. Elena moaned in surprise as an unexpected contraction rolled over her and Cleo soothed her, murmured about the afterbirth and a short time later bundled up the placenta in one of the towels and tucked it next to the baby.

When all was done, she felt the mother's belly, and thanked her lucky stars that the rock-hard uterus she felt beneath her hands was contracting and healthy. They didn't need to battle a haemorrhage as well as a birth in the front seat of a small vehicle.

Felipe tore open the sterile packet so she could reach over and take out one of the cord clamps.

She eased baby away from mother for a moment so she could see the infant's belly, clicked the little clamp shut over the thick cord an inch above the baby's skin and the next clamp half an inch further towards the mother's end of the cord.

'I don't have scissors, but the ambulance will. I didn't need the clamps if I'm not cutting the cord but it's safer to do it in case someone accidentally stretches the cord and it breaks or the placenta somehow ends up below the baby. I've seen a baby's blood volume compromised like that before.'

Felipe stared at her. Then shook his head.

Cleo narrowed her eyes. 'What?'

'Nothing.'

# CHAPTER SIXTEEN

FELIPE COULD NOT help but stare at her. This woman he had left on Sunday morning, mere days ago, who had re-appeared in his life like a breath of fresh air. She knelt on the road, smiling at a stranger. As calm as if Elena had just given birth in a labour ward suite.

'I'm looking at you. So composed. Matter-of-fact about this moment.' He shook his head. 'I have seen many births as a student doctor but none as reassuring as this emer-gency with no one for back-up.'

She smiled at him. Her face was softer than he'd ever seen, as if she were totally content with her world.

Inside himself something shifted. A fracture of time, a blending of past and present, so that at this moment he remembered the velvet of her skin beneath his hands and yet could study now the curve of her cheek as she bent over the mother and murmured to her.

The scent of new baby and blood, burnt rubber and the press of bodies was in his nostrils, and yet there was a lightness to the moment he could not believe. She was amazing. Something else shifted. The urge to fight for her, to rise above the obstacles lying between them, stirred in his chest. Was there any possibility of a future with this woman? Because he wanted her for his own.

His hand clenched. He had wronged Cleo when he had

walked away from her without giving them a chance. He remembered the generous giving of her lovemaking, her full attention when he had been speaking of his past, how incredible their connection had been. But he'd still walked away.

She broke into his thoughts softly. 'I had you here for back-up.'

'*Sí.*' In this instance. He hoped he would have been of use if needed, but once before he had been unsuccessful when attending childbirth. He winced as a painful memory suddenly returned to haunt him. One that had changed the course of his work because briefly, years ago as a student doctor, he, too, had considered working with mothers and babies.

He'd tried to resuscitate an infant he'd helped to birth but it had not gone well and the baby had died. No matter that later the autopsy had proved the baby had lacked a functioning heart. The trauma of it had been enough for him to know that the life and death stakes of working with newborns in Obstetrics was not for him.

His Cleo had stepped up and taken the braver path. He had taken the path of caring for people at the other end of life—when no one expected miracles. But that was good, too, because it was his passion now and all was as it should be.

His brow furrowed. He hadn't thought of that infant in years. He hadn't thought of a lot of the things that now dominated his mind when he was around this woman.

Enough. Later. 'Here comes the ambulance.' She did not understand just how extraordinary she was. He was realising again how much that intrigued him.

The ambulance wailed to a stop with the onlookers now standing back, and very swiftly Elena and her baby were safely bundled inside the large vehicle.

Cleo's hands had been disinfected thanks to the ambulance personnel, though her cream dress had marks that would not be so easily cleaned.

When the ambulance pulled away, a muttering Alba had bundled the remaining washcloths and towels into a black disposable bag and marched them straight to the rubbish bin. As they rode up together in the lift, Felipe saw Alba steal glances at Cleo as if she couldn't decide if she were a good woman or a disaster waiting to happen.

His midwife had her eyes shut and a gentle smile on her face as she leaned back against the wall of the elevator. He watched the gentle rise and fall of her breasts and skimmed the vivid red marks on her dress and shook his head again.

Alba spoke tightly. 'I will find her a gown to wear while I try to save that dress and she washes.'

Felipe considered her ire. Knew it wasn't aimed at Cleo but against people who imposed on guests of his grandmother by bleeding on them.

Cleo opened her eyes. 'Thank you.'

He recalled her speaking to Elena and realised she actually spoke his language quite well, and he wondered why he hadn't noticed that before. There must be a story in that, too. It was surprising how badly he wanted to know all her stories. 'We will return to my villa as soon as you've washed. Grandmother will understand.'

He watched her consider the marks on her dress and the spots of blood on her legs. 'Perhaps that's a good idea.' Another rueful scan. 'Before I touch anything or anyone.'

All would be forgiven, he thought, after such heroics, but held his peace. Maybe he was making too much of this. Her actions were, after all, those of any woman with her medical experience.

But he knew the changes inside him, the ones his grandmother had seen, had shifted yet again.

Had he always held himself back from meaningful relationships? Been cool and aloof until finally he had found someone who had broken through that shell and shaken him badly, like Cleo was shaking him to the core now?

He thought of the couple downstairs, their new baby arriving with such drama but, thankfully, safely. That had also shaken him.

He wasn't like his own father, who'd had trouble connecting with any other human being. He was a good man, could be a good husband and—dared he think it?—could also be a good father one day...

The lift doors opened and Alba hustled Cleo away.

He took himself to the nearest bathroom to wash his own hands and ensure he was presentable before he returned to his grandmother, whom he knew would be avid for news.

He remained pensive.

His grandmother eyed him shrewdly. 'You look shocked. Is the woman well?'

'Mother and infant are well. You have had a baby born in your street.'

'Not the first. Better than a stable, I imagine.'

'Indeed.' He smiled at his grandmother. 'Does anything faze you?'

Old eyes twinkled. 'The way you look at the midwife.'

'Really.' He could believe that. Little escaped his grandmother's eye but now she'd see even more. He didn't comment further but it was something he would have to think about soon. 'Where is Sofia?'

'She has gone to refresh the baby in the guest room.'

'With your permission we will take our leave when she returns. Cleo has a need to change her clothes after her heroics downstairs.'

His grandmother sat back and raised her brows. 'Her heroics? Aren't you the doctor?'

He smiled. 'The mother was giving birth, not undergoing chemotherapy. That's never been my speciality.'

She waved a veined hand. 'In my day, the doctor did everything.' Then she leaned forward. 'Are your emotions truly engaged with this woman?'

'She is Sofia's midwife,' he said evasively.

'That was not what I asked. Have you finally allowed someone to become close to you?'

Footsteps and the topic of their conversation appeared at the door just in time. 'Ah, Cleo. Come in. I was just telling my grandmother how lucky we were to have you here for the birth.'

# CHAPTER SEVENTEEN

CLEO STOPPED AT the door, aware of the raised tension in the room. She'd heard the word for midwife. And she looked a mess. Both occupants were immaculate as they waited for her to enter. She did, slowly, and stopped short of the chair where Doña Luisa sat.

'We were fortunate everything turned out well for all involved.' She looked at Doña Luisa. 'My apologies for my appearance. Alba has been very kind to sponge my dress but I'm afraid...' She trailed off.

Doña Luisa waved that away. 'No need for apologies. Felipe has already been singing your praises.' The older lady's eyes were fixed on Cleo as if looking for something she couldn't quite see.

Sofia returned then, pushing the pram and a sleeping baby, and if Cleo wasn't mistaken it seemed Felipe was very happy at her arrival.

'On that note we will take our leave to return another time,' he said.

Doña Luisa raised her brows but she did look tired. 'Send Sofia to me tomorrow. In the morning, and she may stay with me until siesta.' She glanced at Felipe. 'You and Cleo may return for dinner tomorrow night if I am well enough.'

There was something going on here that Cleo couldn't

grasp. Byplay she didn't understand, and that seemed to include her, between grandmother and grandson that hadn't been evident when they had first arrived. Had she caused that? She hoped not and kept quiet.

Sofia kissed her grandmother's cheek and lifted the baby from the pram. Doña Luisa's face softened as she glanced down at the sleeping infant.

She murmured, 'She is beautiful, like her mother.'

Sofia smiled and said, 'We will see you tomorrow.'


Going back in the car, Sofia seemed pensive. Finally she said quietly, 'She is definitely dying?'

'Yes.' Felipe spoke softly as well, and his sadness underlay the single word. 'But on her terms. She tells me her life has been well lived. And too long, apparently.'

'Is there anything else you can do for her?' Sofia wiped a tear from her cheek.

'She is done with the treatment and now it is time to keep her comfortable. I watch her closely.' Felipe gently touched his cousin's hand.

Sofia lifted her chin. 'I apologise for being difficult when you first found me. She said she asked you to come for me. That she was the one who found out about Terence taking my money.'

Felipe smiled gently at her and Cleo wanted to cheer for his kindness. '*Sí.* But if I had known the extent of his crimes, she would not have needed to ask me. I would have come anyway.'

'I understand.' She looked at Cleo. 'Perhaps my cousin is not quite as horrid as his father was.'

Cleo felt the humour of the situation. And let her eyes travel over the two dark heads, and their identical stubborn chins. She said to both Sofia and Felipe, 'I'm glad for you. If your family can help when somebody lets you down, that is better. And even less reason for me to be here if Sofia is going to be spending more time with her grandmother.'

Maybe she could get away earlier than two weeks, which would be a very sensible thing to do.

Sofia leaned forward and touched Cleo's knee. 'Do not think you can go yet.' A fierce look at her cousin under black brows. 'I don't trust him completely.' But it was said playfully.

'Why not? What can he do? You have your own house.'

This time it was Felipe who laughed, out loud, until his shoulders shook. Sofia stared at her cousin in amazement. 'I had no idea you could do that.'

'Cousin. Please. Cleo will think I am always sour and serious.'

'Imagine.' Sofia rolled her eyes, her tone dry. 'Have you seen him laugh, Cleo?'

Cleo's heart squeezed. She had. They'd laughed quietly together as she lay in his arms, about some silly anecdote she'd told him about her work. Laughed as they'd showered together in her small bathroom. Laughed, standing at the window of her flat, at the antics of the seagulls, the only other creatures awake.

'Now I have,' she said with forced lightness, avoiding the tell, but her cheeks felt hot. Thankfully Isabella chose that moment to stir in the bassinet and Sofia was instantly distracted.

Felipe raised his brows at her pink cheeks and smiled at her until her cheeks heated even more. 'Stop it,' she mouthed.

But inside she warmed as well because some of the instant rapport they'd shared on Saturday night had returned since the birth on the street.

She turned her head quickly to look out the window before her red cheeks caused comment from Sofia, but there was still that full awareness of the man sitting next to her.

His thigh next to hers, though not touching. The warmth of his nearness, the powerful shifts of his body, the scent of his cologne, which she would never forget.

When the baby had settled and peace returned to the rear of the car, Felipe touched her shoulder.

She pulled her thoughts from how she could extricate herself from the mess she'd landed in and looked at him.

'Will you plan an outing tomorrow, now that Sofia will be spending time with her grandmother?'

She was struggling with this shift between them. She didn't know if she had the headspace for tomorrow right now.

'Perhaps. We will see how Isabella is through the night tonight.'

He started to say something then stopped and said, 'Of course.'

He settled back and said no more and she wondered what he had been going to say. Then stopped herself.

The next morning Sofia rose bright and happy and Isabella lay content in her carry bassinet. Cleo had risen each time Isabella had woken in the night and with subtle suggestions Sofia had grown more confident to settle the baby quickly and for longer periods between. Unfortunately, it was harder each time for Cleo to fall back to sleep. The odd way Felipe had watched her after the birth of Elena's baby kept returning to unsettle her; even his voice had changed when he'd spoken to her.

Perhaps she could leave by the end of the week as Sofia was doing so well.

After breakfast, Cleo stood at the upstairs window and watched Sofia and Isabella be driven away by Felipe's driver. Sofia had grumbled a little at it being just eight thirty and Cleo smiled at the early start Felipe's grand-mother had demanded. She was clearly wasting no more time.

Was the house empty of its master? Cleo hadn't seen Felipe leave. Blue skies and sunshine tempted her to see something of the city and be back before lunch. Sofia had cleverly downloaded a taxi app to Cleo's phone so she could summon a lift when she wanted to move about the city.

Cleo liked that idea of the freedom to see what she wished and then to call a driver when she needed to move on.

A knock sounded at the door and, on opening it, Maria handed her a note. She took it reluctantly. Even though she'd never seen his writing before, she knew it was from Felipe.

So he was still at home and she would not escape from him so easily. She really shouldn't be excited by the thought of that but her darned pulse rate had jumped un-mistakably.

'Tea is served in the library,' Maria said, and turned away.

Cleo unfolded the paper.

*I wish to speak to you. F*

She could actually hear her heart beating. Well, that was the end of a quiet sightseeing tour around Barcelona on her own. Maybe he would suggest she wasn't needed any more, which would be the most sensible thing because she was finding it harder and harder not to remember cer-tain intimate moments between them.

She descended the stairs, took a deep breath and opened the library door.

'Good morning, Cleo.'

'Good morning, Don Felipe.'

He raised his brows at her. 'Perhaps if I kissed you every time you called me Don, you would stop doing it.'

She raised her brows back. 'I would stop because if you did that I would not be here to call you anything.'

'I believe that, too.' The smile he gave her made her tingle. 'Did you sleep well?'

'Yes, thank you,' she lied.

'Neither did I.' Matter-of-factly. He smiled broadly at her and it was the first truly open smile she'd seen since her apartment in Coogee. Despite herself, she laughed.

'I'm sorry to hear that.'

He nodded but didn't comment. 'So today, at least until Sofia returns, I would like to spend the morning with you.' There was no question in the statement and she shook her head at his arrogant assumption.

'Not "May I spend time with you?"' The way he was looking at her now made her think that sightseeing was the last thing on his agenda. His tone reminded her of the night they'd first met. The dashing dancer hero, arrogant, overpoweringly handsome, offering her wine and suggesting they take a walk. She'd gone that time, had been a fool once, and doing the same thing in Barcelona while in his employ would be doubly foolish. But she was seriously tempted to blow him a kiss and say yes.

'I have already made plans.' Her voice hadn't sounded as definite as it should have, if she was being honest with him or herself.

'Really?' His brows rose but his smile stayed. He was playing with her. 'What are they?'

Her mind raced as she tried to remember the places she wanted to see. 'I have an app on my phone for the taxis going into the city and I'm going to the Sagrada Familia.'

His face softened. 'Gaudi's most beautiful church is certainly worth a visit. May I come with you?'

'Do I have a choice?' She shook her head again at his cheek but happiness bubbled up and she gave in to it. Why should she miss out on this man's company and his no doubt stellar tourist-guide capabilities? The chance of spending time alone with Felipe made her belly tingle. She was a fool, yes. But a lucky one.

'Of course. But I would like to come with you.' And there he was, giving with one hand and taking away with the other. His handsome face laughing up at hers. Making her sigh with what could have been between them— if only. Spending the day with him would only make it harder to leave him in the end.

'Why aren't you at work?'

'I spent several hours there in the early hours of this morning and I have just returned from there again. I am going back this afternoon.'

She instantly saw the sudden flattening of his mood. Her heart sank. 'Don Raymond?'

'*Sí*. He is at rest now.'

She leaned in and touched his arm. 'I'm so sorry for your loss.'

He looked down at her. 'Thank you. He has told me many times to appreciate his presence and not moan about his departure.'

She smiled but it was very hard. She had the feeling Felipe didn't have too many true friends.

She gave in to the cause of diverting his thoughts. 'What time would you like to leave?'

He looked at his watch. 'The earlier the better. As soon as Carlos returns with the car. The crowds grow large as the day wears on.'

Huge crowds did not sound fun. 'Why is that?'

'In the Sagrada tickets allocate a time to go in but not a time to leave. One could lose a full day inside.'

She nodded. She just needed to collect her handbag. 'Then as soon as possible sounds ideal.'

'Good.' He smiled at her. 'Another day I would like to take you at sunset to see the golden light streaming in through the windows.'

Another day? Was he planning more trips? Instead of asking that, she only commented, 'You sound enamoured of the place.'

'I will tell you that story later.'

Half an hour later they were seated together in the rear of Felipe's car. He touched her hand. 'Today we relax. Not business. Just friends.'

Could she do that? Pretend this Spanish aristocrat was just a friend of hers? Cleo Wren, Australian midwife, sightseeing in Barcelona with Felipe, her sexy flamenco dancer?

This was how they'd started all this. With a dancer she'd found irresistible and a walk, holding hands.

The chemistry between them sizzled and crackled just sitting in the car. His body heat so near to her thigh, his mouth curved and wickedly teasing. His eyes watching hers with a banked desire.

What would a morning of dropping the barriers between them do to their relationship? Or was she too much of a coward to find out?

'We can try,' she said.

When they arrived, parking behind one of the huge tourist buses, Felipe was the one who hopped out swiftly and opened her door, leaving Carlos ready to pull back into the traffic. She guessed he would be picking them up later. So that meant it was just Felipe and her.

The car disappeared around the corner in the rush of traffic and Felipe took her hand and threaded her through the vehicles when the lights turned red on the corner.

He didn't let go of her fingers and the heat from that steady pressure travelled the length of her arm.

'Aren't you afraid people will see you holding my hand?'

'Tourists? No.'

'I thought you are a famous person here?' Indeed, women were already looking at him but not so much with recognition as appreciation.

He smiled at her. 'It is true I know people, and many know me, too, but you are my friend from Australia and what is the use of trappings and responsibilities of wealth if one cannot use them? Also, we have early access to a tourist site.'

He strode to the exit gate. Nodded to the guard and of course they were waved straight in. She wanted to stand outside and gawk for just a moment at the Sagrada before going inside. It was huge. Incredible.

'You come here often?'

He smiled, his eyes amused and also reminiscing about the past. 'My nurse, my nanny who looked after me when I was a child, she brought me many times because it was her Sunday church. She still prays here weekly. Before she worked for us, and afterwards, too, she told me stories of the church. There were many stories. I have a house here she resides in now.'

His face had softened again, a smile reaching to the lines playing around his eyes as he thought back to those times. 'This place gives such peace to the soul, this temple.'

Temple. She savoured his use of the word. The Sagrada

was a temple. Soaring into the sky with ornate towers and the intricate sculpture that seemed to decorate every wall and surface no matter how high or wide she looked. But huge coloured fruit? On top of the towers?

'Come. We will enter from this side instead of the other where the crowds and tour guides are holding their discussions before going inside.' He drew her up the steps, pointing out the apostles and Christ and the myriad stories carved into the stone, and she saw yet another facet of Felipe. The man touched by his childhood church.

He was indeed an enthusiastic Catalonian. Like the dancer she'd first met. Proud and eager to share something he loved with someone who appreciated it. 'I will take you to the other entrance when we come back at sunset another day.'

Then they were inside, and Cleo's breath caught in her throat.

It was as if she stood in the middle of a giant cathedral forest with huge white trees holding up the golden roof of the world. The corded trunks of the enormous central columns reached up, drawing her eyes to the lace of the ceiling. Hundreds of multicoloured windows spilled light into the centre and the people were dappled in shifting leaves of colour. The morning sun painted beams across the floor and the walls and the rows of pews in blues and greens and golds and reds. Her breath caught in wonder.

Oh, my. She held her chest at the wonder of it. 'I wish I could lie on the floor and just gaze up.'

# CHAPTER EIGHTEEN

FELIPE DRANK IN the expression of wonder on her face.
Found just what he'd hoped he'd find. Saw the awe and
the way her eyes caressed the magnificent walls and ceiling of the Sagrada. There was even a glint of tears in her
sapphire eyes.

He watched her crane her head awkwardly, almost
overbalancing, and moved behind her and pulled her back
against his chest to steady her. 'Lean on me. Look.'

And then she was resting against him. His arms came
around her and he held on lightly to her hips, her beautiful hips, his fingers feeling the heat of her curves, soak-
ing in the firmness of bone beneath his hands. He knew
these hips.

The scent of her filled his lungs until his mouth dried
with his need to taste her again. Hot, explicit memories
flooding him of the night neither of them had slept.

God would forgive him for having carnal thoughts in a
holy place. His nanny would be horrified. How could he
have been such a fool to think that he would ever be able
to forget Cleo?

In his defence there had been much he'd needed to do
in his rush back to Barcelona, but he was beginning to realise that even if he had flown back to Spain without her,
another trip to Australia would have happened before too

long. And she would not have slipped away from him because Diego and his Jen were his link to her.

'And you say your nanny used to come here on Sundays for the service?' Her soft voice, still reverent with respect for the beauty around her, broke into his thoughts. Cleo would have been scandalised with his thoughts in this place of God, too. Or maybe not. Perhaps one day he would find out.

'*Sí*. Every week. For the worship.'

'How amazing would that feel. To be a part of a service here.' She sighed and leaned back more firmly against him and the irony of her forgetting she was being held by him, oblivious to the feelings he had for her, mocked his control. Her rapt attention remained on the ceiling and the walls, and every now and then she shifted against him to change the angle of her body and he tried not to groan out loud.

His body responded despite himself, and he had to force his hands to relax against her body. 'A Sunday service? Yes, that can be arranged.' He would do that for her.

Minutes later she whispered, 'I can see why you said those that come inside stay for hours.' She moved her head in wonder and her hair brushed his face. He wanted to take one of the strands in his fingers, roll it around and then kiss it but he inhaled the scent of her instead. As she spoke her body settled more firmly against his.

'It would take days, weeks, perhaps even months of study to observe most of the intricacies inside and out.'

'*Sí,*' he agreed, but he could hear that his voice had grown taut with his need to turn her around and see into the depths of her eyes. To taste her mouth. Flatten her breasts against his chest.

So where could this madness lead?

An affair lasting just a few days? Weeks? Possibly months?

Or to a wonderful life for two people who loved and laughed together?

Or perhaps it might end in a nightmare of a marriage like his parents had suffered. The factor that had kept him single all these years. No. He was not his father— but he also knew that after Cleo's own painful marriage, her freedom was important to her. Her whole world was in Australia.

Could the woman in his arms live in Spain? For ever? With him? He could not live permanently in Australia with all his family responsibilities. Suddenly all the very good reasons why he shouldn't have started this liaison came crashing back.

He gently put her aside and she blinked and focussed again. Stepped another pace back as she realised she'd been held by him and had enjoyed it. Had used him mindlessly as she'd lost herself in the architecture.

As if she had felt utterly safe in his arms.

That made him smile and want to snatch her back. Foolish woman didn't even know when she was in danger.

He cleared his throat. 'In the afternoons the light streams in from the other side. It paints the walls and the floor like this does now, but in different colours.'

Her sigh was long and heartfelt. Filled with wonder. 'It's the most beautiful building I've ever seen,' she said.

'*Sí*. It is a masterpiece.'

She stepped further away from him, saw the tension in his face, but then her eyes strayed again, and he almost had himself back under control despite the 'oh' noise she breathed, and he raised his brows as her gaze came back to his.

She put her hand over her mouth as she noted what her gyrations against him had cost his self-control.

'Your fault,' he teased.

Her face went pink and he enjoyed her consternation.

'Oh. I'm so sorry. I was using you as a leaning post.' Her cheeks grew even pinker and he wanted to touch the warm skin and feel the heat.

'I enjoyed it.' He tormented her, unable to help himself, then took her hand again as they wandered amidst the soaring columns past the tourists and the guides and the security. Occasionally he nodded at someone in the crowd but his attention remained on Cleo.

After another hour he glanced at his watch. 'Is there more you wish to see here today?'

He saw her peer down at her own watch and her beautiful eyes widened. 'Oh, no, you've been very patient.'

'It is no hardship.'

Her face was soft, content, at peace. With her hand in his she said, 'It's beautiful. And I can tell you love it here, too.'

He'd loved being here with her. 'That as well. But perhaps coffee before we head back to pick up Sofia?'

# CHAPTER NINETEEN

WHEN THEY CAME out again into the bright sunshine Cleo couldn't help looking back at the soaring, lacy, over-the-top façade behind her.

The Sagrada's glory stunned her with so many intricate stories woven through the architecture. Surreal in its complex vision and endless in its opportunities to find another story. And then another. And another.

Almost as surreal as allowing herself to plaster her back against Felipe's chest so she could tip her head up. As if her body had been planning the opportunity to lean into him. The solid steel of his arms keeping her balanced. The warmth of his breath against her hair. Good grief, she'd been rubbing herself against him, and he'd let her, welcomed her.

But he'd offered first and somehow she didn't think he'd disliked the opportunity.

Where was this going? Even he must see that the more time they spent together the harder it would be to forget each other afterwards.

There was no winning for either of them in any sort of long-distance relationship, living on opposite sides of the planet. She'd committed to a relationship of unequal standing before. Mark's family had badly wanted him to marry another doctor, not the midwife, and his mother had finally had her way with Mark's new wife. And that had happened in the same city, the same continent. Look where that had left her. Broken and betrayed by a trust she should never have given.

Wouldn't Felipe's important friends and his wider social set expect Don Felipe Gonzales to marry a woman of his own kind?

She couldn't take another betrayal. And this man, a man who'd picked her up and seduced her all in one night, who made the heads of every woman he passed turn and smile, and who could snap his fingers and get any woman he wanted, must be a massive risk to her heart.

What had happened to her decision to be a loner? Rely only on herself? To build a secure and fiscally sound platform that nobody could take away from her?

It would be a huge jump of faith to fall in love with and stay with a man from the other side of the world. Somebody so different culturally, socially, financially... She needed to stop whatever this was between them now.

'Thank you for taking me to the Sagrada. And for being so patient,' she said stiltedly.

He slanted a sideways glance at her, his fingers still firmly intertwined with hers.

The heat in his gaze was making her belly thrum. And his arm brushing against the side of her body was as seductive as all get out. She was having a hard time not leaning into him again. She needed distance or she'd fall against him and make him wrap his arms around her once more.

Hadn't she just had that discussion with herself?

Disaster beckoned. Cleo shook his hand to pull her own free.

He looked at her, let her go then touched her pink cheek with one finger and laughed. Pointed across the park.

'We'll go to that little restaurant there. Sit outside and you can stare at the towers while you drink your coffee.'

'I'd like that.' She would. And then she could calm down. Stop thinking too much about the uncertain future and what might not go right. Take time instead to savour what was going on just at this moment.

She'd wanted to see the sights of Barcelona and he seemed to know instinctively how to improve her experience.

She walked, her empty hand now feeling strangely bereft, and as she did so, she breathed slowly and calmly and settled her raging hormones as best she could. She was probably reading far too much into what had happened.

Perhaps he would have had the same reaction to any woman who'd leaned against him like she'd done. And yet a small voice inside whispered that she did Felipe a disservice.

When they were settled under the leafy green of an overhanging tree she sat back in her chair and gazed across the park at the Sagrada.

'It's such a crazy, wonderful, amazing building. Like the little of Barcelona that I've seen.' And felt. Just like Felipe was wonderful.

He echoed her thoughts. 'Like what is between us?' His voice floated across the tablecloth in a deep, teasing murmur.

Her gaze sprang from the building to his face. 'You think so?'

'I know so.' He pointed to it and then at the two of them. 'Crazy. Wonderful. Amazing.' He repeated the words back at her.

'It's all rather a pickle,' she said softly. Sighed heavily and shook her head as he watched her with a smile playing around his sexy lips.

Before she could think what to say next the waitress reappeared to take their order and saved her.

By the time the orders were taken Cleo wasn't sure whether it would help or create more damage by bringing up the subject of that one night that always seemed to shimmer between them, even here at a small café table in front of the Sagrada.

'So,' he said, and picked up the glass of freshly poured water in front of him, 'in my house…' he sipped, put the glass down, then stared straight into her eyes '…do you think of me when you're in your bed?' Felipe obviously had no qualms about asking such a personal question and she could feel her poor cheeks, the same ones that had only just cooled down, heat up again. For goodness' sake!

His words lifted the hairs on her arms. She could lie. Pretend she was oblivious to his charms, but he would know that was a farce.

Instead she lifted her face to his and held his gaze. Then to pay him back she picked up her own glass, never taking her eyes off him, sipped, and said coolly, 'Why wouldn't I? You're a wonderful lover.'

He didn't smile, like she'd thought he would. She went on in a more serious tone. 'Now I work for you. So I am not the same person who slept with you that night.'

'We did not sleep.'

With that comment her anger and frustration flared. 'What exactly do you want from me, Felipe?'

The waitress arrived with their coffees and hurried off.

He leaned forward, his mouth near hers. 'And that is the best question you have asked all day.'

'Why?' She stirred her coffee briskly and almost threw down the spoon.

'Because it is my question, too, and I do not know the answer.'

She pushed away the small confectionery that had accompanied the coffee, suddenly feeling ill with the loss of something that should have been bright and shiny and filled with promise. Instead it could lead to something sordid, hiding from his grandmother and Sofia. 'There is no answer. I can't risk another night in your bed.' Because it would be an even greater wrench to leave. Even that one night they'd shared had probably spoiled her for anyone else. 'What was between us is impossible here, now and in the future.'

'And yet...' The words hung between them. 'I cannot stop thinking of how much I want you in my bed.'

Heat suffused her. 'In my experience that is not unusual for men.' She stood up abruptly. 'We should go. Your grandmother will need to rest soon and Sofia will need help with Isabella. One of us has to work.'

'I also have to work.' He threw a generous bill on the table and came around the back of her chair but she was already stepping away. Looking left and right as if the car would appear miraculously.

It did. Carlos pulled up right next to them.

Felipe opened the door for her and she scooted across, making room for him to climb in from the kerb. Who cared about those aristocratic women who blocked the door?

Once they were inside, she said, 'I believe Sofia has settled well enough for me to go home at the end of the week.'

He studied her as if trying to see what lay beneath her words. 'Why the sudden need to rush away?'

She stayed on point. Sofia. Always Sofia she should be concentrating on. 'I have nothing to add to her mothercraft skills. She is a natural.'

The car drew around the corner into a street she recognised as his grandmother's and went past the café. Except for a long streak of rubber on the road there were no signs of yesterday's accident.

They stopped in front of Doña Luisa's apartment and Carlos alighted to open Felipe's door. Felipe climbed out and then waited for her to follow.

'I'd like to stay in the car, if that's okay. Your grandmother doesn't need me to stand around while you collect Sofia and Isabella.'

He studied her and she took the opportunity to study him back. She'd ruined the morning, but he didn't seem to hold it against her. 'As you wish. Carlos will stay here.'

With the air conditioner on. She needed cooling down. Felipe walking away gave her the chance to return her breathing and her skin tone to normal. She sat in the car in solitary splendour, avoiding the eyes of the driver in front.

She stared at the plush leather and the wood trim, the cut-outs for glasses and the tiny refrigerator. The uniformed driver at Felipe's beck and call. She would be at his beck and call if she became his mistress. She was out of her league here. He was out of her league and she would not be the Australian plaything until he tired of her.

Because he would undoubtedly tire of her.

She was too far from home.

But then what was at home for her?

Felipe had suggested once that she had the right skills to work in palliative care. Where? For Felipe in the hospice? But where would she live? Could she even work in Spain? Could she shift her focus from general nursing in her medical retrieval job and occasional midwifery at the hospital to palliative care? She had already shifted in some ways with her current work.

Why not? Working side by side with Felipe. Caring for those who needed respectful acknowledgement of their own wishes and being a bridge between grieving families and the celebration of a life that was almost gone.

She stared out the window into the street, watching an older lady dressed in black snap her cane on the footpath as she walked past.

Was her Spanish good enough? This was silly. She had a flat in Coogee. Yet that was not insurmountable. She owned it or most of it anyway and could easily rent it out.

Was she being a coward and losing the chance to really see if she and Felipe had any kind of future?

Why was she so tempted to find out?

She knew why. Because she was falling in love, if she hadn't already fallen in love, with the multifaceted, incredibly wonderful Felipe Gonzales. And why was she fighting it so hard?

Because Felipe would break her if he betrayed her like the last person she trusted had.

She needed to climb onto that plane and head straight back to Australia.

Not plan how to spend more time in Felipe's company. That would surely be the end of her.

There was a tap on the window and she turned, expecting to see Felipe, but instead it was a young man who looked vaguely familiar.

'*Gràcies.*' The man smiled hugely at her and kept nodding. His head had a large bruise in the middle of his forehead.

Ah. Elena's husband from last night. She slipped across to the side of the car and opened the door. 'How is the mother and her baby?' she asked.

'Both well. Both well. *Gràcies.*'

'*De nada.*' She nodded back. 'Congratulations to Elena and to you.' The man smiled again, before moving on.

Felipe appeared beside her, glaring at the man as he

hurried away almost as if he wanted to follow him and demand to know what he was doing.

'He's the husband from last night, remember? Elena and her baby are doing well.'

Felipe's brow cleared. His stiff shoulders relaxed. 'Of course.' Had he been jealous? A little thrill of pleasure ran through her. Did he care enough about her to want to warn off other men? 'I should have told you,' he said. 'I rang the hospital and checked their condition. They must live around here.' His admiring look made her feel warm. 'They won't forget you.'

'Or I them.'

But she thought again of his instant alertness towards the man who'd spoken to her. Surely he hadn't been jealous? Maybe he was just concerned for her safety. But not with Carlos there...

'Where is Sofia?'

'She has decided to stay here with my grandmother. Doña Luisa has deteriorated I think since last night. Perhaps now that the visit she was waiting for has come to pass she can finally relinquish the struggle. Sofia wants to stay with her.'

He circled the car and slipped into the back seat next to her.

So Sofia wasn't coming?

And she, Cleo, Sofia's mothercraft helper, wasn't with her.

What just happened there? she wondered as the car pulled away from the kerb.

'Shouldn't I stay and assist Sofia, if she is staying at your grandmother's?'

'The baby is asleep and my grandmother also is asleep in her chair. Sofia was holding her hand. I think she has realised that there is not much time left.'

Ah. That was it then. She wasn't needed any more. 'I should go home.'

He turned to face her fully. His eyes were dark and determined. 'I would prefer if you did not leave. You still have most of your contract to fulfil. I would be indebted to you if you could settle Sofia into my grandmother's apartment. That is what they both wish now, she tells me, but she will need your help. Especially now.'

He sighed, and now he'd erected a barrier to prevent his emotions showing, but she knew he was preparing himself for the loss of Doña Luisa, the most important woman in his life. 'It is not an easy thing for the uninitiated to understand the finality of death.'

That was true. 'Especially a new mother.'

'I agree.' He smiled slightly but the hint of sadness was back in his eyes, and she wanted to lay her hand on his arm in comfort, but his arm moved away as if he knew what she was thinking. That hurt. Which was a warning she should take heed of.

'I have a proposition for you.' His gaze held hers. 'Would you consider assisting the nurses in the care of my grandmother at the end of her life? Sofia wishes to stay, but it is too much with a new baby, and the actual nursing, she has no idea what that entails, but she wants you with her.'

Cleo frowned.

'It is not what you came here for.' This time he lifted her hand and briefly squeezed her fingers. He was still allowed to touch her, it seemed. His warmth seeped into her. 'Will you do this for our family?'

Not what she had come here for, no, yet she had come to help Sofia. And that young woman's need would be great if she wanted to stay with her grandmother until the end. 'May I have some time to think about it?'

'Of course.' He nodded.

Something in his voice alerted her to a trace of humour. 'I'm not sure I trust the way you said that. How long have I got to decide?'

He smiled at her. 'It will take half an hour for us to arrive at my house, where we are to pack Sofia and Isabella's things. That should be long enough.'

She looked at him exasperatedly. 'Really?'

'I did not arrange this but I can see, if you are willing to be taken advantage of again, how much it will help us all.'

So many reasons for not doing this. The greatest one seated beside her. And perhaps so many reasons to stay if she was brave enough. 'But your grandmother doesn't really know me.'

'She does not know the nurses either and Sofia has told her of your care during her labour.' He shrugged. 'They have cooked this up between them so be sure that my grandmother is choosing to do what she wishes. She is not a woman who pleases other people for the sake of politeness.'

She shook her head at him. 'This suits you, too, though. Doesn't it?'

The glint in his eyes had nothing to do with his grandmother. 'That you are here for an extended time? Yes.'

Was he seeing possibilities between them or did he really believe she would be of benefit to his grandmother and his family? Or both?

She probed further. 'I would be a stranger, looking after your grandmother in her final hours…'

Now he turned serious. 'You are no stranger to me. You are no stranger to Sofia.' He smiled at her and the warmth and depth of his appreciation made her breathless.

'I believe that very shortly you will not be a stranger to Doña Luisa either and she, too, will sing your praises.'

# CHAPTER TWENTY

Now that he had Cleo in Spain he didn't want her to leave again. Hated the thought with a passion that surprised him and yet didn't.

Sofia's request had shocked him but the more he thought about it the more sensible he could see it was.

He loved his grandmother and he wanted her to have the comfort she deserved in her final days. His grandmother's very efficient nurse lacked the heart of the woman beside him.

That his cousin also wanted to be there for the difficult time ahead, losing her grandmother before her eyes, impressed him, and his cousin's common sense in asking for Cleo made him look at Sofia in a new light. She was growing up fast.

'I know this is a lot to ask.' He believed she would do it. He would pay her well, but already he knew that held no factor of influence in her decision.

Cleo leaned back into the chair beside him and closed her eyes for a moment. 'I'll do it. I'll stay. And I will do everything in my power to keep your grandmother comfortable.'

He had no doubt she would. Felt relief wash over him. And not just for his grandmother. For himself, too. 'Thank you.'

'Then I will go home.'

He would worry about the last statement later.

He watched a worried frown cross her face like a small cloud and wanted to smooth the wrinkled skin.

Felipe added, 'I will contact your place of work about the change. Though they will wish to confirm it with you, of course.' He considered how much he was asking her to trust him again.

'And so that you know you can go at any time I will book an open first-class ticket for you to use whenever you wish.'

'Are you reading minds now?'

He laughed. She was a treasure. 'If I were you, I would want those questions answered.'

'Thank you.' Her turn to smile. 'While I am needed and wanted, I accept your terms.'

'Thank you.' He pulled out his phone. 'I will phone ahead and have Maria pack Sofia's luggage. Would you like me to ask her to pack yours, too?'

She shifted in her seat and he saw her discomfort. Despite his usual impatience, he paused. 'I can wait if you prefer to pack your own.'

She smiled at him and it was worth the frustration of standing around when he had so many other things to do.

'I would prefer that.'

He took out his phone and while his conversation with Maria was conducted, he studied her profile.

She chewed on the edge of her lip and he wanted to touch that gentle flesh and tell her to stop but he didn't want to stir up all her reservations again.

She wasn't the only one thinking about how much more difficult this would be when the time came for her to leave. Yet deep inside that feeling of relief continued to spread through him. Tendrils of calm that he recognised came from the presence of the woman beside him.

Perhaps because now he could share the truly heart-breaking goodbye to his grandmother with someone who understood. Strange how he was so sure this was true about a woman he had known for so short a time.

He did not know how he knew but he did. Knew in his heart it was true.

She would be with him when the time came. There was deep comfort in that thought because before Cleo there had been nobody he would have turned to for comfort.

Less than a week ago he hadn't even known that he needed anybody.

The car stopped at the bottom of his stairs and Maria already stood at the door with the first of the luggage. He would go to his office and arrange the things he'd promised Cleo he would arrange. Hopefully, by the time he had done that she would be ready to go.

# CHAPTER TWENTY-ONE

HALF AN HOUR later Cleo walked down the steps of Felipe's palatial home and wondered if she would ever see it again.

When she got to the bottom, instead of sliding straight into the car, she stopped and turned back. The footman put her small case in the boot and then disappeared around the side of the house.

Above her, the stairs reached steeply to the front door, the windows glinted above and to the right of the façade on the second floor she could see the room that had been hers with a small balcony that had looked over Barcelona.

She'd be living down amidst all those buildings and people for the next little while before she went home to Australia.

She didn't like to put a time limit on it, but she was thankful to be able to stay a little longer, thankful that she could help these people who had come into her life like brilliant comets and would no doubt shoot out again just as quickly when all this was over.

She thought about this morning with Felipe at the Sagrada, was fiercely glad she'd have that time to look back on later, but playing this game with the dancer Felipe was over.

She thought about Sofia's confident mothering but also the young woman's need to have a sounding board, seeing as she was without a partner to be that support person.

Yes, there was still some need for her there.

And she thought about Doña Luisa facing life's greatest challenge and what she could do as a silent pillar of support for others. Surprisingly she felt at peace about her choices.

None of this was about her.

So that meant none of this was about Felipe either.

It was all about Doña Luisa and Sofia creating memories that would carry the young mum through the next weeks, months and years of remembering her grandmother.

She turned back to the car. Felipe, already seated in the back, offered her a quick smile. 'Your place of work has agreed. They will email you, and your flight has also been arranged.'

'Thank you.'

'*De nada.*' Then he returned his attention to studying his phone. He didn't speak and she was glad of that.

She had her own thoughts to occupy her.


A short time later, when they arrived at the apartment in the city, they were met at the door by Alba, who seemed perhaps a few degrees warmer than she had been on Cleo's first visit.

'I'll see you in a few minutes.' Felipe went on ahead to see his grandmother.

Alba directed Cleo to her room. 'Señorita, Sofia and the infant are across the hall from you. Doña Luisa's room is at the end of the hallway.'

The room she was shown to seemed too large, filled with light, and had two open slatted doors as well as the tiniest balcony. A small round table and one spindly chair had been squeezed onto the balcony overlooking the street.

Carlos deposited her cabin bag at the door and carried the rest into Sofia's room.

Alba opened a connecting door to a generous private

bathroom tiled in green and gold, with a sink with gold taps similar to the one she had washed in after Elena's baby's birth.

'Thank you, Alba. How is Doña Luisa?'

Alba scowled. 'She is resting. The nurse has left her exhausted from washing her. I would do better than that lump.'

Goodness. Not a reassuring reference from Alba. 'And Miss Sofia?'

'In the library, talking to the woman.'

'Thank you.'

Alba nodded and left. Cleo considered if there would be more help for Alba in running the house if two more guests were added to her workload. Cleo could lift some of that load, too, if she was allowed to. But first she wanted to talk to Sofia and the nurse.

She quickly unpacked, hung her few things in the wardrobe and slid her small toiletries case into the bathroom, then tied back her hair and washed her hands. It was time to see what she could do to help. If possible, she'd like to slide discreetly into the household without alienating anyone. They'd had disruptions enough.

She could hear the nurse before she saw her. Her voice held an aggrieved tone as she gesticulated to Sofia and waved in the direction of the kitchen.

When Cleo arrived, the nurse, a tall, uniformed, big-boned thirty-something Spaniard with dark hair and an unsmiling mouth, did not appear pleased to see her.

Cleo tried not to feel depressed at her unwelcoming stare.

Cleo smiled and held out her hand. '*Bon dia.* Do you speak English?'

'Yes.'

'Hello, then, I'm Cleo.' She held out her hand and reluctantly the woman took it. 'I was Sofia's midwife and am now her guest. You are Doña Luisa's nurse?'

The woman nodded curtly. 'I am Rhona. They say you are to help me?'

'Lovely to meet you, Rhona. I understand Doña Luisa is not well today?'

'She is failing. There was much excitement yesterday. Today she is happy to sleep.' A hard stare. 'Don Felipe tells me you are to help.'

'I am here to support Sofia, who wishes to help. Between the three of us I'm sure we can make Doña Luisa comfortable and feel cared for, without exhausting Sofia, as a new mother, as well. Don't you agree?'

'Oh, yes. I see.' A lot of the starch left Rhona at that. Gently, Cleo asked, 'I'm sure you have much experience nursing terminal patients at home?'

'Not in the home, no, but in the aged care hospital.'

Cleo smiled. 'Aged care is a special field. You must be very caring.'

Rhona unbent another fraction. 'It is important to remember that one day this will be yourself at the mercy of the nurse. And act accordingly.'

'I couldn't agree more. I am a midwife and nurse, so I understand when someone we are caring for is vulnerable and needs reassurance and the support of others.

'Would you agree, Sofia?'

'I know it helped me to have you there.' She nodded. 'Even though you couldn't take the pain or do the work of labour, I never felt afraid. This is what I hope to share with my grandmother.'

The last of Rhona's stiffness left her. '*Sí.* This is what I wish, too.' She sighed and looked at Cleo. 'I accept your help and the support of Nurse Sofia as we all care for Doña Luisa.'

Then, almost shyly, 'It is true I found her weakness made the work much heavier this morning. Perhaps it would be more gentle on her to have assistance when she cannot help herself.'

'And I will be a support for Sofia as she sees for the first time the transition from life to death.'

The nurse stared at her as she thought about that.

'Yes. That, too, is a good thing.' She dipped her head. 'I'm sorry I was not more welcoming.'

'You have nothing to apologise for. Thank you for your understanding of my presence.'

Felipe entered the room at that moment and Cleo searched his face for signs of distress or concern. He looked tired but not cast down. As an oncologist he would see this often. But as a grandson this was a first, and a tragedy. 'She wishes to see you, Cleo.'

Cleo glanced at Rhona and the woman waved her in.

'I will eat and drink tea and then perhaps we can make her more comfortable when next we reposition her.'

Felipe escorted Cleo back along the magnificent hallway past paintings and priceless objects to the darkened room. He paused outside the door. 'I have no idea how you did it but I do believe Rhona likes you. The nurse certainly seems more than resigned to your arrival now.'

'We are all here for the same reason. To care for your grandmother to the best of our ability.'

He smiled. 'Still, you have done well to smooth feathers that my grandmother said were very ruffled.' He gestured with his head towards the door and lowered his voice even further. 'There has been a rapid decline but perhaps it is as the nurse says and she is simply exhausted from all the excitement yesterday.'

He smiled in reminiscence. 'She was very excited to

meet the baby and have Sofia back in Spain. You have helped there, too.'

'I'm glad. Are you coming in with me?'

'No. Go alone. I will wait out here.'

The darkened room of Doña Luisa held the scent of lavender and the aroma of candle smoke. The smoke came from a small altar with two candles and a gilt-framed image of Jesus.

Cleo hadn't thought about the Catholic significance of terminal illness in Spain but she should have. She could see how that would be a large part of Doña Luisa's transition out of this world.

As a non-Catholic she'd have to ask Felipe or the nurse later if there was anything she needed to be aware of regarding Doña Luisa's religious needs. Perhaps the emergency number of her priest as well.

She passed further into the room and saw the papery skin and yellow tinge of Doña Luisa's skin against the pillow. Her breath caught and she eased it out discreetly. The physical change from a woman who'd walked with a stick to one lying in a bed barely able to raise herself up on her elbows was stark.

'Come closer, so I can see you.' Doña Luisa's feeble voice called her towards the bed.

There was an ornate but strategically placed chair so Cleo sat, creating enough space not to crowd Doña Luisa but close enough for easy conversation.

A swathe of silver hair lay tucked into one side of her pale face. Lines of tiredness—she didn't think they were of pain—were etched deeper into her cheeks.

'Good afternoon, Doña Luisa. Is there anything special you would like me to do?'

The older woman huffed out a small laugh. 'You seem

to be achieving what needs to be done. There is nothing wrong with my hearing and my grandson thinks you've calmed the nurse.'

On that tart note she closed her eyes. With eyes still shut, she said, 'I am glad you are here to help my family. To help Sofia, but most of all to help my grandson. When I am gone, he will have no one he allows close.'

Cleo didn't know what to say to that. She didn't think he allowed her close either.

'He watches you constantly. Do not discount the power you have to help him.' Then she sighed.

'My wash tired me. Rhona means well but she pulls me around like a sack. You will help her be more gentle.' Another sigh. 'I will sleep and talk with you later. The pain medication makes me drowsy.'

'Do you have pain at the moment?'

'No. It has left for the time being.'

'Good.' Cleo assessed the sheets pulled up to the pale chin and noted the freshness and precision of the tucking in. Signs of an old-school nurse.

Though Doña Luisa's tidily brushed hair and the lingering soapy smell of lavender attested to the thoroughness of the sponge bath, a little looseness in the sheets and perhaps a chink of gentle light would be good. She'd suggest that diplomatically later. For the moment there was nothing she could do except let her sleep.

Seeing Felipe's grandmother surrounded by the things she loved, comfortable and fresh, with her family in attendance was comforting to everyone as well as for Doña Luisa. It must be helpful to know all the resources she needed were here and there was no reason to move to a hospital for the end unless she wanted to.

Cleo rose. 'Rest well.' But the woman in the bed was already asleep.

Sofia and Felipe waited for her outside the door. The young mum was leaning on the wall while absently patting her baby's bottom. She straightened when Cleo came from the room. 'How is she?'

'Tired. She's sleeping.'

'How could she have gone so quickly downhill?' Sofia asked.

'Sometimes it is the way,' Felipe said quietly.

'And she tells me there is nothing wrong with her hearing so I shall move away from her door.' Cleo drew them with her and smiled. 'Your grandmother is still seeing humour in the world. I hope I have the chance to know her more fully before she chooses to leave us.'

'As I do,' he said as they all moved to the main rooms. Felipe glanced at his watch. 'I must go.'

And that was that. It shouldn't have shocked her, but it did. Had she become so used to him being around?

Of course he had to go.

'I will be back tonight around seven to see my grandmother.'

This wasn't his house and he had a life. Hers was here for the next week or two. Then she would go home.

# CHAPTER TWENTY-TWO

ALL AFTERNOON AT the hospice Felipe's thoughts returned to his grandmother's apartment in the city centre. Concerned for his grandmother, for Sofia and also for Cleo.

Had he been fair to Cleo to ask her to remain? Had he asked too much of a woman he had known for so little time? Yet he felt he knew her better than others he had known for years. Felt he could see to the heart of her and knew with certainty she would care for his family at this time.

And into the future, but that was for later.

He did not doubt that if anyone could ensure his grandmother's comfort and the tranquillity of the carers around her it would be Cleo. He was using her, but she didn't seem to mind. Because she gave freely to others, that was her way, as she had given herself to him, and he was learning that one day soon he would give himself to her.

Even his cousin Sofia had surprised him. She held depths he'd not only underestimated but had failed to appreciate before.

Perhaps he was more like his father than he'd thought. Looking at members of his family as problems that needed to be solved instead of as people who needed to be considered and listened to for their wishes.

He had friends, of course, but none now who were close except perhaps Diego, but he had left Spain years ago. He had colleagues at his hospice, people who admired his work, but apart from Raymond, a man he'd shared medical school with, he had allowed very few people to get close to him. He had many acquaintances but no confidants.

Except he'd told the midwife things that he'd told no one else. That very first night in Australia.

Why was that?

Perhaps because at first he'd known he'd never see her again and some magic about her had encouraged openness. It had felt surprisingly good to be so candid with someone for once. Such was her charm. But he'd quieted his reluctance to share by saying he would leave and never see her again.

And how had that worked for him?

He almost laughed out loud. Who would have believed that a woman he'd met in an unguarded moment would change his views on life so much and become such an integral part of his life, and his family's lives, in so short a time?

And his grandmother fully approved of her. The last thing he had expected from a woman who had been parading aristocratic Catalonian women in front of him for years.

Enough of these deep thoughts.

He was better here, working while his *àvia* slept for a few hours. Waiting for a phone call in case his grandmother's condition changed, seeing to other patients' needs and grieving families, daily staff and administrative issues that had piled up in his absence, Felipe worked steadily to free himself from the overload, and in between short conversations with Alba to check he prayed for his grandmother.

When he returned to his grandmother's apartment just before five that evening the lift doors opened to the faint strains of 'Nights in the Gardens of Spain' by Manuel De Falla. The recording had been one of his grandmother's favourites but he hadn't heard it played in her apartment for years.

The volume was turned so low it was almost a murmur but the whispering orchestra added an undercurrent of life and soul into the darkness of the approaching night.

Alba's mouth twitched when she saw he recognised the music, though her eyes were sad. 'The priest has been. And now the baby has been lying next to her,' she said.

Felipe followed her silently to the door of the darkened bedroom, where he leaned against the frame. He could hear his grandmother's laboured breathing but the scene was peaceful.

Alba slipped away, no doubt to the kitchen.

In the corner the nurse sat knitting and back from the bed. Cleo reposed calmly, with hands crossed, almost unobtrusive in the gloom, reading a small book.

In the background the subtle whisper of the music flowed over them all.

On her bed his grandmother lay on her side, packed with pillows for comfort, her face soft and relaxed, and beside her lay Isabella, one small arm free from her blanket, a tiny starfish hand clasped around her great-grandmother's finger.

The baby's eyes were wide open, and next to her on the pillows on the other side of the bed, Sofia lay asleep.

The room resonated with a gentle flow of breathing from the players in the tableau and Felipe felt serenity seep into him even though he stood on the fringes.

As if she sensed him, Cleo turned her head to meet his eyes. She smiled and the cares of the day blew from his shoulders like leaves in the wind.

He nodded his appreciation of the ambiance of the room and moved to leave them to it.

Silently Cleo stood and gestured for him to take her seat.

He waved her away but she shook her head and walked towards him, her eyes on his face. She touched his arm as she passed. 'Please, sit,' she said quietly. 'Savour the moments you deserve to share more than anyone, for they are beautiful.'

Then she walked from the room and his grandmother woke and turned her head slightly to see him. Her smile was a gift he'd almost missed.

He went closer and leaned over, kissed her cool cheek. 'Good evening, my little grandmother,' he said softly.

'It is,' his grandmother whispered as she closed her eyes and smiled. He thought she'd gone to sleep, but without opening her eyes she said, 'Thank you for bringing them to me. All of them. They are blessings.'

Her breathing became heavier but the smile remained and she soon dropped into a deeper sleep again.

He sat with her for another half an hour until the baby had fallen asleep, too, the quiet clacking of the nurse's knitting needles rhythmically soothing, not something he would have thought possible in connection with Rhona.

Cleo came to the doorway and patted her stomach, pointed to him enquiringly.

Yes, he could eat. Perhaps like a horse, because he hadn't stopped for anything since midday, and now his appetite had returned with a vengeance. He glanced at the nurse, who nodded that she would stay, and followed this amazing woman he had found across the world through to the dining room. His gaze was drawn from watching the way Cleo walked to his grandmother's empty chair.

He knew his *àvia* would not be sitting there regally to chastise him ever again.

# CHAPTER TWENTY-THREE

CLEO WAITED AT the door for him to join her and when he glanced at the empty winged chair in the formal lounge she knew the direction of his thoughts. Her heart ached for him.

'Your grandmother says she feels less strong tonight,' she said. 'But there have been many moments today when we enjoyed listening to her reminiscences.' She smiled at him. 'She is a wonderful woman.'

'She is.'

'I hope you know that many of her memories centre around you. You've given her great joy.'

He inclined his head and waited for her to sit. She did but glanced up at him as he moved to his own chair. He looked so solemn and she remembered his grandmother's wish, uttered so frequently, that he should not be cast down.

She thought of the small poetry book his grandmother had asked Alba to find and give to her. She wondered if she should tell him about it.

The pages held children's poems and Doña Luisa had said maybe one day she would read them to her own children and remember her. It was a battered book, and hadn't looked valuable, so she had accepted it in the spirit with which it was offered and thanked her. Before she could mention it, Alba carried the dishes in and set them on the table.

'Just the two of us?' He looked questioningly at the empty places.

She nodded. 'The nurse has already had her meal and Alba has put away something for Sofia when she wakes.'

'Of course, you are aware of all that goes on. You astound me.' He studied her, his eyes warm, the way they seemed to be all the time when he looked at her now. When had that changed? she wondered. Perhaps since the baby was born in the street?

He said, 'Are you a chameleon that fits into any background? You've only been here two days.'

'Everyone has been very kind.' She shook her head. 'You've missed all the fun. We have been told many secrets by your grandmother. I think Sofia will never be overawed by you again, especially after hearing of your exploits as a child.'

His smile was half-hearted. 'None of it is true.'

'Sorry.' She shook her head. 'But I believe your grandmother.'

He raised his hand ruefully and she saw a little lightening of his seriousness. 'I don't want to know what she told you. No doubt Sofia will share inappropriately later.'

Then his face changed. 'I take that back.' He frowned at himself. 'I believe I haven't appreciated Sofia enough. That will alter when I know my cousin more in the future.'

'I'm glad,' Cleo said simply. 'She's amazing. So good with the baby. So good with your grandmother.' She waggled her brows. 'And you were very good to have saved her from that man.'

He even smiled at that. 'Not what Sofia said at the time.' Then he sighed. Solemn again. 'I should have been aware of her danger earlier but that is for another time...' He turned to her and shook his head. 'I can't believe the difference I saw, walking in here tonight. Thank you, Cleo.'

Cleo felt the sting of tears and fought hard to keep them from overflowing, which they could so easily do. The last few hours had come at a cost and she was weary, but the night could prove a long one yet.

She'd be surprised if Doña Luisa saw the sun rise tomorrow.

Her greatest concern now was for this man. He loved his grandmother dearly. She'd come to realise that. She could see his needs but was trying desperately not to heighten her own feelings for someone she might still have to leave.

When she didn't answer he said, 'What you've achieved here is a priceless gift that I can never repay.'

Her brow furrowed. 'You say that as if this organising of me being here for your grandmother is not your right.' She looked away and then thought of all the people this man helped. The insights from meeting his staff. Their love for him. The stories from his grandmother of his kindness to her. She understood him better now. Some things she'd seen for herself, some things she'd been told by others, and some things she just knew in her heart were true.

Couldn't he see? Or was he too used to keeping most people at arm's length? She remembered their first night together. Was it because his father had told him at seven not to hinder the family with his emotions as if he didn't deserve to be loved?

'You're a man who has dedicated your adulthood to creating support and quietude at the end of people's lives. If I can go some small way to providing that serenity for you here, then it is only what you deserve, and what your grandmother deserves.' She felt that with every fibre of her being. 'It is a privilege to be able to help your family. It's not a favour, Felipe.'

He looked a little stunned. 'I…' He stopped, but in the end he nodded his head and said simply, 'Thank you.'

She continued, 'I will relieve the nurse soon. Sofia has sat with your grandmother most of today. I rested before you came home. I'll do the night shift and watch her overnight.'

'There is no need. I will stay with her.'

'Of course.' She smiled at him. Exactly what his grandmother had said he would say. 'But either the nurse or I would like to be there as an assistant if needed. It is your grandmother who requested that you have support.'

He pushed his plate away. 'I don't need support.'

'I have no doubt. I'm also hoping that you will allow me to unobtrusively follow her wishes. If that is acceptable to you.'

He looked at her from under dark brows. 'Don't use your cajoling ways on me.'

She opened her eyes wide. 'I wouldn't dream of that, Don Felipe.' She remembered too late that he'd said he would kiss her every time she called him that.

He raised his brows at her, another brief flash of humour, but then it faded.

She added, 'I'll be dozing in the corner and no nuisance to you.'

'And if I refuse to be babysat?'

She smiled. 'Then I will leave your grandmother to explain her wishes—which I'm sure she will when she wakes and finds you there alone.'

Which was how it came about that in the early hours before dawn, in that time of transition between worlds when Doña Luisa's breathing changed, that Cleo was there with Felipe. Briefly Cleo slipped away from the room.

'Sofia,' she said. The young woman looked up with

startled eyes from where she was feeding her daughter and then she stilled.

'It is time?'

'Almost, I think. Would you like to take Isabella and kiss your grandmother's cheek in farewell?'

Sofia nodded and, carrying Isabella, she went in and said her last farewells beside Felipe, who sat very still in the dark.

Then Sofia touched his shoulder and left the room, tears streaming down her face. She leaned against the wall outside the door so she could sob quietly, out of her grandmother's hearing.

This brought Alba, whom Cleo had also woken at the woman's request.

Then, as per his grandmother's instructions, she stood beside Felipe as he held his grandmother's hand.

She knew she hadn't come uninvited because one unintentionally imploring glance he'd cast over his shoulder when she'd returned said how much he appreciated her support.

This was the woman who had raised him, loved him when his father wouldn't, had been his mentor and his mother, and he was losing her.

The gap between each indrawn struggling breath grew greater, and the rise of her thin chest grew less, and then the cycle began again. They both knew the outcome and waited patiently. Felipe sat bowed with his hand in his grandmother's and Cleo stood behind him, her hand on his shoulder, until finally Doña Luisa Gonzales breathed her last.

'She has gone,' he whispered, and dropped his head to kiss the still hand beneath his.

'She will always be with you. Love is like that.'

* * *

Cleo and Sofia didn't move back to Felipe's house the next morning, though the funeral was set for four days later. Against her better judgement Cleo had agreed to stay until then.

Sofia spoke to Felipe about interviewing staff to open her house again while Cleo was there to help but he offered his cousin full access to Doña Luisa's apartment if she wished to live in the city. Sofia had been stunned but gratefully accepted the generous offer.

This way, Alba, who was lost and uncertain and grieving for her mistress, would have a new focus, to help care for Sofia and Isabella's daily needs for as long as she wished.

Cleo had seen little of Felipe, who had disappeared into Doña Luisa's office with the solicitor the first day and later with the priest to make the arrangements for the funeral. He'd then gone home to his own house after a brief goodbye.

She told herself that the distance he created between them was what she'd expected to happen. He had no need for her now. Like her husband had had no need for her when he'd found a richer, shinier woman.

But it was too late. She loved him. Had been in love with him since that first night they had lain together in her bed in Coogee, despite her denials.

He'd captured her heart by his absolute wonder in her. Their connection, though she'd tried to pretend it had just been sex, had pierced her in a way she doubted any man would be able to do again.

She wished she hadn't agreed to stay for the funeral, damn it, but Sofia had begged her not to leave yet.

They didn't see him at all the next day, though he rang

and spoke to Alba and a note had come in Felipe's bold writing inviting her to lunch on the day prior to the funeral.

She'd assumed that Sofia and Isabella would be joining them.

On the day before she left Barcelona, the day she was to lunch with Felipe, Cleo woke to a brilliant blue Catalonian sky and shafts of golden light that reflected off the many mirrors and onto the ornate ceiling.

In two days she would be home at her Coogee flat, where her life would be a far cry from the elaborate halls of this city apartment or the grandeur and soaring ceilings of Felipe's mansion on the hill.

At the breakfast table a huge, barely open, long-stemmed rosebud sat to the side of both her and Sofia's plates. 'And what is this?' she asked Alba when the maid came back in with the coffee.

Alba, too, was wearing a small red rose in her buttonhole.

'April the twenty-third in Barcelona is Lovers' Day.' Alba smiled. 'Everyone gives roses. Traditionally it was the man giving a rose to his true love, and her giving him a book. Nowadays everybody gives roses, not only to lovers but to family and colleagues... It's a beautiful day!'

'Like Valentine's Day?'

'Perhaps. If you go into the city, all the stalls in the city centre will be selling roses. Sofia and I are going for a walk this morning with Isabella in the pram to see them.'

'I thought Sofia was coming to lunch with Don Felipe and me?'

'Not today,' she said, and unsuccessfully hid her smile. 'He will come at twelve and you must wait here for him.' The look she gave Cleo said clearly that she was not to go down on the street where she could get into any mischief, such as finding babies to be born.

They'd be alone?

In a town full of rose stalls?

With lovers everywhere?

Could it get any worse, with an ache in her heart that she would have to hide and her wanting more? Dreading his friendly dismissal of what had grown between them?

She had thought they had grown closer recently. Much closer. But it seemed that had been wishful thinking on her part. Apart from the note, he'd not even spoken to her since his grandmother's passing.

Once Cleo's duties were done. Her assistance given. His needs met.

But it was too late for her. She'd let her guard down, had foolishly begun to think maybe Felipe wanted more, wanted her in his life. She'd even dreamed, tentatively, of the future, but that had been before he'd distanced himself from her.

He had no need of her now.

He didn't care for her like she cared for him.

Felipe had never promised her a future.

Perhaps when she returned home it would pass. Love at first sight was impossible. Wasn't it?

Why was everything so tragic? She needed to go home and she couldn't. Not until after the funeral.

Perhaps she should just accept the last time she would be with Felipe alone…she laughed bitterly at that…with a chauffeur, and savour her small slice of time with him to keep for ever. As long as she expected nothing.

The way he had stayed away the last couple of days had made it clear she'd done her job and she could go now. So much for a connection.

But deep inside a tiny flicker of forlorn hope refused to be extinguished. He had held her hand at the Sagrada. He had smiled at her with warmth and appreciation and wanted to see her happy. Today was their last chance. Tomorrow would be a formal occasion and then she would be gone.

She would know when he arrived.

Would he be her warm Felipe or would he be the grim-visaged aristocrat with the solid walls of formality around him?

Despite Cleo's preference to wait for Felipe downstairs, at twelve she sat in the formal lounge in her white dress, which Alba had restored to its former pristine state...and breathed.

Breathing was good. Mindful. Calming.

'A penny for your thoughts.'

She jumped. 'I must have been daydreaming. I didn't hear the lift.'

He inclined his head. 'You look lovely.'

'You look very elegant yourself.' He always did. No matter that he wasn't formally dressed, anyone could tell he was an aristocrat. 'Where are we going?'

'We will drive around the city to show you the sights as we have kept you too busy.' So the Felipe she got was the noble showing the visitor his city. His Barcelona. His tone was formal. Not like the Felipe in Australia or the Felipe at the Sagrada. Austere.

He had said she looked lovely. But her tiny fledgling hopes of softness, of closeness between them died. 'You haven't kept me too busy.'

Sightseeing with him acting like this wasn't attractive anyway. 'Though thank you.' She allowed herself to be ushered into the lift, but she already felt like a burden to him, merely a task he felt he needed to complete.

She wished she could just get on the plane today.

He stood beside her, so tall and handsome, and she was having trouble not touching his arm, just one touch, but he was incredibly formal. Aloof. The aristocrat he was through and through, and she realised with despair that she was so not the woman for him. She should have known that. She had known that.

His reserve dashed her mood and made her want to turn back. The faint drift of his cologne teased and she wished she'd dabbed herself liberally with her own scent to drown his out. She should never have come.

He handed her into the car, past Carlos at the door, and sat back. At least Carlos seemed friendlier.

On the seat in front of her, where Sofia had sat so many times, was a huge bouquet of long-stemmed, glorious red roses.

He sat next to her. 'They are for you.'

'Lovely,' she said, trying to smile. 'But we are not lovers.' Oh, Lord, why had she said that?

# CHAPTER TWENTY-FOUR

FELIPE OPENED HIS eyes wide at her flat voice. 'The roses, it is a tradition.' She didn't like roses? She'd seemed to like the ones growing at his house. 'They can also be between colleagues, even friends, and I hope I may have at least grown towards that standing with you?' Felipe was at a total loss. He'd expected her to display pleasure. Given him one of her beautiful smiles. Perhaps a kiss, or maybe that would have been too much to hope for.

He could read nothing on her face. But her mood was odd. Funny how he had trouble sensing the moods of others but with Cleo he could tell straight away when something wasn't right. He knew his nervousness to make this right today made him seem less approachable, almost grim, but he couldn't help that. He was damnably tense. On edge to do this in a way she would remember. So much depended on her answers.

'They're beautiful,' she said. But there was a lack of enthusiasm in her tone he didn't normally associate with Cleo. Was he wrong? Did she not care for him at all?

This armful of roses had been a romantic gesture prior to walking her in Gaudi's beautiful Park Güell and asking her to stay in Spain.

To ask her to allow him to take the time to court her

properly. To discuss the obstacles and how they would surmount them together.

To propose marriage to her so soon after his grandmother's passing was too fast even for him—but he had come today to at least begin.

The wall between them had never been as formidable as it was now. Or was that because he so desperately wanted to break it down?

Or, more damning, was it that now she actually had her ticket home she was already gone in her thoughts? 'Is something wrong, Cleo?'

This outing was so important and yet it seemed doomed already. Already the distance between them grew wider.

'I'm tired.' She did look weary and he cursed himself for not checking on her over the last two days. 'It's been a very emotional week.' She finally looked at him. 'You must be too exhausted to play tour guide.'

That stung a little. 'I am not playing.' Nothing frivolous now, that was for sure. Though he had planned a few lighter moments that he'd thought she would appreciate.

'Like you weren't playing at being a flamenco dancer?'

He frowned at her. 'I was not playing then either. In my soul lives such a man. I thought you knew that.'

Silence. He tried a new tack. 'But that is not what I wanted to talk to you about.' Something had gone very wrong at the outset and his plans were failing fast.

'What do you want to talk to me about, Felipe?' Her tone wasn't encouraging and he wished he could take her back to the house and start again with this day. He'd thought to take her for a walk in the Park Güell with a picnic basket, and share their first kiss since far too long ago. But already he knew his plans were ashes at his feet.

'Perhaps you would consider moving to Spain and working with me at the hospice?' he said, far too abruptly. That had been one of the strategies he'd thought might interest her if she decided to stay. Stated alone, without context, it seemed overly demanding and even he had heard the harshness in his tone.

She froze. 'In what capacity?'

'I once said I could imagine you at the Hospice Luisa.' He softened his tone. Tried to make her see his vision for the future—but only if it was her vision, too. He tilted his head to study her. 'I said I could see you as one who stands at the gate and comforts those going and those who must say goodbye.'

Like she had just done so admirably for his sweet *àvia*.

She shook her head. 'No. I can't.'

'But what if you were a teacher of the gatekeepers? The mentor? Someone who shared those skills that I saw so eloquently in my grandmother's household?'

'No.' Vehemently.

He found himself pulling back from her strong denial. The word sounded like a death knell to all his hopes.

She turned away. 'This is what you wanted to talk to me about?'

'One of the things. That and perhaps moving in with Sofia.' The last thing he'd thought of when he'd realised that asking her to stay with him in his house as he courted her was not fair to either of them. But really he was floundering against her reserve.

He was very afraid now that if he mentioned love to her she would open the door and get out of the moving car.

How could he have got it so badly wrong?

Surely she wasn't immune to him? That day at the Sagrada. Her warmth and compassion in the early hours of the morning his grandmother had passed. Their one incredible night together in Sydney had affected her, he already knew that. She'd told him so on his jet.

Every day since he'd let her in a little more, accepted his need of her, his love for her, until she took up space in his world and was embedded firmly in his heart.

But perhaps he had got it wrong. Perhaps his grand-mother, too, had got it wrong—though that would be a first.

Or, more likely, he felt a little of the tension in himself ease at the thought, he had simply rushed his midwife and spoiled everything.

All was not yet lost. It was just today that was lost.

That he could believe. All he could do was retreat and regroup and approach her again later. But he would not give up. If he had to follow her to Australia, then he would. He would never believe she was immune to him.

But if she left, and he followed, and she said no, then he would have to believe she did not have emotions towards him. Emotions he had seen with his own eyes—and that he shared for her.

'Have I been thoughtless in proposing we meet up today? While you are probably still tired?' He resisted the urge to grip his hair and pull it in frustration. Could he do nothing right with this woman? 'But I knew tomorrow at the funeral it would be impossible for us to talk before you left.' She didn't comment and he accepted his mistake. There is no hurry, he told himself. Give her time.

'Would you like me to take you back to the house?'

'Yes, please.'

# CHAPTER TWENTY-FIVE

CLEO'S LAST DAY in Barcelona dawned dismal and dreary, like the face she saw in the mirror.

Outside, later, the sky hung leaden like her mood and the wind had a cool bite as she waited for the second black car that would carry her, Sofia and Isabella to the funeral.

A taxi would take her to the airport straight afterwards.

Her small bag was packed beside her and the tickets printed for the journey home. Tickets found also on her phone, because she liked to have the paper copies as well for extra insurance.

She'd more than fulfilled her commitments to all of the Gonzales family and she wanted to leave as soon as possible.

Even Doña Luisa's insistence that she be there for Felipe had been completed. She'd done so well there that, well, he'd offered her a job in his hospice.

Gee, thanks.

Stupid her, wishing for more. She'd known a long-term relationship with Felipe had been a dream, but one look at the distant man who'd come to take her to lunch yesterday and she'd known he'd been lost to her.

He'd looked almost afraid she was expecting more from him than he wanted to give.

She'd been afraid he'd offer her a monetary bonus for loving them all. That would have hurt as well.

On the drive back he'd barely spoken to her, though he had caught her arm as she'd gone to get out at the apartment. 'Please, take the roses. I want you to have them.'

She'd taken them, to make him feel better. Even though they'd made her feel worse. Had buried her face in the red velvet petals in the lift as her tears had dripped onto the mosaic floor. Thank goodness nobody had been home.

He'd promised her nothing and she had no right to be disappointed that this was how it ended.

Oh. Yes. Except for the opportunity to work at the hospice and remain as a companion to Sofia.

The funeral was held in the cathedral in the centre of Barcelona and the huge church was almost full. The rows of dignitaries and heads of state felt overwhelming to Cleo. Felipe and Sofia sat in the first pew and slotted in perfectly with all the exalted personages.

Cleo fitted perfectly at the back with Alba and Rhona and Carlos.

But when the long, traditional service was done with much pomp and ceremony it wasn't over yet. Sofia had asked Cleo to go to the graveyard with her and reluctantly she'd agreed.

She could leave for the airport from the cemetery but she could not go to the wake. Enough.

Fewer people were present at the graveside service as only a few were invited to the private ceremony.

What she couldn't help notice was that apart from Sofia there was no one who approached Felipe in a genuine way to offer their condolences. Yes, there was respect, and acknowledgement of his loss, but no warmth. He really had no one. Where was the warmth?

After the greetings and handshakes he stood back from others, emitting a solitary demeanour that demanded he be left alone. Without support. Her heart ached for him but that was nothing new.

As the service closed and the first clods of earth were scattered, Sofia, with Isabella in her arms, walked up to him and touched his shoulder. Then she hugged him and, to Cleo's surprise, he hugged her back. The first time she'd seen that from him. But his face remained a forbidding mask.

Sofia kissed his cheek, said something quietly, and then she turned and walked away to talk to other people.

Felipe remained at the graveside alone and finally Cleo couldn't stand it.

She crossed the grass, past exquisitely dressed groups of two and three people in designer black, until she stepped in front of him.

She lifted her chin and met his eyes. 'I'm so sorry for your loss, Felipe. I consider myself fortunate to have spent some time with your grandmother. She was a very strong woman.'

For the first time all day an expression crossed his face as he looked at her and the desolation in his eyes made her gasp. Unconsciously her arm rose to grip his arm and she squeezed it to comfort him with her fingers.

'Another woman I love leaves me,' he said. The wind tossed his dark hair and she shivered at his pain.

'Like you will leave me.' He'd said it very quietly and she looked up.

Startled.

'It will be a little different when I leave,' she said, 'because you don't love me.'

Instead of answering, he looked down at the grave and said, 'Now, Àvia? You think this is a good time?' Then his face softened and he whispered, 'Then rest well, my little grandmother.' He took Cleo's arm and steered her away from the crowd.

'Do you know what she said?' He didn't look at her as they walked. 'She said, "Do not let her get away."'

'Who?' Cleo was a little worried about the way this conversation was going. At the crowd they were leaving behind. Had Felipe lost it in his grief?

He looked down at her but at least his face was no longer impassive. 'No. I'm not going mad. My little grandmother told me she would haunt me if I let you get away. And I nearly did.'

She tried to pull her arm away. 'Um… I'm leaving, Felipe. My flight goes in four hours.'

'I promise that if you still wish to catch it when I am finished, I will get you there in time.'

He ushered her with his hand at her elbow to the car where Carlos was waiting. Felipe spoke quietly and Carlos nodded. When they were in the back seat together, Carlos shut the door and stood a few paces in front of the car door to prevent anyone approaching them.

He turned to her, then took both her hands in his. She lifted her chin. 'What?'

'You are never afraid, my midwife. And I would never do anything to make you afraid.' He kept hold of her hands but more gently now. 'I see I must work harder for you. Must open myself up, but I find this so hard.' His eyes searched hers.

'I don't understand.' She didn't.

'Yesterday, inside I was a young lover playing Romeo, yet on the outside I came across as cold and forbidding as my father.'

'Romeo?' She shook her head. 'Where was he during that conversation?' A small glimmer of light hit her.

He smiled. 'Emotion of the heart. It is hard for me to show. It makes me sound formal when I try to let it all out.' He shrugged without releasing her fingers.

'You were nothing like Romeo yesterday.'

Then he smiled and his face finally opened up to show the man she loved. 'But I will work on it. You will help me. You will always bring out the passionate dancer in my soul. If anyone can do it, it is you. For you are my angel. My midwife.'

She shook her head. Too much. Too fast. Too dangerous to believe in.

'You see my problem?'

She still felt confused.

'I love you.' He shrugged those beautiful shoulders and she felt her pulse speed up.

Three crazy words she'd never expected him to say. But he didn't give her time to question him.

'I did not know, until after that babe was born in the street, that I love you with all my heart. I have done ever since that first night.'

Nope. He'd left her without even a word. 'I don't believe you.'

'Did you know, that first morning, I stopped and looked back at your window, where I had left you, and was so torn?'

How could that be true? Not one word of the future had he spoken. She would have welcomed even one.

'And what happened to all my clever plans yesterday, my love?' He shook his head. Bewildered. Searching her face for the answers.

'Yesterday?' She said it carefully.

'I was full of plans but nervous like a boy.' He sighed. Disgusted with himself. 'Later I wondered if I'd scared you with my serious face because I wanted you to say yes to what I asked you so badly.'

She remembered. 'Yes, you did. Scare me.' She nodded. It had scared her that he didn't care about her at all. Not one bit. But maybe that wasn't true? But she still didn't fully understand him. 'You wanted me to work for you so badly?'

'No. Yes. I am doing it again. I just wanted you to listen to my plans for our future. And part of that could be work, but most of it is you and I together. But it was a shambles.'

She couldn't deny it. It had been.

He smiled ruefully. 'And here was me with a picnic basket in the boot and a trip planned to the Park Güell to ask permission to court you slowly.'

She blinked. 'I beg your pardon?'

'We will do it all again and this time it will work.' He shook her hands. 'If only you do not climb aboard that plane this afternoon.'

Cleo's mind raced as she pieced everything together. He'd been nervous, not aloof. Scared, not arrogant. Afraid she'd say no. Afraid she didn't want him. Not asking about work. Or moving in with Sofia. But about the possibility of a future. With him. Together. Her confident, passionate, sometimes arrogant Felipe was a mess because of her? He'd been adorably nervous and had made a mess of it all.

Had she made him nervous because he'd cared so much that she agree to his plans? That's what he'd said.

'And you were so hard and unbending, my love. So angry and determined to leave,' he said.

Yes, she had been that. Looking back. Firmly in protection mode. 'You offered me a job.'

He dropped her hands and lifted them to his face. 'My last resort to keep you here until I could move mountains and seduce you.'

She sat back. A small smile finally played around her lips. Now she recognised him. Here was her passionate flamenco dancer. 'So your plans are to seduce me?'

He nodded. Decisively. 'Absolutely, but again my grandmother would haunt me if that was all. No, my love. My plans are to make you my wife and live with you to the end of our days, teaching you again and again how much I love you.'

And he had her.

Right there. That was all he needed to say.

'Dear Felipe.' Though there was a touch of exasperation in her tone. 'A little straight talking would have helped you yesterday. Do you know why I think straight talking would have worked?'

'Tell me.'

'Because…' She swallowed. She'd known herself, had thought it, cried over it, but had never said the words, and would have to admit it out loud for the first time. 'I love you. Have loved you from the first moment I saw you in that cantina.' She leaned her head into him and tapped his chest with her finger. 'You are so hot.'

'I know,' he said with an arrogant lift of his brow, and she laughed.

But the laughter died when he pulled her close, slid his arms around her waist and lifted her onto his lap. Thank goodness Carlos was blocking the view.

He rested his forehead against hers. 'I adore you, and thank heaven for the night I found you, my beautiful Cleo.'

He looked down at her, their faces close together. Said softly, 'So, when we go for a picnic, and I bring more roses, and we walk in the park, will you listen to my reasons why you should spend your life with me?'

'Yes, I will listen, my passionate flamenco dancer.'

And then he kissed her, his relieved sigh deep and heartfelt as he cradled her face. She closed her eyes and sank into him, her arms around his shoulders, his big hands warm and gentle.

Finally, she'd found the man she'd thought she'd lost when one dawn he'd walked away from her.

# CHAPTER TWENTY-SIX

*Six months later*

THEIR FIRST WEDDING was held in the small chapel underneath the Sagrada Familia. Weddings below the church, where there were soaring archways, were not common. After all, it was a crypt, where Gaudi, and others, rested eternally.

Only those with a certain postcode could be married there, and luckily Felipe had the right house. The architecture rose in stunning archways, a circular room with a flower of small chapels and the pulpit in the centre. Light streamed in through careful structures in the walls.

Felipe's old nanny beamed and quivered with excitement from the front pew next to Alba and Carlos. On the other side of the circular vaulted room Sofia and Isabella both looked gorgeous in pink and smiled at him.

Felipe stood tall at the altar with his cousin Diego next to him. Later there would be another wedding in the grand cathedral and the enormous reception would be held in the town hall. But Felipe had wanted this tiny, intimate gathering first, in the place that had been so special to him for so many reasons.

And now she came.

The music began and the tiny congregation turned. Beside him Diego stirred as his Jen appeared at the door in palest pink.

But Felipe had eyes only for the woman behind the bridesmaid. His bride. His Cleopatra. His queen.

And she looked every inch the queen with her head held high as she walked slowly but confidently towards him. His heart swelled as the music did, and her eyes met his. Such love shone out at him. He adored her.

He could do nothing else for he had never been so happy and hopeful for the future with his beautiful Cleo coming to stand by his side. To be his wife. His love.

And tonight, after the second wedding and the main reception, Felipe had a surprise for her. Tonight he would teach her the first steps of his dance so that for ever, together, they would dance as one. Then he would carry her to his bed and love her with all the joy in his soul.

\* \* \* \* \*

# MILLS & BOON

## Coming next month

### A PUP TO RESCUE THEIR HEARTS
Alison Roberts

'Off the sofa, Lucky,' he commanded. 'We've talked about this before, haven't we?'

Lucky jumping down was enough to break that stillness for Stevie. She was moving further away from him – towards the fireplace.

'This mantlepiece…' She stepped onto the flagstone hearth to reach up and touch the massive beam of wood that was embedded in the wall. 'It looks like a whole tree trunk. It's incredible. How old *is* your house?'

'Dates to about mid-eighteenth century I believe. The wood burner doesn't look too out of place, though, does it?'

'It's gorgeous. And I love how you can stack the logs on either side like that. Did the flue from the log burner just go inside the original chimney?'

She was leaning in, to peer up into the space and Josh didn't think to warn her not to touch the inside of the chimney. It hadn't occurred to him that there could still be some ancient soot clinging to stonework until Stevie straightened and pushed that curl back off her face, leaving a huge, black streak in its place.

'Oh, no…'

'What? Have I got something on my face?' Stevie was touching her nose now, and then her cheek and then she saw her fingers and laughed.

'Don't move…' Josh walked past the fireplace to where the living room led into his kitchen. He grabbed a clean tea towel, ran it under the tap and went back to Stevie who used it to wipe her hands and then her face.

'Have I got it all?'

'Almost.'

Without thinking, Josh reached out and used the pad of his thumb to wipe a remnant of smudge from her cheek. Close to her mouth. So close, he could feel the corners of her lips. And how incredibly soft her skin was… It was his turn to stop in his tracks, suddenly overwhelmed with what he could feel. And see. The way Stevie's gaze was locked on his, the way those gloriously tawny eyes darkened and…oh, man… the way her lips had parted again. And this time, he just knew that she *was* waiting to be kissed.

That she *wanted* to be kissed.

*Continue reading*
A PUP TO RESCUE THEIR HEARTS
Alison Roberts

*Available next month*
www.millsandboon.co.uk

# COMING SOON!

We really hope you enjoyed reading this book. If you're looking for more romance, be sure to head to the shops when new books are available on

## Thursday 21$^{st}$ January

To see which titles are coming soon, please visit
**millsandboon.co.uk/nextmonth**

# WE'RE LOOKING FOR NEW AUTHORS FOR THE MILLS & BOON MEDICAL SERIES!

Whether you're a published author or an aspiring one, our editors would love to read your story.

You can submit the synopsis and first three chapters of your novel online, and find out more about the series, at **harlequin.submittable.com/submit**

We read all submissions and you do not need to have an agent to submit.

## IF YOU'RE INTERESTED, WHY NOT HAVE A GO?

**Submit your story at:**
harlequin.submittable.com/submit

# MILLS & BOON

# LET'S TALK
## Romance

For exclusive extracts, competitions
and special offers, find us online:

facebook.com/millsandboon

@MillsandBoon

@MillsandBoonUK

**Get in touch on 01413 063232**

For all the latest titles coming soon, visit
**millsandboon.co.uk/nextmonth**